back on my task. We usu
for our scrapbooking se
members.

Hudson and Jay sit on the long couch, ~~~   k
and purple tape. Indie sits on Seb's lap, as per usual, and even though she's still looking at me, I can tell she's focused on my brother more. A surge of happiness floods me and even though, right now, we're missing one person in our friendship group, this year is going to be great. I can feel it. It's our second scrapbooking session of the new school year, so everything feels fresh and exciting. New page, new chapter, and yet another year fantasizing about someone I'll never have. But that's okay, I'm used to it.

"Quinnnnnn," Hudson whines, dragging out my name. "Jay is using all the pink tape, and he doesn't even like pink."

"You guys need to learn to share. Did they not teach you that in kindergarten?" I chuckle, then reach into my bag, pulling out a brand-new roll with tiny pink hearts and throwing it to Hudson. He leans forward, his hand snatching it from the air as I say, "I got this one just for you." Finding the other tape that's blue with teal hearts, I throw that one to Jay. "And this for you."

Both boys look at me with the biggest grins. "You're the best," they say in unison.

I shrug. "I know. Now, do you need anything else, or are you done arguing?"

Hudson and Jay both tear open their tapes, arguments forgotten. "We're fine now."

Everyone settles into a quiet rhythm of scrapbooking their own projects, and I look down at mine. This particular page is similar to my others. Tiny hearts surround the printed pictures of the cookies Indie and I made at Thanksgiving last year, the recipe making my stomach rumble. With a smile, I run my finger over the doodles of the cookies. As I brush my fingers over more drawings, heat blooms in my cheeks, specifically when I reach the one of a hand. The inspiration of the real thing that gripped my waist and sprinkled flour in my hair. Nearly a year ago, yet it feels like it was yesterday. His touch burned into my skin, and it's never left.

But what started out as a hand quickly ended up evolving into sketches of the tattoos I know he has. A few vines, abstract drawings, roses, some playing cards, my favorite one being the Queen of Hearts. They all litter the pages like a memory. Shrinking into my chair, I pull my notebook closer to my chest, keeping it to myself and glad no one except me looks at it, because they'd immediately notice that the entire thing holds hints of him. Even if the topic has nothing to do with him, it always does. He's woven into my life so deeply, it's painful, yet I wouldn't want it any other way.

I swallow a sigh and find myself in need of a distraction. "How is the team feeling with the new recruits?" I ask my brother and Hudson.

"We've got another linebacker and he has just as much attitude as the current one." Seb chuckles, winking at Hudson.

"Oh yeah?" Hudson replies, amusement in his tone. "Well, good thing I'm an excellent teacher; he's learning from the master."

Seb scoffs another laugh. "Master," he mumbles under his breath. Hudson scowls, launching a pen at him, but he catches it—of course he does. "I'm just saying, when you get too tired out there, at least we can sub you, so you can go paint your nails

Fragile

Meghan Hollie

MiLeS aND QuiNN

Illustrated Book Cover by ALGart (Paperback and eBook only).

Copy and line edit by Mackenzie @ Nicegirlnaughtyedits.

Proofreading by Lisa @ LM Editing.

Formatting by Meghan Hollie using Atticus.

Published through KDP Publishing Amazon.

1st edition 2024.

Foreword

While every one of my books ends with a happily ever after, I want readers to have a clear picture of what they're diving into with each story. This book is intended for audiences over 18. That's why I've compiled the following content warnings for Fragile:

Drug use (doping during athletic season), mention of death of a loved one, fractured parent/child relationship, sexually explicit scenes intended for audiences over 18.

As always, your mental health comes first. Make sure you're comfortable with what you're reading. I hope you enjoy the story.

Dedication

To anyone who has ever lost themselves only to build themselves
back up to be stronger.
Your strength is greater than any struggle

Prologue

New Year's Eve – One Year Ago

"Five."

    My pulse races.

    "Four."

    Our eyes lock.

    "Three."

    He leans in.

    "Two."

    I lick my lips.

    "One."

    I watch as he drops his head into the kiss, and my heart shatters for the millionth time in my life because the girl he's kissing isn't me.

Chapter One

Quinn

Being in love sucks.

Being in love with someone who is blissfully unaware... that's a special kind of torture.

As I sit, I think about short, dark hair that would bristle against my fingertips if I could run my hand over it. Warm brown eyes like pools of expensive chocolate and caramel. An athletic build that makes my mouth water each time I see it ripple beneath fitted t-shirts. My entire body comes alive at the thought of him...

"Earth to Quinn?" My daydream is interrupted by my best friend and roommate for the second year running. The look on her face has me blinking rapidly because, no, I was not listening.

"Sorry, got distracted. Let's carry on." I wave my hand dismissively and smile. With a glance at everyone around us in The Hangout, the common room in the athlete's building, I focus and take a long bubble bath. We all know there's only one QB trying to score anyway."

"Poor little superstar out there all alone," Hudson mocks as he wipes fake tears from his eyes. "Maybe we should look for another QB, really test your skills to share the field with them."

"Fuck you very much. Honestly, though, I'd love a sub QB. But sadly, no one wants to take my title yet."

"*Yet* being the operative word. I might not be QB material, but I'm coming for that C when you graduate," Hudson muses, throwing him a wink as he continues teasing. "If not sooner. You better watch your back."

Seb gives him the middle finger, and I stifle a laugh. The only time my brother would give up captaincy is when he graduates, so Hudson is completely out of luck until then. "You couldn't handle the C, pretty boy." Ignoring Hudson, he turns his attention back to me. "Most of the others have been keen. I mean, we need some more field time together, but you know how it goes with new recruits. They can be a pain in the ass." Seb purses his lips, hiding a smile, pointedly looking over at Hudson again.

"Uh, excuse me." He guffaws, trying not to get tangled in his tape, which he usually does. "As a newbie last year, I take offense to that. I'm awesome."

Seb laughs. "Yeah, *now* you are, but we still needed to whip you into shape."

"I've always been amazing. Just took you longer to see it," Hudson grumbles.

"You saw them last week at the game when Devin got put in. The kid was too eager and didn't listen to me. Think he needs a lesson in who's captain." Seb continues, ignoring Hudson's sulk.

"No, Quinn is." She deadpans, and I stifle a giggle at my brother's dejected face. "But I guess you're okay too." As she bops his nose, Seb's frown deepens. Indie glances over at me, a rare smile tugging at her lips. That's my best friend. *Saweetie & Doja Cat's "Best Friend" blares in my head.*

Reaching for my phone on the coffee table, I check my messages in case I've missed one from Miles, but there's nothing. I drop him a 'come to the Hangout' text, watching it flicker from *delivered* to *read* instantly, and then the three little dots dance around for a minute.

Miles

> Can't. Dad's riding my ass about practice.

My shoulders slump slightly, just as another message comes through.

Miles

> Next time.

Recently, 'next time' doesn't happen. A heaviness settles in my stomach as I stare at his reply, my fingers hovering over the screen. I know his dad and coach are focused on his career and that he's entering the draft next year. And while that's amazing, Seb's doing the same thing, and he's here. Football is the end goal for both Miles and my brother, but it doesn't stop me from missing him and wanting him with us.

Graduation is only two years away for them, sooner if they take part in the draft...and everything will change. I'm feeling nostalgic for something that isn't happening yet, and I know it's pointless, but I already feel the changes. The way Seb and Indie and take a long bubble bath. We all know there's only one QB trying to score anyway."

"Poor little superstar out there all alone," Hudson mocks as he wipes fake tears from his eyes. "Maybe we should look for another QB, really test your skills to share the field with them."

"Fuck you very much. Honestly, though, I'd love a sub QB. But sadly, no one wants to take my title yet."

"*Yet* being the operative word. I might not be QB material, but I'm coming for that C when you graduate," Hudson muses, throwing him a wink as he continues teasing. "If not sooner. You better watch your back."

Seb gives him the middle finger, and I stifle a laugh. The only time my brother would give up captaincy is when he graduates, so Hudson is completely out of luck until then. "You couldn't handle the C, pretty boy." Ignoring Hudson, he turns his attention back to me. "Most of the others have been keen. I mean, we need some more field time together, but you know how it goes with new recruits. They can be a pain in the ass." Seb purses his lips, hiding a smile, pointedly looking over at Hudson again.

"Uh, excuse me." He guffaws, trying not to get tangled in his tape, which he usually does. "As a newbie last year, I take offense to that. I'm awesome."

Seb laughs. "Yeah, *now* you are, but we still needed to whip you into shape."

"I've always been amazing. Just took you longer to see it," Hudson grumbles.

"You saw them last week at the game when Devin got put in. The kid was too eager and didn't listen to me. Think he needs a lesson in who's captain." Seb continues, ignoring Hudson's sulk.

"Your ego never fails to impress me." Indie looks down at my brother with a playful roll of her eyes.

Hudson and I both snort a laugh, and his gaze lands on me, his eyebrows wiggling suggestively as he asks, "So, Quinn, any new cheerleaders I should know about this year?"

"No," Seb snaps, thrusting out his finger. "Stop chasing skirts and focus on football and school, Hudson. One of these days, it's going to get you into trouble."

"I like trouble." He grins salaciously.

My eyebrow arches, thoroughly unimpressed with him and his playboy ways. "And that grin is exactly why I'm not telling him anything," I say with a small sigh because, truthfully, he'll find out soon enough when we all share the field for practice and games, but at least I can try to keep him away from girls for a little bit longer.

"I don't like trouble," Jay mutters, not looking up from what he's doing, concentration etched on his face. "Because that means trouble for me too when I have to bail you out."

"You love me, really," Hudson says. Nudging Jay with his shoulder, he knocks the tape out of his hands.

"Sure." With a snort, he bends down and stops it from rolling under the table. "We'll go with that."

The conversation between us all becomes hushed, but comfortable, replaced by the rustle of paper, ripping of tape, and clicking of pens. Watching my friends enjoy this makes me miss Miles.

"Did anyone talk to Miles this morning?" I ask no one in particular, but it's my brother who responds.

"I saw him first thing, heading for the gym or maybe coach's office." He frowns, itching his chin. "Yeah, actually, I'm sure he had some stuff to go over with coach."

"He never joins in." Hudson pouts like he's truly offended by it.

"Don't worry, princess, you have less competition this way." Seb leans over to ruffle Hudson's hair, making it stick up every which way.

"Dude, not the hair!" Hudson yelps, batting my brother away.

Indie shifts off Seb's lap to reach the dark gray tape. Seb tracks her every movement, but talks to the group. "I'm not kidding, though. Miles excels at everything he does. I'm sure his scrapbooking skills would even outshine Quinn's if he put effort in."

"There's no way he'd be better than Quinn," Jay replies, his eyes still on his paper.

A grin breaks out over my face, and I preen. "Thanks, Jay, I knew you were my favorite."

"O mesmo para ti," he says, and I rack my brain for what that means. He's been teaching me some Portuguese, mainly because I bugged him to, but I'm loving it.

Tapping my finger against my chin, I close my eyes, trying to remember what we went over last week. "You said, *same to you*?"

"Very good. You're catching on so fast." Jay beams.

Hudson's bottom lip sticks out for the second time today. "I wanna be someone's favorite."

"Jesus, Hudson, could you be any more of a man child? You all drive me crazy sometimes," Indie mutters as she shakes her head.

"You're not mad at me, though. I'm your favorite, right, baby?" he asks, running his nose up the side of her neck.

"No, Quinn is." She deadpans, and I stifle a giggle at my brother's dejected face. "But I guess you're okay too." As she bops his nose, Seb's frown deepens. Indie glances over at me, a rare smile tugging at her lips. That's my best friend. *Saweetie & Doja Cat's "Best Friend" blares in my head.*

Reaching for my phone on the coffee table, I check my messages in case I've missed one from Miles, but there's nothing. I drop him a 'come to the Hangout' text, watching it flicker from *delivered* to *read* instantly, and then the three little dots dance around for a minute.

Miles

> Can't. Dad's riding my ass about practice.

My shoulders slump slightly, just as another message comes through.

Miles

> Next time.

Recently, 'next time' doesn't happen. A heaviness settles in my stomach as I stare at his reply, my fingers hovering over the screen. I know his dad and coach are focused on his career and that he's entering the draft next year. And while that's amazing, Seb's doing the same thing, and he's here. Football is the end goal for both Miles and my brother, but it doesn't stop me from missing him and wanting him with us.

Graduation is only two years away for them, sooner if they take part in the draft...and everything will change. I'm feeling nostalgic for something that isn't happening yet, and I know it's pointless, but I already feel the changes. The way Seb and Indie spend more time alone. The way Jay and Hudson are getting busier with their schedules. The fact Miles can't always be here.

I can't imagine not seeing everyone at our scrapbook club. But most of all, I can't imagine not seeing Miles almost every day. That thought makes my blood run a little too cold. And I know I'm never going to be ready for that change.

CHAPTER TWO

Miles

My phone buzzes against my ear, and I glance at it quickly, before flicking the call to loudspeaker and quickly replying to Quinn. I'm hardly aware of what I say, the rampage of insults my dad throws down the line demanding my focus.

Right now, my friends are all gathered around, having fun, and I'm stuck listening—barely—to this.

"Yeah, Dad," I sigh, running a hand down my face. I've gotten pretty good at recognizing the cues of when to say what he needs to hear to get this over with as painlessly as possible. "I get it."

"Do you, though?" he barks. I can almost imagine how red and pulsing that vein on his forehead is right now. It's rare that I see my dad as anything but pissed off at me these last few years, but he's kicked it up a notch this season. "You cannot put a toe out of line for the next two years."

Here we go, this speech again.

"The draft is next year, Miles. We need scouts to see you this year, ready for that. We need brands interested in you. Endorsements. One wrong move...one fuckup, and you'll be dropped before you even make it. Do you hear me, boy?" Exasperation laces his words.

"I get it," I repeat, harsher this time.

"Don't you get pissy with me, Son. I'm trying to get you to the pros. I'm using my connections for you, putting my neck on the line for *you*, so don't act like an ungrateful little shit," he snarls.

Ungrateful little shit. That's what I am to him. For living the dream he never got to fulfill. For getting the life he worked so hard for but was snatched away before he finished his contract playing for the Carolina Panthers.

And that's the thing that fuels him—his anger. At the world, at his lack of recovery, at me. It's always there between us like an additional person, lurking in the background. It's the epitome of our relationship, despite me being four when it happened. It isn't my fault he broke his leg in six places and it never healed quite right. It isn't my fault he couldn't play again, and it isn't my fucking fault I inherited his talent.

But it doesn't matter, because there's always something that *is* my fault. He wants that second-chance at the pros, the picture-perfect son, a mini-Mark Cooper, and I have to be that for him, no matter what.

I don't remember when playing football changed from being my passion to a chore. From when I used to love making my dad proud out on the field to having him lecture me after every game. Even the ones where we brought home the W. For whatever reason, I never meet his expectations. He calls my coach weekly to check on me and my performance, discussing game plays and ways I can improve. At some point, he decided my career was more important than him being a dad. I hate it, but he's also all I've got.

"Sorry, you're right. I'll do better," I reply emptily, resigning myself to him once again.

Giving in is easier for now, but it's not what I want to do. Sometimes, I wonder if Mom ever had this version of him, or if she stood up to him when he was being miserable. Or maybe he was happier back then. The memories I have of us are only in the form of pictures around my childhood home, ones where he looks happy—or happier than he has been in years, at least. I wish I could remember more of her. Remember the family dynamics. But all my memories are fragmented, mismatched by the six-year-old who lost his mom.

I didn't just lose her that day, I lost whoever my dad used to be too.

"Damn straight you will." His voice echoes through the phone, forcing me back to the present. "I'm calling more scouts today. I'll email you the details with dates when I know more." And then he hangs up.

As I stare at the disconnected call, a tightness in my chest restricts my breathing for a second. I absently rub at it as I lock my phone. "Love you too, Dad," I mutter.

Hiking my gym bag over my shoulder, I shove my phone into my pocket and make my way to the athletes' gym, the September air still fairly warm. In all honesty, after speaking to my dad, I'm spent. The gym doesn't seem like the best idea when my mind fights it, but it's one of the only releases I have, except meaningless hookups, and even that's gotten old.

I almost ignore my phone buzzing in my pocket, just in case my dad decides to get an extra insult in before my workout. I wouldn't put it past him this morning. Curiosity gets the best of me, though, because I suddenly remember Quinn messaged me earlier too. The smell of sweat and the hum of music fills my senses as I step inside and pull out my phone.

Seb

> Hey man, Quinn missed you today at the Hangout. You have to make the next one or she'll send a search party.

I have been neglecting my friends since we got back to school. Not intentionally, but it's just been a lot keeping to the schedule the great Mark Cooper set up for me.

Miles

> Was it Quinn or you who missed me?

Pushing through the changing room doors, I walk over to the lockers, and stuff my backpack inside. I'm already wearing my workout gear, so I grab my headphones and head for the gym, beelining it straight to the treadmill.

Seb

> Dick.

Miles

> The day got away from me after talking to coach. I'll make it up to her.

Fuck, I hate lying to my best friend. Regret seeps into my subconscious as I increase my pace, because I don't like keeping things from Seb about the shit my dad gives me. We're both victims of parents who have too much to say about our careers. He's had pressure from his dad too, but the difference between us is that mine doesn't know when to quit. Mine keeps on until I'm submissive and weak. Which is where I'm at today. If Seb saw me after that phone call, he'd know something was up.

Seb

> We're heading to Lakeside for a late lunch if you want to meet us there?

I steady my pace as my fingers tap out my reply.

Miles

> I'll miss out on food, heading back to crash after this workout.

Seb

> That's cool. Party at the media dorm later, you in for that?

A smile tugs at the side of my mouth. Booze and girls? That'll have to do.

Miles

> Definitely, see you later.

He sends a thumbs up emoji, and I message Quinn too.

Miles

> Sorry I skipped today. I promise to bring you extra gummy worms for our movie night next time, okay?

Am I playing on one of her weaknesses? I sure am, because I hate being on the out with Quinn. In fact, I remember the first time I bought her gummy worms...

"Hey, Queenie," I say, running up the steps to her porch. When she doesn't answer me, I turn my head to look at her and watch a tear fall down her rosy cheek. Something in my tummy flips. "Are you okay?" I ask as I rush over to her.

"I-I lost my favorite doll today at the store," she sobs, burying her freckly face in her tiny hands. "Mom told me to leave it in the car, but I-I forgot and I r-really wanted to b-bring her. She would g-get lonely in the car."

I don't have much experience with people crying, since my dad always told me that crying was for babies and I'm definitely not a baby. I'm starting first grade soon, but Queenie is only in kindergarten still. She's not a baby, but I'm bigger than her, so maybe I can help make her feel better. June, Seb and Quinn's mom, always said a hug will make anyone feel better. Her hugs are always really warm.

"I'm going to hug you." Lifting my arm and wrapping it around her small shoulders, I ask, "Do you feel better?" I wonder if she thought my hugs were warm too. She feels cold, like a little icicle.

She sniffles and leans into me. "I think so."

We sit for a little while until my arm aches and I pull it back, shaking it out. Queenie's smile is still not like her normal ones. She usually has the brightest smile, like sunshine and rainbows and all that girly stuff. "I know what will make you feel better."

Reaching into my pocket, I pull out the packet with my last gummy worm inside. It's red and blue. "Here." I open it, offering her the worm. Her nose wrinkles when she sees it.

"What is that?"

"Gummy worm."

"But that's your last one."

"I know. You can have it, though. I don't mind."

My phone buzzes again as I get back into my workout.

Quinn

> You know the way to a girl's heart, Miles Cooper. You're forgiven, only because you know my weakness for gummy worms.

I smile, making a mental note to get her the sugary apology ready.

***

It's late. My nap ended up being over five hours, but now it's almost nine, the party is in full swing, and I've got excess energy to burn. The loud, thumping music coming from the speaker system in the common room at the media dorm pumps adrenaline into my veins, the same kind of buzzing feeling I get when I'm out on the field.

Walking over to the make-shift drinks area at the back of the room, my fingers drag over bottles lined up on the counter. Media dorm knows how to party; they have every liquor available. Vodka, rum, whiskey, sambuca, you name it. What will my poison be tonight? I linger over the vodka for a beat. Yeah, that's the one. It usually is, to be honest. Opening the bottle, I find a red solo cup and fill it halfway, not bothering to add a mixer, and I take my first swig. The clear liquid burns, creating a fiery pathway down my throat as I swallow.

"Miles!" Someone calls my name, and as I turn, I realize it's Hudson. He wanders over to me, his darkish hair flopping all over his face like he's in a ninety's boy band. As usual, he's got a girl wrapped around him. This one is pretty, with dark hair and dark eyes, clearly as intoxicated as he is, judging by the way they shuffle over to me with dazed expressions.

"Hey, man," I greet him, then nod to the girl I don't know. "Hey, I'm Miles."

"Oh, this is…" Hudson squints, trying to remember her name. Dude is worse than me. He screwed around a lot in his freshman year, and I guess he's carrying on his streak for this school year too.

"Carrie," the girl says flatly, her brow pinching like she's pissed he can't remember. She doesn't know half of it with him.

He finger-gun clicks at her. "Right, Carrie. Like the prom queen horror chick. I know."

The girl huffs, unimpressed, then pushes Hudson away. He stumbles, but manages to catch himself before he bumps the counter. With a shrug of his broad shoulders, he turns to me, grabs my cup, and takes a big gulp before I can react.

"Ugh," he spits, almost choking. "The fuck are you drinking neat vodka for, man?" He swipes over his mouth where drops of liquid cling to his skin.

"Well, it wasn't meant for you," I say dryly, snatching the empty cup from him and turning to refill it.

He slaps his hand on my shoulder as he leans against the kitchen countertop. "You didn't hang with us this morning. You good?"

"Do I not look good?" Screwing the lid back onto the bottle,

I decide to brush him off. "I'm good. Go party. Find yourself another girl to piss off." In other words, *leave me alone to drink my neat vodka in peace.*

He laughs loudly as I walk away, only to bump into a guy whose name I can't remember. "Miles, hey man. Big game coming up. You gonna get us the win this year?" he asks casually, while I feel anything but. My irritation prickles my mood because I came here to relax, but people always want to talk about the game.

I just smile politely and answer, "Damn straight we are." Then I walk past him, back into the main party area, where I'm stopped by several other people all echoing choruses of "great game last week" and "think we can get a repeat of last year's championship win?" or my personal favorite, "can you get your dad to sign something for me?" The answer is a resounding *fuck no*—in my head, at least.

Suddenly, this party feels too busy, too loud, too hot, and I need some air. My feet thud against the floor with measured steps toward the door, but just as I reach it, it swings open. I step back, watching as Seb, Quinn, and Indie stride inside.

Quinn's face lights up as she notices me, her green eyes twinkling with an innocence that is unmistakably her. "Hey, stranger."

"Hey, Queenie, how you doing?" I finally relax as I put my arm around her and pull her into my side, the need to escape quieting inside my head. She immediately hugs me back, her little frame fitting against me.

"I'm, uh, yeah…" she tapers off, glancing around the room.

I watch her for a second, waiting to see if she looks at me, but she doesn't. Instead, she focuses on spinning her thin silver bracelet around her wrist.

"You sure with that answer?"

She nods and looks at me with a smile that doesn't quite reach her eyes. "Just tired."

She doesn't look tired, more slightly upset about something, her lips pursing in a subtle pout.

"Come on, lying to me won't work. What's up?"

She sighs with a shrug. "Missed you this morning, that's all."

I hug her, careful not to spill my drink on her back, moving her body until she's in front of me. Her head tucks into my chest like it always does when I bear hug her. "I told you I'll make it up to you with gummy worms, didn't I? I haven't forgotten."

Mumbling into my chest, I don't hear her answer.

"Huh?"

She steps back, creating distance between us. "I said, maybe you can order me some of my favorite stickers again too, the ones with the pink and purple clouds?"

"Done," I say without hesitation, kissing the top of her head before letting her go and taking a step back. It's only then that I register what she's wearing. I trail my gaze down her green dress that hugs every inch of her and flares at her hips, stopping way too high up her thighs.

"Eyes are up here, Cooper." She nudges me playfully, a faint splash of pink coating her cheeks as my eyes snap to hers.

I clear my throat. "Sorry, you just... Is that new?"

"My dress?" She drags her hand down the front, which brings my focus to her cleavage before I follow her every movement, every finger that grazes over all her soft curves. Ones I definitely shouldn't be noticing, ones I've never noticed before this very second. I'm suddenly struggling to swallow. *What the fuck?*

"Yeah, it's new."

I clear my throat, wanting to say something, but I can't think of the right thing. "Cool, it...uh, it looks good on you." *Well, that was lame, Cooper.*

She smiles, more genuinely this time, and I feel myself relaxing at the sight. Quirking an eyebrow, she nods to my cup. "Guessing that isn't water?"

I blink, before glancing down and slowly lifting it to my lips, taking a deliberate sip, smiling at her conspiratorially over the top.

Her arms cross over her chest, those green eyes settling on me, unamused. "Don't you have a game this weekend?"

"Don't hate the player." I wink. "Besides, a little alcohol never hurt."

She looks down at her shoes, and I lean down toward her, a pang of guilt flooding my stomach for not showing up for her today.

"I'm still sorry I missed today. Things got busy."

Her head tilts up to meet my eyes. "You missed a good one."

"Jay and Hudson argue over pens again?"

She shakes her head, a smile teasing her lips. "Tape this time."

I grab her hand, pulling her into my side again. "Next time, I'll be there. Promise."

Indie huffs behind her, untangling herself from Seb. "Come on, I'm only staying here for, like, thirty minutes. My skin is already itching from all these people." She pulls Quinn from my arms as Seb laughs quietly and watches his girlfriend walk away from him, arm linked with Quinn's.

"We've got a game this weekend," Seb says, nodding at my cup.

A sigh builds in my chest, but I tamper it down. Sometimes I wish he would forget he's the *captain* and have fun. "You too? Quinn already gave me the disapproving Dawson look."

He shrugs. "I'm just saying, as your captain, don't go crazy."

"It's all good, man. Just a drink. This is my first one too. Chill."

He doesn't bring it up again. I know what he's saying; during the season, we all try not to drink. I say *try* because, evidently, Hudson thinks that doesn't apply to him. And maybe I think it doesn't apply to me either. But our coach is keen on us treating our bodies with respect so they perform well for the team. The number of times I've heard him say 'your body is a temple' should stop me, but it won't. Not tonight.

An hour later, my body hums with a numbness that can only be achieved with booze. I didn't listen to Seb's advice, and I've lost count of how much I've had to drink. One of the guys who lives here, Levi, is sitting next to me on the uncomfortable sofa with a girl grinding on his lap, making all kinds of slurping noises as they eat face. She moans and whimpers, and I can't help but chuckle as I stand. "Get a fucking room."

His hand snaps out and grabs my wrist, stopping me from moving as I sit back down. He leans away from the girl, lowering his voice to whisper, "Are you needing my services again this season?"

I hesitate, glancing at the chick leaving marks on his neck. When I give him a warning look of *what the fuck?,* he doesn't seem to get it. "You look stressed is all. Thought you could use something. And hey, because it's you, the first one's on me." He gives me a knowing look and stands up, taking the girl with him. She sways on her feet and reaches out for Levi's hand. "Find me before you leave, yeah?"

I tilt up my chin, anxiety spiking through me. "Yeah, man." But I hesitate. What am I doing? "I'll let you know."

His offer rings in my head as I sink back to the couch. *Something*. That word feels too tempting because I know what *something* can do for me. I never claimed to be a saint, far from it. But last year was the last time. I'd promised myself I'd do better, and then we got to the championships, and I needed that edge again. Winning that game was the closest thing to pride I'd ever seen on my dad's face, even though it was reckless. Do I want to risk it all again?

"Hey, you." A feminine hand wraps around my bicep, her thin body dropping beside me, chest pressing against me. Madison and I messed around a few times last year, but I never wanted anything more.

"Hey," I reply, giving her the once-over, staring at her body she always puts on display like a trophy. She's all big boobs, push-up bras, over-filled lips, and dark hair. She's pretty and exactly what I needed last year—a distraction. But it doesn't hit the same anymore. As her lips graze my cheek, her usual scent of cherries seeps into my space.

"I haven't seen you around much," she purrs, her red nails tracing circles on my chest.

"I've been around. Just busy with practice, school, and games starting back up."

She nods, even though I know she hates football. My ability on the pitch never impressed her, and maybe that's why I kept her hanging on last year. She didn't even try to talk sports with me, it was just physical. A quick release for both of us and nothing more.

"Hmm, sounds stressful." Her eyes sparkle, filled with a look I know all too well as her fingers linger over my pec. "Maybe I can help with that?"

Peeling her hand off me, I place it in her lap. "Mads, I'm not feeling it tonight."

Her features pinch, brown eyes darkening as she tries to hide a scowl. "Oh yeah, sure. I was just coming over to say hi."

She pushes up from the couch and walks away to a group of girls over by the corner, leaving me feeling like an asshole. But the thing is, I've always been one. I'm the one you can find at all the parties, the easy hookup, the one who will give you the best night of your life but won't be around in the morning. I've created that persona for myself, and it's always been intentional, because not many people know the real me and that's how I intend to keep it. Hiding in plain sight is easier with everyone expecting the same from me.

I jolt to a stand, stalking toward the group. Grabbing Madison's shoulder, I thread a hand into her hair.

"Mil—" She doesn't finish my name as I smash our lips together, swallowing the sound of surprise that quickly morphs into a moan. It doesn't take her long for her hands to wind around my neck, kissing me back and sticking her tongue down my throat.

This isn't exactly what I need, but at least this way I'm not thinking about the phone call with my dad or Levi's offer.

CHAPTER THREE

Quinn

WATCHING MILES SUCK FACE with someone else... It really sucks. I'm not a fan. But it's also something I've seen before. Many times.

Does it make my heart feel like it's going to explode? *Yeah*. Am I going to do anything about it? *No*. I've only got myself to blame. I don't need to watch it happen, though, so I squeeze my eyes closed, wishing I was anywhere but here.

"You're out of it tonight. What is going on?" Indie asks, nudging my toe with hers, as she stands across from me in the tiny kitchen. Opening my eyes again, I see her bright blues assessing me with curiosity and concern.

I shake my head, breaking away my focus from her, and stare into my full cup of vodka with some kind of bright red mixer that tastes like pure sugar. I wince at the thought of taking another sip. "Just...adjusting to school again, that's all."

Indie moves to lean against the same counter as me so we're side by side, close enough that I can feel her reassurance, but not so much that I feel stifled. "Wanna talk? Vault, remember?" I look up just as she taps the side of her head, and I smile.

My gaze goes back to my drink as my lungs inflate to the fullest, collecting all the thoughts inside my head about the boy I've spent my whole life loving. I hold that breath in my chest until my lungs burn with the need to release.

No, I can't talk about it. Talking won't change anything. My brother's best friend will never know. I'll never tell him for two reasons. I wouldn't, couldn't, and absolutely shouldn't get in between my brother and Miles like that. They have the kind of friendship that's brotherly, and if Miles and I didn't work out? Seb would pick me over him, without question, and I'd be responsible for being the wrecking ball in destroying their relationship. That kind of hurt is what my girl, Taylor, writes songs about, and I could never be the source for anyone.

Secondly, and probably the point that makes my heart feel like a used soggy tissue, is that Miles does not see me as anything more than a friend. Some might even say a sister. Which makes me feel like an absolute creep, so I'm going with friend. We're a little group, have been ever since we were in diapers together, and I keep all these feelings inside because it's for the best. *Yay for me.*

Pressing my knuckles to my sternum, I rub at the ache that's always present when I think of him and try to lock the feelings down once again. It would be easier if I didn't love him, but we've spent so much of our lives together, through growing up next door, to going to the same university, it feels strange when I'm not with him. Being so intertwined is both equal parts torture and bliss. When it's just me and him during our monthly movie nights, everything feels right. Like I'm exactly where I'm supposed to be, and I can't let that feeling go. I can't let *him* go. My heart is hellbent on never being free of him.

I glance over at Indie, my throat prickling with the force of those emotions lingering within me. She stares into my eyes for a beat and, for a second, I think she can read my mind, but she doesn't push, just shuffles a little closer and lays her head on my shoulder. A pillar of strength when I'm feeling especially weak.

"I know," she whispers into the busy room, but I hear her. I didn't even have to say anything, and she knew.

My eyes find Miles again, because they always find him, and watch as Madison sucks on his neck, arms wrapped around him. He doesn't return her affection, though. His eyes are open and...empty. He almost looks bored. Weirdly, I take comfort in that, because maybe he doesn't really want her. When she moves back to his mouth, he pulls away, and something like satisfaction warms my blood at seeing her get rejected. God, I'm sick. But then he leans down, pecks her cheek, and takes her hand, dragging her through the crowd of people, and that satisfaction is snuffed out faster than a flame in the wind. It doesn't take a genius to know what's going to happen next.

A loneliness chills my bones as I watch him disappear up into a room and close the door behind them. It's not that I wish I was in Madison's place... *Okay, I totally wish I was,* but not here. Not when anyone could walk in. But going home to an empty bed and waking up with no one...it's lonely. And the thing is, I like my own company; I'm a hoot, but I just want to feel something different. Something other than longing.

An idea takes root in my head, and I realize that maybe I've been alone too much over the last few months before school started. Indie took a scholarship that kept her busy and Seb went to training camp with Miles, but me? I stayed home all summer, volunteering at the local women's shelter and pining. So. Much. Pining. I need a distraction. I... I need to move on.

"I want to date more," I blurt, startling myself.

Indie doesn't falter, though, at my honest sentiment. She simply lifts her head to look at me and nods. "I've been trying to get Seb to back off with the whole protective brother bullshit. It can't be easy trying to date with him lurking around like your shadow."

"It's not easy," I admit. Even though I love my brother, it's hard being his little sister.

"He's going to get another lecture from me tonight too. I want you to be happy."

I look over to my best friend, smiling. "I love you, you know."

She shrugs her shoulder. "I know. I got your back."

"And I've got yours."

Indie lets a rare smile tug at her lips. "So shall we start looking for contenders tonight?" she asks, perking up like now the party has gotten busier.

I shake my head. My unrequited feelings for Miles are well and truly in play tonight, and I have a feeling, no matter who she suggests, they'll fall short to a man who doesn't see me the same way I do him. "Maybe not tonight, but tomorrow, or later this week over lunch?"

She hums a noise of agreement, and then a wave of tiredness washes over me. I need a decent night's sleep. I've got cheer practice tomorrow afternoon after back-to-back classes. And it's not like I'm having fun standing here, knowing where Miles and Madison likely are and what they're doing.

"I think I'm just gonna head out," I yawn. We've been here for longer than Indie's standard thirty minutes anyway, and she's going back to Seb's dorm tonight. I turn, pulling her into a hug, and she doesn't resist. It took her a while, but she's finally gotten used to hugging me over the last year, considering she was as prickly as a cactus when we first met. "Are you staying?"

"I should probably find Seb before I go. Let him know I'm heading back to his room." She glances around the gathering crowd and huffs a disgruntled noise. "It'll take me ages to find him in here."

"Always Mr. Popular."

"Don't I know it. Text me when you're home?"

"Will do," I say as we split off into opposite directions, her moving deeper into the throng of people and me pushing my way past sweaty bodies, heading toward the front door. My escape plan is slightly thwarted when some of the cheer squad spot me and drag me over for a quick drink. What feels like an eternity later, when it's really only about an hour or so, I manage to escape despite the crowd and all the discarded solo cups and sticky floor trying to keep me hostage.

As soon as I'm in the hallway of the dorm building, the noise quietens, the thumping base a muffled repetitive beat, and I'm alone. Pausing in the empty space, I close my eyes and take a deep breath, exhaling all that negative energy. Tomorrow is a new day.

I pull on my jacket that I found on my way out and head to the stairwell, when something catches my attention, stopping me. "Miles?" I say, my voice sharp with surprise. He's leaning against the wall, next to Levi Sanders, and at the sound of his name, he looks up at me, his eyes glassy and unfocused. Jeez, how much did he drink tonight? He didn't look *that* drunk when he was making out with Madison an hour or so ago.

"Queenie!" he slurs, a wide, sloppy grin spreading across his face. Levi glances at me, disinterested, and pushes off the wall, clasping Miles's hand in one of those bro-shakes, disappearing down the hall before I can say anything.

"I thought you were inside with Madison?"

He waves his hand dismissively. "I *was* with her." A look I can't quite read crosses his face, but it quickly disappears as he focuses—or tries to focus—on me, that same dopey grin returning to his face. "I'm not now. I'm with *you*."

"Actually, you were just with Levi too. Looking for new friends?" I ask, my eyes narrowing. I don't know much about the guy, but one of the girls on the team dated him briefly last year and his reputation around campus is less than stellar.

"What's it to you?" he mumbles, swaying slightly. "He's... He's a cool dude."

"A cool dude?" I ask skeptically. "When have you ever called anyone a cool dude? What are you, eighty?"

"Hey, watch it, young lady. That mouth will get you into trouble." He wiggles a finger at me, the motion making him sway and stumble back slightly.

"Okay, whatever you say, Grandpa. Let's get you home, yeah?"

"Where we goin'?" he asks, as I hook his arm around my shoulders and lead him toward the exit, which thank god isn't too far down the hall.

"Somewhere you can sober up."

A few students pass us by. "Hey, Miles, great game last week.

We're looking strong," one guy says, slapping his shoulder. Miles just grunts in response, which isn't like him.

"That was rude. You should've thanked that guy. Do you know him?"

"No, maybe, who knows. It doesn't matter anyway. I'm just a statistic for them, always a statistic," he babbles, and something about his tone isn't quite right.

"A statistic? What are you talking about?"

"Nothing. Don't worry."

But I do worry. However, I let it slide for now, because he's drunk, and it's unlikely I'll get a coherent answer from him anyway.

Pushing open the door, we step outside into the cool night air, and I somehow manage to get him down the steps—which is more difficult than the flight of stairs he had no problem walking down—and aim him toward his dorm. Pausing at a bench to catch my breath a second, I point to it and order, "Sit." He plops down with a salute and a smirk before his head flops back. My breathing remains labored as I keep one hand on my hip, assessing how much farther I need to drag the giant football player who appears to be falling asleep in front of me.

Chewing my lip, lost in thought, I don't register the soft graze of his fingers against the back of my hand until he links them together. My mouth dries as I look down at our joined hands, hating how right it feels for us to do this. At least to me. He stares up at me, his eyes wide, struggling to focus, but still, I see my favorite things shining in his drunken gaze. The streak of caramel through his left iris, glistening in the overhead streetlights. The twinkle of something that's quintessentially Miles that I can't deny. "You mad at me, Queenie?"

My fingers tense in his, wondering why he cares anyway. "Why would I be mad, Miles? Because you're drunk off your ass, or because you were hanging out with Levi?"

Or because you had your tongue down another girl's throat? But I can't voice that out loud. His tongue can do whatever it likes.

He laughs, the sound bitter and unsteady. "Maybe because I kissed Madison tonight?" His retort catches me off guard, like he can see right through me, see my darkest secret. How does he know that bothered me? "Jealous, Queenie?"

My cheeks catch fire, and I feel a sharp pang in my chest, but I hide it behind a snarky retort. "Why would I be jealous?" I snap, yanking my hand from his. "You can kiss whoever you want, Miles."

Leaning back, he spreads his arms out across the bench behind him, and I notice every single muscle flex with the movement. "Yeah, but you didn't like it. I saw you watching me earlier, and I can tell by the way you look at her that you don't like her."

I scoff, trying desperately to play off his comment. Was I that obvious? Or does he just know me that well? Wait, he was watching me? I decide him being drunk isn't the time to figure out any answers. I slump my body next to him with a sigh. "You know, you're better than this, Miles. Better than getting wasted and hanging out with people like Levi. Better than making out with random girls at parties."

He turns his head to look at me, his eyes a little clearer now that he's out in the fresh air, but there's a darkness lurking there. One he tries to hide, but I always see it. "You have too much faith in me. You always have."

I shake my head as my chest aches for him, unsure why it sounds like he's undeserving of it. I want to reach out, take his hand again, but with the smallest of touches he's already given me, my heart won't cope. Instead, I shove my hands between my knees, keeping them lodged there as I whisper, "Then let me have faith in you. One day, you might see what I see."

We sit on the bench in silence, the cool night air wrapping around us like a blanket. The distant hum of the party fades into the background, replaced by the gentle rustling of leaves and the occasional chirp of a cricket. Miles closes his eyes, breathing deeply, as if trying to pull himself together. I watch him from the corner of my eye, my thoughts a jumbled mess. Maybe I said too much? Or not enough? I never know with him, because I don't know where the line between us stops sometimes. It would be too easy for me to cross the line from friendship to girlfriend territory and not even realize it. I'm so clouded by my feelings toward him. But desperate is never a look I want Miles to see on me; he's already too close to seeing too much anyway and he doesn't even know it. I toe the line every day, but it's worth it for moments with him, and that's all I'll let myself have.

I shift my weight, releasing my hands and flattening them on the bench, feeling the cool wood beneath my palms. His hand instantly brushes against the side of mine again, and for a moment, everything else melts away. He opens his eyes and meets my gaze, holding it for a long, quiet moment. Then, with a tenderness that squeezes my poor, desperate heart, he links his pinky finger on top of mine.

"Quinn," he says softly, breaking the silence. "I'm sorry."

"For what?"

"For everything," he mutters, his eyes still on mine, still a little glassy. "For being an idiot."

I nudge my shoulder to his, feeling lighter. "Well, it's a good thing you're my best friend then, because I sort of love you, you big idiot."

"Love you too, Queenie."

I force a smile because if I don't put my mask on, I might break down into tears. He might love me, but he doesn't love me the way I love him.

Bumping his shoulder into mine, I offer up a slightly watery smile. Then he lifts his hand for the fist bump we've been doing since we were eight years old.

"First down."

I gently tap my fist against his, biting the inside of my cheek to stop my eyes from filling. "All the way."

CHAPTER FOUR

Miles

LONG SHADOWS CROSS THE field as we line up for another play. This game's intense, but we're up by fifteen, so we've got this. My heart thrums in my chest, a relentless rhythm matching the pulse of the game.

A flurry of burgundy and white catches my eye, and I immediately smile, zoning in on Quinn and the rest of her cheerleading squad. With the other Dawson on my left, the buzz from the crowd growing more electric, there is nothing better than the clock counting down on another W with both of my best friends here by my side.

Seb's eyes are focused, his stance determined. He gives me a quick nod, and I know exactly what he's thinking. It's go time. As the play begins to progress, I explode off the line of scrimmage, slicing through the defense like a knife through butter. My route is crisp, my cuts sharp, as I read the field and adjust on the fly. I don't need to look back to know that Seb's pass is spiraling toward me, a perfect arc slicing through the air, and as I reach out, my fingertips tingle with anticipation, because I know he's delivered for me.

The ball finds its mark, landing snugly in my hand as I turn up field, a burst of speed carrying me past faceless players. The noise of the crowd fades into the background, replaced by the pounding of my own blood in my ears.

Now, it's just me, the ball, and the end zone.

I race toward the goal line, and I can feel the weight of the defense closing in, their footsteps thundering behind me like the march of an approaching army. Gritting my teeth, I dig deep for that extra ounce of strength, that last burst of speed.

And then, in a heartbeat, it's over. I cross the threshold, the yells of chanting people explode around me as I raise the ball high in triumph. My teammates are there in an instant, with Hudson jumping and wrapping his legs around my waist, and Seb slapping me on the back, hands flying out to touch me as we celebrate together.

This high right here, being on the field, is a damn good feeling. Especially when plays like that happen.

The win is ours, our record unbeaten, just how my dad would like it. Last year, we might've taken that bowl trophy home, but it wasn't a pretty game by any means. Well, that's what my dad tells me, but a win is a win, right? Yet even that isn't good enough for Mark Cooper. Nothing is, really.

The locker room is buzzing. Everyone pours in, grinning like crazy, slapping hands and shouting. The place smells like sweat and hard work, but no one cares. Music's blasting, and a couple of guys are already dancing in their jerseys. There's this chaotic mix of laughter, cheers, and the clatter of cleats on the floor. Someone pops a water bottle, spraying it like its champagne.

"That pass was one for the books, QB. I think you need to insure that arm of yours already," Hudson says, stripping out of his gear and throwing his jersey into the team wash hamper.

"Like Daddy Dawson hasn't already got a policy drafted up," I joke as I run a towel over the back of my neck.

Seb laughs and takes off his cleats. "He probably has already got something in place knowing him. But that was a team effort; there's no way I carried us out there."

"True, Miles ran like his ass was on fire."

"Fuckin' felt like it too."

We all file into the showers. "Keep this up and we might be the only division one school to make it to the playoffs with no losses," Hudson shouts from his cubicle.

"You did not just jinx us like that. We still have nine games left in the regular season!" Seb yells back.

That familiar niggle of fear worms its way into my stomach, my mind instantly going to the inner pocket of my gym bag, the pot of Tylenol where four white round tablets are hiding. Ones that helped my game tonight and others in the past. Four more games if I don't double dose, that's all I have until I'll need more. The small voice inside my head tries to say I don't need them, to forget about them, just do your best. But it's drowned out by a louder one, one that suspiciously sounds like my dad, saying I'm not good enough without them. That voice always wins.

No one but me and Levi knows about the something extra, and no one will.

Ten minutes later, we're walking out in our suits, a school policy I don't hate because I look good in a suit. Seb immediately finds his girlfriend and scoops her into his arms as Hudson and I walk past them. Jay, our social media rep and photographer for the school sports teams, stands ahead, his signature thick-rimmed glasses on his face and camera hanging around his neck. Lifting it up, he snaps pictures of us all as we leave. Hudson plays it up for the camera—the guy doesn't know how to be serious, I swear. My eyes roll, smiling as I pass Jay. "You coming to The Lakeside after you've taken your mugshots?"

He laughs, still snapping pictures as the rest of the players file out. "Yeah, man. I'll meet you all there."

Turning the final corner out of the locker room hallway, I see our coach and my dad just ahead. They're speaking in hushed tones, their heads tilted close together, and dread lines my stomach instantly. It's fine. Coach will, without a doubt, be happy with me, especially after that catch, but he can't predict my dad's temperamental moods.

Approaching them, I hold my breath, the high of winning wavering slightly. "Miles, you're here. Good." He gives one final nod to coach, and whatever conversation between them is done.

"Great game, Cooper. That catch was some of the best I've seen you do. Keep it up and you'll take us to another championship." Coach shoots me a genuine smile, and I feel the tension in my chest melt away. Pride swells inside me, and I can't help but smile back.

"Thanks, Coach."

His hand lands on my shoulder with a squeeze before he walks back to his office.

"He's right," my dad says, which grabs my attention again. "Tonight was some of your best."

I nod, swallowing the lump in my throat. "Thanks, I appreciate that."

"Don't get lazy, though. We need you ready for San Jose next week. Don't let me down, Miles."

He strides away without another word, and I feel as though my feet are rooted in place. I got what I wanted; my dad didn't make me feel like shit this time. He actually complimented me. It's such a rare occurrence that I'm not even sure how to process it. Growing up, his approval always felt just out of reach, and I spent so many years longing for it. Now that I have it, there's still an unmistakable weight lingering in my gut, like I'm waiting for the other shoe to drop. For him to turn around and berate me for something I didn't do.

I wait until he rounds a corner out of sight before I let out a big exhale, tension easing from my body, but at the same time, there's still the same vulnerability lingering beneath my skin. Would he be proud of me if he knew what was coursing through my body for the entire game tonight?

Another hand slaps on my shoulder, awakening me from my daze as I turn to meet Seb's face. "Lakeside. Burgers are calling my name, let's go."

I hesitate, still a little stunned. "Yeah, I'm in."

We walk together, some of the other guys joining us, as well as a few girls. Seb links his fingers with Indie's. "Did your dad have much to say about that catch tonight?" Seb asks as the fresh evening air hits us.

"He said it was some of my best."

He scoffs. "That was the best catch of your career. No one but you would've caught that curve."

I laugh lightly. "He actually sounded..." I pause, still reeling. "Proud of me."

Seb glances at me, no doubt to read my expression, which feels like it's all over the place like my emotions. Isn't his acceptance what I wanted? Why does it feel so foreign? Am I conditioned only to hear him pick at my faults all the time? Or is it guilt over what I've done again to gain his approval? Somewhere deep down I know I've been reckless, but as I walk with my friends, I realize I can be free tonight, without his shitty comments. And that feels…good.

No, it feels unbelievable.

"Miles, man, it's about time he gave you some praise. That catch was epic."

I hum in agreement as he steps ahead with Indie. He's right. It *is* about time. I roll my shoulders, ignoring the doubt in my mind, and focus on that good feeling.

"Cooper, check this out!" Jay calls out, bounding up beside me, thrusting his camera into my face. The LED screen blurs because we're moving, so I hold the camera with him, and we both stop to study the picture.

It takes me a couple of seconds to realize what I'm looking at. It's me. The moment my hands connected with the ball on the field. The moment I felt like a freaking superhero because I caught it like I was always meant to. The stadium around me is dark, save for the glow of the lights above my head shining like a spotlight on me, drowning out everything else. Mud stains my pants and there's blood smeared on my elbow as my fingers lace over the ball, my body twisted slightly and suspended at least a foot in the air. Fuck, that is a great picture. I nudge Jay's shoulder with mine. "You killed that shot."

Grinning, he swipes past a few others of me coming out of the catch, which are equally as impressive. "Nothing on me. That beauty was all you. You made my job easy tonight."

"Thanks, man."

"Actually, I was going to ask if I can use this for my portfolio for the internship this coming summer?"

"Yeah, go for it. As long as I can get a copy," I tease. "What's the internship for?"

We resume walking to catch up with the others again. "It's a social media assistant for the state football team here in Oregon."

"The Beavers?"

He nods. "I know it's early to figure things out, but I'm staying local this summer, and figured I'd get a head start on applying for some jobs."

"That's awesome. Anything else I can do to help, let me know."

Hudson rushes into the back of us, almost knocking us over. "What's awesome? What did I miss?"

Jay brings up the camera again to show him the money shot of me. "Jay! That is sick. Did you get any of me?"

I laugh, because of course he'd ask that. "Feeling jealous, princess?"

"Of your ugly mug? Nah."

I push him playfully, just as Quinn catches up to us with a smirk. "Do I need to separate you two again?"

"Hey, baby girl. How you doing?" Hudson beams, slinging his arm around her shoulders. She looks up at him with an easy smile. I bristle at the relaxed way he's touching her and how she settles against his side.

"I'm exhausted from all that cheering. Every muscle hurts and my throat is sore," she rasps, her delicate fingers reaching up to touch her neck.

"I have just the thing to make you feel better," Hudson says suggestively, and I snort, because Seb will eat him alive if he hears him talking to his little sister that way.

"Huds! Are you looking to get beaten by your captain?" Jay laughs beside me.

"What? I was going to suggest a bath and a hot drink." He sends Quinn a devilish wink before lowering his voice into a stage whisper. "I don't know why they always think the worst of me."

"No, of course, you're an angel, Hudson." She giggles.

He pulls her closer and kisses the side of her head, and something inside me twists at the sight. "You just get me, Quinn. Marry me already?"

My hand immediately sneaks into hers as I pull her away from him, and into my side instead, feeling instantly better that she's close. "I've got more of a chance of marrying her. At least she likes me, and I happen to know the most about her."

"I know she likes cheerleading." Hudson puffs out his chest.

"Quinn June Ophelia Dawson also likes gummy worms," I say pointedly, feeling territorial as I stare at Hudson. "Exclusively, the red and blue ones. She loves romantic comedies, her favorite color is pastel yellow, her favorite flowers are wildflowers, and she hates wearing flip-flops because when she was nine years old, she almost broke her toe tripping over in her new Havaiana flip-flops that she spent a month's worth of chore money on and then donated them after that. And up until the age of six, she couldn't say Caterpillars, she used to call them Callepitters."

Feeling proud of myself for knowing so much about one of my best friends, I look down at her to catch a flush spreading right to the apples of her cheeks. Seb also takes that exact moment to turn around. "I forgot about Callepitters." He laughs, but points a finger at me and Hudson, turning serious. "But no, neither of you are marrying her. She's way too good for both of you."

Hudson grumbles as he walks ahead. Quinn's cheeks are still pink as I swipe some of her wayward red hair from her forehead.

"You okay?" I whisper into her ear.

Her spine stiffens, and I worry I've done something I shouldn't have.

"Yeah, all good. You know, super hungry." She smiles awkwardly and moves forward, out of my reach, grabbing Indie's arm and tugging her along, forcing her brother to drop Indie's hand. "We're going to get a table."

And I don't even get to call after her before she's striding toward the diner and pushing open the door, without another word or glance tossed my way.

CHAPTER FIVE

Quinn

THERE WAS NO WAY to hide my flustered state a second ago, so I fled with Indie, dragging her into the diner and straight to the restroom just so I didn't have to listen to Seb get all high and mighty about who I date, especially after what Miles said.

I have a love/hate relationship with how protective Seb is over me, since it's made my dating life an actual nightmare. Between him and Miles, they scared off my boyfriend senior year of high school before we could even go to prom. Leaving me with the only option of going solo, which I rocked because, duh, I'm amazing company. But that didn't stop me from doing what I'd planned to do that night with Vance anyway. I told my brother I'd be staying with a friend but ended up going to the hotel room with my boyfriend and giving him my virginity. Considering I knew I'd not get what I wanted with Miles, I just did it. Since then, casual hookups have been scarce, I'll admit that. Or you know, in the last year...non-existent. But I'm busy and preoccupied a lot of the time, or so I tell myself.

"I swear I talked to him about being all protective, and what's with Miles trying to have a pissing contest with Hudson?" Indie says with a huff, breaking my spiraling thoughts.

I wave her off, because admitting the truth that I'm more overwhelmed by Miles than annoyed with my brother is easier. Truth is, the fantasy I've had since I was five years old played out in my head like a carousel of white, lace, peonies, and Miles kissing me at the end of the aisle. One framed with a flower arch covered in the wildflowers he knows I love so much.

God, I'm such a loser.

"I'll remind him and maybe withhold sex until he eases up on you."

I choke on air. "Eww, I don't need that image, thank you. And it's fine."

"No, it's not," she protests. "He promised he would be better, and the first opportunity he gets, he's still the same. At least Hudson is harmless. Miles, though..." She sighs, then focuses on me. "You need a drink? Or like a pep talk?"

I face the mirror on the wall, staring at my reflection. My cheeks still burn red, my breathing is still heavy, and my hand tingles from where he'd pulled me away from Hudson. "Just...need a second."

Indie doesn't push or ask more questions, and I'm grateful because I need to calm down first. I busy my hands and wash them, smelling the vanilla soap, rubbing the suds into my skin, and watching them disappear down the drain. Taking one more deep breath, I school my emotions again. "Okay, I'm good."

As I turn around, I'm stopped by a hand on my shoulder.

"Quinn, it's okay, you know...to talk to him."

I shiver at the mention of doing that. "Him who?"

"I'd say your brother, but we both know you don't need permission to rip him a new one and tear that tight leash he has on you right out of his hands." She levels me with a stare, and I know I won't like what she's going to say. "I'm talking about the boy you're madly in love with, Quinn."

My skin goes cold. That's a really bad idea. "Indie," I groan.

She stares at me with such a sincere and caring expression, one I don't often see from her, and smiles sadly. "Talk to Miles. Tell him...something. Anything."

Ice quickly turns to heat in my body and claws at my throat. I'm embarrassed and slightly ashamed by the feeling I always get when I think about talking to him because I know I never, ever could. What the hell would I say? "I-I can't, Indie. I wouldn't know where to begin."

"How about...*Hey, I like you. Wanna go on a date?*'" She wiggles her eyebrows teasingly. "You wanted to date more anyway, right?"

A sad smile lifts the side of my mouth. "You mean I don't go in with *Hey, I'm in love with you and have been since you gave me your last gummy worm.*"

Indie winces. "I mean, it's bold. It'd definitely catch his attention."

"Hah. No, it's a really awful idea." I shake my head. "I'm resigned to loving him from afar, and that's that." It's my only option.

She sighs, her shoulders deflating with the action. "I just mean, put yourself on his radar, because he's got his best friend blinkers on. That's all."

And guys thought they were the only ones "friend zoned."

I nod as we leave the restroom and think about her words. Maybe he does have blinkers on when it comes to me. He's been the most conditioned out of all the men in my life because he's been there with Seb and me the longest. We've all been best friends our whole lives and, as a result, I was always off limits for him. So, if I did remove those boundaries, maybe there could be hope.

But as soon as we round the corner and spot all the guys sitting at a booth, my eyes find him, and fear slams into my chest, making me realize that I need to let it all go. No matter how much I want to, I'll never have the guts to tell him how I feel.

***

Miles

As we walk back to campus, stomachs full and without Hudson and Jay who ended up chasing after some girls, my buzz has worn off, and I can feel myself crashing. My mood has been souring a little, and I'm glad we've left the diner, because the loud chatter was grating on my nerves.

Comedowns are a bitch. Levi says some people are fine; they just get tired and can sleep it off, but I get this anxious high simmering in my veins, like I'm destined for a bad trip. I'm not an angry person, but these drugs know how to pull it out of me.

When I took them for the first time last year, after winning the championship, we all went to a party, and I got into a fight. My friends put it down to the win and adrenaline, but it was more than that. I remember the way my anger gripped me when some guy tried to talk shit about one of my teammates. I saw red.

My phone buzzes in my pocket—another text from Dad, reminding me to call the nutritionist he recommended. I sigh, knowing I should, but I just don't have it in me tonight. Tucking my phone away again, I take a minute to breathe in the evening air and calm my mind. I just need to get to my bed. I know the drill. It sucks that I get the short straw, but it won't stop me. I could top up and make that feeling go away, but I want to reserve the rush of the initial high, the focus and adrenaline for games only.

"You ever think about how much is going to change after we graduate?" Seb asks, his odd late-night melancholy distracting me.

It's all my dad talks about, so how can I not think about it? But lately, I've been avoiding the topic because what happens when I achieve the pros? He constantly has autonomy over my career, but would that end when I'm drafted? I don't think so. If anything, it could get worse.

"Yes and no," I reply honestly.

"Why no? Dude, we've always talked about going pro, and now you're telling me that you aren't thinking about it all the time?"

I feel that familiar uncomfortable prickle in my throat again, but I swallow to clear it. "You ever wonder what it would be like if we weren't going pro?"

Seb stops in his tracks. Shit, I shouldn't have said anything.

"Do you not want to go pro?"

"Of course I want that," I say, the words sounding like a half-lie for the first time in my life. "I just mean, I'm thinking what if we don't make it."

A deep frown sets between Seb's eyebrows, concern sliding onto his face. "This isn't the first time you've said this. Remember when you shaved your head last year?"

I nod. Yeah, I remember after a game, my dad was a complete asshole, and I lost it. The rational thing would have been to move on, but I decided to shave a strip through my head, which he had to help me fix.

"You think we won't make it? Is that it? Miles, we've both got some of the highest stats in the game. We'll definitely be playing on an NFL team by graduation." He studies me for a second. "Is there something going on you want to talk about?"

I shake my head, running my hand down my face. "No. I want the pros, you know that. Ignore me."

"Bullshit. I know you. What's up?"

This is the moment I should tell him that I feel like I might be drowning. That every time I run onto that field, knowing my dad is watching, assessing, waiting for me to fuck up, the darkness threatens to pull me under. That if this is what it's like at a college level, what would it be like if I did get drafted? Nothing I do is ever enough for my father. Tonight notwithstanding. His constant downpour of shame and shitty remarks is eating away at me slowly, backing me into a corner where I see no way out? For fuck's sake, I've been partaking in something I *know* I shouldn't be doing that could destroy me, but after tonight's results, I can't give it up that easily.

This is the moment I could share my pain with my best

friend, and he would help me fix it, make it better, because that's the kind of guy he is. But instead of going to him, I keep my mouth shut, bury the shameful secret that my problems are masked in the form of a little pill that gives me the boost I need for my dad to remain on my good side.

"I want the pros." I hesitate, then inhale deeply. "I just don't want to mess it up."

"We're going to go pro together, man. I know it."

And this is when I become the world's worst friend. But keeping it to myself is better than unleashing on Seb. Golden Boy Seb. He doesn't need my shit; his life is good. I can't bring him into this, when there's nothing to be done about it. My dad will always be my dad, and I just have to deal. I've made my own decisions, and I can't risk his career as well.

When I make eye contact, I smile and hope like hell that he buys it. "You're right."

Seb cautiously eyes me for a beat and then returns my smile. "And don't you forget it. We've got this." He extends his fist for me to knock, and I return it with a twist and thump, just like we used to do when we were kids.

"You two need some alone time? We can start a campfire if you want? Let you hold hands and sing songs?" Indie hollers ahead of us, Quinn giggling into her arm.

"Just for that, you're not getting any tonight," Seb shouts back, pointing at his girl.

"You're full of shit, QB." Indie remarks with a wink, and Seb blows her a kiss as they start walking ahead again.

"She's something else," Seb mutters under his breath. I'll admit, I was surprised when I heard he'd met a girl a few summers ago and didn't tell me, especially when Indie showed up at CLU last year. He eventually told me the story, and they've pretty much been inseparable ever since. She's fierce and independent, whereas he's soft and stubborn, but they work, and I like seeing him happy. "You know she gave me a lecture about laying off Quinn the other day?"

"What did she say?" I ask curiously.

"Apparently, the whole protective big brother thing is a turnoff for guys." He snorts. "I told her good, that's the point." He winces at the memory. "That was the wrong thing to say, though. It got me another talking-to about how Quinn is the boss of her own life and not me and how I'm stifling her, blah, blah, blah."

I laugh. That sounds about right. "We've always been Quinn's armor, though. She used to like it when we step up for her."

"Exactly." Seb's hands go up in exasperation before itching the back of his neck. "I don't know. I guess it doesn't work now that we're adults. I do see what she's saying, but she's my little sister..."

"I get it, man. I feel protective of her too."

"I know. I always liked the idea that she had both of us looking out for her." A soft smile tugs at his mouth. "But I think it's best to let her do her thing now, and then, when some douchebag hurts her, we step in again. Indie might be right. We should back off."

"You say 'we'..." I give him a pointed look.

"Hey, don't act like you didn't scare off that guy at her junior prom."

I scoff. "He was an asshole." Jason Vance *was* the biggest asshole. I'd heard him talking—no, *bragging*—to his friends about how far he wanted to go with Quinn that night. I knew they'd been dating for a while and, yeah, guys his age would brag about sex, but I still didn't like it. So, I may have had a hand in that one.

"I agree." He nods. "But like I said, now we back off."

Back off? He can't be for real. Queenie is too sweet, too kind to let assholes walk all over her, and college guys are assholes. I should know. I don't realize how hard I'm clenching my fists until I feel the bite of my nails in my palm. Yeah, fuck that. "I didn't get the lecture from Indie. I'm still keeping an eye on her."

Seb half groans, half laughs. "You can't, man."

I slap a hand on his shoulder as we turn the corner, and the campus dorms come into view. "I'll do my best to keep the douchiest guys away from her. I'll be subtle."

"You? Subtle? Unlikely."

Yeah, maybe he's not wrong. But I won't let one of my best friends get hurt.

Chapter Six

Quinn

"Oooh, what about him?" Indie asks with her pointer finger outstretched. She's taking this whole 'Quinn goes dating' thing incredibly seriously. I follow her line of sight and grimace, my nose wrinkling in protest.

"Ashley Prescott?" I question, equal parts horrified and in disbelief that my friend would suggest him. The guy is gorgeous, and he knows it. All wide grins and floppy blond hair, big, flexing biceps, and he's on the lacrosse team. I don't think I want to go there. He also sleeps with anything that has a pulse. "Hard pass."

Indie snorts a laugh as she brushes her blonde curls away from her face, and continues perusing the cafeteria of unknowing suitors, all for my benefit. They squirrel around innocently, going about their day, with no idea they're being scouted by us—or, more accurately, my best friend and her shrewd gaze.

"Hmm, slim pickings here today. I know some guys in my music classes."

I can tell she already knows my heart isn't in it. I'm lovesick, have been my whole existence, and there's no cure. Yet here I am, trying to move on.

I shrug, lowering my chin into the palm of my hand, my gut churning at the thought of not getting what I ultimately want. "There's no point."

Indie's hand slaps down on the table between us, startling me for a second. "There is a point," she insists. Her wide blue eyes pin me with determination. She's a great friend, the best, and I can't imagine my life without her now. "You haven't dated anyone since freshman year, and you can't keep waiting for something to miraculously happen. That's not the Quinn I know."

I wave her off, even though she's right. I'm stubborn and go after what I want. Well, usually. "I'll get over it. This happens sometimes." It's the truth. I go through phases of love and loss without having ever romantically been involved with the person I love. It's like sunshine without the warmth. Ice cream without the sugar high. But the thing is, I wouldn't change how I feel.

Unrequited love sucks. But never having known what it's like to love him, even if it's from afar, that would suck more. I know I only have myself to blame because I expose myself to him almost daily and remain silent. No words pass my lips as my heart ricochets around my chest when he's nearby. Not a single syllable slips out to admit the truth as my body thrums when he walks into a room. I've trained myself well to appear nonchalant, yet inside I'm burning, yearning, and testing the limits of how high my blood pressure can go.

"I'm not accepting that." One thing I know about Indie is, she rarely gives up when her sights are set on something. "You need to date again," she demands. I go to protest, but as luck would have it, Jay and Hudson choose this exact moment to join us at the table.

"Who needs a date? I'm available." Hudson grins, mid-chomp on a carrot stick, placing his tray of food on our table. Jay sits next to him and shakes his head.

I've gotten used to Hudson's advances. Weirdly, I think it's just in his nature to be flirty and he doesn't mean much by it. Unless he wants to piss my brother off.

"No one needs a date," I say, just as Indie announces, "Quinn does."

Excellent. Let's bring more people into this.

I watch as Hudson's grin grows and those dark brown eyes twinkle at me. "I've told you before, Quinn. I'm always down for a little action."

"Oh, well, in that case, please whisk me away and do your worst, because I'm totally interested," I quip. Fluttering my eyelashes at him, he just stares at me, food paused halfway to his lips.

"Wait—"

"It's called sarcasm, Huds. Don't get excited." As I roll my eyes playfully, Jay laughs next to him. He focuses his gaze on me and smiles.

"Como vais, Quinn?"

My brain immediately boots into Portuguese mode, the little I know, but I hesitate, thinking about how I want to say what I need to. "Estou de boa... E tu?"

His smile widens as he pushes his black-rimmed glasses up

his nose. "Very good pronunciation. You're doing well. I'm all good, though, if you don't count the fact that Hudson here"—he elbows his friend in the ribs—"needed rescuing from a hookup gone wrong at two a.m. this morning."

Hudson grunts and chews through his mouthful before answering. "She went all clingy on me. I freaked. She locked the door to her dorm and everything. I felt like I was trapped. The only way out was to tell her my best friend was outside having an anaphylactic shock and I had his EpiPen."

Silence dances over us as Indie frowns at Hudson. "Your logic is warped. Have you ever tried honesty?"

Hudson scoffs. "I told a girl once I was horny and wanted to have sex with her, and she slapped me and left. Honesty makes me an asshole, apparently."

I stifle a laugh. Good for her, I'd slap him too. "With charming words like that? I'm shocked." I mock gasp.

"I know, right?" Hudson agrees, then shoves more food into his mouth.

"You're hopeless." Jay snickers before devouring his pasta.

Hudson growls but says no more, and when he emerges a few minutes later from his now empty lunch plate, he locks eyes with me again. "So, why do you need a date?"

"I don't *need* a date. I *want* a date. There's a difference," I insist, just as another body joins us and my skin prickles with awareness. I know exactly who has just sat next to me because my body is attuned to his nearness.

"Hey, Miles, we're just helping Quinn get a date."

"And you and Seb are not going to sabotage," Indie adds with a pointed look.

I glare venomously at the people in front of me, my so-called friends who are insistent on meddling.

Hudson ignores me, continuing to talk to Miles. "You get the email from coach about the meet later?"

"Yeah, we're reviewing tapes before the game."

Hudson nods, and then Miles turns to face me, his brown eyes curious. "You want to date Hudson?" he asks, his low baritone voice hitting me square in the ribs, reminding me who I really want in this façade. Something rattles inside me like a loose screw, unsettling me again.

"Listen, I'm available—" Hudson begins.

"I was asking Quinn," Miles cuts him off, his tone firmer than he'd usually speak, with an unreadable look in his eyes. "Well? Is that what *you* want?"

"Yeah, I want to date." I fluster for a second before adding, "But not Hudson." I cast an apologetic glance to him and return to Miles. "I want to be wanted by someone and get butterflies and have someone care enough to be around me without you and my brother ruining it." I'm practically hissing, my sudden anger surprising me too.

My nostrils flare as I stare at him and he stares back, but nothing changes in the way he's looking at me. I don't know what I expected to happen, for him to suddenly confess his love for me? *Hilarious.*

"You don't date much," Hudson interrupts, breaking our eye contact as Miles looks away. Misplaced disappointment lines my stomach as I drag my gaze to the boy who's more giddy puppy than linebacker. "So, I'm going to guess your type. Clearly, it's not great if you don't want *me*." He leans toward me to whisper loudly, "Which is a mistake, by the way." Leaning back, he continues. "I love love, and I'd be a great choice." His eyes glitter with excitement.

"No, Huds. You love hooking up," Jay counters, placing his fork on top of his empty plate.

He waves off Jay and begins searching the crowd around the room. "Let's see who we've got here, then. We can't have you going without sex."

Groaning, I lower my head to the table with a light thud. This was a bad idea. "I said *date*. I know this might be foreign to you, Hudson, but people can date without sex to begin with."

Hudson scoffs at my comment, not stopping his search.

"I wish I could help you and get him to stop," Jay offers apologetically as I look up at him with pleading eyes. "But I've known him for years now, and he's like a dog with a bone."

Hudson rubs his hands together, mischief emanating from him. "Not him," he says as he scans the room eagerly. "Nope. No. He's not the one. No. Ahh, what about Zach Mackenzie?"

"The hockey player?" I ask, just as a grumbly noise echoes next to me. Was that Miles?

"Yeah. He's over there," Hudson says, pointing behind me, distracting me from overthinking the noise I think Miles made. Turning to rest my chin on my shoulder, to look subtly, I see Zach. He's standing in front of the drink fridge, one hand leaning at the top as he flexes his hand against the door, and his muscles pop a little with the movement. I can't deny the guy is insanely good looking, with his t-shirt rippling across his wide, muscled back. His dark hair is cropped short to his head, and his blue eyes are a stark contrast to his dark skin. The guy is a walking orgasm. "Oooh, Quinn is ogling him."

Another grumbling noise next to me. I definitely didn't imagine that one. He's probably assessing the need to intervene and how to stop anyone from getting within fifty feet of me, but if he thinks he can stop me, he'll have to answer to an incredibly determined Indie and now, apparently, Hudson too. "I am not ogling." Zach's beautiful, but he's not the boy sitting beside me. And that is yet another reason I know I should start dating again—less exposure to my one true love, and more exposure to people I can learn to love. Foolproof, right?

"He's fresh out of a relationship. His ex left him just before we got back this semester. I don't know the full story, but he could be a fun time. Or are we looking for a long time?" Hudson asks and, truthfully, I don't know.

"Uhhh," I fumble, wringing my hands under the table.

"I think she needs to get railed." Indie surprises me, and I spin to face her, mouth dropped open.

"Indiana!" I chastise.

She shrugs, casually sipping her water. "I speak the truth."

"What about Killian from my photography class?" Jay suggests. "Do you know him? Tall guy, blond hair, lives in my dorm, usually at most parties we go to."

"I know who you mean, but—"

"Not him," Miles mumbles, but no one acknowledges him.

"There's also Dylan. You know the drummer in my classes?" Indie interrupts, but all it does is fog my brain, and I feel my frustration like a frog in my throat. Am I not allowed a say in any of this?

"Pfft, a drummer?" Miles nudges me, eyebrow raised. I open my mouth to respond, but don't get the chance.

"Or Guy from my business class. He's always nice and super smart," Jay suggests, just as Miles sighs, and I see his hand run down his face from the corner of my eye.

"Everyone, please—" I begin.

"Hey, Zach!" Hudson bellows, and I wish more than anything a giant sinkhole really would open up to swallow me whole. With strides of a true athlete, Zach strolls over to us with grace and speed, and when he gets to our table, I realize I've shrunk into myself.

"What's up, Parker?" He addresses Hudson with a smile, but it doesn't reach his eyes. They remain sad. Yeah, this guy is clearly still heartbroken over someone, and this is a terrible idea.

"Do you know Quinn?" Hudson asks, presenting me to him like a game show host. Where is that sinkhole, please, lord? I sit up straighter to offer a polite greeting.

His blue eyes land on my green ones, and he smiles. It's honest and sweet, and I still can't deny he's really cute. "Yeah, you're Dawson's little sis, right?"

I nod. "That's me. Also known as Quinn." I wave and smile back at him, just as another growl rumbles through Miles.

"Why are you growling and mumbling over there, Cooper?" Indie asks, mirth lacing her tone.

His brown eyes narrow on her. "I'm not growling," he says indignantly. "But if I *was* growling, I'd tell Mackenzie here to get lost and find another girl to hit on." He changes in an instant and flashes a calculated grin at Zach, causing tension to slice through the table. Jeez Louise, is it hot in here?

Zach's eyes go wide as he straightens and steps away from me. "I'm not, I mean... Quinn, you're great and really beautiful, but uh... I just got out of a relationship, and I'm not really looking for anything." The poor guy looks like he might throw up, which does wonders for a girl's self-esteem.

My cheeks flame, the heat creeping under my skin like a

disease, but I'm a pro at hiding how I'm feeling. "That's okay. I'm also not looking for anything. These guys ran away with the matchmaker idea. Ignore them."

Zach looks around nervously, and as he finds all eyes on him, a little blush colors the apples of his cheeks. "Okay, cool. There are some guys on my team who—"

"No," Miles booms, and everyone swings their attention to him.

"No?" I choke out, staring at his stupidly handsome scowl.

"No hockey players," he says casually, stabbing his fork into his salad and ignoring my death glare.

The balls on this guy. If I didn't love him, I'd hate him. "Oh, and football players are better?" I challenge.

"Yes, we are." He swings his gaze to Zach. "Sorry, dude, she won't be dating anyone from your team."

Faking a thought, I tap my chin. "I didn't realize you were the boss of me." I turn to Zach with a flirty smile. "If any of your teammates are single, tell them I'm throwing a party in a few weeks, and I'd love for them to come."

Zach's eyes flick between Miles and me, but then he nods and smiles. "Sure thing. See you all around."

Hudson makes a low, whistling sound. "I can't wait to come to your party, Quinn. Wait, I'm invited too, right? No, don't answer that. Of course I am."

For the second time today, I roll my eyes at Hudson. "Yes, you're invited. All of you are." I look at Miles and scowl. "Except you." Because I'm feeling petty. And despite his protective stance today, he doesn't want me. He wants to keep me safe. Well, maybe safe is boring. Maybe I'm done playing it safe. Maybe I'm done with possessive, growly boys who have no intention of doing anything about it.

He guffaws, but I see a little smirk lift the side of his mouth.

Even though it was a spur-of-the-moment idea, I'm having this party. Now I need to rally my best friend into helping me organize it.

CHAPTER SEVEN

Miles

WHEN YOU'RE FACED WITH a decision for your future, no one tells you how many roads there are to take. No one tells you that it's so multifaceted when you make decisions for yourself as an adult. There're needs versus wants, right and wrong, morals and dilemmas. But that gray area? The in-between, it's huge. Often, the answer to what we want and doing what's right isn't always the same.

The little white pill weighs heavily in my hand. A tiny, embossed line on the one side grazes against my fingertips as I sit at my desk in my room.

Waiting.

Battling with myself, because I know the consequences. I know the risks.

Yet, every time I think of being able to impress my dad, I take it. Consequences be damned. Rinse and repeat. This is my third game doing it—fourth, if you count last year. And each one, I've gotten a better reaction from him. Can I do this without help now? The question plagues me. I hate the low and the mood swings and the shitty feeling afterward, but the high from knowing my dad is proud of me again? I can't stop chasing it.

My phone buzzes on my bedside table. I glance over, and it's like he knows I'm about to do something that could fuck up my whole career.

I place the pill back on my desk, next to the Tylenol pot I keep it in, and swipe the screen, mustering up all the energy I have to lift it to my ear. "Morning, Dad."

"Did you call him?" Dad's voice is sharp, no greeting, no warmth—just straight to the point.

I hesitate. "Uh...not yet."

"You *what?*" His tone drops, lower, more dangerous. "I told you days ago, Miles. And I've sent reminders. How hard is it to pick up the damn phone and make an appointment?"

"I was going to, but—"

"But what?" he snaps, cutting me off. "Too busy? Too tired? You've got an excuse for everything, don't you?"

My heart starts pounding harder. "I just... I forgot, okay?"

"Forgot?" he repeats, voice rising. "This is your career we're talking about. You think anyone else is going to forget to take care of their body? You think the competition's out there slacking off like you?"

"I'm not slacking," I say, but it comes out weak, almost defensive, and I hate myself for sounding that way.

"Really?" he barks. "Then where are you right now? Hmm?"

My throat tightens. "I'm, uh, just—"

"Stop stuttering, Miles," he hisses. "Where. Are. You?" Each word resonates like a slap, his anger rising with each one.

"I'm at home," I admit quietly, wincing in anticipation.

"You're supposed to be at the gym!" He's past the point of exploding now. "I gave you a schedule for a reason, and you're ignoring it? Do you even care about this? About any of it?"

"Of course I care!" I blurt out. "I just needed a break, Dad. I can't—"

"Oh, right, a break. Sure. Because you've earned that, right? With all the hard work you're putting in? You didn't even call the damn nutritionist!" He lets out a harsh laugh. "You don't want this bad enough, Miles. You're wasting time, *my* time, and you don't even realize it."

His words slice into me, guilt and something much darker curling in my stomach. I grip the phone tighter, attempting to stay calm. "I'm trying," I reply through gritted teeth.

"Trying isn't good enough!" he yells. "Trying gets you nowhere. Action gets you results. You keep this up, and you're going to end up like everyone else—mediocre. Is that what you want? To be just another guy who didn't make it because he couldn't stick to a simple plan?"

I'm silent. I don't know what to say. I *hate* when he talks to me like this, like I'm already failing before I've even started.

"Miles, I'm telling you this because I know what it takes. And if you can't handle the pressure now, then maybe this isn't for you."

That hits even deeper. I bite my lip, my chest tight with frustration and rage I can't release. "I'll call the nutritionist," I mumble, just to end the conversation.

"You better," he says, voice cold as ice. "And get to the gym. *Now*. I don't care how tired you are. If you want this, you'll do what needs to be done. If not, I'll stop wasting my time."

"No," I whisper, defeated, but hating that I'm succumbing to him. "I want to do this."

"Then get your ass in the fucking gym and call the nutritionist. You'd better not be this sloppy at tonight's game."

Just then, I hear the faint call of a flight number in the background. He must be at the airport. I swallow hard, dread creeping up my spine. "You're coming?" I ask.

"Of course I'm coming. Why would I not?"

My chest tightens at the thought of screwing up again, of him watching from the stands, eyes burning into me every time I miss a pass or hesitate on the field. The weight of his expectations pressing down on me is suffocating.

"You better not embarrass me."

The line goes dead before I can respond.

The dial tone I'm so accustomed to greets me, and my grip tightens around my phone, before I launch it across my room with a deafening roar. Anger grips me in its fierce jaw, as I watch the device smash into the doorframe and land with an echoing crack. My breaths are heavy, weighted, and harsh as adrenaline courses through me all the way down to my toes.

I stand in a rush and grab my gym bag, slinging it over my shoulder as irritation makes my skin crawl. Why the fuck can't I just tell him to fuck off? Even in my haze, I know why. My fists open and close rhythmically as the pill catches my eye again. The elephant in the room, my saving grace and my damnation. I'm moving toward my desk before I can register what I'm doing. This is my only option to get him off my back. I've worked hard my entire life, but it's never enough, and I need an edge. I need this.

So, I take one and pocket the rest, heading out to the gym, just like he wanted. I pause by the door, staring down at the spiderweb crack on my phone, that spreads from the corner of the screen. Damaged. Broken. Tainted. Just like my relationship with my father.

***

The first quarter is a whirlwind of intense action. Seb is on fire, his passes precise. Our offense is clicking, and we're moving the ball down the field with a rhythm that feels unstoppable. Hudson, our outside linebacker, is anchoring our defense, making crucial tackles and keeping the San Jose's offense in check. I'm in the zone, blocking hard, running my routes, and waiting for my moment.

I've barely thought about the fact that my dad is here. I didn't see him before the game, which is for the best. It meant I could focus and get my head where I needed it to be.

On the next play, I move to the line of scrimmage. The snap comes, and I rocket off the mark, breaking into my route. I glance back just in time to see Seb's eyes lock onto mine. The ball spirals through the air toward me. I leap, fully extending as my fingers make contact with the leather. Pulling it in, I secure the ball tightly as I hit the ground. First down.

The crowd goes wild, and I can hear the chants of our fans, their energy feeding into our performance. We huddle up, and Seb's eyes are blazing with determination.

"Great catch, Miles," he says, clapping me on the shoulder.

"Great throw, QB."

We line up again, and I see the San Jose defense adjusting, trying to read our play. But Seb's too smart for them. He changes the play at the line, calling an audible. I nod, understanding my new route. The snap comes, and I'm off again, cutting through the middle of the field. Seb's under pressure, but he stays calm and releases the ball just before a defender gets to him. It's a perfect throw, and our tight end, Chris, catches it in stride, sprinting down the sideline for another big gain.

By the fourth quarter, we've built a solid lead, but we can't let up. The opposition is fighting back, and we need to stay sharp. I glance over to the sidelines where the cheer squad stand in their uniforms and spot Quinn immediately, her flame red hair pulled up into a ponytail and a beaming smile on her face as she waves her pom-poms at me. "Go eighty-eight!" she yells, and I can't stop the smile from spreading across my face.

Just as I refocus and go to make my break, a hulking guy named Derek, blindsides me with a late hit. Pain explodes through my side, and I hit the ground hard. The referee's whistle blows, signaling a penalty, but it's too late to stop the surge of anger that rises within me.

I push myself up, ignoring the pain, and get in his face. "What the hell was that?" I shout, shoving him.

He smirks, unfazed. "Welcome to real football, pretty boy. Too busy staring at the ass on the side of the pitch to notice me? That's your too bad."

When he flicks the side of my helmet, that's all it takes. My fists clench, and before I can think, I'm shoving him again. He stumbles back, but then surges toward me. "You're a fucking asshole!" I shout, just as he gets one decent right hook to my ribs, exactly where he knocked into me. The pain of his hit registers, but it doesn't stop me. The field erupts into chaos as players from both teams rush in, trying to tear us apart. I can hear the crowd roaring, the mix of cheers and boos adding to the frenzy.

Seb and Hudson are there in an instant, pulling me back. "Miles, calm down!" Seb yells, his grip firm on my shoulder. "What's gotten into you?"

"Let it go, man," Hudson adds, his voice urgent. "We need you in the game, not on the bench."

Derek is led away by his teammates, grinning like he's won. He hasn't won a fucking thing, the prick. I take a deep breath, trying to rein in my anger. But as the ref passes him, I see his face contort in fury as he throws his helmet off, and I know exactly what's coming for me next.

He reaches me in four strides. "Eighty-eight, you're off too. I don't care who started it," he says, his voice leaving no room for argument.

Seb and Hudson loosen their grips on me. "Miles, go cool off," Seb mutters, but I barely hear him. The anger and adrenaline still course through my veins and cloud my thoughts.

As I make my way to the sideline, Coach approaches, his expression a storm of rage and frustration too. Hooray, it seems everyone is pissed tonight. "Miles, that was reckless. We needed you out there, not getting into fights!" he barks, his voice a harsh whisper meant only for me.

"Fuck," I whisper. "I know, Coach, I'm sorry," I manage to say, but it sounds hollow. The reality of my actions sinks in, and I realize how much I've let my team down.

I slump onto the bench, my head in my hands, the pain in my side a dull throb compared to the ache of how much I've fucked up tonight.

And worse? My dad is here somewhere, watching the whole thing.

Fuck.

CHAPTER EIGHT

Quinn

I HAVE ONE GOAL in mind as I jog toward the locker room entrance. I need to check on Miles. After he was benched, he wouldn't look at me again; he focused on the game and shut out everything else. And even though the team won, he stalked off to the locker room just before everyone left the field. I took the fastest shower of my life and changed before heading down here. I know I shouldn't be here, but I need to see him.

Players pass me by in a blur of suits, but I'm not paying attention to their faces.

My brother spots me and steps in front of the locker room door, blocking my way. "Quinn, he's not in the mood for a pep talk," Seb says.

"What makes you think I'm going to do that? I want to check he's okay." Glaring up at him, I will him to move but he doesn't.

"Trust us, you'll want to leave him alone tonight," Hudson

adds, making me bite my cheek to stop from snapping, but it's no use.

My jaw clenches. "No, I want to see him."

I have to.

Seb sighs and hangs his head low. "His dad is in there right now. Coach just left. It's not pretty."

"I don't care. He needs his friends."

"Quinn, please," Seb begs, frustration lacing his tone.

"I'm not interested in what Miles the football player is doing right now. I need to know that my best friend is okay."

I'm done with this conversation. If his dad is in there, making him feel like shit, I'm not going to let that happen because, knowing Miles, he already feels like shit without people drilling it into him. I force my way past Seb and Hudson and smack my hands on the heavy door, pushing it open.

Immediately, I can make out the edges of a voice, harsh and cutting, though the words aren't clear. It's obvious he's shouting. Berating. Furious. My feet stutter and my pace slows in anticipation.

I chew on my bottom lip as I debate what to do. I know I shouldn't eavesdrop, but the pull of curiosity and concern is too strong. Miles got kicked out of the game, and he'll feel awful for fighting. He never fights, so something isn't right. I inch closer to the door, the cold metal handle brushing against my arm.

Through the narrow crack in the doorway, I see Miles sitting on the bench, his white shirt half open, with his suit trousers on. It looks like his dad barely gave him a chance to get dressed. His shoulders are hunched and his head down as his dad looms over him, gesticulating wildly, casting dark shadows over Miles as he paces across the room. I strain to hear, pressing myself as close to the door as I can without drawing attention.

"How could you be so goddamn careless?" Miles's dad's voice finally comes through more clearly.

When he spins around, I see his face is a mask of anger, his jaw set in a hard line. It makes me shrivel, and I'm not the one he's directing it at.

"I don't know, Dad," he mumbles, sounding dejected. "It was just a bad game."

"A bad game?" He huffs incredulously. Stopping his pacing, he faces Miles once more, leaning forward and jabbing his finger toward his son, venom pouring from each word as he spits, "That was more than a bad game, Miles. You were a disaster out there—both in your attitude and your fucking playing. Maybe if you're head wasn't up your fucking ass, you wouldn't have been so sloppy." He straightens, ticking off faults on his fingers, which, in my opinion, weren't event that bad. "You missed that block in the second quarter, you fumbled the ball in the third, and let's not even talk about that fight that finally got you taken out of the game. All things I know should never have happened. You're better than that. *I* trained you better than that. You're not some pathetic wannabe out on that field. Your Miles fucking Cooper. I expect you to fucking act like it."

Miles flinches with each accusation. I want so badly to walk in there and give him some kind of reassurance, but that probably isn't going to be enough tonight. The knot in my stomach tightens as I wait helplessly behind a door I'm not sure I should open.

"You let your team down." His dad continues, letting his sour mood emanate from him, not bothering to filter his emotions. "You let *me* down. I worked so hard to get you to this point, and this is what you do with it?"

A loud bang startles me, and I realize it's the sound of his dad's fist hitting the metal lockers. Suddenly, the door I'm leaning against flies opens, and I stumble forward as Seb storms past me. I hadn't even realized he was standing behind me. "Woah, woah, sir," Seb cuts in, standing between them in the middle of the room. "With all due respect, Miles isn't the only one on the team."

I'm rooted in place, my body frozen. I don't know if I should follow my brother, but at the last second, my foot catches the door before it closes completely. Not that I can move, caught between the doorway and the room. Mark Cooper is frightening, and I don't know how to react.

Turning his wild eyes to my brother, he hisses a dark laugh. "I'm well aware of that, Sebastian. I'll be reporting to your father too. I don't think he'll be pleased to see how distracted his star player was out there."

Seb rears back in disbelief.

"That's enough!" Miles bellows. Fury flares his nostrils as he stands, knocking his helmet to the ground. "You need to leave," he growls, his voice deeper and darker than I've ever heard before.

The room feels smaller. I'm pretty sure I've stopped breathing.

Mr. Cooper's mood becomes deadly, suffocating even. When he takes one menacing step toward Miles, my heart lurches. Surely, he wouldn't... I don't have to see him to know his teeth are gritted as he hisses loud enough to be heard, "This isn't over." With that, he turns and leaves, the black cloud following him, wrenching open the door being propped by my foot and brushing past me without a care.

"Can't fucking wait," Miles mutters, running a hand down his face.

My mouth opens and closes, but I have no idea what I can say to make this better. Tentatively, I walk over to the bench and sit next to him. My brother does the same, but it's like Miles hasn't noticed, his gaze glued to the floor. I can feel the tension radiating off him, like he's trying to hold himself together.

Growing up, we all knew that Mark Cooper had a temper; I've just never witnessed it like this before. It's a lot of the reason Miles spent so much time at our house, especially since his mom passed. My parents used to say that he was grieving, and he needed to work through it, but it's been *years*, and nothing has changed, it seems.

I move my hand closer to his, where he grips the bench with whitened knuckles, and brush my pinky finger against his. He jolts at the movement, his eyes immediately going to our hands. When his eyes rise to mine, they're so full of emotion that it steals my breath for a second.

I want to do anything I can to make him forget about every harsh word. He doesn't deserve this, no one does.

Seb clears his throat. "Miles, I'm sorry about your dad."

Miles shakes his head, but his hand wraps over mine absently, squeezing it. "I just want to go home," he murmurs. "I need to sleep."

I exchange a glance with Seb.

"Miles, it's—"

"Please don't. Whatever you're about to say, just don't," he pleads, trying to keep his voice even. "I just want to sleep it off."

"Alright," I say softly, then stand, not dropping his hand.

"Let's get you home."

Seb stands too and pats Miles's shoulder. "We're here for you, man. Don't forget that."

I extend my other hand in a fist like I always do. "First down."

He hesitates, and my heart stutters, but then, his hand gently knocks against mine. "All the way," he whispers, with a ghost of a smirk. It doesn't matter that it lacks his usual conviction; he said it, and that means he hears us.

Miles drops my hands and says, "Give me a second to finish getting dressed, and I'll meet you out there."

***

We walk Miles back to his dorm, where he tells us about a thousand times he will be fine and to leave him be. My brother can clearly sense my hesitation because he puts a hand on my shoulder, directing me to face him as soon as he closes the door.

"We'll leave him tonight. I want to come with you to see Indie quickly, and then I'll come back here and be across the hall. It's fine, Quinn."

I nod, but I'm distracted.

How can I be okay with leaving him when he feels so low? How am I meant to sleep, knowing he is hurting? More importantly, how can I take that pain from him? I can't, and I know he needs time, but it makes me ache.

As we get to my dorm, the faint hum of music greets us. Paramore, I realize.

"I told her to go home and wait for us," Seb states, as if hearing my thoughts.

Opening my door, I see Indie sitting on her desk chair. "Hey," she says, putting her book down. "How is he?"

"He's feeling like shit," Seb sighs as he runs a hand over his hair. "I'm hoping he just needs sleep." Walking over to Indie, he gently kisses her temple.

"I'm worried about him," I say, finally vocalizing my thoughts. "I don't think he's been himself this year."

Seb sprawls out on Indie's bed. "Things haven't been easy for him. Mark is a piece of work. I'll get his head on straight, though."

"Hmm." I acknowledge what my brother is saying, but everything in my body and mind is telling me that I need to do more, to figure out how I can help him. "I'm going to shower."

I wash off the game and the whole day, trying to think of scenarios and things I can do to lift his mood. It all feels superficial now, because this, what his dad said tonight, those things can't be taken back. They're permanent.

With a sigh, I reach for my towel, quickly dress, and return to my room within ten minutes. Seb is still on Indie's bed, but she's moved to be next to him now. I put my cheer outfit to one side and begin brushing my hair, my thoughts still on Miles. Always on him.

"Soooo," Indie begins in a tone that I rarely hear from her. It snaps my head up, and I turn to face them on the other side of the room, curiosity piqued.

"Why does that 'soooo' feel fully loaded?" I narrow my eyes at her.

She flicks her tongue over her lip ring rhythmically before answering, a habit when she's nervous. "I know the timing isn't great, but I might've found you a date."

For a moment, I'm frozen, processing the information. Then, a million questions flood my brain. None of which I have the energy to ask. "Oh?"

"He's in my music class. You might know him. He took the same AP Calc class as you last year. He's six feet tall. He's nice, a little quiet, plays the cello, is super talented, and his name is Alex."

My hands instantly go clammy, and I place my brush down, wringing my fingers together, unsure how to deal with the anxiety that's suddenly racing through me. "I don't remember an Alex, but maybe I'd know him if I saw him?" My feet trace the length of our room and back again. I don't know how to feel about actually going on a date. We talked about it, and it was all my idea, but actually knowing someone is interested, and it could happen, that's scary. It feels final, like I'm somehow betraying something that never actually existed between Miles and me. Which is completely insane to even think of us as a *we*. He is him and I'm me. There's no us.

No matter the timing of it, I can't help but feel like this is my opportunity to move on. To stop obsessing over someone who doesn't have a clue about how I feel.

Turning to face them, I notice Seb's lack of enthusiasm. Indie's influence, no doubt. "And you don't have anything to say about this?" I ask him.

His gaze briefly flits to me, but Indie cuts in. "Tell her how happy you are." Her death stare, usually reserved for when Jay and Hudson bicker, makes even my brother shudder.

When his eyes meet mine, the same color reflects back at me. His mouth firmly placed into a forced smile that fools no one. "Thrilled," he grits out, and I have to curl my lips inwards to stop a bellowing laugh from escaping.

Indie sighs loudly. "He is happy for you."

"Absolutely." I chuckle. "And you're not going to butt in at any point, right?"

"I will not sabotage."

"Was that so hard?" Indie asks.

"It was, actually," Seb retorts.

The reality of having a date with someone who knows of me and isn't deterred by my brother, well, that makes me little bit giddy. "I've got a date." I test the words on my tongue, and they feel odd.

Seb grunts in disapproval. He's always been the best big brother, but thanks to Indie, I'm finally feeling like I can spread my wings a little more. "Oh god, what do I wear? Where am I going? Is it casual?" My heart rate kicks up a notch, and I can't tell if its nerves, fear, or excitement. *Try everything.*

"I have his number for you. I wasn't about to give yours out, because girl code and all."

"You're the best."

She shrugs and reaches for her phone, pinging me his details. "I know."

My brother stands, packing away his laptop and notebook. "I'm going back to check on Miles." He leans down to whisper something to Indie that I know I don't want to hear, judging by the color of her cheeks. And the mention of his name brings back that guilt. Should I be thinking about dating when he's hurting? God, I sound so ridiculous. He doesn't care about me like that. Sure, he cares. Miles is so incredibly caring and thoughtful; he always has been, but he doesn't see me like I see him.

Resolve fires into my bloodstream. I need to get a grip. I can still be there for him as a friend if he needs me, but I need to move on.

Opening my phone, I see Alex's details and force a swallow. Why do I feel so nervous? My fingers hover over the keyboard, the words blurring together. It's just a text. A simple message. Why does it feel like such a big deal?

Come on, Quinn. It's not that hard, I think to myself. But the more I think about it, the more my stomach twists. What if I say something wrong? What if Alex doesn't reply? What if he thinks I'm boring? A thousand what-ifs swirl in my mind, making me want to lock my phone and go back to lying on my bed.

"You okay over there?" Indie asks. When I look up, I realize my brother has gone, and I didn't even notice him leave.

"I've never texted a guy asking him out before. What do I say?"

"You could say… 'Hey, Alex, it's Quinn. Indie mentioned that we should hang out sometime.' Simple, direct, and it opens the conversation."

Covering my face with my hands, I groan. "It should be easy. I tend to ramble, though, and he might think he's made a mistake before we've even met."

"You? Ramble? I never realized," Indie teases.

"Oh, she's funny today," I quip.

Indie rolls her eyes, coming to sit next to me, playfully nudging me with her shoulder. "Quinn, it's just a text. Alex is not going to dissect every word. Just be yourself."

I peek at her through my fingers. "Easier said than done. What if he thinks I'm weird?"

"Newsflash: we're all weird. And if he doesn't appreciate your unique brand of weirdness, then he's not the right guy for you," Indie says firmly.

I consider it, then nod slowly. "Yeah, that sounds good." I open my phone again, typing out the message. After a moment's hesitation, I hit send and toss it to the side like it's on fire. "There, done," I say on an exhale.

"See? That wasn't so bad. Now, the hard part is over."

I laugh nervously. "Yeah, now I just have to wait and see if he replies."

Indie grins at me. "He will. And if he doesn't, it's his loss. You're awesome, Quinn. Don't forget that."

I smile, feeling a little bit of the tension ease from my shoulders. "Thanks, Indie. I don't know what I'd do without you."

She winks. "Probably still be staring at your phone. Now, let's go do something to take your mind off everything. How about we watch that terrible movie we've been avoiding?"

Anything to distract me sounds great.

CHAPTER NINE

Miles

"Fuuuuuuuck." I wake up with my head pounding, the remnants of last night hanging on like a bad smell. My mouth feels like it's stuffed with cotton, and my eyes squint against the light filtering through the curtains. I didn't even drink anything last night, but the combination of stress and a comedown have made me feel worse than any alcoholic hangover.

I already know it's going to be a rough day. Dragging my tired body out of bed, my muscles protest, especially the ones on my side where I took the hits on the field. Lifting my shirt, I gently graze my fingers over the skin that is turning purple near my ribs. "Great," I mutter to myself. Painkillers are a must. Reaching for the Tylenol pot, my fingers skim the side, pushing it off my nightstand and dropping to the floor. "Dammit," I hiss, grimacing as I lean down to pick it up and unscrew the lid. For a moment, I stare at the amphetamines inside rather than the painkillers, twirling the container in my hand, hearing the pills rattle inside, reminding me of how little it helped last night.

I quickly stuff the pot into my duffel bag, wanting to forget all about last night, and reach for the other box of actual Tylenol this time.

Standing in the middle of my room, I try to distance my thoughts from yesterday, but it's useless. The memory of Dad's yelling from last night crashes over me like a wave. His voice, sharp and bitter, echoes in my ears. The humiliation of Seb and Hudson having to intervene, the look of pity from Quinn that hits worse than my dad's words ever could. I glance at my phone on the nightstand, the screen cracked from when I threw it against the wall in frustration before the game. A reminder of how things are spiraling out of control.

I decide I don't need a shower right now, so I stay in bed for a while, trying to muster up the energy to face the day. My stomach churns, both from the comedown and the guilt gnawing at me, and probably hunger, since I've normally eaten three times by this point.

Grimacing, I grab my phone and try to read through an injury prevention assignment we're working on in my sports physio class. When this was given to us, I felt excited because I spend my life working with trainers and physios preventing injury on the field. I had a good idea of what I wanted to do, how I was going to execute the assignment, but now, staring at my notes, it all feels pointless.

Last year, I decided my degree would be in sports physio. My dad has no idea, but Seb's dad told us how important it was to set our future selves up for anything beyond football, and it resonated with me. It was easy to combine with football and, more importantly, it felt natural to me. I was good at it. My grades were always highest in these classes, so it made sense. Now, though? I feel the intense need to give it all up, and I'm well aware that's just my current headspace.

Closing the app, I heave out a frustrated sigh at the fact I can barely concentrate.

Eventually, I drag myself out of bed and into the shower, hoping the hot water will wash away my sour mood. It helps a little, but not much. I pull on some sweats and a hoodie, figuring I'll just hide out in my room for the rest of the day.

My phone buzzes with messages from my friends, asking if I'm okay. I send back quick, half-hearted replies of "I'm fine. Just need a day to chill." I know they don't buy it, but I don't have the energy to explain.

Hours pass in a blur of mindless scrolling and napping. The sunlight shifts across my room, and I stay put, trapped in my own little bubble of self-loathing. My stomach growls, but the thought of facing the dining hall keeps me holed up. I snack on some stale chips from my desk instead.

Around dinnertime, my phone buzzes again.

Hudson

> Yo, you alive?

I stare at the screen and debate if I should reply. Before I can make up my mind, another message comes through.

Hudson

> C'mon man, you can't hide forever. Party tonight. You need this.

I roll my eyes, but maybe he's right? Do I need to just party and forget about things? I sigh and type back.

> Idk man. Not feeling it.

> I'm not taking no for an answer. Be ready by 8. I'll pick you up. And I'll bring burgers, I know you've been in your room all day and not eaten.

I groan and toss my phone aside, flopping back on my bed. Part of me wants to stay hidden away, but another part knows that I can't keep avoiding reality forever.

At 7:45, I force myself to get up and change. I go for my usual party gear: jeans, a clean t-shirt, and a hoodie. My reflection in the mirror looks like crap, but it'll have to do. Just as I'm lacing up my sneakers, I hear a knock on the door.

"Hey, Miles!" Hudson calls out from the hallway. I grab my phone and wallet, then take a deep breath before opening my door.

"There he is! Thought you were gonna bail on me," he says, thrusting a paper bag from Lakeside into my hands. The smell of meat and melted cheese greets me like the best thing I've ever smelt.

"Almost did," I admit as I follow him outside.

"Well, I'm glad you didn't. You need this, dude. Besides, everyone is busy tonight on dates, even Quinn."

My skin bristles at that little snippet of information. "Quinn's on a date?"

"Yeah, and no one I picked was good enough. She went with Indie's choice. Can you believe that?"

Offering a weak smile and a nod, I can't figure out how that news makes me feel. I'm happy she'll be happy, but I wish I'd met the guy first. What if he's an ass? What if she needs help? No, she's Quinn. She's completely capable.

As we walk to the West dorms, I eat the burgers—plural, because Hudson gets it—and I try to push the thoughts of Quinn, my dad, and the mess I've made out of my head. The night is young, and for a few hours at least, I can pretend everything's normal. Hudson chatters away about the people who'll be at the party, the latest girl he's hooked up with, and some new game he's been playing. I nod along, grateful for the distraction.

Walking up the steps to the building, Hudson claps me on the back as we head inside. "Let's have some fun tonight, yeah?"

"Yeah," I say, forcing a smile. "Let's do this."

I can handle fun. I hope.

CHAPTER TEN

Quinn

"WHAT'S YOUR FAVORITE PIZZA topping? And please don't break my heart and say it involves pineapple," Alex asks, his face a picture of hope.

"Well," I begin, chuckling awkwardly as I glance at the menu set in front of me. "The thing is, I feel like I need to defend myself for liking pineapple..."

His hand flies to his chest, clutching at his white t-shirt. "No, you can't like pineapple on pizza."

"I can and here's why. It can serve as a sweet to something salty or spicy, like jalapenos or nduja sausage. It's juicy and delicious and it's the best fruit in the world. Why wouldn't I put it on pizza?"

"Because it's wrong. Any Italian would be crying over this." His blue eyes sparkle with his teasing.

"Good thing I'm not Italian, then."

When he smiles at me, I notice his gaze flick between my lips and my eyes. He has a really pretty face, super symmetrical, regal even, and his hair is perfectly smooth. He's nothing like how I thought a cellist would be. But then, what did I expect? Tattoos? Hair that's dark and sexily long and messy on top but not too long? Sharp jawline and big muscles? Oh wait, no, that's just Miles. I think about him for a second and how he replied to my text earlier, short and vague. I didn't like it, and as much as I try not to care, I do.

"So, what are you majoring in?" Alex asks, and I focus back on my date. My kind, handsome, and funny date.

"I've already declared psychology. But I'll also keep my arts electives and extracurriculars. Then I'll do a master's in art therapy."

His eyebrows rise. "Wow, you're impressively organized."

"I think I've always been this way. I like having my life planned."

"I like that." He nods, focusing on my mouth again, a soft smile curving his lips.

Is this the moment I should feel butterflies at the thought of kissing him? Of having his lips touch mine, but all I feel is...my phone buzzing in my jean pocket. "I'm sorry, my phone is going crazy." I sit up slightly to pull it out and see several messages from Miles, none of which make sense. He's clearly drunk, asking me where my 'dromflgherd' is. It doesn't seem like he's got all his capabilities. "I'm sorry, my friend is drunk texting me right now. I just need to make sure he's okay," I say to Alex without looking up.

"It's all good. I'm going to head to the restroom."

When he leaves, I open the text thread with Indie to ask if

she's with Miles. Then I open Miles's again to reply.

Quinn

> I don't know what a dromflgherd is, but I think you need to get home to bed. Either that or take up kindergarten spelling again.

I don't get a reply from him, but Indie texts back.

Indie

> Yeah, he's here. We're at a party on campus. Don't ignore your date on account of him!

I huff a laugh at Indie's insistence, just as Alex sits back down. His scent of clean soap washes over me, and I realize it's all wrong. He doesn't smell like Miles, and I don't like it. I want his woodsy scent to surround me, to drown in the subtle fresh smell of him. But that's not what I've got. Instead, it's Alex, and he's so nice. Super-duper nice, in fact. I acknowledge that I should want that, not Mr. Unavailable. I pocket my phone again and look up at the boy who *is* available, who likes me and is easy to talk to, and I will myself to feel something, anything more than friendship. My phone buzzes against my butt again, but I ignore it. I know he's with Seb and Indie so he's fine.

Alex's warm smile greets me when I look at him. "I've settled the check, so we can go whenever," he says confidently, and that only falters when I frown and contemplate. "Not that I want tonight to be over; I just didn't want you to pay for dinner," he adds hastily.

"Oh." I feel myself blushing. "That's really...nice of you." There's that word again. *Nice.* I'm going to study a thesaurus tomorrow. "Thank you," I say honestly. "I didn't expect you to pay for me."

His cheeks deepen in color too. "My mom raised me right."

"She sure did."

There's a beat when I think he might lean over the table, try to take my hand, or be bold and kiss me. I feel like I'm suspended in the air, fighting with the idea that I should want that, but also scared that I'm leading him on in some way. How can I give my heart to someone else when it belongs to another? *Chill, Quinn, it's a first date.*

Clearing my throat, I smile and pick up my jacket draped around my chair. "Shall we go get ice cream? My treat."

"I'd like that."

Good. Okay, great. It gives me more time to psych myself up to kiss him.

***

The walk isn't far from Alex's car. The gentle lapping of the nearby lakes is a distant sound as we wait in line at Scoop Dawg, the ice cream parlor in town. After a few minutes of silence, I notice Alex shuffling next to me. Glancing at him, his blond hair glistens in the overhead lights as his arm flexes behind his neck where he rubs the same spot. "You okay?" I ask.

"Yeah, yeah." He swallows hard and drops his hand. "Actually, I was wondering if I could or should hold your hand. But then I didn't know how to grab you without making it weird and startling you. Not that I'd grab you, but uh... Well, then I worried my hands are sweaty and maybe you don't want to hold my hand. What am I even saying?" he trails off, looking to the sky and closing his eyes. "I'm sorry, that was the least cool I've ever been."

I chuckle because it seems I may have found the male version of myself. Rambler, overthinker, nice guy. Maybe that's why I'm not feeling much for him? We're too similar? "You and I are more alike than I realized," I admit.

"Is that good or bad?"

"I don't know yet." And that's the truth. Alex is sweet and kind, and I'm having a good time with him. I'm just not herding a whole kaleidoscope of butterflies in my belly either. But maybe that could come with time. The only person who ever made me feel like that is Miles.

I keep my gaze on Alex, and he keeps his on me. Just as I feel the brush of his fingers against mine, the server yells, "Next!" jolting us apart and breaking the moment.

Stepping up to the brightly lit counter, my mouth waters at the creamy selection before me.

"I'll take one scoop of double chocolate brownie with salted caramel sauce on a waffle cone, please." It's my go-to from this place because it's insanely good. Not for my sugar levels, but great for me. Alex orders the same, and I wonder if he normally would have ordered something different. You know, like one of those guys who orders whatever the girl gets so she likes him? Although, I don't think he would, based on his opinions of my pizza toppings.

"I guess you can be forgiven for your pizza choices because your dessert one is pretty good."

"Thanks," I say, licking the cool dessert that makes my tongue freeze. "Good to know I'm redeemable." I laugh softly. When I swallow, I realize Alex is watching me and not in the kind of way that tells me he's wondering what my ice cream tastes like. Probably because we have the same, but still. His eyes are like two hot pools of lust... It could be that he just really likes ice cream. But when he swallows and licks his lips, staring directly at mine, I still feel nothing.

Am I broken? I think I'm broken.

My phone buzzes in my bag consistently, but I ignore it. When it rings again, I know I can't ignore it this time.

"I'm sorry. I should check this." I wince, breaking my gaze from Alex, swiping to open my phone, just as another call comes through. I end up answering it. "Miles?"

The line is quiet, save for the heavy breathing on the other end, and immediately I home in on everything I think I can hear, plugging my other ear. "Miles? What's going on?"

He sighs, long and hard. "Quinn."

Quinn, not Queenie. He calls me Quinn; it's just not unusual for him to use it over the nickname he gave me. But the way he pleads my name tonight has my heckles rising.

"What's going on?" A desperate need to help hits me like a freight train and my feet are twitching to run to him. To fix whatever he means without even knowing what he's talking about.

"It's not enough," he mumbles. "Never enough," and then there's a rustling sound, almost like he dropped the phone. "Fuck," he shouts, sounding farther away.

"Miles? Are you there?" My voice raises.

More fumbling, followed by a sigh. "I'm here, where are

you?"

"I'm…out." I glance at Alex, who is looking over the lakes and pretending not to listen.

"On a date?" he slurs, and I decide I really don't like this. He's drunk and alone and where the hell are all our friends?

"It doesn't matter. Where are you right now?"

"Outside your dorm."

I run my slightly sweaty palm down the side of my face at his answer. "Is Seb with you?"

He doesn't say anything for a little while, and the silence feels like its heavily resting on my chest, like I'm waiting for a bomb to explode. If only he could tell me where he is.

"Quinn?" he breathes.

"I'm here," I whisper, my heart racing.

"I need you."

CHAPTER ELEVEN

Quinn

"SORRY, ALEX, BUT I really need to go. My friend needs me," I say, trying to mask the anxiety in my voice. Alex's eyebrows pinch with concern, and I wonder if he can tell how worried I am. I managed to get Miles to tell me he's outside my dorm. Why, I have no idea, but that's where I need to go.

"Okay, let's go." He nods, already reaching for his keys.

The drive back to campus is quiet, the kind that makes my thoughts louder. I can't stop thinking about Miles.

I need you.

His words play on a loop in my head. I'm helpless. Lost in those three words. Like a dagger to my heart, I couldn't ignore him.

When we pull up to my dorm, I immediately spot him slumped on the steps, looking completely out of it, his head lolled to the side of the wall, his arms slack by his sides. My breath hitches at the sight.

Flinging open the car door, I rush over to him. "Miles, what happened?"

His eyes open and they light up slightly when he realizes it's me. "Queenie, you came."

"Of course I came," I whisper.

"Come on, let's get him inside," Alex says, taking charge. I'm grateful, because I don't think I'd manage it myself. Together, we lift Miles to his feet and, let me tell you, lifting a six-foot-five guy who has muscles upon muscles, that's no easy feat for a lanky cellist and a cheerleader. Yet somehow, we manage to get him to my room. He's babbling the entire way, sometimes coherent and sometimes not.

Miles slurs, leaning heavily on Alex. "Hold up. Who is you? I mean, why are you? Wait, I'm Miles. Do you have gum? I'd kill for some gum," he mumbles, squinting at Alex.

Alex grunts, turning away as Miles leans closer to him. "He could probably do with gum, and a shower."

"Alex is a friend, Miles. He's helping me get you inside," I reply without looking at either of them. Grabbing my keycard from my back pocket, I swipe it, awkwardly pushing the door to my dorm room open. We fumble inside, and let Miles flop onto my bed, where he rolls over with a grumble.

Sweat coats my skin. That was harder than getting to the top of the pyramid at a game.

I glance at Alex, feeling another rush of appreciation. "Thanks for helping. I know this isn't an ideal date activity."

"No problem," he replies, giving me a small smile and looking down at a snoring football player in my bed. "You sure you're okay with this?"

I realize it doesn't look great, the guy I just met, who has been nothing but nice to me, just helped me get a friend back to my dorm without questions. It's a mess of a situation, but not one I'm willing to think about too much. "Yeah, I'll manage. He's just had a rough night," I say, looking at Miles and feeling a pang of worry.

Alex chuckles softly. "Yeah, but you're a good friend. Not everyone would do this."

We stand there for a moment, not saying anything, only listening to the quiet purr of Miles. I can't help but wonder what might've happened between us tonight if Miles hadn't interrupted. I know I wasn't feeling it, but I don't know how he felt and that makes things really awkward. I'm not about to kiss him when the love of my life lies unconscious on my bed.

"Listen," Alex says, breaking the silence and taking my hand in his. I'm not surprised to find that his hands aren't sweaty at all like he worried about earlier. "Call me sometime, okay?"

I smile and nod, though my mind is still spinning. "Thanks, Alex. Really."

He leaves, and I feel awful that my first thought is how relieved I am he didn't try to kiss me. I focus back on the football player in my bed and sigh, running a hand over my hair. I notice his phone on the bed, having fallen from his pocket, so I pick it up and put it on the charger. A notification from Levi Saunders lights up the screen, but I can't see the message. What does he want with Miles?

Miles groans, making me jump slightly as I turn his phone over so I don't get caught looking.

I pull my own phone from my jean pocket and text Indie.

Quinn: Miles is in our dorm. Long story, but he's wasted. I'll catch you up tomorrow, but can you stay with Seb tonight so I can sleep in your bed?

Her reply comes almost instantly.

Indie: Fuck, we've been looking for him. He slipped out of the party, although I didn't think he was that drunk. I'm sorry if he ruined your date.

He wasn't that drunk with them? My brow furrows as I walk over to the mini fridge in our room, pulling out two bottles of water. When I turn around, Miles is sitting on the edge of my bed, looking clear-eyed and composed—definitely not drunk.

"What the—?" I start, but the words die in my throat as he stands, moving toward me in one smooth motion. He plucks a water bottle from my hands, and I just stare, my jaw slack. This isn't the same guy who was slumped outside my dorm less than thirty minutes ago. This isn't the same guy who was sending me drunk texts, either. No, this guy isn't drunk at all.

Miles twists off the cap and takes long, deliberate gulps, rippling the edges of the rose inked below his throat. I can't help but watch as his throat works, each swallow making something in my chest tighten. He drains the entire thing, then wipes his mouth with the back of his hand. "Thanks, I needed that," he says, his voice calm, steady.

I blink as my mind tries to piece together what's happening, but it's no use. "What's going on right now?" I'm not sure that question will get me anywhere close to the answers I need, though.

He doesn't reply. Instead, he gives me this sheepish look, like he thinks that flashing me those puppy-dog eyes will make everything okay, like I'll just melt and forgive him on the spot.

Not tonight. Not this time.

"Did you..." I hesitate, clenching my fist at my side, wondering if I'm about to make things worse by asking the most obvious question, but I can't think of any other solution. "Did you *fake* being drunk?"

He rubs the back of his neck, eyes dropping to the floor between us. "I mean..."

That's it? My jaw tightens as I fight the urge to roll my eyes. I shift my weight, crossing my arms tighter. Just say it, Miles.

I glance at him, hoping—no, *begging*—for him to finally look at me, but he's still staring at the floor like it'll magically give him the words. My foot starts tapping, my patience thinning by the second. I can feel my temper rising, burning hotter with every beat of silence.

"Miles," I snap, my voice harder than I mean it to be. "Just tell me."

"Okay..." He swallows roughly as his brown eyes meet mine. "Maybe I did fake it a little bit."

"Miles!" I shout, spinning around on my heels, frustration and confusion bubbling over. I can't contain it anymore. Why would he do that? Why did he feel the need to fake being drunk? So I'd come running? The realization hits me like a punch to the gut, and I feel like such an idiot.

"Wait, I may have embellished the extent of my drunkenness, but I did drink tonight," he admits, his voice soft.

"What does that even mean?" I screech, throwing my hands in the air. "Are you doing this to be all protective over me again? Did Seb send you here? Are you two trying to sabotage my date?"

"Woah, no." He holds his hands up. "I swear, Seb doesn't even know I'm here."

"Then why? Why are you here, pretending you're drunk, pretending that you need me?"

"Shit, I..." He falters, running his fingers through his hair, clearly scrambling for an answer that will make sense.

"Alex was nice, the date was nice." My voice rises in anger. "Despite the fact that we didn't agree on pineapple being a pizza topping, it was nice, and now it's..." Shaking my head, my breath comes in heavy, ragged bursts as my arms drop ramrod straight by my sides. "It's nothing!"

He steps closer, and I'm engulfed in his familiar scent, the warm mix of cedar and spice that's always felt like home. And I hate it. I hate that even now, when I'm furious, I want to lean into him, to let him calm the storm inside me. "Quinn, I'm sorry."

Stepping back once, then twice, needing the space between us, I bump into the door with a soft thud, crossing my arms in front of me again like a barrier. "Well, this time, I'm not accepting it."

His face tightens, his mouth opening as if he wants to say something, but instead, his lips press into a thin line. As he exhales sharply, his shoulders slump with clear frustration. Finally, he mutters, "Pineapple does belong on pizza, by the way."

I blink at him, caught off guard. I want to stay mad, but his eyes meet mine, and there's a flicker of something familiar—something that makes my heart stutter, no matter how hard I try to resist. I swallow hard and bite back a smile that I refuse to let free. "I know," I mutter. "That's what I told him."

He stares at my mouth for a second, running his tongue over his lower lip. "Did he kiss you?" With each movement toward me, I can feel the heat of his body approaching like the sun rising in the morning. That moment just before the dawn breaks when you know something is in the air. And just like the sun, I feel helpless to stop him.

"N-no," I splutter, practically choking on the word.

He hums, never taking his eyes off my lips, and I don't know what to do with that. The dormant traitorous butterflies suddenly flare to life inside my chest, causing the ruckus I'd been waiting for all night.

"He wanted to kiss you."

The air vacates from the room at a rapid pace and my lungs claw at my ribs. "H-how would you know? You weren't watching."

He steps closer, his voice low enough to send a tremor quaking through me. "Trust me, he wanted to taste you."

Those big brown eyes fall to my lips again and linger there until I absently lick them. I can't speak, can barely breathe with the weight of his eyes on me, with him so close.

"I fucked it up," he whispers.

My immediate instinct is to comfort him, to say he didn't, to tell him that I didn't really want Alex to kiss me anyway. But I stop myself. Because the truth is, he *did* stop tonight from becoming something more, and that was supposed to be *my* decision, even if I wasn't into it. It doesn't matter—he still took that moment from me.

"I didn't mean to ruin your date," he murmurs, his voice thick with regret.

"But you did," I snap, my voice still tinged with frustration. I see him wince, but I can't take it back.

"I'm sorry," he says, stepping closer so our bodies brush. A wave of sensation sweeps over me, my breath faltering as his touch sends goosebumps racing across my skin. And before I can process the apology or the emotion flickering in his eyes, his hands are on my face, cradling it between his warm palms, angling me so I have no choice but to look up at him. My pulse flutters just below the tips of his fingers, and for a moment, the only thing I'm aware of is him, the intensity in his gaze. A gaze that's full of something so powerful and potent that I can't look away.

And then he leans in and the world stops spinning.

The soft and brief press of his lips against mine sends a shock wave through me—my entire body goes rigid, frozen in place, as though I've stepped into another reality. My mind stutters, trying to catch up with what just happened. Did he— Was that a kiss?

Miles pulls back, eyes wide, as if he's just as stunned as I am. He doesn't move, doesn't let go. He's staring at me—no, at my mouth, his own slightly parted, his breaths shallow, like he's not sure what he's done or how to fix it.

My heart pounds like it's trying to break free. The whisper of his lips on mine echoes on my skin, the sensation burning into me, searing itself into my memory. But it was so quick, so unexpected, that I can't quite wrap my mind around it. Did I imagine it? Have I completely lost my mind, that I'm now imagining him kissing me when he hasn't?

"Huh..." He frowns, his voice is hoarse, unsteady. He keeps his confused gaze on my lips, like he's drawn to them, unable to tear himself away but he doesn't know why. It's the kind of stare that leaves me breathless. It's like he's waiting for permission, or maybe for me to stop him.

But I can't.

Neither of us moves. The air between us is thick with confusion and something else—something heavier, something dangerous.

I can't breathe. I can't think. All I know is that his hands are still holding me in place, grounding me, and I don't know if I want him to let me go or pull me closer. If he lets go, I'll never forget the feeling of kissing him, not now that I know what he tastes like, how he feels. I'll forever be haunted by it. But if he pulls me closer, that means he chooses me. And I've spent my whole life being overlooked that the thought of him actually choosing me feels like something I can't afford to believe in. Not yet.

In his eyes, I see the same hesitation. The same shock. The same lingering question.

What now?

I open my mouth to speak, but Miles adjusts his grip so his thumb ghosts over my lower lip, deepening his frown as he murmurs a gentle *shh* sound. Any words I'd planned on saying dissolve on my tongue in an instant from the feel of his touch. My breath catches in my throat, and my pulse thunders in my ears, so loud they're practically ringing. His dark eyes glisten in the soft light from my lamp as he looks at me intently, studying me like I'm something precious or something he shouldn't have. I wish I could melt into him. Take this opportunity to bare my soul and my feelings and let him know everything I've wanted for years now. His moves are slow and deliberate, like he's memorizing the feel of me, making my hazy head swim with notions of forever. I need to calm down.

But it feels like an impossible feat, when he's here, holding me, looking at me like *this.*

A soft breath escapes me, and it ignites something within him. His fingers weave into my hair, pulling me closer as his lips crash into mine, rough and unrelenting. Fierce and possessive. And my body freezes all over again. Reality slamming into me as hard as his mouth is. This is real. Miles is kissing me.

His hands tighten in my hair, pulling me closer with a growl, and I finally respond instinctively, my body molding against his. My fingers curl into his shirt, as if holding on is the only thing keeping me grounded. I kiss him back, pouring years of unspoken longing into the heat of the moment.

His tongue sweeps into my mouth with a sudden unrelenting desire that pools in my core. The taste of him, faintly sweet, floods my senses, and I'm lost in it. The world fades away—there's only him. His breath, his touch, the heat radiating from him like we're both on the verge of unraveling.

A moan escapes between us, and I don't know if it's me or him but just as suddenly as it began, it all shifts.

He pulls back abruptly, breaking the kiss with a sharp gasp, as if he's come up for air after being underwater for too long. His hands drop from my hair, trembling slightly, wild eyes darting away from mine. I watch as his chest heaves and he stares at the floor.

"Miles?" I whisper, my voice barely audible. Inside I'm shaking, vibrating from what was desire that's now been doused with ice water and it's left an ache in its place.

But he doesn't answer. He takes a step back, then another, his eyes wide, panicked, like he's just realized what he's done. "Shit," he mutters, his hand pressed over his mouth.

I try to think of something to say, anything, but nothing comes out. I can't begin to process my own thoughts, let alone consider the ones he's having.

"I—" His voice falters, and for a second, he looks like he might try to explain, but nothing prepares me for what comes out. Clearing his throat, he frowns. "That was...uh, nice."

I wince, my face contorting. "*Nice*?" I ask, dumbfounded.

"I should go," he whispers, more to himself than to me. He makes jerky, uncontrolled movements, running his hand through his hair as I stare in disbelief.

Robotically, I move away from the door, not sure what else to do as I helplessly watch everything I'd feared would happen manifest in front of me. *He's leaving because he didn't mean to kiss you. He doesn't want you*, a voice whispers in my head.

Then, as soon as the door opens, he's gone, rushing out and leaving me standing there, stunned, my heart pounding painfully in the empty silence.

CHAPTER TWELVE

Miles

DAMN.

I fucked up.

I fucked up in the most epic way.

Not only did I kiss Quinn. I then told her it was nice. *Nice*.

I'm a liar and an asshole.

It was more than nice.

And that isn't something I should be admitting at all.

What the fuck is wrong with me?

I'm not sure what possessed me to kiss her. The only time I even thought about it in the past was when we were younger. I told Seb she wanted to marry me, and he punched me straight in my nose and told me I was a jerk and to find another girl. I guess that warning became less effective over time, because I ploughed straight through that boundary tonight.

I felt like I *had* to do something. I just didn't expect it to be a kiss. And I didn't expect her to kiss me back like that.

The moment my lips touched hers, it was like everything in my body jolted to life, because holy fucking shit can she kiss. I briefly remember panicking because kissing has always been transactional for me, a part of a bigger act to get off, but that... Damn, that was something entirely new.

I might've been a tiny bit drunk when I came in here tonight and yeah, okay, I embellished said drunkenness when I saw her with that guy. But I sure as shit am stone-cold sober after that bolt of lightning struck through me.

Kissing Quinn was like waking up on Christmas morning to snow.

I'm in trouble.

It's like my eyes are opening for the first time, and through my new sight, I don't see my best friend's little sister anymore. I see this grown woman who has curves that make me drool and long red hair that makes me want to wrap it around my fist. Freckles that speckle the bridge of her nose in the most perfect way. Noticing Quinn is natural; she's always been beautiful. But she and I have never been that way, I've always only ever been protective of her. Until two minutes ago when I pressed my lips to hers, and I felt something else... Possession.

The cool almost-morning air hits me as I step outside, and I take a deep breath, hoping to clear the fog in my head. As I walk across campus, the sky starts to lighten, but the sun hasn't risen yet. The world is quiet, and it feels like I'm the only person awake.

Once I get to my dorm, the place is deserted, which is for the best. I'm not in any mood to bump into anyone. Hell, the only thing I can think of is her and how soft her lips are, and how the fuck I've never kissed her before today. Well, I know how. My best friend told me I couldn't but, damn, if I had done it sooner, Seb wouldn't have been able to stop me.

So now, how the fuck I'm supposed to deal with not kissing her next time I see her?

***

"Yo, Miles! You in?" Seb's voice echoes down the hall, followed by his familiar knock—a rapid-fire staccato that's impossible to ignore. What's also impossible to ignore is the uneasiness creeping into my body, as I frantically spin around the room, looking for nothing yet unable to stop moving. As though as soon as he enters my room, he'll know something is wrong just by being in here. *Chill the fuck out, man. He doesn't know you kissed Quinn. It's not like she's here either.*

"Yeah, give me a sec," I shout back, taking a deep breath and deciding to distract myself with packing for our away game. The less eye contact I give him, the better it'll be. Pulling out my bag from under my bed, I throw it on my desk and chuck in some gym gear to make it look like I was in the middle of something. I head to the door, nearly colliding with Seb as he bursts in.

"Man, this place is a disaster," he says, laughing at the discarded clothes scattered across the floor, my desk chair and hanging out my drawers. He's got that easygoing grin on his face, which would soon vanish if he could see inside my head that's filled with images of me kissing his little sister.

"Yeah, yeah. You're one to talk," I retort. Shoving him playfully, I pray my brain will stop sabotaging me. Walking to my desk to resume my packing, my stomach stops flipping out long enough to distract him from noticing my nerves.

"I hear you stayed at Quinn's last night?" He saunters over to my bed, pushing off the mound of laundry that I still need to do and plopping down with no indication that he knows. But I still panic.

Pausing my hands, gripping the edge of the zipper, the metal pinches into my fingertips at the force I'm holding it. My heart stalls like an old, rusty chevvy that's had its day. RIP me. He knows. He can tell I kissed his sister. Oh, shit.

Looking over to him, with a million apologies and justifications on the tip of my tongue, I open my mouth, and just as I do, he interrupts. "I was with Indie when she texted her last night," he says before I blurt everything out.

Oh, fucking hell. Everything deflates in my body as I release my grip on the zipper and fight the urge to sag with relief. "Yeah, man," I force out, clearing my throat. "I passed the fuck out. Lucky it wasn't on a campus bench." It's a lie. I didn't pass out at all.

He nods. "Quinn is the saint we don't deserve. She's always got our backs."

"Yeah," I agree, looking down at my bag as nausea swirls in my stomach.

"Did she keep you up all night?"

His question catches me off guard, making me turn to him sharply, my mouth falling open in surprise. "W-what? Why would you ask that?"

My pulse feels as though it's rushing around my body at warp speed.

"Because she snores like a wooly mammoth?" he says as

though I should remember that.

"Oh…" I deflate again, adrenaline ebbing. "I wouldn't know. I sort of left early. Sobered up pretty fast." I somehow manage to keep my voice light.

I continue searching my drawers for my hoodie, one that I don't even need to pack, just to keep myself busy. That was really close. Too fucking close. I hate lying to him, but also, I didn't think I'd ever need to lie about accidentally kissing his sister. But am I lying if he doesn't ask? *Fuck my warped logic.*

"Have you heard from your dad?" Seb asks. His voice is casual, but I can hear the underlying concern. "He gonna watch the game tomorrow?"

A deep sigh escapes me, followed by a casual shrug, finally picking out the hoodie I was looking for but don't need. "I don't know. Last time we talked, he was still pissed about me getting thrown out of the game. Got another speech."

"You didn't even start the fight."

"Yeah, well, he's got his own ideas about how I should play," I say, trying to keep the bitterness out of my voice. "But maybe he'll watch. Who knows?" *Who cares?*

"I'm here if you want to talk about anything. But want my advice?"

"Pretty sure you're going to give it to me anyway."

"Ignore the bullshit. Focus on the game. Your dad, girls, school, none of that matters on the field."

I inwardly sigh this time, zipping my duffel closed. Guilt twists and churns in my gut. Seb's always got my back, and here I am, keeping secrets from him, secrets that could destroy our friendship.

"Let's go to the gym. You look like you need a workout," Seb says, getting to his feet and walking to the door.

I need something, alright.

CHAPTER THIRTEEN

Quinn

"I'M NOT SAYING YOU need to diversify your glitter gel pens, but your book is a lot of blue, that's all." Hudson shrugs with a smirk that's all trouble as he sticks a bright pink butterfly onto his page. "Any particular reason for that color choice, Jay?"

Jay scowls at him. "No reason, and you aren't one to talk with your pink book."

"There's nothing wrong with pink."

"I'm not saying there is, but like you said, there are other colors in the rainbow, Hudson."

"Will you two stop it, please?" I snap, slapping my hands to my knees a little too forcefully with the pencil I'm holding.

Both pairs of eyes swing to me, wide and surprised. "Sorry," Jay and Hudson mumble.

Sighing, I put down my pencil. "No, I'm sorry," I admit, running my hands through my hair. "I'm just tired today."

"Date go that well, huh?" Hudson asks as his eyebrows wiggle suggestively. "Did he play you like a violin?"

"Dude, he's a cellist. How the hell is he meant to play her like violin?" Jay asks with a creased brow.

My body tenses at the mention of it because a part of me had forgotten about the date altogether. Too hung up on the fact that Miles kissed me and then disappeared. Does he even remember kissing me? Did he do it because he was drunk? Was it so bad that he couldn't face me? So many what-ifs have plagued me all day. I almost canceled the scrapbook club so I could mope and bury myself in chocolate, but I hate letting people down.

"I don't want to talk about last night," I mumble, but not quietly enough, because Indie stands and marches her biker boot-loving self over to me, grabs my arm, and shouts over her shoulder. "Carry on scrapbooking, you two. No arguments or no more pens and tape. We'll be back."

As my best friend drags me into my brother's room, I'm grateful Seb and Miles aren't here.

She sits on the edge of his bed, crosses her legs, and looks at me pointedly. "Spill."

I sigh, meandering over to the desk chair and sinking into it. "I don't know where to start."

"The date. Then tell me what's made you sad, because I never see you like this."

I tell her everything, the 'nice' date with Alex and how Miles ended up kissing me and pretending he was drunk. When I'm done, I could easily cry my heart out, because the more I think about it, the more I realize he kissed me and there's a really good chance he might regret it.

"He kissed you?!" Indie yelps.

"Yup."

Jaw slack, she finally closes her mouth. "Wait, he wasn't drunk?"

"Nope."

"Why did he do that?" She's fuming at that knowledge, her arms flying around.

With a shrug, I sigh. "I don't know."

Her beady blue eyes narrow at me. "Why aren't you madder?"

"Because...?" I don't know why I pose it like a question. The issue is, why did he kiss me and then ghost me? I feel the pinch of anger ignite in my gut as I look helplessly at Indie.

"Get pissed at him, Quinn," she demands, slapping the mattress. "He interrupted your date, he chased him away, kissed you, and then bailed."

She's right. He did do all of those things. I stand, suddenly feeling the adrenaline rushing into my body. "I am pissed." I begin pacing the room. "He kissed me."

"And sabotaged your date," Indie adds.

I gesture to her with a 'thank you' look. "And I'll never get that kiss back."

She huffs. "Asshole."

I storm over to the bed and sink down next to her, crossing my arms over my chest. "Complete asshole," I mutter with less conviction.

"How dare he," she says, hooking an arm over my shoulders. My irritation subsides just as fast as it came, though, because even if I wish I'd had my first kiss with Miles under different circumstances, getting pissed doesn't help me much. It reminds me that we kissed and nothing else has happened. Indie must feel my mood shift because she asks, "Have you spoken to him?"

I shake my head. "But we go away tonight for the game, remember?"

"Ah, shit, I forgot I said I'd go to that. Why is football suddenly my life?" she groans.

I chuckle. "Because you're in love with the quarterback. It'll be fun though. You drive and we'll have an epic playlist." I fiddle with a random thread coming from my sweater. "It'll keep me from going insane thinking about Miles."

"Sold." Indie pauses for a second. "Anything else on your mind? You have that look."

"I don't have a look."

Indie stares at me pointedly, and I already know I'm going to fold because there's one name that keeps ringing in my head from last night. It's kept ringing in my head over and over and the worry has built right alongside the anxiety of him kissing me.

"You don't think any of the team would do anything stupid, do you?"

"Define stupid, because if you're talking about the situations with girls that Hudson gets himself into, then I'd say that's really stupid."

"Yeah, that boy is something else," I pause, contemplating what to say. "I meant more like..." I hesitate again, should I even be bringing this up? But if I can't talk to my best friend then who can I talk to. "...maybe, like, drugs or something."

Her eyes widen. "You don't think someone is doing drugs, do you?"

"No, no no." I backpedal as my hands become clammy. "I read an article about a pro player being tested for drugs, and I just got worried about any of the guys doing it."

Jesus, that was fast thinking. My heart is strumming in my throat.

"I don't think the guys we know would do it. They all have too much to lose."

I nod. "Yeah, you're right." Except I still have a niggling feeling in my gut about Levi. Maybe they're just unlikely friends. I don't know if I should outright ask Miles, or just keep an eye on things. That is, if I can ever face Miles again after last night.

Indie nudges my shoulder with hers. "You know, I'll never judge you for anything, and if you want to hate him, I'll hate him too."

"Thanks." I smile softly. "I'm not sure I could ever hate him, though."

"I'm not sure he deserves you being so good about him."

Shrugging, I stand, ready to go back to our friends. "He needs someone in his corner. You didn't hear his dad the other day."

"I didn't, but you also need someone to fight for you, too."

***

Indie and I are some of the last ones to arrive to wave off the bus for our away game. The team's already there, the chatter and energy buzzing around us, as luggage gets flung into the lower compartment with heavy thuds. I glance over at Indie, who's busy checking her phone.

Just as we're about to step onto the cheer bus, Seb appears out of nowhere, blocking Indie's path. "Hey, where do you think you're going?" he asks, raising an eyebrow, a smirk on his face.

"The other Dawson has claimed me today," Indie shoots back, pocketing her phone.

"But you're *my* girlfriend." Seb pouts, sticking out his bottom lip in an exaggerated manner. "I want to ride with you."

Indie stares at him, a sly smile playing on her lips.

"I'm pretty sure you'll survive a five-hour bus ride without me."

"Maybe I don't want to."

"Maybe you should stop holding up your team and get on the bus, Seb."

He sighs dramatically, but a smile tugs at his lips. "Fine, go. But I'm mad."

"Oooh, mad Sebby, my favorite." She winks, blowing a kiss to him before stepping toward her car. Seb shakes his head, chuckling as he watches her go.

As I turn, I spot Miles walking across the parking lot, headphones on, a deep scowl etched on his face.

My stomach knots at the sight of him.

Seb notices me watching him. "He got a shitty email from his dad when we were training in the gym last night, put him in a weird headspace again."

"Another one? Does the guy ever give him a break?" I mutter, deflated.

"Doesn't feel like it lately. I've got him, though. Don't stress, little sis," Seb says, before joining his teammates.

The memory of the kiss plays in my mind like a home movie and a sliver of guilt creeps into my gut for not telling my brother. Not that he needs to know anything about my love life—in fact, the less the better.

I watch Miles fling his bag with ease into the lower deck of the bus and a really big part of me wants to rage at him, but the look on his face has me re-thinking my anger. I don't want to be another person who rages at him, even if he does deserve it. I want to be the one he comes to when he needs help.

Another part of me wants to run up to him and ask a million questions. The first one being, does he think the kiss was a mistake? The thought makes my heart ache. So, I shake it off, forcing myself to focus before I go back to overthinking him kissing me at all. I know worrying won't solve anything, and it's not the right time to try to talk about this with him.

So, I concentrate on things I can control, like cheering my little heart out at the game tomorrow.

Chapter Fourteen

Miles

Seb shakes me awake, his hand firm on my shoulder. "Hey, man, time to get up. We have pre-practice warmups and breakfast."

I groan and roll over, the dull ache of exhaustion settling in my bones. "What time is it?"

"Time to move your lazy ass." Seb laughs as he yanks the covers off me. "Come on, we need to be downstairs in fifteen."

I sit up, blinking against the harsh morning light filtering through the curtains. My head feels heavy, and my thoughts are a jumbled mess. Last night, I barely made it to the room before collapsing into bed. No dreams, just a deep, unsettling darkness that swallowed me whole. Maybe that was a blessing. No time to think about Quinn or that kiss. Or the crappy email my dad sent me with a long-ass list of his expectations of me.

Dragging myself out of bed, I pull on my practice gear, the

fabric feeling rough against my skin. I splash some water on my face, trying to wake up, but the cold sting does little to chase away my mood. Seb's all ready, his energy a stark contrast to my sluggishness. "You good?" he asks, concern flickering in his eyes.

"Yeah, just tired," I mutter and avoid his gaze. I don't want him to see the turmoil brewing beneath the surface. While he grabs something from his bag, I find my wallet and push it into my back pocket, looking around for my phone. "You see my phone?"

"Yeah, I put it in the closet," he says casually, as though that's normal behavior.

"Because...?" I prompt.

He looks up at me. "Because I need your head in the game, and you don't need any of daddy dearest's pep talks today."

I huff a laugh, both because my best friend is being good to me like he always is, and because he knows my dad has the ability to derail my game. What he has no idea about is how my doping can do that all by itself.

We head downstairs, and my stomach tightens with each step. I need coffee. Strong coffee. As we enter the breakfast area, my heart stutters when I spot Quinn across the room. She's laughing with Indie, her smile lighting up the space. She looks so effortlessly beautiful it almost hurts to look at her.

Panic claws at my chest, and I freeze, my brain scrambling for an escape. "I, uh, forgot something in the room. I'll catch up with you later," I tell Seb, my voice tight. Before he can question me, I turn on my heel and bolt for the door.

The cool morning air hits my face as I step outside, my breaths coming in shallow gasps. I need to clear my head. There's a diner across the street with a flickering neon sign. It looks like the kind of place that serves terrible coffee. Perfect.

I push through the door, the bell jangling above me, and take a seat at the counter. The place smells like burnt toast and old grease. A tired-looking waitress shuffles over and pours me a cup without asking. As I wrap my hands around the mug, the warmth seeps into my cold fingers. Taking a sip, I grimace at the bitter taste. It's exactly what I need.

As I sit there, my thoughts spiral back to Quinn. How does she feel about the kiss? Does she regret it? Was she as surprised as I was by how good it felt? She kissed me back, so she was clearly into it, and that equal parts scares me and makes me feel something I've never felt with anyone else before. The memory of her lips on mine is a sharp, sweet ache that I haven't been able to forget.

I want to talk to her, to know what she's thinking, but the fear of the unknown paralyzes me as soon as I lay eyes on her. The idea that I might have messed everything up is yet another thing for me to think about. I can't afford to lose another person in my life. I can't afford to let anything get to me. I need to keep it together. *Is that what you're doing with the pills? Keeping it together?* The angel on my shoulder, who suspiciously looks a lot like Quinn, coos into my subconscious.

And that's my other issue. The secret I've been carrying, the weight of it pressing down on me every time I play. Should I tell her about the drugs? Would she understand, or would she just see me as a screw-up? My hand trembles as I reach into my sweats pocket, touching the small, white pill in the plastic packet that I grabbed before I left the room.

I know I shouldn't, but I pop the pill into my mouth and down the rest of the cup, the bitterness masking the familiar tang of the drug. The caffeine and the pill together should give me the edge I need, but I'll probably take another just before going out there too. I have to keep it together, at least until after the game. My dad's emails have been a constant reminder of what's at stake. If I mess up again, there'll be hell to pay.

Shoving my thoughts aside, I leave the diner and head back to the hotel. Each step feels heavier than the last as the weight of my secrets pulls me down. Seb's waiting for me outside, frowning. "Where'd you go? I thought you said you were going to the room."

"Just needed some air," I say, forcing a tight smile.

He gives me a skeptical look but doesn't push it.

We join the rest of the team for warmups, and I focus on the motions, trying to let the routine calm my nerves. My body moves on autopilot, but my mind is a storm waiting to downpour. I can't let anyone see how off I am. Especially not Quinn.

As we stretch and run drills, my eyes keep drifting to her. She's across the field, her focus on her own teammates, but every now and then, she glances my way. Every time our eyes clash, my chest constricts. Fuck. I really can't afford to be this distracted.

I shake my head, trying to clear it. For now, the game is all that matters. We need this win in a few hours, and I need to prove I can handle it. Even if it means keeping secrets and pretending everything's fine. The pressure is suffocating, but I force myself to breathe, to concentrate.

I need to be strong. For the team, for the game. For myself. Even if it means hiding the truth.

***

The locker room is a frenzy of celebration. We won. The exhaustion from the game is creeping up on me fast, but the victory has everyone buzzing, the adrenaline still coursing through our veins.

After we've showered and are dressed to the nines in our suits, the team heads to the hotel bar to keep the party spirit going. Apparently, they're happy for us to have beer if some of the seniors order it. Not the best logic, but I'm too drained to join in.

"Where the hell are you going, Cooper?" Hudson asks as I try to slip away, needing some quiet time.

"To sleep, man. Have a drink for me, okay?"

"Party pooper."

"Yeah, yeah. Get lost. Go party," I say, pressing the button for the elevator.

My feet are heavy as I lumber to my room, swiping the keycard. I suddenly get an overwhelming scent of cinnamon, and my head snaps to the second bed in the room where I see Quinn sitting, with her laptop open. My heart skips a beat, surprise and confusion washing over me. "Quinn?" I say, my voice tinged with disbelief. "What are you doing here?"

She offers a small, awkward smile, taking off her headphones. "Seb asked if we could switch rooms for the night. He wanted to be with Indie," she says with hesitation. "I didn't think you'd mind..."

"Right. That makes sense. No, it's fine that you're here. Of course it is."

With a grimace so unlike her, she closes her laptop. "Really? Because I can ask if there's another room. Maybe that would be better."

My feet move toward her bed before I can stop them. "No, no, it's..." I stop myself and take a breath. "It's fine, Queenie. I want you here."

We're both quiet for a moment, the air thick with unspoken words. She clears her throat to break the silence. "Okay, thank you."

Turning back to my bed, I take off the tie that suddenly feels too tight. "You don't have to thank me, I'm glad you're here," I admit, because she's still my best friend, no matter what. I want to be around her; she's comfort, she's safe, and I need that.

She doesn't make an attempt to put her headphones back on, and the weight of our last encounter feels like a physical presence standing between us. Quinn and I have never had awkwardness between us before, and I'm not sure how to deal with it now. I've been hiding, ignoring things, sure, but I also know I can't keep doing that. My fingers run down my shirt, unbuttoning the top few buttons so I can breathe again.

In and out. In and out.

But it doesn't work. I know we need to talk, clear the air, but how do I bring up the kiss? *'Hey, do you remember last night when I kissed you? Well, funny thing, I've been wanting to do that again, I think? Which is weird...because we don't do that.'* Yeah, that's terrifying.

She takes a deep breath, her exhale wobbly, and it makes me turn my head.

"Listen—" I say, at the same time as she says, "Are we—"

We both laugh, the room growing stifling with unsaid words. "You go," I offer.

She licks her lips, and it's that exact moment I know I'm screwed. All I can think is how I want to be closer to her, to feel her, to learn even more about her, because Quinn isn't just the girl that's been in front of me my whole life, she's strong and so fucking beautiful. *Does she feel the same?* The question plagues me. "Are we ignoring the elephant in the room, or do you not remember anything from last night?"

Relief and anxiety battle within me. I run a hand through my hair, exhaling slowly. "Fuck," I admit, my voice barely above a whisper. "It's been driving me crazy, honestly."

Her green eyes pierce mine, and for a moment there's complete silence, the only sound the rapid thumping of my heart.

"Crazy good or crazy bad?" she asks, tilting her head with an unreadable expression on her face.

The edge of that cliff feels like it's right there beneath my feet. I could lie and lose her, but that thought tears me up inside. "Just crazy," I settle on, rubbing the back of my neck.

"Do you want to forget about it?" she asks, and that twists my insides further.

I take a tentative step toward her bed. "I don't know how to handle this."

"Okay, then answer me this: Have you been ignoring me on purpose?"

Guilt eats at me, because yeah, I have to a degree while I've tried to sort my head out today. "I just didn't know how to figure this out. I didn't want to make things weird between us."

"A little late for that," she mutters, but doesn't meet my eyes.

She's right. It's weird. So, I guess it's now or never. I need to tell her. I take one deep inhale and brace myself.

"Quinn, I shouldn't have kissed you."

Chapter Fifteen

Quinn

I SHOULDN'T HAVE KISSED you.

His words hit me like a punch to the gut, a sharp, painful twist in my chest that makes it hard to breathe. I struggle to keep my cool, to maintain some semblance of composure, but it feels like everything inside me is shattering.

He regrets it.

He thinks it was a mistake.

The reality, stark and raw in front of me, is unbearable. The heavy feeling deepens in my chest and spreads across my entire body. I turn away, pretending to fiddle with the edge of my sleeve, desperate to hide the turmoil raging within. I knew this might happen, had prepared myself for the possibility, but hearing him say it out loud is so much worse than I ever imagined.

It feels like my heart is breaking, piece by fragile piece, and there's nothing I can do to stop it.

"Oh," I say, my voice trembling as I try to hold back the tears prickling my eyes. It takes every ounce of strength to hold it together because, inside, I'm being torn apart. But I can't break in front of him. That rage that felt so potent with Indie has well and truly died with a simple sentence.

"I shouldn't have kissed you," he says again, turning to face me, and a quiet sob pushes through the front I'm putting on.

I swallow hard, trying to keep my voice steady. "I get it," I whisper, unable to look at him. I can't stay here. I need to get out, to put some distance between us before I completely fall apart.

I stand up, moving mechanically to my bag at the foot of the bed. My hands tremble as I start gathering my things, shoving my laptop, clothes, and headphones back into my duffel with quick, jerky movements. "I'm gonna get another room. This was..." I shake my head, vision blurring. "This was a mistake."

"Quinn, wait," Miles says, his voice filled with regret, but I can't look at him. I can't bear to see the guilt or pity in his eyes.

"No, it's fine," I say, my voice strained. "I'll just... I'll find somewhere else to stay tonight. You don't need to worry about it."

"Quinn, please, just stop for a second," he pleads, stepping toward me, but I shake my head, zipping up my bag.

"I don't think there's anything left to say," I whisper. I sling the strap of my bag over my shoulder and force myself to take a deep breath as I walk toward the door. And then I feel a presence behind me.

Close. Really close. Too close.

The heat from his body pours over my own like a soothing balm, all while feeling like an electric charge buzzing around us.

I don't think I can handle him purposefully touching me right now. The thought that he would hug me like he always does, like I mean something to him when I know I don't mean enough, would hurt too much.

"Quinn, I'm sorry, but I need to say this," he begins, and the remaining shards of my heart fall to the ground at his feet. "I shouldn't have kissed you..." *Please don't say it again. I can't handle it.* "Because you deserve more than a drunken kiss. And now that I know exactly what you taste like, I want more."

My head snaps up in an instant, and I spin around to find his eyes assessing me with such intensity it steals my breath. "W-what?"

He takes another step, closing the distance between us, until his body brushes softly against mine. "I shouldn't have done it because it complicates things. Because you're my best friend's sister. Because you're *my* best friend. But I don't regret it. Not for a second."

I blink, hope and confusion storming around my heart. "Y-you don't?"

He shakes his head lightly, his gaze falling to my mouth. "I can't regret something I don't want to forget."

Licking my lips, I swallow hard. "So, what does that mean?"

A smirk lifts the side of his mouth, and the glint in his eyes is new, as though he's seen something he wants for the first time. It's breathtaking because it's him. He's looking at *me* like that. His knuckles dust across my jaw, and I fight to close my eyes and lean into him more. "It means, I want a do-over. I want to ruin our friendship because I need to kiss you again." He leans his head toward me, almost letting our lips brush, but not quite. "And again," he breathes, his minty breath engulfing my senses.

I nearly whimper. "And again," he says finally, pulling back to study my face. "Until I earn all your kisses."

My heart kicks against my ribs. He wants to kiss me. Miles Cooper wants to kiss me. More than once. If I thought I'd spent my life swooning over him, that all pales in comparison to having him here, wanting me like this.

I hesitate for too long, lost in my own euphoria.

"But if you don't want that, I'll back off and let you date your musician. I'll be your friend and leave it at that." He moves his hand to cup my jaw, his calloused fingertips scraping against my skin in the headiest way, as he drags them into my hair. My head tilts up to look into his eyes, and my body responds, heating and pushing toward him, desperate for more. I wet my lips as I attempt to control my breathing, desire and need pooling low in my belly just as I lean forward, almost touching.

"I don't want to date the musician," I say breathlessly.

His eyes flicker with surprise, and yet confident smirk blooming on his lips tells me he'd hoped I'd say that. "You don't, huh?"

I shake my head, lifting onto my toes to brush the tip of my nose to his.

"Kiss me and mean it, Cooper."

I catch a glimpse of a smirk again before he pushes me fully against the door and slams his lips to mine.

CHAPTER SIXTEEN

Miles

FOR THE SECOND TIME in my life, I'm kissing Quinn.

My Queenie. The girl who has been under my nose my whole life.

Those beautiful green eyes pierced me when I turned up tonight, and I tried so hard to act normal, but that went about as well as a fumble at the touchdown line. I couldn't pretend. The moment I walked into her space, that smells like her sweet cinnamon scent, she did the most Quinn thing she could possibly do and outright asked me what was going on. And just like that, I wanted to kiss her again.

Which is what I'm doing now. Her lips move against mine like she's always kissed me, like she was made for me. The overwhelming and entirely new feeling of possession roars its way into my blood again, making me pulse and vibrate with need for her. I tighten the grip I have in her hair and feel her moan against my mouth as I sweep my tongue along hers.

Breaking away briefly, I stare down at her. My favorite color isn't reflected back at me yet, her eyes closed, and her lips look swollen from my kisses. "Quinn," I breathe, and I'm rewarded with her emerald eyes opening and burning with lust for me. "Fuck, you're beautiful," I whisper before kissing her again.

I don't know how long we stay kissing, but it's not enough. When she pulls away, breathless, I take a tentative step back to give her some air.

She swipes across her puffy lips, holding her fingers there. "Wow, I mean, that was—"

"Yeah. Agreed," I say on an exhale.

"What should... I mean, the... Uh..." She squints, as though she's thinking really hard.

"Have my kissing skills made you incoherent, Queenie?" I muse, a smile playing on my lips.

She scoffs and waves her hand. "No, yeah." She pauses and thinks. "Definitely something going on. My brain isn't braining."

I chuckle and reach for her hand, pulling her to me, and she comes willingly, fitting against me perfectly. It blows my freaking mind how natural it feels. All of it. "So..." I begin, slowing my gaze over her delicate face. "Wanna watch a movie?"

"Movie," she repeats mindlessly and stares at me for a beat before wriggling out of my hold and walking to her bed, her hands laced in her hair. "Wait, what the h-e-double hockey sticks just happened?"

"I kissed you."

"Again."

"Again," I confirm, watching her face morph from confusion

to surprise and pretty much staying that way. "Is that okay?"

"Okay?" she repeats with a huffed laugh. "Yeah, it was more than okay. I mean, we should talk about it, right?"

I nod. "I know, and we will." I bring her toward me to kiss again. Now I've started, I can't seem to stop. She wraps her arms around my neck, letting me kiss and taste her exactly how I need to before I whisper against her mouth. "But let's just chill for a bit, okay?"

She nods, seemingly in a daze, and I walk to her bag, taking out her laptop again, passing it to her. She taps a few keys, waking it up as she sits on her bed. "What were you watching?" I ask as I flop down next to her.

"*Insidious.*"

A startled sound escapes my mouth as my gaze darts to her. "You know that's scary as shit, right? It's not a happy ending like you're used to and it's sure a shit not a comedy."

She shrugs. "Trying something new is good for you, and I'm sure I can handle it."

Yeah, but maybe I can't if she gets scared and climbs into my lap. I know what we're doing is new, and I'm towing some kind of 'best friend' line here, but my control will waiver when we're alone now that I know what she tastes like. I can't let that happen yet. Not with Quinn.

"What's that face for?" she asks, amused, as she breaks into a grin. "Don't tell me the big, strong football player is a scaredy cat?"

The jab to my ribs has my body curling in on itself, and a burst of laughter erupts from both of us. We're a mess of limbs and teasing pokes until I grab her wrists and pin them above her head. Her warm body fits perfectly beneath mine.

Our breaths make a heavy soundtrack in the room as we stare at each other.

My heart thuds so loudly, I swear she can hear it. As her lips part slightly, I can feel the rise and fall of her chest, matching the quick rhythm of my own breathing.

The look in her eyes pulls me in, like gravity. It feels inevitable. I lean closer, our lips just a breath from one another's, and even though we've already kissed tonight, I want more. Which is a bad idea. My eyes flicker down to her ruby lips and then back up to her green eyes, searching for any sign that I should stop, but all I see is her, waiting for me to make a move. And it would be so easy to do.

"Quinn," I murmur, my voice barely more than a whisper. I can feel the tension crackling in the air between us, and I'm so close now that I can feel her breath on my skin. "I'm not afraid." Except I already know that's a lie. I'm scared of this, of her, of what we could be and how I'll inevitably mess it up. Suddenly, my throat feels thick as I try to swallow past it. "But for once in my life, I'm going to exercise control."

She searches my eyes for a beat. "Control?"

"I don't want to jump into the deep end here. You're my best friend."

"Okay," she says hesitantly. "You know I'm not fragile, right?"

I smirk at her response. I know she isn't. She's the strongest person I know. "You might not be, but maybe I am."

She nods, something that looks like understanding crossing her face. "Well, let's watch the scary movie. Unless your idea of a good time is sparkly vampires and sexy werewolves again?"

I chuckle lightly, burying my head into the crook of her neck, breathing her in as I do. Fuck, she smells so good. "You know how much I wanted Jacob to get the girl. That's unfair."

"I know, poor baby." She pats my back in the most condescending way and some of that fear dissipates because this is her. My Quinn. When I lift to meet her face, she's smiling at me, and my heart double taps. "But Edward was far superior. Now get off me, you big brute."

Reluctantly, I move off her and roll to sit on the bed. Two seconds later, her sweet scent washes over me as her body joins mine. When she presses play, the sinister music filters into the laptop's crappy speakers, somehow making it more disturbing. I shift in my seat as an image of a boy in his bed in the dark comes on screen, and I glance over to Quinn out of the corner of my eye. She's chewing on her bottom lip like it's her favorite flavor of gummy worm, so I lean over her and grab her the bag I brought for her instead. "Give those lips a rest, I'll need them later." I peck a quick kiss to her temple.

A gasp of air escapes her, and I can't help but smirk as I turn my attention back to the movie.

As the evening progresses, I become more aware of Quinn next to me. Her breathing, her subtle movements, her scent. Even though that's always been etched into my brain as something uniquely her. But tonight, it feels different. It feels like I'm seeing things differently and I'm a little terrified. It's like flying without a parachute, because I have no fucking idea what I'm doing with Quinn. I can't just turn on the charm and get into her pants. I mean, I could, but that's not what this is, I already know that much. I need to think about being what Quinn needs, and wants, in a guy.

Honestly, I have no idea if I can do that, but after one—no, two—tastes of her, I'm not giving up that easily.

Even if I'm in over my head.

Even if I'm keeping things from her.

One thing I know for sure is that I want Quinn Dawson.

Chapter Seventeen

Quinn

THE BED IS WARM this morning. Almost unbearably so, but I like it. The early morning light filters through the hotel curtains, casting a warm, golden hue across the room as I blink a few times to get my surroundings. My body feels weighted to the mattress and that's when I realize the heat of another body pressed against mine. As I become more aware of my surroundings, I remember Miles. Him kissing me. Him falling asleep after watching quite possibly one of the most disturbing films I've ever seen. How he slept, I'll never know. I couldn't, and it had nothing to do with the creepy horror movie and everything to do with him sharing my bed.

His face is nuzzled into the back of my neck, his breath steady against my skin. His tattooed arm drapes over my waist, encasing me below two dice etched on his skin and above is my favorite one, the half royal flush of cards that I so desperately want to run my fingers across.

For a moment, I stay still, unable to will my body to move because he's here with me, next to me. My heart beats a little faster, not out of nervousness, but out of excitement. I don't know if that's enough for what I'm feeling. I don't want to move, fearing that any shift might wake him and shatter this bubble I've found myself in.

But eventually, I do shift slightly, and Miles stirs, lifting his head groggily. His eyes, still heavy, meet mine. There's a beat of silence, when neither of us knows what to say or do. The events of last night rush back: the football game, the celebration, the kiss we shared, and the eventual decision to share the hotel bed. It all feels a bit surreal now, in the light of day. Who am I kidding? I'm in bed with the boy I've loved my whole life, it's completely surreal.

"Morning," he murmurs, his voice rough with sleep. He offers a small, sleepy smile that makes my heart flutter.

"Morning," I reply, my voice just above a whisper. I don't know what's expected of me now, what the right thing to do is. But Miles seems unbothered as he stretches, his arm leaving my waist as he rolls onto his back giving me room to turn to face him.

"Did you sleep well?" he asks.

"Yeah, I did. You?"

"Best sleep I've had in a while," he says, turning his head to look at me. His gaze is steady, and I feel a blush creeping up my neck. God, he's pretty in the morning.

"We should probably get up," I say, more to myself than to him.

"We should." He hesitates before grabbing me again, deftly

turning me, dragging my back to his front. "But I want to stay here for a little longer."

My nerve endings are shot. I feel raw, exposed, desperately begging my brain not to word vomit that I'm in love with him.

I'm in bed with Miles. I'm in bed with Miles. Miles kissed me. Yeah, no matter how many times I say it in my head, it still feels like I've entered the multiverse. Any moment now, there's going to be another version of me prancing into the room, demanding I leave because I'm in the wrong world.

Any minute now...

"You're tense."

Of course I'm tense. "I'm...not sure what to do."

"Just relax. Let me hold you." He buries his face into the back of my neck again, and I'm back to melting. Melting into his arms, feeling like I never want to leave this space. Until my stomach gives out the biggest protest for not having breakfast already.

Miles chuckles behind me. "Hungry?"

Turning in his arms, our eyes immediately lock, and I take in every inch of him. Sleepy Miles isn't one I see often, and he might be my favorite yet. The caramel in his eyes is brighter in the soft light, his lips poutier than usual, and his hair on top of his head sticks up in all directions. I lick my lips as he stares right back at me, unabashedly taking me in the same way I'm doing to him. "Starving."

The corner of his mouth twitches just as he flops on to his back, covering his face with a groan. "You can't say it like that and expect me to be a gentleman."

"Since when are you a gentleman, Miles Cooper?" I prop myself up on my elbow, looking down at him, my hair dusting

MEGHAN HOLLIE

over my shoulders.

Poking his cute face out from under his arm, his eyes sparkle with mischief. "Since today."

"I see."

"Or maybe since last night, if I think about it." His arm drops, revealing the rest of his face.

"Hmm." I lean a little closer, enjoying the way his gaze dances with anticipation. My pulse kicks up as I consider teasing him a little.

Before he can react, I press a quick kiss to his cheek, his warm skin against mine. He turns to catch my lips, but I pull back just in time, leaving him hanging.

"Hey!" he protests, laughter erupting from his chest that quickly turns into a pout.

I grin, the energy crackling between us. "You'll have to be quicker than that."

His face lights up at the challenge and, in a second, the moment shifts into something else entirely. My insides tingle as I shift off the bed, backing away. The playful look on his face quickly morphs into something much hotter. Much darker. I have to clamp my mouth closed to stop a whimper from escaping.

Our eyes still locked, once my feet hit the floor, I squeak and turn around, hauling ass to the bathroom when two strong arms wrap around my waist, lifting me with ease, spinning us around until I'm catapulted onto the bed with a soft thud.

I swipe my hair from my face, open my eyes, and take in the muscled, bare-chested, insanely hot football player hovering above me with the darkest eyes devouring every inch of me. I'm not ashamed as I do the same to him. My eyes snag on each and

142

every piece of ink on show, the rose and vines that start at his strong throat, to the compass near his left pec, all the way down to the trail of dark hair between his muscled V-shape hips. The masterpiece of him is overwhelming.

I'm unable to help the smile that breaks through at the thought of him being here with *me*. "You caught me." I giggle as he leans closer, the subtle scent of him as intoxicating as the look on his face.

"I caught you," he repeats gruffly. "Now gimme those lips."

He closes the distance between us, capturing my mouth with his, softer than I thought he would, and I weave my fingers into his hair, holding him there. Lowering his body to mine, I revel in the sensation of him being pressed against me, kissing me, wanting me. Every sweep of our tongues takes me higher, and I know he feels it too when he deepens the kiss, pressing into me harder, like we're both on the edge of something dangerous, something I can't pull away from, even if I wanted to.

Then, my stomach rumbles again, louder and more obnoxious this time, breaking the moment.

He lifts slightly, smiling down at me, sated and so insanely sexy. "Come, let's get breakfast. Bus is leaving in an hour."

We dress quickly, me in the bathroom and him in the hotel room. I don't trust myself not to throw myself at him if I see more of his naked body.

Downstairs, we find the hotel bar and order water and two coffees.

"Morning, sunshine," I sing-song, spotting a very hungover looking Indie walking toward us.

"Ugh, don't," she mumbles, grabbing my glass of water and chugging it. "How are you so chipper?"

"Good night's sleep," I say casually, but Indie narrows her eyes at me. She glances between me and Miles, her eyebrows raising slightly.

"Uh-huh," she says, a knowing smirk forming. "What time does the bus leave?"

"In an hour," Seb says, coming up behind her, wrapping his arms around her waist and kissing her neck.

"Let's go eat before I drag you back upstairs," Seb says to Indie, but Miles and I both hear it because my brother is as subtle as a steam train.

"Dude, your sister heard that."

"I don't ever need to hear it again, either." I shudder.

Seb looks sheepishly over at us both. "Sorry, sis."

I roll my eyes, crossing my arms. "Yeah, well, you're not sorry enough."

Miles smirks, leaning in. "This is why I'm glad I'm an only child." I can't help but steal a glance at his lips when I notice he's already doing the same thing to me. Our eyes hold for a beat, Miles's hand slipping under the table to rest on my thigh. And then Seb laughs, breaking the spell, reminding us that he has no idea what's going on between us. He doesn't move his hand, though, and it grounds me, stops me from completely freaking out.

Miles manages to turn away, making small talk with my brother again, but not Indie. My best friend's narrowed eyes are locked on mine, as though she's trying to telepathically communicate. Something tells me her intuition has peaked and she knows that more happened between Miles and me. I just hope she doesn't say anything to Seb. Not yet.

CHAPTER EIGHTEEN

Miles

THE HANGOUT ISN'T A place I've spent much time outside of parties. Occasionally, we'll break out the Xbox. Which is what Hudson and I found ourselves agreeing to do about an hour ago. It's after classes and there's no practice tonight so we've got a rare night off. My immediate thought was to ask Quinn to my dorm, but then I remembered she volunteers at the women's shelter in town on Wednesday evenings. So here I am, getting beat at a fucking game of *Call of Duty*.

"Dude, you're not even trying to watch my six. Come on!" Hudson wails.

"My joystick keeps sticking. It won't let me fucking shoot!" I shout back.

When you're playing video games, it doesn't matter if you're sitting shoulder to shoulder, if you aren't shouting at each other, it's not as fun.

"Fuck!" Hudson curses, just as we both lose the game again. "I give up." The controller hits the coffee table with a thud and Hudson slumps back into the couch.

"We can play another night," I suggest.

Hudson huffs and we sit in comfortable silence, scrolling our phones for a second, when a text from Quinn comes through, telling me she's finished at the shelter and will be getting the bus back soon. This kind of text isn't new for us, since she usually lets me know where she's going and if she's safe. But now I feel a surge of something else too alongside our friendship, and I'm trying to come to terms with it.

I'm also desperately trying to take things slow with her because I refuse to mess this up.

With Seb being her brother and my best friend, talking to him about it is out of the question. He's way too protective, and I'm not ready to deal with the fallout that could bring. Hudson, on the other hand, might be a wild card, but he's my best option right now. He and Quinn are friends too, and maybe he can give me some insight without blowing everything up. I glance over at the man in question, watching the way he smirks at whatever he's seeing on his phone, wondering if I can trust him to keep this between us. Eh, fuck it. I need to talk to someone before I explode.

"So, can I ask you something?"

"Oh, shit." Glancing at me with an odd expression, he sits up straighter, dropping his phone to his lap. "Is this like a bro-to-bro thing? Are you... Do you need advice?"

I run my hand down my face. "Yeah, I need advice." I then pin him with a stern stare, pointing my finger at his face. "But you dare tell a soul, and I will end you."

"*You are* coming to me for advice!" he yelps, practically jumping from the couch. "Oh my god, fuck. This never happens. Well, I'm your guy, the best man for the job." He brushes his hair from his face and looks at me with a dopey grin. "Hudson Parker – Advice Guru. And to think you're the one who started it all."

My eyes roll back in my head. "You about done?"

"I'm so excited." Clearing his throat, he schools his expression. "Hit me with it."

"Fucking hell," I mutter. "Okay, so here it goes."

Hudson rubs his hands together in glee, and it's really fucking hard to concentrate when he's acting like he's in a candy store or some shit. "So, like, say you're with a girl, and you kiss—"

"Dude, I do more than kiss girls—"

"Hudson," I chastise, snapping my fingers to get him to focus.

He shakes his head. "Right, okay, kissing girls, I'm listening."

I take a deep breath. "Like I said. Say you kissed a girl, and you liked it more than you would normally?"

His brow furrows. "Do you not kiss girls often?"

Exasperation claws at my nerves. "No, I do, but... Fuck, I don't know, like a girl who is more than just a hookup, you know?"

"Oh, okay, I'm with you."

The couch bounces beside us, and I hadn't even realized that Jay walked into the room. "What is he with you for? You aren't concocting some kind of orgy with a bunch of people, are you?"

"I mean..." Hudson debates, just as I firmly say, "No!"

Then, without missing another beat, Hudson says, "Miles

needs advice."

My hands raise in frustration, then drop to my lap with a thud. "Hudson, what did I just say to you twenty seconds ago? You have to keep your mouth closed."

He shrugs. "You haven't even said anything yet. Just told me you kissed a girl and you liked it."

"Isn't that a song?" Jay muses.

"Probably."

"Guys!" I say through gritted teeth. This was the worst idea ever, and it's only getting worse.

Hudson slaps my chest, chuckling to himself. "Listen, if Jay ever gets over his hateship he has with this chick in his class, he can come to me for advice now, because I'm clearly the best at it. Right, Miles?"

"You haven't actually done anything yet, except raise my blood pressure."

"He constantly does that for me. Also, I don't have a hateship," Jay grumbles, sitting back against the couch.

Hudson snorts. "You do, first step is admitting you have a problem. And yours happens to have blue hair, a nice ass, and a quirky attitude."

Jay flips him off, and I stiffen, my entire body tensing at the offhand comment from Hudson. Yet another day I'm reminded of the tightrope I'm walking when it comes to football, and everything I've got on the line. *But you don't have a problem, Cooper. This is temporary.*

The reality is, bringing Quinn into any of it is a terrible idea. And here I am, discussing the option of what the fuck I should be doing if I like her more than a hookup. Fuck. Abort, *abort*.

Hudson's hand lands on my shoulder, drawing me out of my

thoughts. "I'm sorry, buddy. Kissing. Girls. Not just hookups. I'm all ears. Go."

"This was a mistake." I stand, shrugging him off and storming toward the door.

"I'm listening now, dude, come back!" he yells as I push open the door, his voice growing more distant as I pick up my pace.

A tug on my arm has me turning around when I come face to face with Jay.

"Did you seriously go to Hudson for advice? We both know I'm the one you should've come to."

I hesitate, unsure what the hell I should do now. "Yeah, he was just there, and I was in my head."

Jay hums an acknowledgement. "Well, I'm here if you still need to talk?"

I pause. What could be worse than talking to Hudson? Is this the worst idea? I know I don't want to bring anyone else into my other activities, but Jay is the more level-headed of the two, so fuck it. And this is just about Quinn, nothing else. "And you won't blab it to anyone?"

Jay crosses his heart with his fingers. "Swear it."

I run a hand over my hair, hoping my second attempt might go better. "So, there's a girl I kissed. And it felt different. Like, really different."

Jay raises an eyebrow. "Different how?"

"I don't know. It wasn't just physical, you know?" I scuff my shoe against the ground, looking down at it as nerves make my palms sweaty. "It felt like it meant something more."

He nods slowly. "And this girl, she's not just anyone, is she?"

I swallow hard, the weight of what I'm about to admit pressing down on me. "No, she's not just anyone."

Jay's eyes narrow slightly. "So, what's the plan? You going to talk to her about it?"

As I shrug, the weight of uncertainty weighs me down. "I know I should. But the thing is, what if she doesn't feel the same way? What if she wants me for what I'm known for, just a hookup? Or what if things get complicated?"

Jay chuckles softly. "Man, relationships are always complicated. But look, if you really care about her, you should talk to her. You can't let the fear of what might happen stop you from finding out how she feels."

I nod, appreciating his honesty. "Yeah, you're right."

Jay claps me on the shoulder. "Good luck, man. And remember, if Hudson or anyone else gives you crap, you can always come to me."

"Thanks, Jay. I appreciate it."

"Anytime. You coming to Quinn's party tomorrow?"

My brow creases. "Party?"

"Yeah, the one she invited the whole hockey team to. You were there, the other day in the cafeteria. We're hooking Quinn up, remember?"

Fuck. I remember, alright. Unease washes over me at the thought of seeing her with anyone else, but I tamper it down—barely. "Yeah, I'll stop by."

And make sure no hockey player gets their mitts on her.

CHAPTER NINETEEN

Quinn

"REMIND ME WHY I agreed to this again?" Indie grumbles, yanking her arm out of my grip.

Honestly, I don't even know myself. This party was supposed to be so I could meet guys. Planned in anger when Miles was trying to sabotage my dating life, but now...things are different, I think? Am I off the market? Do I even want to throw this party anymore? My gut tells me it's a bad idea, but so many people are coming and the people pleaser in me can't let them down. I'll just hang around, avoiding all the guys I invited. Yeah, that'll work.

"Because you're my best friend and you love me," I say pointedly. Besides, if I have to suffer through this, all the while wishing I was alone with Miles instead, then I'm gonna need my best friend as backup.

She rolls her eyes, but follows me across the hall to the common room anyway and grabs a string of fairy lights from the box I borrowed from the arts department when I was feeling indignant and determined—which I do not feel anymore. What I wouldn't give for another movie night with Miles instead. "Fine, but I'm not climbing any ladders," Indie says, interrupting my wandering thoughts.

"Deal." I nod, handing her the tape. "Just start hanging these up around the edge of the room."

Before she makes her way to the corner she turns to me, checking to see who's around us and lowering her voice. "So, are we going to talk about the fact you shared a hotel room with Miles?"

My eyes go wide and do my own double take around the room. Seb and Miles both managed to tell Coach they would ride back to campus with us, so we haven't had a chance to talk yet. "We, um, well—"

She gasps. "If he hurt you, I'm ready to go to war."

"No, no." I place my hand on her arm. "Nothing like that. We watched a movie and maybe kissed more. He apologized for how it played out and he wanted a do-over."

Indie conceals a squeal, and I can't help but giggle. "Oh my god. Did you just kiss?"

I nod. "But we haven't talked about anything properly. I don't know if we're a thing or not. Or if I should ask him."

Indie twists her mouth, thinking. "So why are we having all these guys over for this party if you might or might not be a thing with Miles? Are you going to talk to any of them?"

Biting my lip, I say, "I'm not going to be rude, but I don't know..."

"I think you should keep your options open for now. You

haven't made any promises yet."

I shrug, because is that even what I want? I don't think it is. But we haven't exactly figured it out either.

"Wait," she says, grasping my arm. "What do we do about Seb?"

It's one of the main questions I've considered, but I'm not ready for him to know. "I don't know. I hate to ask, but…"

She groans. "You're going to ask me to keep a secret, aren't you?"

I force a pleasant smile and flutter my lashes at her, my hands tucked under my chin. "Pleeeeeeeease. Only for a little while. I don't even know if there's anything to tell yet."

She frowns at me for a second. "Fine. But you owe me…again. First, this decorating, and now, secrets. I'll add it to your tab."

"I love you," I say, wrapping my arms around her.

"Yeah, yeah." Rolling her eyes playfully, she moves to the corner to hang the lights.

I turn my attention to the glittering foil curtains that one of my girls, Lily, from the cheer squad brought by earlier today, hoping they aren't too tangled. Indie fusses with the fairy lights, muttering under her breath about the tape not sticking properly. "Why can't we just use those command hook things?"

"Because we're out," I tell her, holding up the curtain to assess. "Just do what you can."

She grumbles some more, but goes back to work. I manage to get the foiled curtains hung by the doorway and near the kitchenette entrance, then head over to the snack table to make sure everything is set up. The table is piled high with chips and cookies, while solo cups line the edges, along with several mixers and a couple of bottles of vodka that Lily had from a party she threw recently. Oh, and my favorite gummy worms, of course. But that has a memory playing in my head like a home movie.

"When I'm big and old, like Mom and Dad, if I sell all my toys and buy you a ring, will you marry me?" I ask, chewing on a gummy worm he bought for me at the store. They're my favorite candy now.

"You'd sell all your baby dolls for me? Even the ones that burp and poop and stuff?" Miles asks with his mouth full. Mom says he shouldn't talk with his mouth full, but he does it anyway.

"I'd do anything for you. You're my best friend."

Miles passes me another candy, the red and blue one, and I smile because that's my favorite. "You're my best friend too. You and Seb."

"Yeah, but you don't wanna marry my stinky brother, right?"

He shakes his head. "I think I'm supposed to buy you a ring, instead of you buying me one," he mumbles, shoving too many gummies in his mouth, but it's okay, because I only like the red and blue ones and he's eating the other colors.

"So, you'll marry me?"

"Sure." He shrugs, swallowing the big mouthful.

"Good," I say as I reach for another candy. "Because you make my heart beep real loud."

"I do?" he asks, looking at me strangely.

"Yeah."

"You're weird." Laughing, he stares into my eyes, and my heart thumps so loudly in my chest I want him to hear it so he'll believe me. "I'll get us some more gummy worms."

"Quinn, where do you want these?" Lily asks, snapping my

attention back to the room. She's holding some white and gold balloons.

"Over there by the couch." I point it out, trying to refocus on the tasks in front of me.

***

An hour later, the decorating is finally done, and the common room looks amazing. I decide it's time for phase two of the evening's preparations. I grab Indie by the arm, and this time, she doesn't try to pull away.

"Quinn, where are we going? Aren't we staying here?" she asks, confusion in her voice.

A mischievous grin takes over my face. "It's makeover time."

"Oh, no way," Indie protests, digging her heels in. "I'm not getting dressed up. I'm fine in this. I like—"

"Your jeans and your boots. I know. But tonight, you're wearing the dress that I bought for you. And before you object, it's black."

Indie grumbles, but she doesn't put up that much of a fight. Once inside, I push her down onto my bed and go get the dress I found last week with her in mind. Springing out of the closet, I hold the dress on the hanger, "Ta-da!" I sing-song.

Her eyes sweep over the black minidress, and I catch a flicker of interest in her expression. There's no way this isn't a perfect Indiana Beck dress. It has a black slip underneath with a sheer mesh overlay that resembles an oversized T-shirt. It's perfect for her. When I see her roll her eyes in resignation, I know I've nailed it.

"Ugh, fine. But just to be clear, this is the only dress I'll accept, and the boots stay."

"Noted," I say, satisfied at how well I know my best friend. She tugs off her t-shirt and holds out her hand for the dress, and I have to suppress a squeal of glee.

While she's getting dressed, I start working on my own outfit. I also found a new dress when I bought Indie's, and while I got it originally to catch a guy's eye, I'm now only hoping it'll draw the attention of one guy. Nerves swim in my belly as slip off my clothes and into the dress. I think about seeing him and not touching him tonight, and I already don't like the idea.

Indie clears her throat, and I spin around, having changed too. "Happy now?" she mutters.

"Very," I say, beaming, squashing all these feelings brewing inside me. "You look gorgeous. Now, let's do something with your hair."

"Quinn, seriously, this is overkill." She groans as I start fussing with her hair.

"Nonsense," I say, pinning a few strands back of her wild curls. "You're going to look amazing, and you might even have fun tonight."

"What is this fun you speak of?" she teases as I lightly tug on a curl. "Hey!"

"Fun, Indiana, is something you need more of."

She mumbles something I chose to ignore, as I pin back a few tendrils of her golden locks giving her a boho beach vibe. Perfect.

"Come on, let's go to our party."

As soon as we enter the room across the hall, the place is filling with familiar faces from class and some of my squad too. "Hey,

Quinn, we brought mixers and snacks!" calls one of the girls.

"Amazing, the table is just over there by the door," I shout back, looking around the room for a familiar set of brown eyes that make me weak.

Suddenly, two big arms scoop me up from behind. I let out a squeal and turn to see Hudson, slapping his chest. "Oh god! You scared me!"

"Did you just call me god?" He smirks as he puts me down.

"Not like that!" I squeak.

"Relax," he laughs. "The place looks great. You smashed the party vibe."

"Thanks," I say, glancing around him, wondering if he's here alone. "Did you come here alone?" I ask, hoping it doesn't sound as obvious.

"Jay is on his way. Not sure about Miles and Seb. They were at the gym with me earlier, but I haven't seen them since," he says, distracted, looking around, and my good mood sours just a tiny bit. What if he doesn't come because I told him he wasn't invited? It was a joke at the time, but now things have changed, and he's the only one I'd like to see here. "So, any of your squad single?" He wiggles his eyebrows.

Huffing a laugh, I sigh. "There's no stopping you, is there?"

"Noooooope," he drawls, then kisses my cheek and runs off into the crowd.

And I try my hardest to pretend I'm not searching the crowd for someone too, whilst secretly praying he actually shows up.

CHAPTER TWENTY

Miles

THE BASS THUMPS THROUGH the walls as I make my way into the girls' dorm. I arrive thinking it's going to be your typical college party: red solo cups, bad decisions waiting to happen, and the faint smell of something burning in the tiny kitchen. But when the door pushes open to their version of The Hangout, all I can see is yellow. The whole place is a sea of different textures of sunshine, some glossy and metallic, some glittery. Indie and Quinn really went all out. I even spot a life-size cut-out of Harry Styles in the corner.

I push through the throng of people, my eyes scanning the room for her.

"Miles!" Seb shouts from across the room. He's waving me over, with his girl firmly planted across his front and a possessive arm over her chest.

"Hey, lovebirds, where's Quinn?" I ask.

"Being the social butterfly, per usual." Indie nods behind me "Weren't you uninvited to this party?" she asks, but I wave it off, ignoring that little detail in favor of turning and immediately finding her. How can I not when she looks like *that*? Damn. My eyes drink her in and my knees wobble at the sight of her. *What the hell is happening to me?*

Her soft red hair flows in waves, free of her bow she usually wears, as she flicks it over a shoulder, showing whoever she's with that perfectly symmetrical smile of hers, cushioned with pillow soft pouty lips as shiny as glass. My gaze travels down her petite, curvy frame as saliva gathers in my mouth at the dress she's wearing. It's light blue, short, and hugs every sinful inch of her body. Hot freaking hell. She looks insanely good.

Don't even get me started on the heels.

Fuck. Me.

A groan builds in my chest. I'm so fucking screwed. It's like I've spent my entire life wearing glasses and now I've got perfect vision when it comes to her. One kiss, one moment, and she's all I see.

As I watch her, I notice she's surrounded by guys. And not just any guys—hockey guys. Goddamn them for keeping her attention. Clearly, it's attention she wants to give, though. She's relaxed and smiling and...flirting? My hand sweeps down my face, trying to stop the grimace I can feel spreading.

The need to do something roars in my head like a siren. But what the fuck should I do? Claim her for everyone to see? Fuck, I didn't plan on pissing off Seb tonight so I can't do that. Maybe Indie was right, and I should have stayed away tonight. This party was set for her to date more, and maybe she still wants to do that? We never said anything about being together officially, or even exclusively.

Doubt tightens my jaw as I watch guy after guy fawn over her, and she laughs with that musical sound I can't hear over the music, but I can see the guys are entranced. How could they not be? She's pure sunshine. But I want her to be my sunshine girl, not theirs.

Yeah, I need to do something. Turning to Seb, I tap his shoulder, directing his attention to the groupies around his sister. "Dude, the entire hockey team is getting real close to Quinn over there."

He raises an eyebrow, following my gaze to where Quinn laughs at something one of the guys said and my blood turns green with envy. "So?"

My head snaps to him. "*So*?!" I repeat, only much higher pitched than he did. How is he so calm about this?

He shrugs. Fucking shrugs. "Not my circus, not my monkeys," he mutters, taking a sip of his drink. "Quinn's a big girl. She can handle herself."

"What the fuck, man?" I admonish. I see Indie snickering in my periphery. "That's because of you, isn't it?" I ask her.

"My girl barely got a look in with so many guys because of this behemoth's actions scaring them all away, so yeah, I told him to back off."

Okay, so maybe I have a shot? I laugh internally at myself. I am 100% sure mine is out of the pot of names Quinn is allowed to date. Maybe she doesn't want me, maybe she went through with this party because she wants to keep her options open. The idea churns my stomach, but I wouldn't stop her. I wouldn't like it, but I wouldn't stop her. Damn, I wish I'd been clearer about what I want.

My eyes zero in on another guy who is approaching her with a look that says a lot more than 'I wanna be friends.' Guy looks familiar. Oh shit, is this the date guy?

"Who's this guy too?" I nod toward them.

"Oh, that's Alex. You know, the cellist? He and Quinn had a date that I believe you interrupted," Indie says with a tone that tells me she knows more than she's saying.

I swallow the lump stuck in my throat, unable to tear my gaze away from Quinn. Alex approaches her, taps her shoulder, and she turns with a bright smile that knocks the wind out of me, throwing her arms around him in a hug that makes my fists clench. I watch with bated breath as his hand drifts lower and lower until it grazes the top of her ass. My blood boils to dangerous levels, to the point I might explode. *That fucking hand.* I wonder how easy it would be for him to play his instrument one handed, because dude's about to lose at least one of those paws.

My jaw aches from pressure, my head spinning with the notion that I don't want anyone touching her. I'm about to do something stupid and reckless, and I don't think I can stop myself.

Before I know it, my feet are striding toward them, the force of each footstep practically echoing in my head, wondering if I have actual steam coming from my ears because it fucking feels like it.

The distant sound of Seb calling my name should stop me in my tracks, but I'm too far gone now. If he questions me, I'll play it off as being protective of her, but right now, my tunnel vision is homed in on Alex's hand.

I should keep my cool. I should let her do her thing. I also should know better.

But clearly, I don't.

As I approach, I get a front-row view of exactly where he's groping her, and my teeth grit together. "Move the hand, or fucking lose it," I hiss.

They both turn to face me, but that damn hand stays in the danger zone. "Oh, hey, Miles," Quinn says as she shrugs off his arm, pretending to adjust her dress in the process. "I didn't see you come in."

The relief is instant the moment I see his hand drop, and I try to read her face.

"Hey, man, how you doing?" Alex says causally, interrupting my perusal of Quinn, as though he didn't hear my threat a second ago. "Crash any other dates lately?"

I turn my glare to him, my teeth still clamped together. He's trying to be a smartass, and I know how I feel about what I just saw. I don't want to make a scene. But I also can't let him win. "Seems to be yours is the only one I enjoyed crashing," I say, pulling Quinn into my side, throwing a territorial arm over her shoulder.

Alex's eyes glitter with annoyance, glancing at my arm and back to me, and the unmistakable tic of his jaw has me suppressing a smirk. Until he looks down at Quinn with enough interest that makes a growl rumble deep in my chest. "You know," he says, voice casual but deliberate, "we never did rearrange another date. How's next Friday sound?"

Before Quinn can answer, the words are out of my mouth. "She's busy."

Her head snaps to me, and I can feel her glare even without looking.

"Oh, is she?" Alex arches an eyebrow, crossing his arms.

"Yeah, she is," I say, and my tone leaves no room for argument.

Quinn shifts against me, clearing her throat. "Alex, could you grab me a water?" Her voice cuts through the tension, cool and composed, but she shrugs off my arm this time—and not as subtly.

Alex hesitates, eyes still glued to mine, then notices my arm drop. His smirk widens. "Sure," he says, way too pleased with himself, before walking off.

The second we're alone, I know I've screwed up. The noise of the party fades, leaving us in this bubble where it's just us. Turning to see her face, my eyes trace the delicate curve of her lips, the freckles dusting her nose, and the piercing green of her eyes that seem to shine even in the low light. There's a pull between us, magnetic, impossible to ignore. I don't know how I ever managed to before.

"What was that about?" she asks, her voice sharp, but there's no real heat in it.

I shrug, trying to play it off. "Guy stuff."

She snorts and shifts slightly, but we're still close enough that our arms brush, sending a jolt of electricity through me. I see the flicker of something more on her face, mirroring my own feelings. The air around us feels thick, laden with everything we're not saying, everything I can't seem to say. Like, *I want you, don't go home with him, pick me instead*.

My hand itches to reach out, to bridge the gap between us, but I hesitate, not wanting to ruin her night, settling for a brush of my fingers against hers instead as I turn to face the room again. Her breath hitches, catching my attention once more, a flush blooming on her cheeks as she stares at me. She has to be feeling it too, right? Whatever this is between us.

Just then Alex returns, and his presence is like a bucket of ice-cold water. "Here you go," he announces, handing her the unopened bottle.

"Thanks, Alex," she murmurs, her voice a little too high, a little too forced.

The noise of the party echoes around us as we awkwardly stand together, my entire body tense, as though I'm anticipating a defensive move on the field.

"Wanna dance, Quinn?" Alex asks, and I scoff.

"Not a chance," I snap, my body temperature spiking.

Without another word, I reach for Quinn's hand, glancing behind me briefly to see my best friend too busy with his girl to notice what I'm about to do. My fingers thread through hers, and I grip firmly, tugging her to my side. She stumbles for a moment, her palm landing on my stomach, the contact searing through my shirt. But as I turn us both to move, her steps quickly fall in sync with mine, and I pull her away from Alex, my jaw still clenched. The buzz of voices and music fades behind us, but I don't stop until we're far enough from the suffocating tension and heading to the hallway.

Away from him. Away from everything. I'll deal with any fallout later, right now, I need her.

Because the only word I hear with each stomp of my feet is *mine, mine, mine, mine.*

Chapter Twenty-One

Quinn

MILES DRAGS ME AWAY from the party, and I'm not usually one for the caveman effect. But this might be an exception. Seeing him all riled up over little old me, well, that gave me enough satisfaction to last a week, at least.

I'm trying so hard not to giggle at whatever just happened. "What was all that back there?"

His nostrils flare as he pushes the door to the hallway open, the gush of cooler air hitting us both in the face. But he doesn't reply, his frustration evident in his purposeful strides as we pass my room and head to the stairwell.

The door slams against the wall with an echo in the empty space. He drops my hand and paces back and forth for a few seconds before I can't take it anymore. "You looked mad when you came over to us."

"I was, and I still am," he says, his body halting before spinning around, eyes wild as they lock onto mine.

"Why?" I ask breathlessly, my skin rippling with goosebumps from the shift in the air. His presence feels thicker, more deadly tonight, like he might want to eat me alive. And I'd let him.

"Why do you think?" he huffs with an empty laugh as he stalks toward me. I step back instinctively and quickly realize I'm being backed into a corner.

My breath stutters, belly flipping at the look in his eyes. We're mostly hidden in this part of the stairwell, but the thought of being caught thunders in my blood like a volcano ready to erupt. He takes another step closer, completely blocking my escape, the shadow of his broad body blanketing me.

Yet the notion that I've made Miles Cooper jealous still makes me want to giggle so much I have to roll my lips between my teeth to stop a noise from coming out.

"Something funny, Queenie?" His voice rumbles deep, reverberating through my core as we stand this close. My lips slip free from my teeth, but I bite the bottom one between them again as I catch my breath. Blinking up at his towering frame, I nod slowly, unable to hide the reaction.

His hand lifts, thumb tugging my lip free with a deliberate slowness. He trails the dampness down to my chin, and my eyes flutter involuntarily. God, that shouldn't be hot—but it is. He lingers for a moment, grazing my skin with a heat that makes my pulse quicken. The smirk tugging at the corner of his mouth is almost smug, like he knows exactly what he's doing to me.

"You don't like it, do you?" I whisper, more a challenge than a question. "Seeing me with someone else."

His thumb stills on my jaw, and for a second, I think I've crossed a line. But then he smiles, slow and dangerous, his eyes darkening.

"Let me spell it out for you." He moves even closer, brushing his nose against my cheek as he presses me against the wall behind. His hot breath skates over my neck, before I feel a nip at the shell of my ear. I shiver at the contact, my nerve endings spark to life. I can't help the way my body arches closer, craving more, even though my mind scrambles to catch up. "I didn't want him touching you. I didn't want him near you. I definitely didn't want him thinking he could have you." His voice is so rough, so deep, that it sends a thrill I've never known through my body.

A fluttering sensation erupts in my chest, traveling to my throat as I nearly groan. "W-why can't he have me?"

He laughs softly, so softly the only sensation I feel is a puff of air hitting my fiery skin. Pulling back, he rests his thumb under my chin, tilting my head to face his. "Tell me, whose hands would you rather have on you, and be honest. Mine or Alex's?"

I swallow past the lump wedged in my throat and blink a few times, just to let him believe I'm thinking about it, when really, I'm trying not to explode, trying to remain somewhat composed. Now I really have Miles's attention, I'm glowing from the inside. "Well, that's tough to decide..." I begin, just as I hear a growl deep in his throat and his jaw tics once. I can't help the sadistic smirk that pulls at my lips. "I *guess* I'd pick yours."

He lets out a low, dissatisfied sound at my answer, his long, rough fingers trailing along my jawline. The contrast between the calloused edges and my soft skin sends a sharp rush of heat racing down my spine. His hand moves to the nape of my neck, sliding through my hair, and I can feel every tug as he leans in, his breath grazing my opposite ear.

I fight to suppress the tremble building inside me, but it breaks free, and I realize I'm helpless to stop the reactions he's pulling out of my body because this is everything I've wanted. And right now, I'm going to grab it with two hands.

"You guess?" he murmurs, his voice a hushed rumble that vibrates against my skin.

"Uh-huh," I croak. My knees tremble beneath me, and if he wasn't anchoring my head in his palm, I'm not sure how much longer I'd be upright. The multi layers of what's happening all swirl in front of me like ingredients of a cake. Miles was jealous tonight. He wasn't being protective in his usual way; he was pissed someone else was touching me and it wasn't him.

"Maybe I need to show you what my hands can do, hm?"

Yes, please. He pushes his hips into mine, and I feel something much harder against me. Something I very much want to see, taste, feel. "Miles," I breathe.

His lips ghost across the delicate skin of my collarbone. This time, I can't stop the moans. "Yes, Queenie?"

"I-I..." I don't know what I'm trying to say as a flood of desire overwhelms my senses.

He chuckles, finally putting pressure to my scalding skin with his mouth. "So soft," he purrs just as his free hand moves toward my chest and my nipples pucker beneath the material. I couldn't wear a bra today because the back of the dress was so low, but I'm not overly busty so it wasn't that obvious anyway. But now, with Miles having such easy access, I feel like I need the protection of a bra because I'm about to cut through this dress with my nipples. "Do you need my hands here?" He brushes over my aching breast, and I whimper as he moves over to the other one, tweaking my nipple between his fingers. "Or here?"

I lick my lips, my mouth dry as I heave for air. "Everywhere. Anywhere. Please."

He growls deep in his throat, cursing as he lifts me so I'm straddling his leg, the hem of my dress riding so high my whole ass is practically out. Instinctively, I grind my hips, needing friction, needing something. "You think I can deny you?" His hand frees from my hair and my breast, drifting down my sides as he palms my hips, dragging me forward, the pressure intense as I gasp for air. "You think I want another guy touching my girl?"

I bite down hard, swallowing a heady moan. *My girl.* The way he says it feels like a brand, searing itself into my mind. And god, I love the sound of it.

"I know I said we'd take it slow, but I don't think I can do that. Not with you." He continues relentlessly. The intense pressure from the angle he has me in, his jeans rubbing against my core, makes me gasp. My hands shoot out to his shoulders to steady myself, and I'm not ashamed of the way my hips begin to rock back and forth of their own accord too. "Not when I need to show you that you're mine."

The weight of "mine" hits me like a punch to the gut, sucking the air from my lungs. I'm overwhelmed and so, so close, focusing on all the things he's never said before. My girl. Mine. God, I need this. I need release. I need him. Heat coils inside me, the beginnings of my orgasm whispering on the periphery, but it's just out of reach.

"Fuck, look at you," he rasps, his voice low. "There isn't anything I want more than to make you come right now." Licking from my collarbone to my earlobe, he bites down gently. "You want to come?"

"Yes, Miles, yes." I nod furiously, digging my fingers into his shoulders, holding on for dear life. "Oh my god," I pant, moving faster on his thigh, the friction of his jeans against my thin panties sending waves of lust rippling through my body. Each movement sends a burst of pleasure that spirals me higher and higher, the pressure building like a storm.

"Love the sound of my name on your lips," he says gruffly. "Ride my leg, Queenie. Show me how much you need it." I can barely catch my breath as the world around us blurs. My skin flushes, heart races, and just when I think I can't take any more, I feel that sweet peak approaching, the crest of the wave taking me under.

My mouth falls open in a silent gasp, and then he pulls me to him, his lips crashing against mine. He captures my moans with his mouth, swallowing each sound as they escape me. It feels primal, raw. God knows he's earned every single one.

I melt into him, surrendering to the rush. Surrendering to him, letting myself believe that this is actually happening.

My body hums with complete and utter satisfaction as he continues to kiss, nibble, and devour me.

It's only when I finally sag against him, my limbs heavy with exhaustion, that reality sets in. We're still in the stairwell of my building.

"So...that happened," I manage, my voice shaky.

He stiffens slightly, his grip tightening. "Are you okay? Shit, I should've thought about where we are. We could've been caught—"

I cut him off by placing my hand over his mouth, those deep brown eyes consuming me.

"It was...amazing." A post-orgasm thrill makes me shiver

again as I release his mouth and press my lips to his. "So hot," I mutter.

"Yeah?" he asks, with a boyish tilt to his head that makes me swoon.

I giggle as he deepens the kiss, threading those perfectly thick fingers into my hair, taking what he wants from me.

Eventually, Miles moves his leg, lowering me to the floor once again. My feet feel like clouds as I stand in my heels, trying to keep my balance. Two big hands smooth down my dress, covering my body, as I fix my hair, then swipe my thumb over his lips, removing the remnants of my lip gloss too.

"As good as you look with shiny lips, I think it'd be obvious if we walked back in there wearing the same shade."

He laughs, light and carefree. "I'd walk back in there with my head held high because it means I was the one kissing you."

His words send another flutter through my chest, such a damn peacock. But then, it hits me—our friends, my brother—they're all at the party. They'll see my flushed cheeks, the kiss-swollen lips, and it'll be impossible to hide what just happened. I'm not ready for them to know. Not yet. I want to keep this moment, keep him, to myself a little longer.

"I need to go freshen up first. Meet you back in there?" I say in a rush, needing to just give myself a second to clean up and process what that was.

He eyes me warily. "I can wait."

I wave him off. "No, it's fine, go back to the party. It'll look less suspicious if we go back in separately."

Nodding, he steps closer, pinching the tip of my chin between his thumb and index finger before pressing a kiss to my lips, then another. "I'd like to come with you because I don't want you to freak out. I'll wait like a good boy on your bed, keep my hands to myself, then take you back to your party. We can arrive separately if you want. But one thing I'm not going to do is make you come, and then disappear. It's not happening, Queenie."

Swallowing hard, I take in the serious expression on his face. "Well," I breathe, feeling tingly all over. "Let's go then."

Chapter Twenty-Two

Miles

Sweat runs down my back as Coach shouts from the middle of the field for us to "move our asses." In our defense, we've been sprinting across the field for over three minutes now, and while all of us have a high fitness level, it's fucking hard.

"Pick up your knees, Parker!" he bellows. "Dawson, I need my captain to be fast!"

Grunts echo along our line up as we all heave for air and push our bodies further and further until, finally, the sweet shrill of the whistle blowing makes every single one of us collapse.

"That was mediocre. Is that what my team is? Mediocre?" Coach spits.

"No, Coach," Seb yells—at least I think it's Seb. I don't look up to check because I might just pass the fuck out if I do and I can't hear over my panting.

"Then get up and show me why you deserve to be on this field and on this team!"

None of my muscles want to move. They protest as I lazily raise my body from the grass. As I sit up, I see the cheer squad making their way to the far side of the field, stretching and warming up. And then a flash of red catches my eye, and in slow motion, I watch with rapt attention as Quinn bends over to put her water bottle down, giving me a full view of her peachy butt. *Jesus, keep it together, man.*

"Cooper, get up and stop staring at the skirts," Coach yells, and it's then I realize I'm the only player still sitting down. Everyone else is at the side, ready to run again. Even if some of the newbies look like they might throw up, they're there.

"Sorry, Coach," I grumble, heaving my body upright, suppressing the exhaustion and running drills with my teammates again.

Fifteen minutes later, we're throwing the ball across the field. Coach wanted this practice to be about cardio and endurance and not plays so here we are.

In the time I've been passing the ball, I've fumbled as much as I've caught, because I have to actively stop myself from glancing across the field. Which is nearly impossible because they're loud, and with the reminder that Quinn is over there, it's much harder to concentrate. Her bright smile can be seen even from yards away. I can feel her infectious energy like a magnet, pulling my gaze her way.

"Cooper, head in the game!" Devin, my teammate, smacks my shoulder, jolting me back to reality. "You're gonna get a ball to the face, dude."

"Yeah, sorry," I mutter, forcing myself to look away. I need to focus. But my mind keeps drifting back to Quinn, her laughter ringing in my ears.

A sudden scream pierces the air, slicing through the sounds of whistles and shouts. My heart lurches, because I know that sound. I heard it enough growing up. Spinning around, I see a figure crumpled on the ground. Quinn. Without a second thought, I sprint across the field, my cleats pounding against the turf along with my heartbeat.

Quinn's face is contorted in pain, her hands clutching her ankle. Her teammates crowd around her, but they make little effort to help.

"What happened?" I demand, kneeling beside her.

"I—I fell wrong," Quinn stammers, wincing as she tries to move her foot. "I think I rolled my ankle."

"Alright, let me help you," I say, my voice calm but firm.

"No, no, I'm fine," Quinn protests, trying to stand. She stumbles, and I catch her before she can fall again. "Ahh, ouch ouch ouch!"

I scoop her up effortlessly, ignoring the murmur of voices and the crowd gathering around us. Quinn's protest is also lost when I look down at her with a look that tells her I'm not putting her down.

Seb pushes through the small crowd and appears at my side. I tense, wondering what he might think of me holding his sister, but as I look over, his face is tight with worry, focused on her. "You okay, Quinn?" he asks, and she gives him a small nod. He deflates and slaps my shoulder. "Get her to the physio, Miles," he orders, his voice low but firm.

I nod, already moving in that direction, my grip on her secure. "I'm on it." I should be more worried about repercussions, of just running over here, acting on instinct, but I'm hoping he won't read into it and plays it off as a friend's duty to help.

"Hey! She's our responsibility," the squad captain clips, her hands on her hips, snapping my attention her way.

"She's hurt," I shoot back, and my tone leaves no room for argument. "I'm taking her inside."

Glancing once more to Seb, he nods and says, "I'll be there in a sec, just gotta talk to coach."

Quinn's arms instinctively wrap around my neck. She's light in my arms, her warmth against my chest a stark contrast to the cold sweat on my skin. I can feel everyone's eyes on me, but I don't care. My only concern is the girl in my arms.

The hallway to the locker rooms is fortunately empty. Quinn trembles slightly, whether from pain or something else, I'm not sure. I glance down at her, to see her chewing her bottom lip. "Hey, you doing okay?" I ask softly.

Quinn nods, her face pale. "Yeah, just hurts. Thanks, Miles." Her voice is barely above a whisper, and I can see the pain she's hiding. Without thinking, I shift her slightly in my arms and lean down, pressing my lips to her forehead. Surprise flickers in her eyes before they soften. A small smile tugs at the corners of her mouth, and I catch a hint of color returning to her cheeks.

I nudge the locker room door open with my shoulder and carry her inside, gently setting her down on a bench. Kneeling in front of her, I gently pull off her sneaker and rest her foot in my lap. The skin around her ankle is already starting to swell and looks a little angrier than the other foot.

"We need to get some ice on this." Grabbing a nearby towel, I wrap it around her ankle for support before slowly lowering it to the floor.

"I'm such an idiot," Quinn mutters.

"Hey, don't say that." My voice is gentle as I look up to her. "I already know this isn't the first time you've sprained your ankle. Remember when we were kids?"

"And I tried to outrun you and Seb to the park?" She huffs an empty laugh. "Yeah, that was really dumb too."

I chuckle because I remember that day. She insisted on racing us, because she had these new sneakers from her dad. They were some fancy running ones, and he'd convinced her she would run faster than Seb in them. We let her take the lead initially, but then halfway there, she stacked it, and I ended up giving her a piggyback the whole half-a-mile back to her house as her tears soaked the back of my t-shirt. "I mean, you *were* pretty fast, until you ate mud."

She groans, her eyes closed as her head falls back between her shoulders, and the sound and image in front of me awakens something inside that I immediately have to tamper down. "I ate so much mud, it wasn't even funny."

"It was a little bit funny." I gesture with my thumb and forefinger. "You all good to wait here a sec?"

She gives me a weak smile, and I leave, walking over to the cabinet in the room and rummaging through the first aid kit, pulling out an ice pack and snapping it to activate, before returning to her to press it against her ankle. Quinn winces as soon as it touches her swollen skin.

"There we go," I soothe, pulling her foot back into my lap as I sit. "Just need to keep this on for a while."

Quinn leans her head back against the wall, closing her eyes. "You're really good at this."

"Good at putting ice on ankles?"

"Well, it's more than that. You should major in physiology."

I laugh, assuming she's joking. "I am."

Her mouth drops open. "Since when?"

"Since this year. I picked Sports Medicine and Exercise Physiology." I let the smirk break free on my lips as I look up at her. "I'm really good at icing ankles, see, so I figured it's a safe bet."

"Ha ha, you think you're funny."

"Hilarious, actually."

She snorts and then winces, her eyes fluttering, when the ice pack shifts over her ankle. "You didn't have to carry me, you know."

"Of course, I did," I scoff. "I couldn't just leave you there."

Quinn opens her eyes, looking at me with a mixture of gratitude and something else. Something that I've seen on her face a handful of times but could never place it until now. Heat. My fingers rest on the front of her leg and suddenly they itch to explore more of her. More than I let myself do the other night in the stairwell. To feel how she can yield under my touch. To drag my hands all over her perfect skin.

My pulse gallops wildly in my throat as I beg my body not to react, but it's too late. I know it is. I can already feel the want traveling around and settling right in my crotch as my body takes over. I'm not in control anymore. Something has switched in my brain from protector to predator, and I'm incredibly thirsty for the girl in front of me.

Moving my hand slowly up her leg, I don't break my eyes from hers. I watch every single micro expression, every shudder, every flicker of pleasure that crosses her face as I caress her skin torturously slow. Her skin is smooth, soft, and just as I get to her knee, I twist my hand to graze behind, tracing over the softest part of her.

She audibly gasps, parting her legs ever-so-slightly, and a moan slips past her perfect lips, begging me to react to it, to her. I barely think before I place her foot down and lunge toward her mouth, connecting our lips in a bruising kiss. Her taste floods my senses, mint, cinnamon and just her. Our teeth clash in a frenzy, tongues dueling in desperate sweeps as I devour her, every ounce of restraint shattering like glass.

My fingers grip the back of her neck, holding her there, deepening the kiss like I'm afraid she'll slip away. Her nails dig into my shoulders, sending sparks skittering over my skin as we press closer, like we're starving for this—each breath, each touch, only making the hunger worse.

Just then, the door creaks open, and we spring apart like two repelled magnets. I practically make it to the other side of the room, wiping at my mouth, just as Seb pokes his head in. "Everything alright in here?"

"Yeah, we're good," I say gruffly, clearing my throat. I point to Quinn's foot. "Just getting some ice on her ankle." *And my balls.*

Seb nods, looking at his sister. "All good, Quinn?"

"Great. Fine. I mean, good." Her lips look slightly swollen, but it's her wild eyes that give her away. She blinks a couple of times before she continues. "I'm sure it'll be okay. Well, no, it does hurt, but I'll be fine. Super, super fine, actually. I'll be...super."

Oh god, kill us both now.

Seb tilts his head, eyebrows knitting. "Did you bang your head too?"

"W-what?!" Quinn laughs, obnoxiously loud, bending at the waist. "No, silly. Just my ankle."

Oh god, I need to step in before she starts singing or some shit. Dragging my hand down my face, I step in front of her, looking at her brother. "She'll be fine. I'll get the physio to look over her too," I say, trying to distract from Quinn's hysteria.

Seb's eyes widen in a 'whatever you say' kind of way. "I've let Coach know you'll head out of practice early."

"Thanks, man," I say, grateful for the reprieve.

Seb hesitates, but closes the door behind him. I turn back to Quinn, who is watching me with a dazed expression.

"What the heck was that?" I ask, stifling a laugh.

"What was what?"

"That! You laughing like a lunatic and saying all the synonyms for good."

"I panicked!"

"Clearly," I snort.

She pauses, a thoughtful expression crossing her face. "Do you think he could tell something is going on with us?"

Panic flares in my gut at the thought that my best friend might not be okay with this. "I doubt it…"

"But…?"

I scrub the back of my neck as I sit next to her. "How do you think he'll react?"

"I'm not sure. But he isn't the boss of me, and I can date whoever I want."

My lips lift in an honest to god belly-fluttering smile as I look at her. "Is that what we're doing Quinn? Dating?"

Her shoulder lifts, a faint blush stains her cheeks. "I guess not yet… We would need to go on a date first."

"Or be exclusive," I reply without an ounce of hesitation, the words tumbling out before I can second-guess myself.

I pause, meeting her gaze, waiting for her response.

I can almost see the wheels turning in her head as she watches me. She bites her lip. "Exclusive, huh?" she finally says, playfully, but I hear something deeper in her voice too.

"Yeah." I nod with a smile, feeling my cheeks heat. "I'd like that."

Her smile beams like sunlight. "I'd like that too."

I shake my head, partly unbelieving of her wanting me. But I focus back on her as her answer settles in, leaving me on cloud nine.

"Come on, Queenie. Let's get you checked out by the physio."

CHAPTER TWENTY-THREE

Quinn

I'M NOT ALLOWED TO do any cheer practice for two weeks.

The news delivered by the physio was less than ideal.

It could've been worse and that's my mantra for right now.

"Get out of your head, Dawson," Miles says, snapping me from my thoughts. Leaning against him, we do an awkward shuffle/hop dance around campus to get to my dorm room, since I refused to take the underarm crutches. And I didn't want to draw that much attention to us by being hauled around campus by a six-foot-four football player either.

"Right," I agree. "Out of my head."

"Two weeks isn't that bad. You won't be off it the whole time either. They're being careful." He shifts his grip, making sure I'm steady. "Just a few more steps."

I nod and bite back a grimace from the pain. My ankle throbs with every movement. If only I hadn't pushed myself to try that new stunt without more practice. If only I had been more focused on the risky move and not staring at the field, waiting for Miles to turn his head again.

"Okay, I know you said no carrying, but I don't care," Miles says before he scoops me up again and walks without breaking his stride, closing the half a meter to my dorm steps. So much for not drawing attention to us.

Once we reach my dorm, he fumbles with the key card, swiping it a couple of times before the door beeps open. Lowering me to the floor, only once he's walked up the stairs, we step inside mine and Indie's room, and I sigh in relief as the sight of my bed comes into view.

Miles closes the door, drops his gym bag down, as I hop over to my bed. "Stay here. I'll get you some ice," he says, leaving me alone.

Taking a deep breath, I hold back tears I've felt ever since we left the physio exam room. "It's fine, it's going to be fine," I tell myself. "You have so much to do in the meantime."

The door opens again, and Miles offers me an easy smile. He walks toward me, looking down at my ankle. "So, the hallway first aid kit doesn't have any ice packs. I need to check the box in your hangout room. Will you be okay?"

Rolling my eyes, I say, "Yes, the clumsy cheerleader will be fine sitting on her bed, not moving."

Reaching out to push him away, he grabs my wrist before I can connect with his stomach and slowly lifts my hand to his lips. He presses a featherlight kiss to my knuckles, all the while burning me alive with his intense brown eyes. "Need anything before I go? I won't be long."

The way his hand lingers in mine has what feels like a family of wild hummingbirds fluttering all over my skin, hellbent on making me break out in goosebumps for him. "I'm good," I croak, watching the smile spread across his face.

"Your phone is here." He picks it out of his pocket and places it on my bedside drawers. "And I'll be fast."

And then he's gone, and my body is definitely a few degrees warmer.

I glance around my room, trying to distract myself from the tingling sensation he's left on my knuckles and in my hand. I could hobble over to my laptop, get some work done for my assignment due next week in business. But I could also just lay my head for a second and rest.

Just as my head sinks into my pillow, my phone buzzes. Reaching to my bedside, I see a message from Indie.

Indie

Seb just told me you hurt yourself at practice today. Do I need to come and take care of you? Because I'm a great nurse, ask Seb.

Quinn

I'm not sure if you mean sexy nurse or actual nurse for him, but either way, I'm good. Miles has it covered.

Indie

I bet he does. I'd ask for details, but I feel like the less I know the better, especially because I'm keeping it all a secret.

Guilt rattles me as I stare at her message.

Quinn

> I'm sorry, we'll tell him soon. I'm just not quite sure how yet.

Or if I want to before we've had time together. It's always been the three of us growing up, and now it's changed. I want to be selfish for a little while. Exclusively selfish.

Indie

> I don't want you to tell him because of me. Take your time, figure out whatever it is. I'll keep it in the vault x

I sigh in relief, because I know we should tell my brother, and we will. Soon.

Pulling open the drawer next to my bed, I search inside for a pot of Tylenol that should be there. "Come on, come on," I mutter to myself while rooting through hair ties, claw clips, and condoms that are still in an unopened box, but better to be prepared than caught without, right? "I swear I had some."

After one more sweep of the drawer, giving up seems inevitable. Glancing around the room, a hopeful look lands on Indie's side; maybe she has some.

I try to put a little weight on my ankle and the pain shoots up my leg like a hot rod pressing against my skin. "Ouch, ouch." I wince, taking a deep breath. "Okay, we can crawl. Crawling is good. Until the swelling goes down, we can crawl."

Slowly managing to angle my leg so my ankle doesn't touch the floor, I butt-shuffle over to Indie's side. On route, I spot Miles's gym bag strewn in the middle of the room, which is closer, and I know for a fact he keeps Tylenol and Aspirin in his bag. "Thank all the gods. Right, keep going. We can do this, Quinn," I murmur, forcing my body to shift toward the bag.

Miles walks back in just as my fingers grasp the strap.

"I got the—" He stops dead in the doorway, holding something that looks like the same package as the ice pack from the stadium earlier. "What are you doing?"

Puffing my hair from my face, I look up at him, panting and awkwardly trying to keep my foot off the floor still. "Oh, y'know, trying to practice interpretive dance."

He tilts his head, but a small smirk plays on his face. "And how's that going for you?"

"Great, can't you tell?" I laugh just as I lose my balance and land on my butt with a soft thud. "I tried to walk, but it hurt."

He moves closer to me, looking down with his arms crossed. "And you couldn't wait for me to come back and help?"

"No," I huff. Waving him off, I slowly shift to my knees, elevating my foot behind me, the soft carpet brushing against my skin. "I'm an independent woman who can take care of herself."

Granted, that statement would be much more convincing if I were on my two feet, hands on my hips, determined glare in my eyes, and not crawling around like a baby. But I'll work with what I've got.

"Quinn, what is it you need?" he asks softly, but I also hear the amusement in his voice.

"Don't worry, I can do it."

"Okay, if you say so," he says, walking away to sit on my bed behind me. "I'll let you do your thing."

As I sweep my hair from my face, I creep forward again, this time steadier. I sneak my hand into his bag, fingers brushing against the familiar red and white container, and I unscrew the lid without hesitation. Slowly, I turn to face him, settling onto my butt and lifting the bottle high for him to see, victory coursing through my veins. "See! I can do—"

"Quinn, no!" Miles shouts just as he lunges toward me with a speed that catches me off guard. His hand connects with mine, knocking the open pot from my hand. It hits the edge of the drawers and explodes open, tablets scattering across the ground like marbles.

"Oh my god. What was that for?" The words escape in a hiss, heart racing from the sudden reaction.

"Shit, I'm sorry," he says, cheeks flushing. "That, uh, that Tylenol is out of date. I don't know why I keep it in here. I should, uh, throw it out. Yeah, I'll do that." He frantically gathers the tablets from the carpet while I watch, bewildered.

Does Tylenol have an expiration date? I guess it does; I just never thought about it. I watch him dart across the ground collecting the tablets when I spot one next to my leg. Picking it up, I immediately know something isn't right. "W-what are these?" I ask, my voice uneven.

He freezes, his eyes wide and filled with something that looks like fear. I follow his gaze to the tablet in my hand. They're small, round, and white, and they're definitely not Tylenol. Miles schools his face and deftly plucks the tablet from my hand. "They're just some extra vitamins. You know, for energy."

I narrow my eyes at him, not buying it for a second. "*Vita-*

mins?"

"Yeah, my dad has me on all kinds of supplements," he says, then crosses the room to sit on my bed again, placing the pot next to him. "It's easier to keep them in one place." I study his face, searching for any telltale signs of deceit. Miles has always been good at lying. I remember him doing it enough to get out of trouble with his dad growing up, but I know his tells. One of them being avoidance. "Come, sit down, let me ice your ankle."

My mind races with questions, but I force myself to stay calm. "They don't look like vitamins, Miles. You said they were out-of-date Tylenol..."

He looks away, his jaw tightening, and then he releases a heavy sigh. "Quinn, it's nothing. Just let it go, okay?" The pleading note in his voice hits me square in my chest like a bolt of lightning, because I know something isn't right.

"No, I won't. You're lying to me. What are they?"

Miles sighs, rubbing the back of his neck, but he doesn't answer me.

"Miles?" I say tentatively, bringing myself to stand on my good foot, ignoring the throbbing pain in my ankle as I hobble over to him. I don't get two shuffles before I'm hoisted upright, and he moves me, depositing me on my bed. His breathing is harsh and unforgiving, his chest heaving against his t-shirt. Still ignoring me, he moves my leg to rest on his lap and gently places the ice pack on my sore ankle.

The silence between us is suffocating. Laden with secrets I didn't know he had. Ones he won't even admit to now. "Is this what you're doing with Levi?" I ask, knowing I've seen them together a few times.

When he doesn't answer, I feel like I've hit a nerve with how his body language becomes rigid and clinical as he adjusts the ice on my ankle. The immediate cooling sensation travels over my skin, easing the throb slightly, but it does nothing to soothe the tension in the air. The icy chill wraps around me like an unwelcome guest, just as the awkward silence lingers, thick and heavy.

Realizing that bulldozing into the conversation might not be the best way to get something out of him, I take a deep breath. "You don't have to tell me, but you know I will help you," I tell him quietly. I can't ignore the fact I've seen something, and I definitely can't ignore anything about Miles.

"They're..." He closes his eyes, swallowing slowly. "They're amphetamines, alright?"

The word hangs in the air between us as I try to reconcile this new piece of information with the person I've known all my life. He opens his eyes, and for a moment, I see a flicker of something—shame, maybe, or regret. "Yeah," he says, his voice rough. "I... I didn't want to tell you. Didn't want you to look at me like that."

I don't know what to say. My tongue feels too big for my mouth as I swallow back what feels like a golf ball. My heart races, thumping loud enough to drown out my thoughts. I feel my palms grow clammy, every muscle in my body tense, coiling like a spring ready to snap. I catch myself biting my lip, an unconscious attempt to keep the wrong words from spilling out.

Each thought collides with the next, leaving me more confused. It's as if I'm seeing him for the first time, and the weight of that realization drops like a heavy stone in my stomach. I take a shaky breath, trying to steady myself, but I end up coughing to clear the thick feeling that feels like it's lodged there.

"H-how long?" I manage to force out.

"A while," he admits, looking down at his hands.

"Why?" I whisper.

"I need them." He meets my gaze, and the tortured look clouding his eyes makes me shudder in disbelief. "To be better. To be whatever it is my dad needs me to be."

"Your dad?" I question, my voice rising. "You can't just take drugs because of him!"

"It's not like that," he snaps back. "You don't understand."

"Then help me understand," I challenge, my pulse pounding in my ears. "Help me understand why you're risking your health, your future, for him."

He lifts my leg and rests it on his pillow before standing up, pacing the small room. "I'm not risking anything. I've got it under control."

"Under control?" I echo, confusion dripping from my words. "This isn't controlled, Miles. This is doping and it's wrong. Not to mention dangerous."

He stops and turns to face me, his expression hardened. "You think I don't know that? You think I don't know how bad I can fuck this all up? But what choice do I have? I'm drowning, Quinn. Drowning in pressure, in expectations." His hand rushes through his hair before he looks away. "I can't afford to fail."

Tears sting my eyes. "And what about the risk of getting caught? What about your health? Your life? What about *you,* Miles?"

"I'm careful," he says, but his voice lacks conviction. "I'm not an addict, Quinn. I just need a little help, that's all."

Feeling a mixture of anger and sorrow, I shake my head. "This isn't help. This is a crutch. And it's going to break you, Miles. It's going to break you, and you'll fall harder than ever. I could—" I stop myself before I tell him how scared I am to lose him before I've had him properly. I can't be that girl.

He sinks onto the edge of my bed once more, his face buried in his hands. For a moment, neither of us speaks. Frustration bubbles within me, at everything he's admitted. But then I look at him, his fingers twitching and his whole demeanor unsettled and fear for him seeps into my bones. He could so easily self-destruct, and he doesn't see it. Or maybe he does, and he really is spiraling. Nothing I feel right now compares to the storm I think he's harboring inside. The thought of him desperately trying to cling onto anything to stay afloat makes my heart near shatter into a million pieces.

"I can't watch you do this to yourself," I say as my voice cracks. I can't handle losing him to something that I can stop.

He looks up, his eyes red. "What am I supposed to do, Quinn? I don't know what to do."

"You can stop." I reach out to take his hand. Determination fires in my blood because I can help him. I know I can.

"It's not that easy." He pulls his hand away, and I hate the way it feels like rejection. Watching Miles in his anger is like standing too close to a wildfire. His normally calm brown eyes blaze with a ferocity I've yet to encounter. I can see the tension in his jaw, clenched so tightly that the muscles in his neck stand out in sharp relief. His hands are balled into fists, trembling with the effort it takes to contain his fury. Each breath he takes is abrupt and deliberate, as if he's holding back a flood of words that threaten to break free. I want him to talk to me. I want him to lean on me.

"Let me help you," I whisper, not wanting to push his anger further.

He groans, pained. "Queenie, I—"

"I can't watch you destroy yourself like this," I repeat, imploring him to hear me. I feel as desperate as I must sound.

"I don't need help. I need to be trusted that I can manage my own shit," he snaps, then spins around like a tornado, ripping my door open as he stalks out.

The echo of the door slamming shut reverberates through the room, leaving a nauseating silence in its wake.

Panic grips my chest as I wonder how to fix this—if it can even be fixed. I can feel the sting of tears threatening to spill over, and for a moment, I fight against them, but it's useless because they fall anyway.

What just happened?

CHAPTER TWENTY-FOUR

Miles

I STORM AWAY FROM Quinn, the sound of my sneakers crunching on the gravel louder than the pounding of my heart. Rage bubbles up inside me, each step I take amplifying it.

The worst possible scenario played out in front of me like a damn horror movie. Someone found my pills and, worse, it made me feel exactly how I knew it would. Like a piece of shit. I could push away that feeling before, but now, I don't know if I'll ever forget the look on Quinn's face.

Closing my eyes, I still see the pity in hers, the way her voice was laced with that infuriating mix of sympathy and disappointment.

I couldn't handle it. I had to get out.

I'm still only wearing my gym shorts and sweaty workout t-shirt, but I don't care. I need to walk.

The anger pushes me forward, and soon the campus streets

are behind me. I'm walking with no destination, just the need to get away. To clear my head. But the thoughts keep coming. Quinn's voice, her worried eyes, her hand reaching out to touch mine. My dad's consistent scolding, telling me I can do better. Everything spins around and around, making my teeth grind. The way she looked at me, like I'm broken. I don't need pity. I need... I don't even know what I need.

My feet find the familiar path into town, the light slowly disappearing behind the buildings, but I hardly notice. Everything is a blur. I need to distract myself, to drown out the noise in my head. I stop in front of a shop window, staring at my reflection. I see a stranger. Red-rimmed eyes, tense jaw, a guy on the edge. Shoving my hands in my pockets, I turn away, continuing down the street.

A few blocks later, I bump into someone, hard.

"Watch it," I snap before I even look up.

"Miles?" The voice is low, familiar. I look up to see Levi grinning at me, his eyes hidden behind dark shades. He's the last person I want to see right now, but something in his easy smile makes me pause.

"Levi," I say, my tone flat. "What are you doing here?"

He shrugs, removing his glasses to reveal his bloodshot eyes. "Same as you, probably. Killing time. I skipped my business class this afternoon."

I grunt my response, not sure what to say next. I doubt he's killing time the same way as me. Judging by his glazed-over expression, he's high. Judging by my standoffish nature, I'm sober and pissed off.

"You okay, man? You look—"

With my teeth clenched, I cut him off with a hiss. "I'm fine.

I look fine. I am fine."

Levi chuckles sarcastically. "Sure, whatever you say. Those pills I gave you really have taken a hold of your anger, huh?"

I ball my fists in my pockets, nostrils flaring at his nonchalant comment. But Levi just keeps laughing, a sound that grates on my nerves even more. "I'm not—" I begin to say, but stop myself and roll back my shoulders, inhaling slowly. "I'm fine."

"You said that already," he says, pulling me by my shoulder to the side of the street, glancing around before lowering his voice. "Listen, have you been feeling this anger a lot since you took the pills?"

I swallow hard, hating that I'm talking to my dealer about side effects. "Maybe," I say softly.

"I can get you something to even you out."

My eyes snap to his, filled with trepidation. "What do you mean?"

"I mean, something more. Uppers. You've smoked grass before, but I mean something else. Something that can make you feel like you'll forget it all. All the bullshit, all the anger. Everything."

Something else. This isn't the first time he's offered. This is his usual MO when he tries to hook you, then sink you. I can't lie to myself and say it isn't tempting, because it is. Just to be freed from all the expectations, all the remarks my dad makes, even temporarily, would be fucking amazing.

Levi's casually leaning against the wall, his eyes glinting with a mixture of patience and anticipation. He's seen me hesitate before, and he's waiting for me to make the move that will deepen my dependence. His presence is a reminder of everything I'm doing to keep demons at bay, yet every fiber of my being screams that this isn't the answer.

But the promise of relief is almost irresistible. The pressure to just give in and let everything else fall away is overwhelming. I could say yes, slip into the familiar embrace of oblivion, and numb everything that's been dragging me down. It would be so easy.

My phone buzzes in my hand, the vibration pulling me back to reality. It's a text from Quinn. I unlock the screen, my heart sinking as I read her message.

Queenie

> Miles, please. I just want to talk. Call me when you get this.

I glance at Levi again, his attention now on his phone too. As I re-read the message from Quinn, a war breaks out inside of me. That Quinn angel is on my right shoulder and the Levi devil on my left. I'm facing a decision that can help me or break me.

Then reality hits me dead center of my breastbone.

There is one person who I can't disappoint. No matter what.

"So what's it gonna be, Miles?"

CHAPTER TWENTY-FIVE

Quinn

MILES ISN'T ANSWERING HIS phone. In fact, he's turned it off. The only indication that he knows I've been trying to get a hold of him was the read receipt I got when he opened my message. That was two hours ago. But that doesn't stop me from continually checking as though he'll magically message me back, like if I stare at it long enough, I can manifest it.

The ice pack he got me has lost its freeze, but my mood is still just as frozen. I can't shake the feeling that he's getting himself into something that will spiral out of control. And it terrifies me. I spent a good half an hour wallowing and now I need to talk to him.

I take a deep breath and try to think clearly. What else can I do from here? I can't just sit around and wait for him to come back on his own, because what if he doesn't?

Grabbing my phone, I text one of the girls, Katie, on the

squad, who had a thing with Levi last year.

Katie

> Yeah, I've still got his number, hang on.

Within a few seconds, I have Levi's number. He might know where Miles is or have some idea of what he's up to. The phone rings, and I hold my breath, hoping he'll pick up.

"Hello?" Levi's voice comes through the speaker, sounding casual but guarded.

"Levi, I know you don't know me, but I'm friends with Miles Cooper. My name is Quinn," I say, trying to keep my voice steady. "I need to know if you've seen Miles. He left in a hurry this afternoon, and I'm worried about him."

There's a pause on the other end, the faint thump of music in the background. "Miles, huh? Yeah, he was here earlier."

"Earlier? What do you mean? Where is he now?" I press, my anxiety mounting.

Levi's tone shifts to become more elusive. "Look, Quinn, I don't really know where he went. We were just hanging out. You know how it is—people come and go."

My frustration spikes. "Levi, this isn't a game. Miles is in trouble. I need to know if he's okay."

"Calm down, will you?" Levi says, sounding annoyed as he purposefully makes a blowing sound, that I'm guessing is him smoking. "I don't have all the details. He left, and that's all I know."

Great. That's not helpful at all. Levi's always been slippery, and now it seems he's being intentionally vague. As I hang up, I'm feeling even more helpless.

I look around the room, trying to think of another approach.

I can't just wait for him to come to his senses on his own. He's in a dark place, and I have to find a way to reach him.

Leaning over to my dresser, I open the top one and pull out the ankle support I know is stuffed in here with my underwear.

The door softly clicks open a minute later, and in walks Indie.

"Hey, how you feeling?" she asks as she dumps her bag on her side of the room.

"Can you help me?" I ask, exasperated with feeling helpless. "I need to find my support so I can go find Miles."

"Woah, wait a damn minute. You're going to walk with that balloon on your ankle?" She gestures to my angry swollen foot, and I sigh. "Quinn, there's no way I'm letting you walk on that."

"It's not that bad," I counter.

"Okay, so show me exactly how you plan on walking out of here," she says, crossing her arms over her body.

Determination to prove her wrong fires in my gut as I pull myself upright, bad ankle hovering above the ground. Gingerly, I lower my foot to the carpet and immediately can't stop the hiss of pain that escapes me.

"Uh-huh, just what I thought," Indie says smugly.

"But I have to find him!" My voice comes out shaky, panic clawing at my insides as I flop back onto my bed. The thought of sitting around and doing nothing is too unbearable. A hurricane of worst-case scenarios swirls in my mind. Desperately, I try to steady my breathing, clenching my fists to keep my cool. The room is silent, Indie waiting for me to either lose my mind completely or burst into tears, I'm sure.

"Let me call Seb. He'll find him."

"What if…" I stop myself, because I might not know where

Miles is, but I know at some point he was with Levi. He might've gotten high or drunk. And I can't send my brother looking for him if he's either of those things. "Indie, I need to tell you something, but it absolutely can't get back to my brother."

Indie takes a slow step toward me and settles on my bed, eyebrows creased. "I'm listening." She places her hand on my jittering knee.

"Okay, Miles might be—"

"Here, I'm here." The door creaks open, and Miles steps into the room, his face haunted as he stares at me. "I didn't mean to interrupt," he says, his voice tense but steady.

The beat of awkward silence echoes like a high note between us all. Indie clears her throat and backs herself toward the door. "I'm just going to hang out in the common room." Indie thumbs behind her before she adds, "I'll be there if you need me."

When the door clicks closed softly, it's just us.

The only sound is the beating of my heart, thudding and vibrating over my whole body.

I look at Miles, his shoulders low, his arms limp by his sides, and my immediate thought is, did he take something tonight? I hate that my mind goes there, but I need to know so I can help him.

Then another part of me, a much louder part, wants to shout at him and berate him for running off when I couldn't follow him. But as soon as I focus on the dark circles coloring under his eyes and the haunted look on his face, I know I need to let him talk first. I need to let him set the pace of how this goes.

"I'm sorry," Miles breathes out. The weight behind his words is heavy, and as he takes a tentative step toward me, I have to stop myself from being pulled to him like a magnet, my body desperate to soothe him. His brown eyes find mine, and the vulnerability in them almost floors me. He looks like the same little boy who lost his mom years ago and needed comforting. "Will you come with me for a second?"

There's still that voice inside my head demanding answers and telling me I should shout until I get them. But this isn't about me right now, it's about him.

I can only nod.

"I'll help you walk," he says immediately as I wobble, getting up to balance on my good foot. The way he wraps his arm around my waist, effortlessly hiking my arm around his neck so I don't have to worry about weight bearing makes all of this so much harder. Now that I know how he and I fit together, it's impossible to forget. He walks us both down the hall, all the way to the shared bathroom at the end.

Opening the door, the place is empty, mirrors lined up behind sinks surrounded by a halo of white lights. Miles interlinks our fingers when he unwraps my arm from around his neck and lifts me toward the first sink.

He fumbles something from his pocket, and I watch him with rapt attention, neither of us speaking as he opens the pot of Tylenol. The few small white tablets dance in the porcelain bowl, softly snicking as they one by one plummet into the dark abyss.

Exhaling a heavy breath, he falls a few steps backward until his back meets the wall with an audible thud. I don't know what to say, my heart is caught in my throat as I watch him battle something within himself.

Right now, I see Miles as he is: raw. He isn't showing me any facade, he's just here trying to deal with something that's threatening to swallow him whole. Something that has left him feeling powerless. He's just a boy who is lost and desperate to find some control in his life.

I can see now why he walked away earlier. The anger leaves my body in an instant because he doesn't need anyone telling him how bad this is. He knows. He just can't find a lifeline to change that.

The silence begins to stifle the bathroom like steam from a hot shower.

"Before you ask, that's all I have."

My mind stumbles over itself, trying to come to terms with what he's doing and how I deal with everything in a way that doesn't put him under any pressure. "Why did you do that?" I manage to stammer. Empathy wraps around me like a blanket I wish I could pass to him.

He picks at his thumbnail, distracting himself before looking at me for the first time since we've come in here. My palms are clammy, and I shove them deep into my pockets, hoping to hide how unsteady I feel.

"Because I got an offer tonight that made me question every-thing," he replies, uncertainty flickering on his face.

My heart stalls as all kinds of scenarios rush through my mind.

"What kind of offer?" The pit in my stomach tightens. I need to know, but I'm also terrified to find out.

He doesn't look at me. "For more. For something stronger. I saw Levi in town, and he... Never mind. It was something that would truly make me forget." He sighs and turns his attention to me. Eyes shadowed with a darkness I've not seen in him before. But then he blinks, softening his expression and that streak of caramel in his left eye glistens and my breath catches at the sight of it. "And tonight, I realized I had more to remember than forget."

A flutter of hope blooms in my chest.

Then taking two measured steps toward me, he leans in and kisses my cheek and brands me as his. As if I haven't spent most of my life already belonging to him, now it feels like he's choosing me and silently begging me to be his lifeline.

Without second guessing myself, I reach up, my fingers curling into the fabric of his shirt as I yank him toward me. Our lips crash together, hard and urgent, as I pull him into a kiss that's anything but gentle. My hands slip to the back of his neck to keep him close. He groans against my mouth, and I feel it vibrate through my chest, spurring me to kiss him harder, deeper, like I can't get enough.

And with him, I know I never will.

CHAPTER TWENTY-SIX

Miles

"Show me your class timetable," Quinn says, perched on my chair at my desk in her cheer uniform. She has practice this afternoon, albeit observing, since her ankle still isn't right, and has already told me in no uncertain circumstances that I'll be going with her.

It's been a few days since I tipped away the pills from Levi. I haven't felt great; the tiredness that grips me some days is crippling. As a result, I've been sleeping like it's my full-time job, even though school and football should be those things.

I've also had headaches to boot. I can't pretend that I'm finding it easy, because it's not. Nothing about this situation I got myself into is easy. Nothing about the slippery slope I was falling down is easy, and getting back up? Fuck, that's even harder.

My sobriety wasn't just about the pills, though, and it wasn't just about impressing my dad. In fact, that's something I'm eager to forget all about. But I knew I had more to deal with. I could feel it bubbling under the surface of my subconscious. It's about detoxing from anger, resentment, and a hatred that were building a fortress around my heart. The things that keep me awake at night, and I'll deal with them...when I'm ready. But I have to start somewhere. First, the habit needs to be kicked.

We've got game seven coming up soon, and then it's one more game until our rivalry game against Washington University. Our boarder war is historical in football, and everyone expects nothing short of a sensational show of sportsmanship and talent. It's going to take a lot of our best plays to make sure we come out on top. And a lot of my own willpower not to rely on a little white pill.

You can do this. One step at a time.

"Miles?" Quinn asks, getting my attention again.

"It's on the pin board above your head." I nod behind her.

I watch her reach up, exposing a sliver of perfectly freckled skin on her hip as she moves. I love her freckles; they've always been so perfectly her, but now I see them and all I want to do is memorize every one. She bites the inside of her lower lip as she scrolls and types on my laptop, her legs comfortably draped over one another. She's too good to me, for me. And I definitely don't deserve her help. But I'm too weak to push her away right now.

My phone plays the message tone I set for my dad last night, so I know to avoid it. Which is exactly what I do. I need less of Mark Cooper's influence and more of Quinn Dawson.

"Okay," she says, slapping her hands onto the desk. "I've got a plan."

"I'm listening."

The twinkle in her eye tells me that I'm about to get schooled Quinn style. This has always been her favorite thing to do, boss me and Seb around as kids. Hell, forget kids, she still does it now. I'm all too happy to oblige and indulge her, though, especially now.

"I have set up the shared calendar on your laptop, and you need to update your phone too. But effectively any downtime you have, I've taken away and given us joint study time, or if it coincides with something else when we're apart, but there are reminders to check in."

"I've signed my life over to you," I say, more as a statement than a question.

Quinn looks up with a determined expression. "And there's one more thing we need to do." She reaches for my phone, which is laying on the bed.

I frown, not understanding. "What are you doing?"

"I'm deleting Levi's number from your phone," she says firmly. "What's your code?"

I don't even hesitate to give it to her. "0312."

Her entire demeanor shifts from casual to frozen. It takes her a few minutes to look up at me, and when she does, the surprise in her eyes glistens. "March twelfth," she repeats.

I nod, knowing exactly what that date is. "Your birthday."

Her eyes flit from the phone to meet mine, as confusion and vulnerability etch on her face. "Why?" she asks, voice trembling. "Why did you use my birthday as your code?"

Suddenly feeling everything she's not saying, I swallow roughly. "Because..." I begin, needing to clear my throat. "You're important to me. Always have been."

Quinn blinks rapidly. "W-what?" she stutters on a breath.

"I mean," I pause, not entirely sure what I mean, because Quinn has always been a part of me. We grew up together and have always had each other's backs. I've never questioned why I used her birthday as my code before now; it just felt right. "You're my Queenie. And maybe now I realize I've been too blind to see what's right in front of me."

Her eyes fill with tears as she takes a shaky breath. "You really mean that?"

I nod again, my voice barely a whisper. "Yeah, Quinn. I do."

The world around us fades, leaving only the sound of our breaths mingling in the stillness. God, I want to kiss her. To tell her that I couldn't do this without her, but I don't want to come on too strong here. And we haven't actually had a conversation about what any of this is for us. Fuck, I still haven't even taken the girl on a date. I don't deserve her.

"Well, that's..." She breaks our eye contact. "I mean, I didn't expect... Your birthday isn't mine, but I could—"

"Quinn?"

"Yeah?"

"Delete Levi's number."

"Right, right, that's what I was doing. Of course."

She unlocks my phone with a bewildered shake of her head and scrolls through the contacts. I watch as she finds his number and deletes it, and I feel a mix of relief and anxiety as a result. It's a small step, but it's a crucial one.

"There," she says, handing the phone back to me. "One less temptation."

One less temptation replaced with another temptation in the form of Quinn.

"Oh, I thought we should probably block your dad's number on game days too. I'll set reminders to do it each time." She taps once more on my computer before turning back to me, and a sudden swell of gratitude has me reeling.

"Hey," I say, getting her attention and patting the side of the bed next to me. "Will you sit with me for a second?"

A flush creeps onto the apples of her cheeks as she hobbles over. I go to stand to help her, but she puts her hand up to stop me.

"I need to strengthen it again. Don't get up. This is good practice."

I nod, though my instincts urge me to help. Quinn's injury is still fresh, but the determination written all over her face tells me helping her would only piss her off. I watch her make her way to the bed with slow steps. She lowers herself cautiously, wincing as she settles beside me.

"How does it feel?" I ask.

She exhales a whoosh of air, glancing at her bandaged ankle. "It's better. Slow going, but better." When her eyes lift to meet mine, there's a moment, an electric current buzzing, and everything unsaid lingers between us.

"Good," I murmur. "That's good."

Quinn shifts slightly, the mattress dipping with her weight. Trying to dispel some of the tension, I clear my throat. "So, uh, thanks for deleting his number and for organizing all of this."

Her clear green eyes don't leave mine as she nods. "It's easier this way."

"Yeah," I agree, my voice barely above a whisper. "It's just... a lot." *I'm a lot.*

Quinn's gaze softens, and she reaches out, her fingers brushing mine. The contact is brief, almost fleeting, but it sends a jolt through me. "You don't have to carry it all by yourself," she says gently.

The words are like a balm, soothing the raw edges of my stress and anxiety. But they also scare me. Leaning on someone, letting them in, means risking more than I think I can handle. Especially when that someone is Quinn, who is such a big part of my life anyway. I could mess it all up. I could lose her.

"I know," I reply, though I'm not sure I entirely believe it. "But sometimes it's easier said than done."

"I get that." Her hand lingers near mine, understanding in her eyes.

"Quinn," I start, but my voice falters. What do I even want to say? That I'm grateful? That I'm scared? That despite everything, I can't stop thinking about her?

She looks at me, waiting, her expression open and patient. It makes it both easier and harder to speak.

"I don't know if this is... if I'm good for..." I trail off, unable to stop staring at her lips and warring with the feelings inside of me.

Quinn's expression hardens with what looks like uneasiness. "If you're good for what?" she asks, her tone carefully neutral.

"For you." The words tasting bitter in my mouth. "I mean, with everything going on, I'd understand if you want to forget everything that's happened between us and keep it platonic."

Her eyes flicker with something—hurt, maybe? Disappointment?—before she masks it. "I see." As she pulls her hand back, the loss of contact is almost physically painful.

"It's not that I don't want to," I say quickly, desperate to clarify. "I want to, so much. It's just...complicated."

"Life is complicated," she replies, a hint of steel in her tone. "But that doesn't mean we should avoid what we want."

Her words strike a chord, resonating with something deep inside me. I know she's right, but it doesn't make it any easier. The stakes feel impossibly high. Our friendship. My college career. The fact that her brother is my best friend. "What do you want?"

Her green eyes clear as she says. "You."

"Quinn," I say again, and this time, I reach for her hand, holding it tightly like she's my lifeline. "I don't want to mess this up. I don't want to hurt you."

She squeezes my hand back, her eyes searching mine. "You won't hurt me."

It's a challenge, a plea, and a promise all wrapped into one. And it terrifies me.

"But what if I do?" I whisper, raw with emotion. "What if I can't do this right?"

She leans in, her forehead almost touching mine. "Then we'll figure it out. Together."

The closeness of her, the intensity in her eyes, it's almost too much. But it's also exactly what I need. The fear, the uncertainty, they don't vanish, but they become more bearable with her by my side.

"Okay," I breathe out, the word fragile.

I can't wait any longer. I step closer, my hand reaching up to cup her face, my thumb brushing her cheek. The warmth of her skin beneath my fingers calms the nerves firing in my chest. I lean in, hesitating for just a second, and then I kiss her—soft, tentative, because I don't want to rush.

But then she leans into me, and my restraint weakens. The

kiss deepens, slow and deliberate, and I hold her closer, my hand sliding to her waist, feeling her melt against me. Everything else disappears, and all that's left is her—*us*—right here, like nothing else in the world matters.

Chapter Twenty-Seven

Quinn

My whole life, Miles has been the guy who made things fun. Seb wanted to build a treehouse, but we didn't have the wood? Miles found old sheets that we pegged to our tree—actually, just his dad's current sheets, which totally got him grounded, but it was worth it. Until it rained, and we all got soaked. But we stayed under the tree, in our fort of not-waterproof cotton draped over our heads and played go fish until the cards were ruined. Miles was also the first, and only one of us, to get tattoos. He got his first when he was sixteen. Seb and I both thought he was badass because our parents would kill us. But Miles didn't care; he got what he wanted anyway.

My point is, somewhere along the way of growing up and accepting responsibility, he lost that fire, that fun-loving personality trait. And I'm determined to get it back.

"Studying sucks," he whispers, bringing me back to the present. Okay, maybe today isn't the best example of getting back his "fun" as we sit in a darkened library, studying. I'm calling this balance, though.

"I know it's boring, but this is in our calendar for this afternoon."

I never thought I'd be in this position, being potentially involved with the boy I've loved my whole life. Then again, I never thought he'd have secrets either. It hurts more than I expected, realizing that there's a side of him I never knew, something he felt he had to hide from me, from everyone.

It's not anger I feel. It's something softer, sadder, like a quiet ache in my chest. I'm confused, trying to understand how someone I know so well could be carrying a burden this heavy without me ever realizing. It's like a part of him was hidden in the shadows all this time, and I never even noticed. I still have so many layers to peel back, to understand what's driven him to this point, what kind of pressure his dad puts on him that he feels like he has no other choice.

Last night when he opened up to me, I hadn't seen much of that Miles for a while, probably not since his mom passed, and even then, we were so young I barely remember everything. This isn't the Miles I thought I knew—the one who was always so strong, so certain, so ready to take on the world. But maybe that's why I offered to help him. Because I love him too much to let him face this alone, even if it means stepping into something I can't fully grasp. I'm not sure if occupying his time and organizing his life is the right thing to do, but I know I can't just walk away. Not when he needs me the most.

Falling in love with Miles was never a choice.

It always felt inevitable.

I can't help but stare at him, his brow drawn, thick lashes framing his warm eyes. He might not be feeling like the boy I love, but he sure looks like him.

Working his thick fingers into his hair that's back to its usual length now on top, he flicks his gaze to me to catch me staring. A wolfish grin spreads across his lips as he leans closer. "You know, looking at me like that, Queenie, will only get you exactly what you're thinking about."

"What am I thinking, Miles?" I ask, feigning confidence.

I watch with rapt attention as he drags his teeth over his lower lip, letting his gaze drop deliciously slow over my face, lips, breasts, and farther where he can't see because of the table we're at, but I feel it, *everywhere*. His attention is like holding your hand above a flame for a second too long. You crave the warmth of it, and even though everything tells you to pull your hand away, you don't want to feel the cool air again. "I think you're imagining kissing me." Shifting his chair a little closer to mine, he deftly spins my chair with a swoosh on the carpet so we're facing one another. The heat of his palms rests heavily on my thighs and something ignites deep in my belly. "I think you can't stop thinking about how badly you want my lips pressing against yours, my tongue sweeping in your mouth, tasting you, licking you, devouring you."

My lips part, but I swallow the gasp, even though it takes a monumental amount of effort. "Impressive," I croak and clear my throat, leaning toward him, making sure I slowly drag my tongue across my lips, drawing his attention there. "I think you're imagining doing a lot more than just kissing, Miles Cooper. And that will earn you a red dot on your calendar if you don't complete the task set." I settle my attention on his lips too, so full, and right there for me to take. "Maybe, if you get your green check, I'll let you kiss me," I say, a little too breathlessly, before pulling away.

My body protests as I shift my chair back to face the table, but my mind knows that if I jump headfirst into whatever it is we're dancing around, I'll lose my head. The kisses we've shared, and the night of the party, play on a loop in my head. I want more. I crave more from him. Impulsively, I want to dive into the deep end. I want to give him everything. But as much as I have spent countless daydreams on him, we can't move too fast.

"Focus, Miles," I coo, still feeling the weight of his gaze on me.

"I am," he says confidently, without making moves to look at his physio textbook he has open in front of us.

"On the textbook, not me."

A huff leaves him as he moves his chair around. "For the record, that was a test to see if you'd soften on me now that I can kiss you and..." He clears his throat intentionally not saying the part that makes my cheeks flame. *Touch me.* "Good news, you're still exactly the same girl who busts my balls. Difference is, now they belong to you, and they'll stay blue for as long as you say so."

I turn to look at him, needing to see his expression, and when we lock eyes, I know he's telling the truth. My body thrums with need, the urge to throw myself at him and let him do whatever he wants to me feels far too tempting. "I mean it. I'm in no rush with you. I like to tease, but whatever happens, you're in charge."

Tingling. Everywhere. I barely register the fact that my mouth is hanging open a little, or that he's the one who uses the pad of his index finger to close it. Tingling like I've been sitting with my legs crossed for too long. Like I've been stung by a bee. All the tingles.

"Okay, great," I manage to force out.

And then he pecks my cheek in the most ordinary way. In a way that has my unrequited love brain flashing forward sixty years when we're married and sitting on our front porch, telling stories to our grandbabies about how we've known each other our whole lives.

Getting these flash-forwards used to be a recurring thing for me, but now, with meaning behind them, coupled with his confession of waiting for me to be ready, my feelings have just been carved into stone.

For the next hour, I try to focus on studying, the textbook in front of me, but I'm too distracted by the way he's hunched over his book, his brow furrowed in concentration. There's something endearing about the way he studies, like he's solving a great mystery, rather than just completing homework. It makes me smile.

I lean toward him, looking over the notes he's taking. "Wow, you really are serious about declaring your degree, huh?"

"Your dad convinced me at the end of freshman year. Figured it would be a good fall back."

My eyebrows raise, but in reality, I'm not that surprised at that piece of information. My dad is a planner by nature, and he always helps those he loves. "My dad's right, but if you tell him I said that, I'll deny it."

He snuffs a laugh. "Secret is safe with me. Now get studying, Queenie. I want ice cream soon, and you're not finished."

I turn back to my almost empty notes page and decide to get

to work as fast as I can. Writing an essay outline for my child psych health and wellbeing core credit. It actually should be easy to focus on because I'm using something I love as the core part of the essay. The baking class I teach at the shelter is my perfect example in how artistic therapies that are planned and consistent can positively impact mental health.

My phone buzzing breaks my focus. Opening it, I see a voicemail from Indie. I slip in my headphones and press play.

"Hey, just checking in. I feel like I've barely seen you this week with my music practice and your *thing*," she says, and I immediately know she's talking about Miles. "Anyway, I know I said the less I know the better, but I decided I want details because you're my best friend and my life is dull without you. Boys take up too much of our time. Girls' night soon?" she asks before pausing and adding, "Ugh, I sound gross and needy. Anyway, let me know. Bye!"

I hang up with a big smile on my face and shoot her a text, pocketing my earbuds again.

Quinn

Are you home tonight? I'll be back around seven if you want to grab dinner x

A loud grumble erupts from Miles's stomach. "Yeah, I'm starving, you all done?" he asks, looking over at me with those brown eyes of his.

"I'm done, too. But I can't do dinner. Indie wants a girl's night."

He pouts. "I guess she can have you for one night." Then

he winks before adding, "Now let's go get you your double chocolate brownie ice cream with salted caramel sauce and put you into a sugar coma."

I smile widely, looking up at him like he hung the moon for me. How can I not be in love with him when he knows my ice cream order by heart?

CHAPTER TWENTY-EIGHT

Miles

"WE'RE GOING TO BE late. Move your butt, Cooper!" Quinn rushes as she power-walks across the street toward the local shelter. Her ankle has been assessed by her head cheer coach, and she's practically back to normal already. It's been eleven days; she's bionic to have that kind of healing speed.

"I know, I'm sorry."

I'm not really that sorry. The reason we're late is because I spent an extra ten minutes after class kissing her like we hadn't seen each other in days. Except it hasn't been days. It's been maybe twenty hours since I left her.

"Watching you shake that cute ass in front of my face is making us being late so worth it, by the way."

"Miles!" she chastises and covers her butt with her hands.

"Oh no, you don't. I want to see the goods," I tease, chasing after her.

"I'm walking faster to get away from you." She hurries along, and I laugh, catching up to her and pulling her to a stop, resting my mouth just below her ear, feeling the ripples of a shudder begin as her body fits against mine. "Here I thought you were running so I could catch you."

"Miles," she whispers breathlessly, and my body responds to her need.

"Queenie," I purr right back, nibbling on her earlobe. God, she even tastes like cinnamon. It's intoxicating.

"We need to... We should... I mean..."

"Speechless again? Imagine that."

Her elbow swiftly, but gently, juts into my gut as she pushes away from me. "I'm never speechless, just tongue tied. Now move it, Cooper." She claps her hands twice to emphasize her impatience, and I follow behind her like a lost puppy. Except with her, I've never felt lost. Instead, I've always felt seen. And I'm pretty sure I'd follow her anywhere.

She swings the door open with ease, and as soon as she's inside, a woman with light gray hair is waiting for her in the small foyer covered in green plants, giant ones with huge leaves. She's petite, with a round, kind face framed by wisps of soft, silver hair. Dressed in a floral blouse and a pair of faded jeans, she exudes warmth. Her hands move with an effortless dexterity as she tends to the plants around her.

"Quinn, my dear!" the woman exclaims, her voice sweet and melodic. She steps forward, enveloping Quinn in a quick, affectionate hug.

"Maeve, it's so good to see you. I missed you last time!" Quinn says, wrapping her arms around her, just as Maeve turns her attention to me.

"And who is this handsome young man?" she asks, her eyes twinkling mischievously.

"This is Miles," Quinn introduces as she smiles at the interaction. "He's helping me with the class today."

Maeve's eyes light up even more as she extends a hand to me. "Well, Miles, it's a pleasure to meet you. I must say, Quinn has never mentioned how dashing her friend is." She gives me a playful wink, making me chuckle.

"It's a pleasure to meet you too, Maeve." Taking her hand, she gives it a gentle squeeze. "I've heard a lot about you."

"Oh, all good things, I hope!" Maeve coos, clutching at her imaginary pearls.

"Of course, only the best," I assure her and return her playful gaze with a charming smile.

"Well, aren't you a smooth talker," Maeve says, still smiling. "Quinn, you've brought quite the gentleman with you today."

Quinn's cheeks flush slightly as she exchanges a glance with me. "Yeah, he's not bad," she admits with a sweet smile. "Figured he might learn a thing or two."

"As long as I get to taste-test, I'm in." Throwing a wink to Quinn, I rub my hands together and revel in the deeper shade of pink that stains her freckled cheeks.

Maeve's chuckle stops Quinn's response as she says, "Come on, you two lovebirds, let's get you set up in the hall." As she walks away, Quinn turns to face me, eyes wide.

"Taste-test?!" she whisper-hisses.

I can't hold back the grin that begs to break free. "Yeah, Queenie, I want to taste...everything." Stepping closer, I dust my knuckles over her cheek, following the blush down her delicate neck and collarbone. Her breathing shallows and those emerald eyes flutter before me like she could collapse into my arms at any moment. I lean forward quickly, pressing a brief kiss to her lips, ignoring the fact that I want more.

"Baking," she whispers. "We need to bake." Reality seeps back into her gaze, the focus widening her pupils once more, but not before she homes in on my lips and takes a deep, satisfying swallow, one that makes me want to combust.

"Baking, right. Let's go." I nod once, taking her hand and following where Maeve went.

***

I look over to Quinn as she opens a leather-bound book, and I see something so surprising it hits me like a freight train. Grief is a strange thing. It twists through time, tangles in memories, but mostly, it's always something that sneaks up on me in the most unexpected moments. I didn't expect it to find me today, but as I'm surrounded by the comforting scent of vanilla and cinnamon, I try to take a deep breath, as fractured memories rattle around my brain. My eyes stay fixed on what Quinn is holding in her hands.

"Quinn, is that..." I pause, because I've only ever seen it on a card from my sixth birthday that's tucked away in my childhood bedroom. "Is that my mom's handwriting?"

Quinn shifts nervously and nods, dragging her fingers over the small writing, and my heart thuds. "It is," she says quietly over the chatter in the room around us.

"Where did you get that?"

"She gave me some recipes for my fifth birthday." She pauses for a second, guilt flitting across her features. "I thought you knew, I'm sorry."

I didn't know. And now, staring at the handwritten card, heartache crashes over me, transporting me back to the boy who suddenly lost his mom. Years have passed since she died, but the pain feels as raw as if it happened yesterday. Seeing my mom's recipes alive in Quinn's hands is both beautiful and heartbreaking.

"I didn't know," I say, struggling to keep my voice steady. "But don't be sorry. I'm glad you have them."

Quinn pauses until our eyes connect again, her expression a mix of sympathy and something deeper. "I've used them a lot over the years. Your mom was an amazing baker, and her recipes are like little pieces of her."

My chest tightens, and I take a deep breath, trying to keep my emotions in check. "I remember her baking with us when I was really young. It's one of the few clear memories I have of her." *Really the only one that I remember.* My head fills with the distant sounds from that day of her laughing, Quinn being covered in flour as she stood on a wooden stool, hip to hip with my mom. The smell of sugar and butter floated around the kitchen as we all made my mom's favorite cookies.

Quinn's eyes soften, and she reaches out, placing a hand on my arm. Knowing she's kept and cherished something so precious to me, and made it a part of her life, makes my heart ache and swell at the same time. I take a minute to look at her, really look at her, and something shifts inside me. I see the depth of her care, something she's always given away so freely. Her and my mom always got on so well, and maybe that's why, because they were so similar. I haven't given it much thought until now.

Quinn is the most caring person I've ever known. The way she's been there for me, holding me together even when I felt like falling apart, my entire life. When my mom passed, she didn't leave my room. When my dad worked twenty-four-seven after that, she would sit on her porch with me while I waited, staring at my house across the street wondering if he'd decide to come home this weekend. And even now, she's holding me together while I try to navigate this. Through everything, Quinn has always been there.

And in this moment, I realize something else. Maybe I've been falling for her for a while, maybe my whole life. If I think about it, I've always gravitated to her, and she's been the same with me. If she was late for curfew, she'd sneak into my house, because it was so much easier than sneaking into her own, and ask me to walk into her house with her. Which only happened once because nine times out of ten, we were together anyway, and both walked in to face the disappointing headshakes of her dad. Then we'd pass out in the cinema room, watching movies, which is why we still watch so many even now. We've spent years being intertwined.

Only, I can't forget that I'm still walking a tight rope, scared to fall, scared to lose things in my life, scared to mess everything up.

The last two years have been clustered with so many bad decisions on my part... But I also know that I have her, and she's here for me and more important than any of it. Always has been, even before I kissed her. Even before she opened my eyes to something more than friendship. So, what if everything I thought I wanted was a lie and there's one thing I want more than anything. What if she's my one?

Not able to draw my attention from her, she begins her class.

"I missed you all!" she coos, her smile warm. "So today, we have my favorite family cookie recipe to make. Who's ready?"

"Who is that?" a little girl with black curly hair asks, nestled next to a lady who I assume is her mom.

Quinn's eyes track me. "Natalia, this is Miles. He's my...friend. In fact, he is one of my best friends," she says proudly, and suddenly I want to hear her say that I'm more than her friend. "He's helping me today just like your mom is helping you."

She carries on, showing everyone how to measure flour correctly. How to make sure you don't overmix the batter, how soft the butter should be to combine with the sugar, all notes I remember my mom explaining to us in my kitchen. I can see the transformation in the faces around her—the initial nervousness giving way to excitement and pride as they realize they can do this. Quinn has a way of making everyone feel capable and important. It's one of the things I love most about her.

I stand at the edge of the table, content to watch her. Her red hair is tied back with a white bow today, a few stray strands escaping to frame her face, and her eyes are shining. She's beautiful.

When she glances my way, her eyes lock onto mine. She smiles a radiant smile that makes my heart skip a beat. "Miles, come over here," she calls, waving me closer. "I could use your help." I hesitate for a moment, but the warmth in her eyes draws me in. As I step forward, she hands me a mixing bowl. "We're about to mix the dry and wet ingredients," she says, her hand briefly brushing mine. The simple touch sends a spark through me.

"Okay," I hesitate. "Are you sure I'm the one who should do

this?"

"Hmm…" She taps her lip. "Maybe you're right, you did almost burn down your dorm that one time."

"Oh, stop it. Am I ever going to live that down?" I chuckle.

"Probably not. But you've got me to help you, so all you have to do is pour this," she says, nudging the bowl already in my hands, "with this." She points to the mixer in front of us.

"So, I really can't mess it up?"

"You really can't. Look…" She points to the class full of whirring mixers and smiling people. "Not everyone here is a pro baker; they just want to have fun."

I realize that Quinn isn't just teaching us how to bake. She's creating a sense of community, a safe space where everyone can contribute and feel valued. Something she's so damn good at.

Half an hour later, we're devouring an entire tray of cookies. She nailed the recipe, because I'm instantly transported back to being a kid as soon as the buttery goodness hits my tongue.

"Good, right?"

"So good," I groan through a mouthful. Quinn's chuckle skates over my skin and grips a hold of something in my chest. "Thank you for today, I really mean it. I had a great time."

The smile she gives me almost knocks me on my ass, but it's her words that make me come alive. "I'm just trying to help you find some joy again, Miles. That's all."

"Maybe you already have."

Swallowing the lump in my throat, I pull her body to me so I can claim her mouth like I've wanted to all day. She tastes like chocolate and cinnamon and everything about her feels like home.

CHAPTER TWENTY-NINE

Miles

"RISE AND SHINE!" THE voice booming into my dark room is far too full of joy to be anyone else but Quinn. I know this because there have been many times she's managed to drag my ass out of bed over the years. And I have so much regret, giving her my spare keycard.

Rolling over, I pull the covers high over my head. "Five more minutes," I groan.

"Miles, you and I have places to be. Get your lazy butt out of that bed."

"Queenie." I pout, pulling back the cover to glance at her through a squinted eye. "Come put *your* ass *in* my bed."

Her head shakes vehemently. "No can do. It's Thanksgiving week, and we are volunteering at the food bank in town."

"We are?"

She nods, pushing back a strand of hair behind her ear, then adjusting her bow at the back of her ponytail. "It's in your calendar."

"But what if I tell you I've pulled a hamstring and can't walk?"

"I'll drag you there," she says way too sweetly.

"Savage."

"Listen, I might be smaller than you, but I'm getting you to that food bank today. We can't go home this year since my parents are taking a lame cruise, which means we're not having my mom's amazing cooking." She frowns, pushing out that plump bottom lip of hers that gets me every single time. "So, I need to do something to help. That includes you."

"You're wound too tight today." I push back the covers so I can take all of her in properly. Her hands firmly planted on her hips digging into the soft skin there as she stares down at me with a quirked eyebrow. "I can help unwind you."

The way her eyes take in every inch of my body, eyes drifting over each tattoo, the roses, trailing seductively down the vines over my chest, and settling on the compass on the left, makes me think she wants something more, but I don't push. "What would help me is if you get out of bed yourself, and I don't break my back trying to do it for you."

I exhale in defeat. We both know as soon as she gave me the pout, I was in. "Fine." Swinging my legs over the side of the bed, I try to adjust my morning wood, but it's harder to do that when my version of a wet dream is standing and giving me orders at the ass crack of dawn. "I'm up." *Quite literally.*

Her green eyes darken the longer she stares at me, and when her tongue peeks out to wet her bottom lip, I almost lose it. "Oh," she says as her gaze lands on the tent in my boxers. "I can go."

"Leaving is the exact opposite of what I want you to do right now, especially when you look so fucking hot."

Quinn lights up like a beacon. "Hot? Me?" She brushes her hands down her perfect, softly curved body before beaming at me. "Thanks."

Standing up, I stretch my body out and watch her take in every inch of me, and I'm not ashamed. I work hard for my body, and I like having her eyes on me. "Yes, Queenie. You." I lower my arms, palming my dick over my boxers to relieve some of the pressure. "If you hadn't barged in here, I would've been thinking about you while I took care of this," I growl.

Her throat bobs as she swallows, and then the sweetest little gasp leaves her lips as our eyes lock. "Y-you think about me?"

Fuck. This girl.

"Yeah," I reply gruffly as I step toward her. "I think about the noises you made that night in the hallway when you were coming all over my leg. I think about those perfectly soft lips wrapping around me and taking everything I give you. I think about having you underneath me, on top of me, all over me, because now I can't see or think about anyone else but you."

Her breath leaves her mouth on a stuttered exhale, and I wonder if I've pushed too far. But as soon as she flicks those green depths to me, they're swirling with intrigue. "Anyone but me?" she whispers, licking her lips.

"Anyone but you, Queenie," I confirm and I hold her stare for a beat to make sure she knows I'm serious. And then it takes all my self-control to get dressed and not think about undressing her this morning.

***

Driving through the narrow, winding streets of Cedar Lakes, our small college town slowly gives way to more spread-out residential areas near the lakes. Quinn hums along to the radio, her fingers tapping a rhythm on the dashboard. I steal glances at her as I drive my pickup, her red hair, tied loosely with a pink bow today, the loose strands catching the light in a way that makes her look like some kind of angel. And fuck, have I ever thought about a girl like that?

"It's just up there," Quinn says, pointing to a building that reads: *Cedar Lakes Food Bank*. I pull into the gravel parking lot and shut off the engine. Quinn gives me a quick smile before hopping out of the car. I follow suit, feeling the crunch of gravel under my boots as we head toward the entrance.

"Luna should be inside," Quinn says as she pushes open the door. The smell of fresh bread and spices immediately hits me, a comforting scent that reminds me of home. Not mine, but the Dawson's home and her mom's cooking. God, I miss her cooking.

As we step inside, a woman with dark purple hair pulled back in a braid leaps out from behind the counter. "Quinn! It's so good to see you!"

She embraces Quinn, and when they let go, she turns to me. "Luna, this is my friend, Miles," Quinn says, and there's that word again. *Friend*. Damn, why does that bother me? "Miles, this is Luna. She's the heart and soul of this place."

I extend my hand, and Luna shakes it firmly. "Nice to meet

you, Miles. Any friend of Quinn's is a friend of mine." She looks between the two of us, and then directs her attention to me. "Think you can help haul some food out of the truck? We've got a big delivery today."

"Absolutely," I reply with a smile. Quinn gives me an encouraging nod as I follow Luna to the back door, where a large truck is parked. The driver opens the back, revealing stacks of boxes filled with non-perishable foods and fresh produce.

"Just start with these," Luna says, pointing to the closest stack. "If you put them near the entrance, the cooks can unload them. I'll be back in fifteen. Thanks, Miles!" she says as she wanders back inside.

By the time the truck is empty, my shirt is sticking to my back, and my arms feel like they're made of lead. Luna didn't make it back, so I decide to go in search of my girl. Walking into the main room, the AC hits washes over me, chilling the sweat on my body. Around me, tables are being set up, each one lined with neatly organized rows of canned goods, bread, and fresh vegetables. It's a well-oiled machine, everyone knowing exactly what to do and where to go.

"Okay, doors open in ten minutes," Luna announces from across the room. "Remember, first round is for food collection, and then in two hours, the second round begins for the soup drive."

I take a moment to catch my breath, wiping the sweat from my forehead, just as I spot Quinn stacking cans on one of the tables, her movements quick and efficient. Walking toward her, I drop my head to her ear and whisper, "There are two rounds?"

She jumps as I brush my hand down her arm. "Oh my god! Make more noise!" Caught off guard, she knocks a can of soup from the table, but I dart out to catch it before it hits the floor.

"Caught it," I say, passing it back to her. "Sorry, I like making you squeal, though."

Quinn folds her lips inward, hiding her smile, and just before I can reach over to release her pink lips, the front doors swing open, taking our attention. A few people start to trickle in, the first wave of the many who rely on the food bank.

"Hey, Quinn," a vaguely familiar voice says, making my head snap up to see Alex. He grabs an apron and parks himself way too close for my liking. "Fancy seeing you here."

I swear this guy is everywhere. I can't catch a break.

"Hey, Alex," Quinn replies, her tone polite but cool. She keeps stacking cans, avoiding his gaze.

My skin crawls from knowing he's next to her. There's nothing wrong with the guy except his interest in Quinn that makes me want to claim her in front of everyone. I move closer, inserting myself between them. "Alex," I say, forcing a smile. "Didn't expect to see you here."

Alex's eyes flick to me, and his smile becomes a bit strained. Good. "Miles. Helping out, huh?"

"With Quinn, yeah," I say pointedly.

"Great," he grits out, looking back to Quinn. "Indie mentioned you were volunteering here today, so I signed up too."

Oh god, he's a do-gooder as well.

Quinn steps away from the table. "I need to grab a few more things from the back," she says, giving me a look that clearly means *don't start trouble*. Disappearing through a doorway, leaving me and Alex alone.

Alex turns to me, crossing his arms over his chest. "So, what's going on with you and Quinn?" he asks, eyebrows pinched.

I keep my expression neutral and focus on passing canned food to people passing by. "What do you mean?"

"You know what I mean." He scoffs, his eyes narrowing slightly. "Are you two more than friends? Because, for what it's worth, I still like her."

Feeling the tension in the air, I take a deep breath. "I don't—"

"Before you lie about it, I thought there might've been something going on when you turned up at her dorm, and at her party too. Plus, we haven't rescheduled the date you interrupted either."

I guess I'm going to have to lay it all out. "Look, Alex." I meet his gaze, figuring he might take it seriously if he can see how serious I am about her. "Quinn and I have been friends since we were born. We're close and, I don't know, something might be happening." Something is definitely happening in my chest, a ruckus at the thought of her with him, but I play it cool. "But I'm not about to offer to braid your hair and have a heart-to-heart about it. It's between me and Quinn."

His head tilts as he studies me. "So, I'm wasting my time here."

"Like I said, I'm not about to talk about it with you."

His face contorts. He clearly doesn't like that answer. With a sigh, I turn to him. "Listen, you should ask Quinn how she feels about you. Least that way, you'll get a straight answer."

"Oh good, no brawling," Quinn says, breezing right back in between us.

"I was good..." Dropping my mouth down to her ear, I whisper, "For you."

Goosebumps spread across her neck, and I have to resist the urge to kiss her, pull her into my body, and show Alex exactly who she belongs to. But she's not ready for that, yet.

"So Quinn, what do you say to a do-over date?" Alex asks, and her entire body stiffens. I'm not going to intervene; the guy has it bad. But I know everything about Quinn, and she hates being pushed into situations. She's headstrong and stubborn like her brother, so I just silently stand near her, smiling at people as they collect a few items from the canned goods in front of me.

"Uh, I actually wanted to talk to you." She hesitates, flicking her gaze to me briefly, and just that little gesture has me screaming inside. My heart ping-pongs around my empty chest, desperate to get to this girl. "Maybe we could catch up before we leave?"

"I'd like that," he says, placing his hand on her forearm with pointed eye contact that makes me want to gauge his eyes out.

Breathe, Miles. Don't punch the beige slack wearing do-gooder. It'll do you no favors.

"I'm just going to get a water, I'll be back," I say before stalking away, saving Alex's life in the process.

CHAPTER THIRTY

Miles

LAKESIDE DINER IS PACKED with people tonight, which is surprising because tomorrow is Thanksgiving. It's also our rivalry game against Washington. I'm bone tired from today at the food bank. Quinn, however, doesn't look even a tiny bit weary. She's opposite me, surrounded by our friends, who opted out of going home this year too, and she has no right to look as alluring as she does. Her hair is swept off her face and neck, the same pink bow decorating her ponytail. The freckles across her nose speckle her perfectly milky skin, and that crazy cute cupid bow looks insanely kissable tonight.

She's in her element, laughing with our friends, and her happiness radiates from her. Quinn has always been full of sunshine, but now it feels like I want to be the one to soak up her rays. Only me. At the very least, I want to be able to touch her in public more. I mean, assuming that's still what she wants too.

It was on tip of my tongue to ask about the chat she had with Alex earlier, but I chickened out.

I make eye contact with her and let my gaze heat up her cheeks, watching as she looks down under the table. My eyebrows pinch just as my phone buzzes in my pocket.

Queenie

> Meet me in the back hallway in two minutes. I want a kiss xo

Head snapping back to hers, the same flush colors her cheeks, and down her neck. That perfect pink making her glow as she sucks in her bottom lip. My girl wants a kiss, she's getting a damn kiss.

Standing, I don't offer any information as to where I'm going, and none of our friends notice as I walk over to the back hallway behind the kitchen, next to the bathroom door. It's pretty hidden here, but I know there's a storage closet that is rarely locked. I accidentally thought it was the bathroom my freshman year.

A few seconds pass that feels like minutes, my body humming with anticipation, and my skin feels hot as arousal builds in my blood. I palm myself over the material of my shorts, thinking of her and how flushed her skin was a second ago, how I did that to her, my perfect Queenie blushing over me. I never knew how wild that could drive me. Stifling a groan, I hear soft footsteps and then I catch her cinnamon scent, and I have to hold myself back from launching at her.

Her steps are shy as our eyes lock, but her words make white-hot heat shoot down my spine. "Hey, hot stuff," she purrs, confidence oozing from her.

One more step closer, until we're almost touching. The little vixen knows exactly what she's doing, and I love it. The playful side to her I don't see often makes me weak with submission, which has never happened before with a girl. I slowly lick my lips, watching her pupils dilate as they track the movement. "I think you needed something from me?" I raise an eyebrow in challenge and wait for her.

The air around us disappears with each step she takes toward me, a gleam in her eyes that makes me want to pull her against me. But what sends me into a tailspin is the sexy-as-fuck smile she has on her pretty plump lips. When she stops directly in front of me, her warm body heat seeps into me. There isn't a single inch of my body that isn't shrouded in sunshine in her presence. "I do need something," she whispers.

I reach to my left and open the storage room door, taking her hand in mine and dragging her inside with me until all that's left is us in the dimly lit room. The distant hum of the diner fades away, until all I can hear is our synced, rushed breathing.

Backing her up to the door, I blanket her body with mine, pushing my aching length into her too so she can feel how badly I want her. Trailing my fingertips down her arm, I feel her hot breaths puffing against me as I move lower until I reach her hands and pin them above her head with a tender thud. "You're making everything really hard."

She chuckles softly. "Evidently." Her hips roll into me, grazing along my rapidly growing dick.

My hand flies to her hip, pinning her in place with a warning squeeze. "Queenie," I rasp. But she doesn't move. If anything, I can feel her pushing more against me.

"I want you," she whispers.

I stare into her eyes, wanting to ask her if she means that. If I'm the one she picked, not Alex. "You do?"

She swallows and nods. "There's only you. Exclusively, remember?"

Adjusting my grip so I can bring the other hand to join it, she gasps, and the sound is so quiet and airy, like it's been stolen from her lungs. I smile as I stare down at her looking so damn beautiful. "Exclusively mine, huh?"

A light laugh falls from her lips just as I bury my head into the crook of her neck, swallowing a groan, and run my nose up the side, up to her ear, watching the dim light shine on the goosebumps rising on her skin.

"Miles..." she breathes out, and then I'm done for. My control snaps, and I'm on her. Our mouths clash in the most delicious kiss. A kiss that is full of need and desire, or years and years of knowing each other but only just now discovering this new side to us. *Us.* The thought of being something with her ripples likes waves in my mind. God, do I want her. She sweeps her tongue against mine, and my entire body thrums, my heart racing erratically. Her hands pull against my hold, desperate to break free, but I don't let her. She's not going anywhere.

I continue to kiss her, never breaking our connection, while my free hand wanders down over her jean-clad thigh. "Can I touch you?" my mouth says, but my mind thinks, *Can I keep you?*

Her encouraging nod is enough for me to let my wandering fingers caress over and over, moving higher and higher until I reach the button of her jeans and flick it open. Delving in, I brush over her lace underwear and find soft skin and her soaked center.

Gently moving back up, I dip inside her underwear and graze over her clit, feeling her body shudder under my touch. This time, I can't hold back my groan, as my head lowers to her shoulder. "Fucking hell, Queenie, what are you doing to me?"

"I don't know, but you're driving me wild. Whatever it is, please don't stop."

Smiling into her neck, I gently nip at her skin, making her arch into my touch more, but I don't apply the pressure I know she wants. "Are you begging me?"

Her chest pushes into mine, but she still can't reach more of my touch. The thought tilts my lips up. "I'll beg if you touch me more."

I take the opportunity to sink a finger inside her and relish the way her eyes widen but flare with heat and her teeth sink into her lower lip. I pause my movements again, drawing out her pleasure as her hips try to seek friction. "I like you like this." Grazing my teeth gently against her jaw, I hum. "Wet, desperate...mine."

"Miles," she growls, and I have to hold back a chuckle.

"Yes, Queenie?"

"Please," she rasps.

That one powerful word is my undoing. I want to give her everything. I push another finger inside her, feeling her body contract around me, as I move my thumb to apply pressure on her clit. It's a squeeze with my hand in her pants, but it's all adding to the depravity of taking her in this tiny room where we could get caught. And I fucking love it. "Anyone could come in right now, you know."

She pants as I work her deeper. "Anyone could see my hands down your pants."

Wetness coats my fingers as I talk, and I know it's turning her on even more. "Oh, you like that. You like that we could get caught. Does my girl have a kink?" I muse.

Her eyes darken, and fuck if it doesn't make my dick harder. "Faster. I need more." She writhes, rocking her hips.

I want to give her everything. But I'll be damned if the first time we have sex is in a public place. She deserves better than that. I might like the idea of getting caught, but there's no way I'd actually let anyone see her like this.

My hand increases speed, along with my thundering heart rate and pulsing cock. She breathes harder, fighting against my hand above her head, but I don't release her. I hold her steady, just as I feel her fluttering around my fingers.

"You gonna come, Queenie? Hmm, I think you are. I think you're going to come thinking we could be caught any second," I whisper darkly as she moans. "I think you're also going to enjoy walking out there, pretending I didn't have my fingers inside this sweet little cunt of yours." I trail my tongue up her neck just as she clamps her mouth closed. The sight makes my blood run hotter. "I can feel you squeezing my fingers like you would my cock. So fucking beautiful." She releases another whimper just as her orgasm hits its peak.

I let her hands go and she immediately wraps her arms around my neck, pulling me to her mouth to swallow her needy noises. I kiss and lick her until she calms, and her thighs relax around my hand. "I love listening to you."

She reaches between us, running her fingers over my hard length. "I want to play."

"I want that too." I gently grasp her wrist, stopping her before I lose my mind. "But we've both been gone a while, and our friends are out there."

She deflates against me. "We need to get better at doing this in a dorm. Preferably yours because you live alone."

I hum, pulling her closer to me for one more kiss.

Pulling back, she looks up at me, flushed and sated. "I want you to touch me when you want to. I want us to do this thing, whatever it is. I want more. Just you."

I don't miss the confirmation in her words and something inside me melts. It's exactly what I needed to hear. "Just me? No one else?"

Her head shakes. "No one else," she confirms.

That makes me want to tell our friends, to march her out to the diner and blurt that she's mine, but I know she's not ready yet. And after everything she's doing to help me be a better person, the least I can do is respect that. Because for as long as we've been friends, nothing about what we're doing feels strange to me. It feels like the most natural thing in the world.

So, I'll be as patient as she needs me to be. As long as I can keep her.

CHAPTER THIRTY-ONE

Quinn

MY FOOT TAPS NERVOUSLY on the floor. The cheer locker room feels stifling, despite the cool breeze drifting in from the open door. I wring my hands together, eyes darting to the clock every few seconds.

The game is supposed to start at 3 p.m., and it's already 2 p.m. He's here already. I know because I saw him walk in with Seb and Hudson earlier as I made my way across the parking lot.

He's here, he's with the guys, everything is fine. We both blocked his dad's number for today, so he can't make him feel like shit over the phone. He's going to be okay. Nothing is going to push him over the edge.

That doesn't stop the questions whirling in my head, the niggle I feel that is interlaced with fear, the kind that tells me something could go really wrong. What if today is too much for him? What if he gives in before the game?

Standing up, I pace the empty room. The squad doesn't usually get here as early as this, and I'm grateful because I'm so strung out. Trying to shake off the overwhelming sense of dread seems impossible. Deep breaths don't seem to help; the air never feels like it's reaching my lungs.

He can do this. *You need to let him do this*. Besides, he doesn't have Levi's number anymore. Taking one deep breath, I focus on the cheer routine for tonight. Okay, it's all going to be fine. I breathe in and out, slow and steady as I smooth down my cheerleading uniform. The clock reads 2:12 p.m.

Is that all? Okay, I need to check on him. It won't hurt, just one little check.

Grabbing my phone and tucking it in into the waistband of my skirt, I head out the door. The muffled sounds of the team filter toward me, getting louder as I turn the corner. I hear it then, Miles's laugh, the one that rattles me to my bones. It's an honest laugh, the kind that I imagine him clutching his belly, head thrown back, thick neck on show, the roses and vine tattoos peeking from his collar.

He's okay. He's in there with his teammates and friends.

Realizing how ridiculous it would be, let alone obvious that we were more than friends, if I barged in there, I need to let him figure this out for himself. Just let him do his thing. Besides, athletes are notoriously superstitious, and if I interrupt his usual routine, that might throw everything. No, he's going to be fine. I don't need to see him. I trust him. I believe he can do this without feeling the need to fall back into old habits.

Resolute in believing in him, I turn on my heels and walk back to the cheer locker room.

On my way back, I notice two figures facing off up ahead. It's too dark to see them clearly, but as I get closer, I realize it's Jay and a girl with the bluest hair I've ever seen. She's gorgeous, all curves and a beautiful face that's now a bit more visible. By the way she's standing, arms crossed and a serious 'hell no' look on her face, it's clear she's not in a good mood.

"Hey, Jay, you okay?" I ask, and his head turns to me in surprise. Pushing his glasses up his nose, he nods my way, and some of the tension evaporates from his shoulders.

"Olá, Quinn," he says, rubbing the back of his neck. Now I really look at him, his cheeks are flushed as though he's been in a heated discussion. Hmm, interesting. Walking closer still, I extend my hand to the girl with blue hair and blue eyes.

"Hi, I'm Quinn."

She looks at my hand, to Jay with a frown, and then back to me, giving me a small smile and a wave. "Georgia."

Retracting my hand and accepting her wave instead, I say, "I don't think I've met you before. What year are you in?"

"Sophomore."

"Oh, same as us. Are you studying photography like Jay?"

Georgia shifts, looking a little uncomfortable. "Err, not exactly. I'm an artist, but I take Fine Art Photography, which is how I met your boyfriend here."

A barking laugh erupts from my mouth, my hand flying up to capture the sound. "Oh." I swallow the next laugh, schooling my face. "Jay isn't my boyfriend. He's my friend, but he's totally single."

"Gee, that doesn't make me sound like the biggest loser. Not just single, *totally* single."

Balking and backtracking I squeal, "I didn't mean it like that!"

"Well, at least I know I can call you if I need a wing woman."

"Jay—" I begin, but am cut off.

"Well, totally single guy, I'll see you in class," Georgia says, bumping shoulders with Jay as she walks past us. "Bye, Quinn."

I look at Jay, my mouth open, and then back again to Georgia, a million questions racing through my brain.

"Don't ask."

Okay, then. Clamping my mouth closed, I roll back on my feet, trying to think of something else to say. Words never usually escape me, but I'm too intrigued by whoever that girl is. I've only ever seen Jay kiss a few girls at parties, I know he hooks up, but he's Mr. Casual. I haven't seen him interact with so much intensity before. "Okay, hate me all you want, but I need to know who she is."

Jay sighs loudly. "It doesn't matter. She's in my class, like she said. She's insanely talented, and we...don't get along. At all. In any way, shape, or form."

"Someone doesn't like *you*?" I squeak in disbelief. "The sweetest guy in our group and she doesn't like you?" I'm gesturing wildly to him, as though he doesn't know who he is.

He laughs, but it's more to placate my ridiculousness. "Anyway, I've gotta go get my SD card for my camera. Até já."

"Adeus," I reply, saluting him as he leaves.

My phone buzzes against my hip, and when I fish it out, I see Miles calling me. Fumbling to answer, I almost drop it twice in my haste to swipe. "Miles?"

"Hey."

"Everything okay?" I ask, desperately trying to keep the shake of nerves from my voice, but it doesn't stop my pulse quickening at the thought that something has gone wrong before the game tonight.

"Yeah, it's just... I..." He pauses, and all I can hear is his breathing—steady, slow, constant. The silence stretches, making my heart race even faster. "I wanted to hear your voice."

My shoulders sag in relief, the tightness in my chest easing slightly just as the realization sinks in. He came to me when he clearly needed something else. He came to me. "Well..." I clear my throat. "Here is my voice, just for you. Are you sure everything is okay?"

"Yeah," he exhales roughly. "It's better now I'm talking to you."

My poor, loved-up heart can't cope with him being this way with me. The flirting is fine; I'm used to it. It's always been more of a joke. But this? This heartfelt side to him. It makes my feelings intensify to supernova status. Like, seriously, the human torch would have nothing on me, and I didn't think that was possible. I've only glimpsed him being this honest and raw a few times in my life, and now he's directing it all to me. I melt faster than a snowman in sunshine.

"I had an email from my dad. I think he's trying to find other ways to get in touch on game days. I didn't open it, but I felt..."

He doesn't need to continue to tell me what I already know. He wanted to take something to ensure he doesn't land on his bad side. He wanted to make sure he was going to play the game of his life for his dad. And this is why I need him to stop, because he doesn't see it, but he is amazing. He's one of the most talented wide receivers at his level, and he doesn't need anything but himself.

"It's okay, I'm glad you called me."

A rush of air brushes against the speaker, and I imagine him tugging at his hair. "I've gotta go warm up in a sec. I just wanted to talk to you. Tell me something. Anything."

My mind stutters on what to say, and I find myself blurting out, "I have on my lucky underwear today."

He laughs, and I think I want the ground to swallow me whole. Why did I say that?

"The ones with the strawberries?"

My embarrassment disappears slightly at his response. "It's disturbing that you know that, and until recently had no intention of getting into my pants."

"I know a lot about you, Queenie. Like how you love to eat fries and dip them into vanilla milkshakes, which, by the way, is illegal. How you always find a song for every occasion, and how you organize your playlists by friendships. Or how you always wear those strawberry panties when it's game day."

Closing my eyes, I cringe. "Did I...show you? Is that how you know?"

He chuckles. "I wish. No, you told me once when you were drunk in freshman year."

I scoff a laugh, half impressed and a whole lot freaked out that he remembers and banks away so much information about me. "Well, there is something you don't know about me," I say suggestively.

"I'm listening," he says with a deepness to his voice that gives me goosebumps.

"I'll make you a deal, Miles Cooper. If you win tonight, score a touchdown, play your heart out on that field, then I'll surprise you after the game."

"Surprise me?" His voice takes on a new edge, excitement mixed with something more intense. Something I'm becoming addicted to.

"Now, chop chop, Cooper. You've got a game to win if you want to score tonight."

He chuckles, and the adrenaline from that noise hits my heart like a shot. "Jesus, where did you come from?"

"Your dreams," I say boldly, the words slipping out before I can second-guess them, but I don't back down. It's out there now.

"You got that right, Queenie," he says with conviction, and it has my stomach flipping. "You've given me the best kind of motivation."

I laugh, but inside, I'm a mess. A jumbled, in-love-with-my-best-friend kind of mess. "And here I thought you might need a picture, so you knew I was serious. I guess I'm more convincing than I thought."

"Woah woah, wait a second, a picture?" he asks, his voice breaking. "I want that. I'm not convinced. I'm not at all. In fact, I was thinking about throwing the game because I'm nervous, sooooo nervous. You know what would make me feel better? A picture from you."

I can't hold back my giggle. "Go play your game, Cooper. And win. First down."

"All the way."

Hanging up while feeling victorious, a full-blown smile warms my face. And just to mess with him a little more, I take a selfie with my tongue poking out and send it to him with the caption, 'Find me later, but only if you're ready for some fun.'

His reply comes through immediately.

Miles

> Challenge accepted, hope you're ready
> Queenie xo

And what does me in the most? Is the little kiss and hug at the end of his message.

R.I.P to my heart.

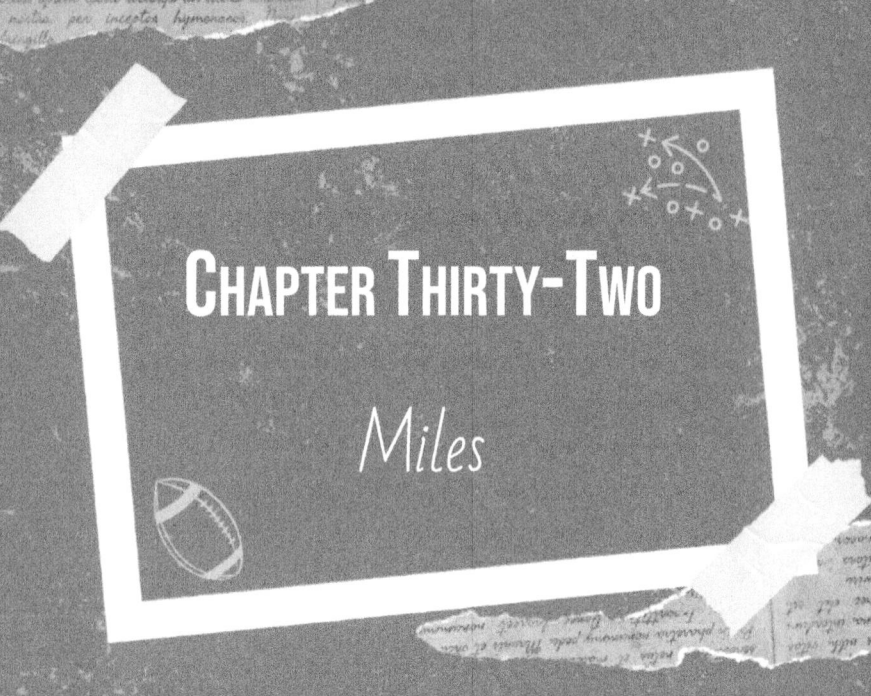

Chapter Thirty-Two

Miles

The roar of the crowd echoes through our Cedar Lakes Stadium, vibrating in my chest as I stand on the sidelines, watching our defense force yet another punt. It's the biggest game of the year, the one that means everything to this town. The rivalry game against Washington. The score sits at 21-14 in our favor, but the nagging thought in the back of my mind keeps whispering that it won't be enough. *I* won't be enough. I've managed to push it aside, but nothing has been easy so far.

Hearing Quinn's voice earlier settled me. That nervous jitter of fear and anticipation, of not wanting to let *him* down disappeared when the sound of her sunshine came down the line. I didn't even have to say much; she just got it.

But out here on the field, with cameras surrounding us, that fear seeps back in, the worry that I'm still not good enough for my dad. Is he watching right now?

I wipe the sweat from my brow, trying to focus on the game instead of the noise in my head.

"Ready to get back out there?" Seb's voice pulls me back into the moment.

"Always," I reply, even though I'm faking the certainty. The crowd's energy pulses around us as we huddle up for the next offensive drive. Seb calls the play, a deep route for me, and I can see the confidence in his eyes. He believes in this, in us.

We break the huddle and line up. I glance over at Quinn once to hit that serotonin level. She gives me a small nod, and it's like she's transferring her strength to me. I dig my cleats into the turf, focusing on the count.

The ball snaps, and I explode off the line, sprinting downfield. My legs pump like pistons, my breath steady. I break past the cornerback, a quick stutter-step leaving him in the dust. The safety's coming over, but I've got a step on him. Seb's pass is perfect, spiraling through the air, and I stretch out my hands, feeling the satisfying thud of the ball hitting exactly where he intended it.

I tuck it in and sprint for the end zone. The crowd's roar increases, and I cross the goal line, spiking the ball in triumph. 27-14. We're pulling away. The team mobs me in the end zone, slapping my helmet, shouting praises, but my eyes search for Quinn. She's on her feet, cheering with her squad, a wide smile lighting up her face. I want to run to her, to share this moment, but I know there's more game to play.

Washington fights back, scoring another touchdown, and suddenly it's 27-21. We're in the final minute, and they're driving downfield, desperate to steal the game from us. My muscles ache, my lungs burn, my mind feels tired, but I can't let up now.

We hold them at midfield, forcing them into a fourth-and-long situation. The tension is palpable as their quarterback drops back to pass. He heaves a desperate throw downfield, and our cornerback leaps, batting it down. Turnover on downs. Our ball. The crowd erupts again, but there's still time on the clock. We need one more score to seal this.

Seb and I exchange a look as we line up for what could be the final drive. His confidence is unwavering, and it gives me strength I need. He calls a simple play to run down the clock, but I know he's looking for an opportunity to strike.

The ball snaps, and Seb hands it off to our running back, who plows forward for a few yards. The clock ticks down. We line up again, this time for a pass play. I break out wide, feeling the cornerback's eyes on me, and then I'm off, sprinting down the sideline.

Seb drops back, scanning the field, and then he sees it. He launches the ball, and I'm there, arms outstretched. The ball is delivered into my palms, and I pull it in, racing toward the end zone. When the cornerback dives, I'm too quick. I cross the goal line just as the final whistle blows.

The stadium explodes in celebration. We've won. 33-21. The team engulfs me, and I find Seb in the chaos, hugging him tight. We did it. We actually did it. More importantly, I did it without anything but blood in my veins.

Through the crowd, I see Quinn pushing her way onto the field. She reaches me, throwing her arms around my neck, and for a moment, everything else fades away.

"You did it, I'm so proud of you," she hums into my ear, eradicating all the noise around us. Right now, there's nothing but her. I let myself sink into the feeling of having her wrapped around me because I need it, I need her, and I don't want to let her go.

For the first time in my life, I feel my heart beating outside of my body.

Because she's holding it in her hands.

"We did it!" Seb shouts next to us, and the cocoon we were in breaks open, letting all the noise back in. Quinn shifts from my embrace to her brother's, just as Hudson claps my shoulder.

"You were on fire tonight. Actual flames, dude."

I smile, absorbing his compliment. "You too, Huds. We fucking did it."

"Party tonight, and I'm going all in."

"Isn't that what you always do?"

He snorts a laugh. "No other way to live." And then he's gone, swallowed by the crowd, scooping up cheerleaders and celebrating. I take a second to look around and revel in the victory, but something in my stomach sours when the fear of my dad's impending commentary grips me, clouding me like a storm. *No, don't let him in.*

A small, soft hand links into my arm, grounding me. "Stay in the locker room. Make an excuse to stick around, and text me when you're alone," Quinn purrs, and my body ignites with a single spark. With a wink, I watch her sway away with her squad, hips swinging, loose hair flowing behind her, and the knowledge that, for right now, she's mine.

***

Trying to get rid of my team is a lot harder than I had planned.

It's like they knew something was going on. I just told them I had to talk to the physio about a twinge I had during the game. Seb eyed me like I was bullshitting him because, by that point, I was already in my suit, so why would I need to see the physio? But he eventually took my word for it and left. Hudson and some of the others, they weren't as willing to leave me until they are one hundred percent assured I'll meet them at the party later. Honestly, I've had easier times sneaking away from my dad growing up.

Finally, I'm alone, and I text Quinn.

Miles

Come get me, Queenie xo

Queenie

I was about to give up hope xo

I chuckle at her response. A few minutes later, she knocks on the door, and it creaks open to reveal her in a short black dress covered in lemons. The deep V of the neckline draws my eyes straight to her perfect freckled cleavage and my mouth waters.

"Hey," I manage to force out, tearing my eyes from my perusal of her body and looking into her green depths.

"Hey." She grins. "The suit is working for you. It always does."

"The dress is working for you. You look beautiful."

"Thanks." She blushes, the apples of her cheeks tinting as she tentatively moves toward me. Her gaze flits quickly to the floor, then back up, avoiding direct eye contact for too long. Every movement is cautious, as if she's hyper-aware of every step she takes.

"Am I making you nervous, Queenie?" I tease, my voice low.

Her wide green eyes lock onto mine. "No," she squeaks. "Don't be silly." She laughs, but it's laced with the nerves she claims not to have. "We could get caught again," she says with a glint in her eyes.

Suddenly realizing why she's acting a little skittish, I take a step toward her, wanting to soothe her in any way I can. "We could get caught. You sure you want to be here with me?" I ask, knowing the question has a double meaning. If we're caught, people will know about us, and I'm pushing that boundary to see where she stands with it.

When she nods slowly, my insides light up. "Now you've got me alone in here, what are you going to do with me?"

She chews on her bottom lip as our hands lace together. "Do *you* have anything in mind?"

Sliding closer to her again, I make sure to place my hand firmly on her hip and pull her into me. "I have everything in mind, Queenie." Letting my gaze lazily travel all over her face, I bring up one hand to trace her mouth with my fingers. "These lips, the ones that cheer for me every game? I want them wrapped around me." She shivers at the contact, so I slowly continue dragging my fingertips down her neck, collarbone, the tip of her shoulder, counting all the freckles as I go, until I link our hands together and bring them to my lips. "These hands that clap for me? I want them all over my body. And these eyes? I want them on me at all times."

"Specific," she says breathlessly, her eyes dilating as she stares up at me.

"You've awoken the beast in me," I say, bopping my nose against hers, the scent of cinnamon filling my head.

"Beast, hmm, I always preferred him to the prince anyway." Her arms wrap around my neck as I crash into her, taking everything she's offering. Her nearness is wreaking havoc on my brain chemistry, and I only have tunnel vision when it comes to her. I definitely know I don't deserve her, but I sure as hell can't give her up when she's a lifeline I desperately seek out.

Needing to have her closer somehow, I dip my hands under the skirt of her dress and grasp her ass as our bodies press against one another. It doesn't seem like enough. I want more. I need to be so close to her, I'm practically under her skin. It's probably not healthy to think that way, but she's consuming me.

Twenty years of knowing Quinn, and it feels like I'm only just seeing her.

Breaking the kiss, I squeeze her ass again, breathing heavily as I look at her full swollen lips. Desire spiking my already heated blood. "Do you have any idea how hard it is to catch a ball while you shake your perfect ass on the sidelines?"

"Worried you don't have the skills, Cooper?" she taunts, the nerves suddenly disappeared.

"Oh, I've got the skills, Queenie, and I can't fucking wait to show you."

"So much talking." She presses her lips against mine. "Too much talking."

Backing her up against the wall next to the row of lockers, I fuse our lips together and devour her with a hunger that I've never felt before. Lifting her hips, I encourage her to wrap her legs around me, and as soon as she does, I lose my mind. Her hands paw at my shirt buttons, lips on mine as she rolls against me. "Miles," she breathes, pushing my shirt open and kissing my collarbone and neck, leaving a scorching trail of kisses, ones that

I want to immortalize on my skin like the rest of the ink there.

I'm dizzy from all the blood pumping around my body at warp speed. Dizzy with having her wrapped around me, needing me, showing me how badly she wants me. Yet somehow, in the midst of her touch and kisses, I remind myself that she's worth more. "Wait, wait, wait," I say, pulling her back up to my face. "Hold up, let me think." Because, right now, the only thing in control is south of my waistband.

"I don't want to wait, Miles. You are what I want." She kisses my jaw again, and I bite back a groan.

"I want you too, but Queenie..." I stop her and pull her face to mine until our noses touch. "You're worth more than a quick fuck in the locker room. I want to enjoy you and take my damn time getting to know every single freckled inch of you."

She whimpers.

She fucking whimpers.

And it takes everything in me not to fold, but she does deserve more. She deserves to be worshipped like the Queen she is.

"Okay, you're right. You're right." She kisses me softly, as though I'm the most fragile thing in her world and something deeper inside me shifts. I definitely feel all the things for her. All the big, scary things that I've never felt for anyone else before. And then, as I'm debating how my world suddenly revolves around her, she slides down my body slowly, eyes locked on mine and keeps moving lower and lower until she's sunk to her knees before me.

"Jesus, Queenie, baby, what are you doing?" I ask, struggling to inhale at the sight.

"I want to do this for you." She looks up at me from under her lashes. "I want to suck your cock."

"You can't say shit like that," I groan, barely holding on to my sanity.

"Please? I've been thinking about it."

"You have?" I manage, half choking at the imagery that particular admission brings. Does she think about doing it when she gets herself off? Jesus, I can't cope. I think I'm about to implode, just as her fingers reach up and trail down my stomach, pausing at my belt buckle.

Nodding, she licks her lips, and seeing the wetness she leaves behind on her bottom lip makes my cock jump in my pants.

"Have you ever…?" I begin, then quickly realize I don't want to know if she has. Why the fuck did my brain go there? But when she shakes her head, euphoria lights up my veins and sparks of fire dance along my skin at the thought of being this girl's first something.

"Please," she begs, her eyes soft, yet full of want and lust. Her fingers move with a slight shake, but the belt undoes in one smooth motion. With a swift flick, my pants button is undone, followed by the sharp, metallic sound of the zipper, loud in the quiet locker room.

Bringing my hand up to her cheek, I caress her skin, completely in awe of her.

She pauses just as she moves her fingertips to brush over the band of my boxers. I thread my hand into her hair to pull out the bow, watching the strands unravel over her shoulders, still gripping just enough in silent encouragement. And then she pushes the material down, freeing my aching cock.

"Jesus," she whispers, coming face to face with me for the first time. The wideness of her eyes and the intrigue glistening in them too makes me feel invincible.

"You know that look on your face does wonders for my ego."

"The eggplant emoji is supposed to be a euphemism, not a real thing."

"Is this the part where I'm supposed to say it'll fit?"

The noise that leaves her mouth is a mixture of snort and laugh. "I'm not afraid of your above average dick."

"Very above average," I correct, gripping myself and stroking once, twice, three times to take away the edge I'm already teetering on.

"Overachiever," she mutters playfully, and then I watch with rapt attention as she brings her hand up to replace mine and her perfectly pink tongue sneaks out and licks the tip. I almost lose my shit right there and then.

"Holy shit," I curse. Her mouth opens, and her heat surrounds me, all of me, taking me to the back of her throat in one swift motion. "Ooh, holy shit," I repeat, because I really am about to lose it. I bow forward, but stop myself by holding on to the wall. The coolness of the stone wall helps me refocus for about half a second before she's dragging her mouth back to the tip.

Looking down, as her head bobs and her hand works the base of me, I feel a growl building in my throat at the sight. It's sloppy, and lacking in finesse, but she makes up for it with enthusiasm and the ability to take me so deeply that my toes curl. This is fucking Quinn Dawson, the girl next door, the girl who bakes cookies and colors within the lines. And now she's giving me the best blow job of my life.

"Fuuuuuuck," I hiss, my hips pushing forward as my grip tightens in her hair. The idea that I'm about to corrupt this innocent girl makes me feel like I'm spiraling out of control.

Heat builds down my spine as she moves faster, gripping harder, and I can barely catch my breath.

"Oh, shit. I'm gonna, you need to—"

I'm cut off by her pushing me all the way to the back of her throat with a determined look, and then I lose it, coming harder than I ever have, my muscles locking and jaw slack as she watches me fall apart for her.

She sucks me once more, eyes still locked on mine beneath me as she slowly pulls away, her tongue lingering on the head of my sensitive cock and licking every last drop. With a hiss, I haul her up as she brushes her thumb over the corner of her swollen lips, and I crash my mouth to hers, tasting myself on her sweet tongue. "You're incredible," I murmur against her mouth. "I can't wait until I can taste you."

Her sharp inhale and the wild look in her eyes tell me she can't wait for that too.

"Is it really happening?" Hudson whispers.

"Maybe it's a mirage, or maybe we're all hallucinating." Jay snickers.

"Get fucked, all of you. I'm here, okay? It's not a big deal." Miles pouts, which is one of my favorite things he does because he gets this little dimple in the middle of his chin when he pushes his bottom lip out. It's adorable.

"Listen, we just never thought we'd see the day when Miles Cooper, the man who is too good for sparkly tape, would get his own scrapbook."

He sighs, waving his hand dismissively. "Like I said, it's no big deal, so stop making it one."

"It *is* a big deal. I'm not about to share my favorite tape or glitter pens with you," Hudson protests, holding his prized materials close.

"Relax, he'll pick his own," I soothe, then turn my head to Miles. "Think of colors that match and might complement each other and we'll get you started."

"Or you can go full on Barbie like Hudson and just use pink," Seb muses, lacking his usual lap companion who had to miss today's session in favor of practicing a new piece on her violin.

"There is nothing wrong with pink!" Hudson cries.

"I'm not great with color palettes," Miles says, ignoring Hudson as he mutters to Seb about the shades of pink he uses. Seb rolls his eyes and bats the back of his head, mumbling something about being a princess.

"You don't have to be. Here, let me show you." I reach for the Sharpie pastel pens, and just as I do, I graze over his knee, and my body feels like it's been electrocuted. Zap, zing, and bam, everything comes to life. Each nerve ending sings for his touch. Every single cell in my body wants him, and it feels impossible to hide. Suddenly, in my mind, I'm back on my knees for him again, doing exactly what we shouldn't have done in the locker room. I'm also incredibly aware that we're surrounded by our friends and my brother, which is why I'm too scared to glance at Miles. If he's looking at me the way I think he might be looking at me, then I'll combust on the spot.

Clearing my throat, I take a second before picking up the pens with shaky hands.

"Okay, so see how all these colors are lighter and most of them complement each other because of the shade they are?" I pick out two colors. "Like, how mint and lilac go well together." Then I reach for the light yellow. "And when you add in another color, it just makes each one stand out more."

He scratches the back of his neck, staring at the pens. "I, uh, you just said a bunch of stuff that doesn't mean a lot to me."

Thinking of a different approach, I set the pens down. "What's your favorite color?"

"Green," he replies without missing a beat and holds my eye contact with a phenomenal amount of intensity.

"Light green or dark green?" I manage to force out, looking away, unable to maintain eye contact. I tell myself it's not to arouse suspicion, but in reality, it's because when he looks at me, I kinda wanna jump his bones. And whatever we're doing isn't public knowledge so I can't do that. *But if you just told people, you could.* The thought doesn't seem as intimidating as it has previously, but I still want to selfishly hold on to Miles for myself a little longer. I've spent my whole life sharing him and now he's mine.

"Look at me again," he says quietly as our friends busy themselves around us. I glance up, and he studies me, well my eyes, for a long time. "Hm, yeah, more of a light green."

Air evaporates from the room rapidly because he's looking at me. My eyes. His favorite color belongs to me.

I fumble, my fingers forgetting how to hold an object as I drop the pastel mint green sharpie. Miles leans over, plucking it from between my legs on the ground.

"Thanks." He winks, and my tongue feels like it's too big for my mouth. Can I even swallow at this point? Who knows?

I manage to nod, though it feels like my head is on a loose hinge, bobbing too much and not enough at the same time. Miles is still leaning close, his scent—a mix of clean laundry and something slightly woodsy—it's familiar and completely enveloping me. It's borderline suffocating, but in a way that makes me want to take a deeper breath, to pull more of him into my lungs.

He chuckles, low and easy, as if he can sense my nervousness and finds it amusing, maybe even endearing. "You okay?" he asks, his voice soft with a hint of teasing

"I'm good," I lie because, truthfully, I feel like I'm on fire and the main source of heat is coming from the apples of my cheeks. I'm probably lit up like a beacon. Glancing around, thankfully no one is paying attention to me.

"Liar," he whispers. "Relax, you're blushing."

Yeah, I freaking know.

I pick up a few of my favorite stickers and place them loosely on the page I'm working on. It's a new page, a blank one, and I need the distraction.

"So do we get to share what we've done at the end of each session here?" he asks, gesturing to my scrapbook.

Panic breaks out a light sweat on my brow. He absolutely, categorically, cannot see my scrapbook. It's filled with pieces of him, us, our childhood and our friendship, but not in a platonic way at all. Anyone with eyes can see I'm in love with him if they saw my book. "We, uh, keep them personal, since secrets and all kinds of things can be in there," I tell him, hoping my voice isn't as shaky as I feel.

The panic subsides when he nods, frowning at his first page. "So, will you help me with my first page? Then I swear I'll leave you alone."

"I don't want you to leave me alone." The words slip out before I can rein them back in. "I mean, of course I can help you."

I quickly busy my hands, ignoring the heat clawing its way around my body. Picking out stickers, tape, and some other colors that will complement the green, I gather them all and thrust the pile into his hands.

He takes it all from me, but I can't meet his eyes, too scared that he'll see the desperation I've spent so long hiding from him. I know we're getting closer, a heck of a lot closer, but I'm still very much in love with him, and I'm not ready for him to see that yet.

"Have you ever seen Miles scrapbook before, Quinn?" Jay asks.

I shake my head, racking my brain. "No, and he used to suck at drawing when we were kids."

"Hey!" Miles protests, poking my side.

"What? It's true. But at least you were always good at sports."

"I knew it!" Hudson exclaims. "He can't be good at everything."

"I am, though," Miles counters, ripping some pale-yellow tape with his teeth, and he's never looked sexier.

"You're mediocre at best. I guarantee it." Hudson laughs as he swirls a pink pen between his fingers.

"Wanna bet?"

Hudson leans forward and surveys Miles's face. "Yeah, I do. Fifty bucks says my scrapbook is better than yours by the end of the year."

"Pffff," he huffs. "Easy."

"No asking Quinn for tips either. That's cheating."

Miles side glances at me, then winks. "Fine, no cheating. I'll still kick your ass."

"Big talk for a guy who has zero artistic talent, according to our scrapbook club leader."

"She doesn't realize how many talents I have," Miles replies suggestively, and it makes me choke on absolutely nothing. To make matters worse, my brother takes that opportunity to look up and frown at me.

"You okay, Quinn?" Seb asks.

Clearing my throat, I smile, eyes watery. "I'm good, I have this cough that's more of a tickle, really, but it's super annoying. I think one of the girls on the squad has it too. I probably got it from her. Maybe I'll get some cough syrup later, or maybe some cough drops. Yeah, I'll go…later." I nod awkwardly, cheeks still warm from my ramble. My brother just replies with a single hum and goes back to his scrapbook. I know he's working on something for Indie, so he's been quiet today, focused, which is good for me. Great for me, because he isn't paying attention.

I can't look at Miles, it'd be too obvious right now.

Jay catches my eye, though, as he shakes his head. "I'm going to grab some water. You look like you need one too, Quinn, come with me?" he asks before getting up and walking away.

I stand and follow him over to the small kitchen area as he pulls the fridge open, passes me a water, and narrows his eyes at me.

"What?" I squeak, even though I know what.

"Nothing," he says, opening his water, twisting the cap slowly, as though he's waiting for me to crack and tell him something. I open mine too and tip the cool liquid into my mouth, and when I look back, he's still watching me.

"Seriously, what?"

Briefly flicking his eyes to the other side of the room, he looks back to me. "So, is it a secret?"

I absently squeeze the water bottle in my hands. "Is what a secret?"

"Sério?" *Really?* he says in his native tongue.

My eyes widen, knowing I'm going to have to come clean to one more person. "Okay, okay," I begin, putting my bottle on the counter beside him. "You have to promise not to say anything."

He makes a cross over his heart. "So, you and Miles?"

"Yeah, for a little while now. But you can't tell Seb." I rush out. "I'm not ready to…"

"Share your guy?"

I nod. "Is that bad of me?"

His shoulder lifts. "I won't say anything; I know how close you all are. Seb is distracted with Indie most of the time, but it doesn't take a genius to figure it out the way you were looking at each other over there."

I groan. "I know. I'll tell him when the time is right."

Jay snickers but doesn't push and starts walking back to our friends. I wait for a few seconds to deep breathe because I know he's right and I will tell Seb…soon.

Taking my spot again, Miles immediately leans toward me.

"Don't forget about our movie night later," he says, a smile playing on his lips.

Begging my body to chill out and be cool, I look up at him. "I haven't forgotten," I reply, trying to keep my voice steady despite the flutter in my chest. "What are the options tonight?"

He tilts his head, pretending to think hard. "I was thinking something scary."

"Is that a private screening or…?" Jay teases, and I raise my eyebrow at him.

"Just our regular movie night," Miles says casually, but the fact he said "our" gives me goosebumps. Ours, as in no one else is invited. Ours, as in me and him. And granted, it's always been that way, but now there's a hint of something more in his tone that makes my heart buck wildly.

"You'll never get an invite to their precious movie nights," Seb says, lifting his head from his book. "They've always done this, except for our freshman year when Quinn wasn't here. But it's just their thing."

I wait to see if he sounds as though he suspects anything, but I realize everything Miles and I do is normal for him. Because we've all grown up together, it doesn't matter if he hugs me or makes me laugh, it's normal for us.

"Are we sure they aren't just having sex?" Hudson's words hit like a bomb, and every muscle in my body tenses. My eyes dart to Miles, who's already looking at me, his expression unreadable but his jaw clenched. Is he freaking out like I am? Or is he annoyed? I honestly can't tell. I open my mouth to say something—anything—but nothing comes out. My mind races, trying to figure out if everyone's figured us out, or if Hudson's just being his usual loud, clueless self.

"Dude!" Seb shouts, turning to us with a look of exasperation. "Tell him that's not happening! He just doesn't get it."

Neither do you. He has no idea how long I've been in love with his best friend, or how many times we've secretly kissed...and stuff over the past few weeks. Guilt gnaws at me. I almost want to blurt it out. Almost.

Miles clears his throat, stepping in, and I breathe a sigh of relief. "Look, Seb's right. Movie nights are our thing, alright? After my mom...well, Quinn used to come over with popcorn and gummy worms to distract me, to keep me company. We've watched every terrible romantic comedy out there, but it's kind of our thing. Always has been."

Jay raises an eyebrow, while Hudson looks suspiciously between the two of us. "Just movies, huh?" he asks.

Miles nods, trying to keep it casual. "Just movies. We've been doing it for years."

"Alright, alright," Hudson finally says, throwing his hands up in mock surrender. "I get it. Movie night is sacred."

I let out a small breath that was stuck in my throat, grateful that we weren't outed yet. But before I can fully relax, Hudson shoots us a sly grin. "But you know, if you're ever in the mood to invite a third wheel, I'm just saying—I make a mean batch of nachos."

Miles chuckles and shakes his head. "I don't know if you're serious or trying to make this sexual."

Hudson shrugs. "Probably both."

As everyone goes back to their own tasks, the tension eases, and I glance at Miles. He catches my eye and gives me a small, reassuring smile, but I still feel on edge. I think it's probably about time we talked about when we tell my brother.

CHAPTER THIRTY-FOUR

Miles

"You've been here before," I say, linking my hand with Quinn's as we round the corner to my dorm.

"Yeah, but that was *before*." She looks around as though she expects her brother to leap out of the bushes, despite the fact we left him back at her dorm, waiting for Indie, after scrapbook club.

"Before what?" I feign innocence, when I know exactly what before she's talking about. Before I kissed her. Before she and I started messing around. Before our friendship became something much more than I thought it would ever be. Just before.

"Before our movie nights had the potential to become X-rated," she whispers as we climb the stairs, and I have to hold back a barking laugh.

"X-rated, Queenie? Is that what's happening tonight?" I tease.

Shrugging, she winks at me. "Play your cards right and maybe."

Jesus, all the blood just shot down to my groin. This girl can absolutely evoke the biggest reactions from my body, and she doesn't even realize how beautiful and sexy she is.

"I'm crap at card games," I say, leaning closer as we reach my dorm. "But I'm really good at other things, you know, sexy things. So maybe we should start there instead?" Wiggling my eyebrow, I swipe my keycard at the door.

As we step into the dimly lit hallway, the sounds of other students echoing faintly in the background, and I can tell she's on edge. She has been since the scrapbook club.

"Jay knows," she blurts, as we round the corner to my room.

I flick my eyes down to her, wondering what she's feeling. "He figured it out?"

She nods. "Pretty much." Pausing, she looks down at her shoes. "I want to tell my brother, but I..." Her eyes meet mine hesitantly. "I like having you to myself."

Stopping in the hallway, I know I'm playing with fire here out in the open, testing to see how far she'll go before she panics. I pull her into me, her head immediately tilting to look up at me. Those green eyes glisten against the luminescent lights above us. "I'm ready when you are. I don't love lying to my best friend, but I can't deny that I'm a little scared too. Plus, I don't hate all this sneaking around. It is kind of hot."

She smiles, before I press a kiss to her forehead, not wanting to push her much more. Holding her this close is a big deal anyway, as any of my teammates could be out here.

I'm not lying when I say I'm scared. Seb jokes about none of us in the group being good enough for her, but has he really thought that through? Does he mean that? Would he really feel so badly that me, the guy who's known and protected her most of her life, would want her like I do?

"Maybe Seb will just figure it out like Jay did," she says casually as head up the stairwell.

Then, I remember the conversation I had with Jay and a very unhelpful Hudson a while back, knowing that probably tipped him off. "I, maybe, sort of, spoke to Jay about this girl I liked a while back."

"A girl?" she asks, stumbling up the last step.

She rights herself, getting to the top step, and I grasp her wrist, stopping her from going further, pulling her back to my front. "It was you. I was talking about you. I didn't know how to express everything. I know I'm still not very good at it." Walking us forward, I feel her body relax in my arms, and I relax too. "I don't think Jay will out us. So, when we're ready to say something, it should be to your brother first."

She hums her agreement.

I reach out and softly tuck a strand of hair behind her ear, letting my hand linger near her cheek. Taking a small step closer, our bodies almost touching, I meet her gaze with a steady, reassuring look. "I'm ready when you are, Queenie." I repeat my words from earlier, meaning every syllable.

We reach my room, and she pauses before opening the door. "You know, we could always skip the movie," she suggests, her voice sweet and sultry.

"And miss out on another terrible rom-com, or have you scared and jumping into my lap with a horror film? Not a chance," I say, dipping my head to kiss her jaw quickly as I push the keycard again to my door, walking her backward into my room.

Smiling, I push the door open and motion for her to enter. She walks over to my bed, flopping down with a familiarity that makes my chest tighten. She's wearing her cargo pants and plain cropped t-shirt that she looks so damn good in. What am I saying? Quinn looks good in everything. She always has.

"I may have brought our favorites. Even if we don't eat them tonight, I'll leave them here for next time." She opens her tote bag on the ground and pulls out popcorn and gummy worms. Watching her open the candy, she offers the first one to me, and I don't even think before I dive in, capturing it with my mouth, my tongue brushing against her fingers ever-so-slightly. Her breath hitches, eyes widening just for a second.

"Who said anything about not eating them tonight?" I hum. Licking my lips, I let the sweet raspberry flavor envelop my tongue. "Mm, so sweet. Pick a movie, Queenie," I say, passing her the remote.

She chuckles as she leans back on the pillows, legs crossed, the hem of her t-shirt riding up higher, exposing that sliver of skin. She scrolls through the streaming options, her focus seemingly on the screen, but I can tell by the way her fingers hover over the buttons that her mind is elsewhere too. After a few seconds, she lands on some cheesy rom-com, that I'm sure we've watched before, but I can't help but chuckle. "I thought we were going scary movie tonight?" I tease, jumping on the bed next to her, leaning in a little closer, so close that our shoulders brush, sending a jolt through me.

"You said I could pick," she shoots back, but there's a softness in her voice that makes my heart skip a beat.

"Fair enough." I settle back against the pillows, but my hand lingers near hers, the temptation to close the distance between us almost unbearable.

My phone buzzes in my pocket, and pulling it out, I see a message from my dad.

Dad

> I need to talk to you, Miles. I'm tired of your excuses. I need to discuss some things with you, and I'm done waiting.

My throat dries like I've swallowed sawdust. I don't want to deal with him. I've managed to ignore him for a while now, brushing him off with the fact that we've got finals coming up and I've been playing well. But I know I'll have to figure all this out soon before it blows up in my face. Just not tonight. Tonight, I need my girl. I turn my phone off and push it away.

"Everything okay?" Quinn asks, staring at my discarded phone.

"Yeah. I don't want distractions tonight," I say, grabbing the remote and pressing play.

As the movie starts, the room falls into a comfortable silence, the flickering light from the screen casting shadows across her face. I can't focus on the movie at all—my mind is entirely consumed by the feel of her beside me, the soft, sweet scent of her perfume, the way her breath hitches just slightly whenever I move a little closer.

Minutes tick by, and I can feel her stealing glances at me, just as I'm doing the same. Every accidental brush of our arms, every time our legs bump against each other, makes my blood rush through me, making it harder and harder to pretend I'm watching the movie.

Finally, I can't take it anymore. "Quinn," I murmur, turning to face her fully, my voice barely above a whisper.

She looks at me, eyes wide and filled with the same anticipation that's been building inside me all night. "Yeah?" she replies, almost breathless.

I lean in to close the space between us as my heart pounds harder. "There's something I've been wanting to do all night," I say, my gaze flicking to her lips.

She doesn't pull away. Instead, she leans in too, her eyes gleaming with anticipation, as if she's been waiting for this moment just as much as I have. "Then do it," she whispers, and that's all the encouragement I need.

I close the gap, my lips brushing hers in a tentative kiss, testing the waters. The moment we connect, it's like a floodgate opens—the kiss deepens, our bodies moving closer together as if we can't stand to be apart for even a second longer. Her hand slides up to the back of my neck, pulling me in, and I respond by wrapping an arm around her waist, drawing her into my lap.

The kiss is slow and deliberate, every movement fueled by the need building between us. I can taste the faint sweetness of the gummy worms we shared earlier, and it makes me smile against her lips.

She pulls back slightly, just enough to speak, her voice husky and filled with need. "What about the movie?" she asks, but there's no real concern in her tone.

"Screw the movie," I murmur. Capturing her lips again, this time, there's no hesitation, no holding back.

She climbs into my lap, her hands sliding under my hoodie,

peeling it over my head, and the feel of her warm skin against mine sends a shiver down my spine. We're crossing lines we've blurred for weeks now, but it feels right—like this is exactly where we're meant to be.

Her center brushes against my length, and I can't help the low groan that escapes me. My hands find their way to her waist, gripping her firmly as I pull her even closer, needing more of her, needing *all* of her. Her fingers dig into my shoulders, and she responds with equal intensity, her kisses growing more urgent, more desperate.

When we finally break apart, we're both breathing heavily, our foreheads pressed together as we try to catch our breath. Her eyes are half-lidded, her lips swollen from our kisses, and I've never seen her look more beautiful. I reach up, tucking a stray strand of hair behind her ear, and she leans into my touch, her eyes closing just for a moment as she breathes in deeply. "I like it when you do that."

I can't help but leave my hand against her skin, reveling in the fact she likes something I do. She leans in, kissing me again, softer this time. It's as if we're finally acknowledging everything, letting it all spill out in the way our lips move together, the way our hands explore each other's bodies.

As the kiss deepens once more, I turn us so that she's lying back on the bed, and I'm hovering over her, propped up on my elbows. Her hands slide up to tangle in my hair, and I can feel the way her body responds to mine, arching up to meet me, her breath hitching every time I touch her.

The shirt she's wearing has ridden up, exposing the more of her smooth skin, and I can't resist the urge to kiss my way down her neck, across her collarbone, moving lower still. The sound she makes—a gentle, breathy moan—nearly undoes me, and I have to take a second to gather myself before carrying on.

My lips brush against the edge of her hoodie, and she lets out a shuddering breath, her hands tightening in my hair. "Miles..." she whispers. The sound of my name on her lips sends a thrill through me every single time.

"Yeah?" I murmur against her skin, trailing kisses along her stomach, feeling the way her muscles tense beneath my touch.

"I want—" She cuts herself off with a gasp as I kiss just below her navel, her fingers digging into my shoulders, as if she's trying to ground herself.

"What do you want, Quinn?" I ask, my voice low and rough with desire as I slowly make my way back up to her, capturing her lips in another searing kiss.

Her eyes open, locking onto mine, and there's something exposed in her gaze that makes my heart squeeze. "I want you," she whispers, her voice barely audible, but there's no mistaking the honesty behind it. "I want all of you."

The words hit me like a punch to the gut, and for a moment, all I can do is stare at her, my heart thundering. I can see the same emotions mirrored in her eyes—desire, need, and something deeper, something that's been there all along, but that we've both been too afraid to acknowledge.

"I'm yours," I whisper. "All of me, Quinn. I'm all yours."

Her breath catches at my admission, and she pulls me down into another kiss, her lips moving against mine with a newfound urgency. The intensity between us ramps up, and I feel like I'm drowning in her—in the taste of her lips, the feel of her body beneath mine, the way her hands roam over my back, pulling me closer.

My hands slide under her shirt, skimming over her sides, feeling the warmth of her skin against mine. I push the fabric up, exposing more of her, and she arches her back, helping me slip it off. The sight of her, almost bare and vulnerable beneath me, takes my breath away, and I pause for a moment, just taking her in.

"You're so beautiful," I murmur, my voice thick with emotion, and she blushes, a shy smile spreading across her face.

Her fingers trace over my chest, over the tattoos that decorate my skin. I know her favorites are on my left arm, the half royal flush of cards. She spends the most time brushing her fingers over the Queen of Hearts.

Slowly moving down to the waistband of my sweats, she runs her finger inside the edge, grazing against my skin, making my body respond in the most primal way.

But then she pauses, and I see the decision cross her face as she shifts upright to pull my sweats and boxers down, freeing me from the material.

As soon as her hand wraps around me, I feel heat shoot down my spine and settle in my balls. The sensation overtaking me with such a force, I thrust into her hand unintentionally. My thighs tense as I realize what I'm doing, stopping myself. "Sorry, that just felt so fucking good."

She grins and squeezes me once more, and I groan. "Queenie, baby, please don't tease me. I'm a strong man, but right now, I feel weak, and I could give in to this feeling so easily."

"Maybe I want you to give in," she purrs, and how the hell I keep it together I'll never know.

"If I give in, I don't think I'll ever stop," I say, running my hand down her shoulder, pushing the strap of her lace bra down. Her entire body shudders as her mouth opens on a gasp.

"Then don't," she pleads, so I use my other hand to push down the opposite strap. As the material falls away, she shrugs her shoulders, and I unhook the bra from behind, revealing her perfect breasts. She gently moves her hand over me again, and I feel my hips flex from the sight of her, the feel of her palm against my sensitive skin. I'm unraveling at an alarming rate around this girl.

"Miles?" she says, bringing my focus back to her face.

"Yeah, Queenie?"

"I want you inside of me."

My heart pounds so hard I can feel it in my throat. Every muscle in my body tightens, desire roaring in my veins, but I force myself to stay still, to give her the space to change her mind, even though the thought of pulling away feels impossible. The need to claim her, to make her mine in every way, is overwhelming—almost suffocating—but I can't lose control, not yet.

"I want that too. Are you sure?" I breathe out, trying to hold on by a thread. "Because once I've been inside you, once I've tasted you, marked you, and made you come, you belong to me only."

"I think..." She pauses, her voice so quiet and breathless I almost don't hear her. "I think I've always belonged to you."

Something inside me snaps. Maybe that's exactly what I needed to hear. I bite back a groan at the idea of being with her as she unbuttons her pants and, suddenly, I've lost all sense of slow and soft. I felt every single word she just whispered to me, the declaration looping around my heart and squeezing tightly. I need to show her how much it means to me.

She lifts her hips, dragging her pants down her toned legs,

and I reach for her panties, looking in her eyes for confirmation I can do what I want to do. Giving me a subtle nod, she lies back completely as I rid her of her clothes.

The sight knocks the wind from my lungs. Quinn bare and on my bed is not an image I'll ever forget. Freckles scatter her soft skin, too many to count, and most are barely visible, but seeing her splayed out on my bed, the contrast of my navy sheets against her pale skin, I feel like I can see constellations decorating her complexion.

My cock nestles at her entrance, encompassed with her heat. Dragging myself over her, I feel her wetness coat me, making me slip up to her clit. "Oh my god," she gasps, meeting my thrusts. "Miles, now. Please."

The tip of me rests exactly where I want to be, and for a second, I forget my head. "Condom," I force out, moving backward slightly.

Quinn's eyes widen for a second, but she doesn't move. "Go," she tells me with urgency, eyes never wavering from mine.

I quickly move, finding the foil packet in my bedside drawer, ripping it open and sheathing myself in record time.

Our eyes connect once more as the frantic need makes way for something else I'm feeling for her. Something that goes beyond all the physical stuff we've been doing. "You ready?"

"For your above average dick?"

I chuckle at her sass, and she laughs, pulling my face down to hers. "I'm ready."

And with one slow, purposeful movement, I'm fully inside of her, and I know in this moment I belong to her too.

CHAPTER THIRTY-FIVE

Quinn

OH MY GOD, OH my god. Oh my god.

I'm having sex with Miles.

Earlier this year, I'd resigned myself to the idea of loving him always from afar and now we couldn't be closer. Skin to skin. Connected in the most intimate way.

"Jesus, Quinn. You feel..." He pushes the words out but doesn't finish his sentence. Instead, he exhales a breath. "I'm going to move, you good?"

I nod, because I need him to move too. As he inches out and pushes back in, the initial burn becomes something much more pleasurable, intense, and makes my back arch. He does it again, and I lift my hips to meet his movements, giving me more opportunity to open my legs farther for him.

The groan that leaves his mouth is the most intoxicating sound I've ever heard, and then he says, "I'm going to lift one of your legs, okay?"

"Yes," I say on an exhale. As he lifts my leg, he moves deeper inside of me, and my entire body comes to life. I'm buzzing with electricity, raw, exposed wires crossing over each other, igniting sparks and flames. "Oh god. Oh god."

He hums a little laugh above me, my leg still wrapped around his tattooed forearm, and the image alone is too much, let alone the sensation. "Hmm, that's it, that's what I wanted. Fuck," he says, pumping into me. "You're perfect for me."

Over and over, he kisses me and makes my body sing for him in ways no one else has. My skin tingles, belly tightening as the impending orgasm whispers around me.

"Touch your clit for me, baby. Loosen up a bit, or I'm going to come real fast."

My hand moves with his command, finding my clit. I apply enough pressure to spur on my orgasm. "Mmm," I moan as he leans down, intensifying the position even more for a second as he sucks my nipple into his mouth. "More. More," I pant like a person possessed. Maybe I am, maybe I've fully moved into the world of delirium because I feel like I'm having some kind of out-of-body experience here.

"More?" he rasps, before pulling out completely and slamming back inside me, hitting a place no one ever has before, and I cry out in pleasure.

My body trembles as he pulls back again. "Miles, god, don't stop," I beg. That sweet spot inside unfurls a new wave of lust into my body as my nails dig into the bed beneath us, my eyes squeezed closed.

"Eyes, Queenie. On me. Always," he demands, and they spring open. His jaw slackens as he moves deeper again, before he hisses against his teeth.

His movements become faster, and he stutters a few times, cursing out loud diving down against my neck as he peppers kisses all over my skin.

My orgasm sneaks up on me. One minute, it's a simmering heat, and then as soon as he thrusts into me and lightly bites on my neck, I'm done for. "I'm...I'm...Oh god, Miles, Miles," I moan, as everything in my body coils tight and explodes into a gazillion stars that blur my vision. He looks down at me, eyes locked on my face as I come, taking in every single moment of this. It feels like I'm floating, weightless, and somehow also completely and utterly exhausted in the best way.

"Fuck, Quinn, I'm gonna—" He doesn't finish, but the low groan he lets out is the sexiest sound I've ever heard as he pistons into me, chasing his release too.

When he's still inside me, my hands gripping his on my one leg hitched up and the other wrapped around him, I still feel the tremors from my release too as he pulses inside me.

I've never had sex that felt so connected. I've never had an orgasm that fast either. He's ruined my heart and now my body belongs to him too. There's no coming back from this, I can feel it in my bones.

He drops his head into the crook of my neck and the feel of his hot breath skating over my skin sends another ripple of heat throughout my body. Humming, he presses a kiss to my collarbone. The gesture is so soft and sweet, and he's kissed me there before, but I'm feeling everything so strongly, as though all the emotions I've locked down for years and years of my life are bubbling just beneath the surface. He's here with me in way I never thought we would be, and it's like a dream. I run my fingers down his biceps, over the muscles that he works so hard for, over his broad shoulders, and I memorize the feel of his weight on top of me, the way he feels inside me. It's too much and not enough at the same time.

Lifting his weight off me, my entire existence begs him to come back, but I don't. The way his brown eyes rake over my face, as though he's looking for something, makes me smile up at him and his messed-up hair. "You're incredible, Quinn. I…" He stops and sucks in a sharp breath. "I don't think you realize how lucky I am to have you."

His words. God, they strike me like a shot to the heart. "I'm the lucky one." *Because I love you.* It didn't matter how many nights we spent together growing up, or how much time I'd mentally begged him to kiss me. I've lost count the number of nights wishing that we would someday take the next step, that he would be my first, that he would be my only. When that didn't happen, I grieved for that, for him, for me because I knew that loving him would be my biggest downfall. Yet here I am, getting everything I thought I'd never have. Getting the one person my heart beats for.

He doesn't argue with that. Instead, he lightly presses a kiss to the tip of my nose and pulls out of me.

I watch him as he discards the condom, and my mind reels from what we've just done. When he settles back into his bed, he taps his chest for me to rest my head. As soon as I feel the steady thrum of his heart beneath my ear, the rest of the world fades away.

The softness of his lips kiss the top of my head, feeling a contentment I've never known before.

"I could get used to this," he whispers, his voice sleepy but sated.

"Me too," I reply, wrapping my arms around him and holding him close.

His fingers trace lazy patterns on my back, and I can feel his heartbeat gradually slowing, syncing with mine. "It scares me a little," he admits after a moment, his voice so quiet I almost don't hear him.

I tense up, unsure of what he means. Tilting my head up to look at him, my eyes search his. "Scares you?"

"How right this feels." He meets my gaze, his expression serious now. "I feel things for you, Quinn, and I don't know where they've come from, because we've only ever been friends, but they're there. Feelings. Big ones and..." He pauses for a second, and I realize I'm not breathing either. "I want to feel them. I think I've loved you across lifetimes, Quinn, and I don't want to stop now."

The world seems to tilt on its axis as his confession sinks in. I want to speak, to tell him everything that's been buried for so long, but all I can do is stare at him, wide-eyed and stunned. I could confess that he's the love of my life, but the words are stuck in my throat, and selfishly I don't want to ruin how special his confession is either.

My voice is barely a whisper when I finally manage to speak. "Don't ever stop, Miles."

He doesn't reply, just leans in and kisses me softly, his lips warm and reassuring. I sink into it, feeling the weight of everything melt away as he pulls me closer. When we part, his arms are still around me, and without saying a word, we curl up together, my head on his chest, his heartbeat steady beneath me. Safe and content, I close my eyes, and before long, we fall asleep, tangled up in each other.

CHAPTER THIRTY-SIX

Miles

THE ROOM IS SOFTLY lit by the morning sun, its golden rays filtering through the thin curtains and casting a gentle glow over everything. It feels like the world outside has paused, holding its breath just for us.

This morning feels like a dream. With her warm body nestled on my chest, legs intertwined under the sheets, her red hair splayed out across my arm and pillow. I want to stay here for the whole day. Something shifted in me last night. It felt real and I don't know if I've ever felt things like that before for anyone.

I trail my fingertips over the soft skin of her arm hugging my stomach, and she begins to stir, her body seeking more of mine even in sleep. As I press a soft kiss to the top of her head, she immediately opens her eyes, snapping her head to look up at me. "Morning, Queenie."

"Morning," she says, sleep lacing her voice. "What time is it?"

"Time for us to snooze a little longer." I pull her body into mine, despite her already being so close. "Mmm, I like this."

She sighs softly, resting against me for a moment before reluctantly untangling herself from my embrace.

"No, don't go," I whine, grabbing for her.

"I'll be right back." Her happiness radiates from her as she stretches, arms reaching up over her head, showing me her perfect body, before she grabs one of my shirts, slips it over her head, and the sight of her as she walks away wearing my clothes makes my chest rumble with possession. I want to follow her, claim her, all over again, but I don't I just watch as she goes into the bathroom.

I power up my phone, knowing there will probably be a hundred messages from the fallout of it being off all night. As soon as the screen comes to life, it rings, and I see Dad's name on the screen. I know I can't keep avoiding him, as much as I want to, so I take a deep breath and answer.

"Hey, Dad," I say, trying to keep my voice normal.

"Finally decided to pick up?" he snaps. There's no warmth in his voice, only irritation. Great, this is going to go well.

"Yeah, I've been busy," I reply, struggling to keep my tone even.

"Busy, huh?" he retorts. "It's funny how you always seem to be too busy to talk to me on game days, you know. It's almost like you're deliberately ignoring my calls."

I wince, because he'd dead on the money. "It's not like that. I've got practice and stuff. It's hard to find a good time to talk."

"Hard to find a good time?" he says sharply. "I've been trying to reach you, and all I get is voicemail. You know, it feels like you're making excuses. It's becoming a pattern."

My stomach knots. "Dad, I'm really doing my best here." *You have no idea how hard I'm trying, so back off.*

"Your best?" he sneers. "I watch the games, Miles. I see what's going on. You get one or two decent plays, and suddenly you think you're the best. Well, that attitude won't work in the pros. It's not good enough. How can you expect people to be interested in your draft next year when you can't even be consistent."

His words cut through me, slicing away pieces of me like always. "That's not true. I'm working hard."

"Working hard?" he scoffs. "I see a player who's lost his edge. Maybe you're not cut out for this. Ever think about that?"

My mind goes blank, numbness taking over, and I'm struggling to process his words, because he knows exactly what to say to hurt me. "Dad, that's not fair—"

"Fair?" he interrupts, voice dripping with disdain. "What's fair is me telling you the truth. You're underperforming, and you need to face it before you lose all interest from teams and scouts."

I can barely hold on. His words are like a cold wave crashing over me. It doesn't matter to him that I wouldn't enter the draft until next year. Nothing matters except the fact he's desperate to ruin my happiness. I don't know how to respond, so I just lie. "Dad, I've gotta go." And I hang up before he can respond.

Quinn steps out of the bathroom, her carefree expression faltering the moment she sees me. My chest feels like it's being crushed under an invisible weight, every breath a struggle, shallow and jagged. My vision blurs at the edges, darkening like the walls are closing in. I can't get enough air, my lungs refusing to cooperate as my heart hammers against my ribcage, faster and faster, like it might explode.

"Miles, what's wrong?" Quinn's voice cuts through the haze, distant at first, like she's shouting from the end of a long tunnel. But then she's right in front of me, her eyes wide with worry, taking my phone from my hands. I want to answer, to tell her I'm fine, or that I'm not fine. I want to say anything, but the words are stuck in my throat, tangled up with the panic that's suffocating me.

She doesn't hesitate. She drops to her knees, her movements quick but gentle, her hands reaching for my face. "Hey, hey," she whispers, and her voice is the first thing that feels real, like a lifeline when I'm drowning. Her hands are warm, firm, as they cup my face, her thumbs brushing lightly against my cheekbones rhythmically, and I try to focus on her. Only her.

"Look at me," she says, and I try—god, I try—but my vision is swimming, the room tilting like I might fall off the edge of the world. My heart is still racing, a wild, erratic beat that silences out everything else. "I'm here. I'm not going anywhere." Her voice is steady, solid, and I latch onto it, desperate to pull myself out of the spiral.

There's something in her eyes, something steady and unyielding, that begins to anchor me. Her touch, the gentle pressure of her hands on my face, grounds me, pulling me back from the brink. The walls stop closing in, my breaths start to even out, the crushing weight on my chest easing just a fraction.

The storm inside me doesn't disappear, but it quiets enough that I can hear her again, feel her presence beside me, pulling me out of the darkness. "I'm good," I whisper, my voice breaking.

She releases my face and climbs straight into my lap, pulling me close to her until all I'm breathing is cinnamon. "I know you are."

I don't know how long we stay wrapped in each other, but it feels like a long time. When I finally release my grip around her, she only adjusts her arms, not dropping them completely.

I inhale her one more time, taking strength from her being here. "My dad called," I tell her with the knot tightening in my stomach, and I find myself kneading her hips for comfort. "He...he..."

"It's okay. If you want to write it down, would that help?"

I shake my head, swallowing down my fears. "He said I'm wasting my potential." I continue on a breath. "That all the work I've put in isn't enough, and it'll never be enough. He said... He said I'm letting him down."

Her hand moves to the back of my head, fingers threading through my hair. "You're not letting anyone down," she whispers fiercely. "You're doing your best, and that's all anyone can ask of you."

I want to believe her, but the knot in my stomach tightens, the doubts swirling in my mind. "He doesn't think my best is good enough," I say, and the words taste bitter on my tongue. "He said if I don't step up now, I'll be stuck, and no one's going to take a chance on me. I'll be forgotten."

She pulls back just enough to look me in the eyes, her gaze steady and full of conviction. "You know he's projecting onto you, right? Because he is. That's what happened to him. He lost his chance to keep his job in the pros, so he's pushing you to get what he wanted."

She's right. That's exactly what's happening here. I've known it my whole life.

"It doesn't make what he's doing okay, though. And when you make the pros, it'll be because you have more talent in your pinky finger than he ever did." She flushes with determination as her eyes lock onto mine.

"But what if he's right?" I ask, my voice trembling. "What if I'm not good enough?"

"You are good enough," she says, unwavering.

I nod, trying to let her words sink in, to let them erase the doubts. But it's hard. My dad's voice is still there, echoing in my mind, a constant reminder of the standards I've been trying so desperately to meet.

"I just don't want to fail," I admit. "Not him, not you, not myself."

"You won't," she assures me. "And even if things don't go the way you want, that doesn't mean you've failed. It just means you're finding your own path, in your own time."

I want to believe her. I want there to be a switch that flips in my mind that can block out all the noise and just listen to her, let her ground me and keep my head on straight. But I don't know how to get rid of his cold voice in my mind.

"You want a distraction?" she asks, pulling my face between her hands and keeping me absorbed in her green eyes.

"Yes," I murmur, and before I know it, we're dressed and she's checking her phone.

"Indie says Seb left our dorm, like, three minutes ago to go into town."

She cautiously opens the door as though he might pop out, but when she's satisfied the coast is clear, she drags me out of my dorm. Being the source of sunshine I need.

Chapter Thirty-Seven

Quinn

When we step outside, the cooler air hits me, and I can't help but shiver. The weather's shifted over the last few weeks, and it's clear that fall is in full swing. I'm just starting to feel the chill when Miles reaches behind his neck, whipping off his hoodie and draping it over my shoulders.

"Thanks, I forgot mine, or maybe Indie stole it," I say with a smirk.

"Keep it," he replies, like it's nothing. "I like you in my clothes." Even though it's not one of his hoodies with his number on it—that only comes out for special occasions—it's a CLU warmup hoodie, and I think I might just keep it.

I grin at him, boldly taking his hand and pulling him toward the studio where we usually have our yoga class, praying I'm doing the right thing. This place always helps me relax, so hopefully it'll do the same for him.

When we get there, the place is completely empty, the usual scent of lavender and jasmine lingering in the space. The room is bright, but the privacy blinds are activated over the glass windows framing the back wall, looking out over the lakes.

But the best part: No students, no teacher. Just us.

"Are we early?" Miles asks, checking his watch, but I know we're right on time.

"Nope, class got canceled today. The teacher's sick. But since the space was free, I thought we could still use it." That, and I texted the teacher when we were getting dressed and she said it's okay.

I walk over to the mirrors and set down my gym bag, then plug my phone into the sound system. As the sound of rain starts filling the room, I quickly gather my hair into a ponytail, adding my bow, a light blue one today. I feel Miles's eyes on me as I slip off his hoodie, leaving me in just my tank top and yoga pants.

I turn to face him, suddenly feeling more naked than we were last night. I know he's seen me like this a thousand times—cheering, working out—but there's something different about the way he's looking at me now. Like he's seeing me all over again.

Grabbing a yoga mat, I toss it on the floor, then do the same for him.

He slowly drops his big body to the floor as I cross my legs and take a breath. "I need to re-center for a beat. Hope you don't mind a little meditation?"

"I don't mind," he says cautiously, closing his eyes and crossing his legs.

We sit there for a few minutes, just breathing in and out, slow and steady. I can feel every muscle in my body starting to relax. When we're done, I catch his eye in the mirror and smile. And when he smiles back, my heart skips a beat.

"So how are you planning on torturing my body today?" he asks, that hint of playfulness sneaking into his voice again.

"I'd never torture you..." I smirk when he narrows his eyes. "But I do have an idea."

"I'm all yours," he says, echoing what he said last night, and my body responds by catching fire and feelings. All those big damn feelings rise right to the apples of my cheeks, showing him how he affects me before I get the chance to say a thing.

Watching him settle his body backward to lean on his hands, his biceps bulging from the movement. My mouth waters as I rake down the rest of his lean, toned body that I know is under his clothes. And then I quickly look away because I shouldn't be ogling him when he needs a distraction.

I focus on the yoga pose I'd saved for us to try next week. It looks easy, but then I've seen couples try yoga poses online before and how easily it can fail. Or be the most hilarious thing you'll see on the internet.

Tilting my head, I double check the pose. "Okay, so basically you need to do a reverse plank."

He frowns at me. "Coach only makes us plank when we're in trouble."

"Then consider this part of your strength training."

He huffs but complies.

Once he's in the right position, hips facing the ceiling, not a shaky muscle in sight, I shimmy down to the ground to sit in between his open legs. Right, this is a great idea, Quinn, take the guy you're desperately in love with and contort your bodies into various positions for fun. Why am I the way I am?

"I think you might need to get closer. Those little legs won't reach my shoulders."

"Little but mighty, I'll have you know."

"Oh, I know. I watch them enough."

As if he just turned up my personal thermostat again, I get hotter. I swear my palms are too sweaty to do this now, and I have regret, so much regret. But I can't back out, not with him cracking jokes and being all flirty. This is what I wanted, him out of his head. "You're distracting me."

"Likewise," he says, tilting his head to the side with a swipe of his tongue over his lips. Dear god, I am sweating.

Ignoring my raging hormones and their ability to control my libido, I move closer to him, planting my hands on the outsides of his legs, and without much finesse, sit on his lap for a second while his hips float, effortlessly still, in the air. "Sorry," I mutter, trying not to wiggle, knowing how close I am to his dick.

"Don't be."

I walk my feet up his body, keeping my hands on the floor until I'm stretched out over him. My ankles barely make it to his pecs, and when he looks down, he chuckles, and that is the only movement his muscles make the whole time. Damn these football players.

Once we both settle in our reverse planks on top of one another, I'm very aware of how small my arms are compared to the height he has off the ground, it makes everything closer. My butt to his crotch, if we're being specific. The diagram showed two people of similar height, and I didn't take into account that Miles has a lot of inches on me.

"Now what do we do?" he asks, his voice laced with amusement that pulses through my body. I can feel every subtle movement of his chest as he breathes, his legs shifting slightly beneath mine.

"We...breathe. Relax," I manage to reply, though the last thing I'm feeling is relaxed. My mind is racing, trying to keep the rising heat in my body at bay. *Don't think about sex right now.* I mentally repeat the mantra, but it's getting harder with every passing second. The closeness, the heat radiating from him, the way his hips rise slightly with each inhale—it's all too much, too intense.

"So, to be clear," he says, his tone dripping with playful mischief, "I shouldn't do this?"

Before I can even process his words, he moves. His hips tilt up, and with a smooth, controlled thrust, he disarms me completely. My balance is gone in an instant, and I gasp as his strong arms wrap around my body, pulling me upright. In one fluid motion, I'm sitting in his lap, his chest flush with mine, his breath warm against my neck.

It takes me a second to find my bearings again before I look down into his eyes. "That's one way to get a girl's attention," I say, breathing heavily against him.

He chuckles, and the sound rumbles through his chest. "Didn't expect that to actually work. We could've both ended up on the floor."

My hands naturally move to his shoulders and interlace behind his neck. "Risky move, considering you've got to catch a ball this weekend," I remind him, trying to keep my thoughts on track.

He runs his nose along the side of mine in a gesture that sets all those lustful thoughts free again like butterflies taking flight.

"Hmm," he hums low, tempting and devious.

His hands wander along my back, rubbing small circles as he drifts over my bare skin across my middle and up until his fingertips graze the edge of my crop top, letting me almost feel his touch but not quite.

My breath catches in my throat, skin tingling under the ghost of his fingers. Pausing, his hand rests lightly just below the fabric, and I can feel the warmth of his palm radiating through the thin material. My body arches, instinctively seeking more of his touch, but he keeps his movements deliberate, slow, as if he has all the time in the world.

His other hand trails down my side, tracing the curve of my waist with the same agonizingly gentle pressure. The contrast between his firm grip and the soft brush of his fingertips is intoxicating, sending shivers down my spine. He leans in closer, his breath hot against my ear as he whispers, "Do you want me to stop?"

The question hangs in the sliver of space between us. Every nerve in my body is on high alert, every sense tuned into him, and I can hardly think straight, let alone form a coherent response. But I don't need to; my body answers for me, leaning into his touch, a silent plea for more.

A low chuckle escapes his lips, and I can feel the vibration of it against my skin. His fingers slip under the hem of my crop top, barely grazing the sensitive skin under my breasts. The sensation is electric, and a jolt of white-hot heat skates down to my core, making me gasp. He isn't fazed, though; he takes his time, savoring each inch as he slowly pushes the fabric higher, his touch igniting a fire beneath my skin until he brushes his finger over my nipple.

"Miles." I'm panting, not sure if I'm pulling him closer or pushing him away. "We definitely shouldn't," I say with absolutely no conviction as I take his top off in one swift move.

"Yeah, you're right, we shouldn't," he replies, kissing the slope of my neck, nipping my collarbone, his hand returning under my top. "But here's another idea... What if we did?"

Somewhere in the distant part of my mind, there's an alarm bell going off. I'm sure it's trying to tell me something, but with Miles's mouth marking my skin and his hands trailing all over me, I can't seem to care. In fact, I really don't care. So instead, I lean in, pressing my lips to his in a kiss that's far more of an answer than any words could be.

He groans, a low, satisfied sound that buries itself inside my body, and suddenly, we're both moving, grinding and pawing at anything we can touch. Deepening the kiss as if he's just as desperate to erase whatever space still lingers between us, I let him take control.

The alarm bells in my mind have gone quiet now, drowned out by the rapid beat of my heart and the overwhelming heat of his touch. This is reckless, stupid even. But it feels inevitable. Right now, the only thing I want is him inside me.

He pulls back, just enough to look at me, his eyes dark and intense, searching my face for something. "Tell me to stop. If you don't want to do this here, tell me now," he says, breathless, but I can see in his eyes that he's hoping I won't. "Because I think you've given me a new kink. Almost getting caught with you turns me the fuck on."

I don't say no because I want him and I'm all in with this. Instead, I grab behind his head and pull him back to me, crashing our lips together in a kiss that's all fire and need. He responds instantly, any hesitation gone as he presses me harder against his length. I need our clothes off, I need him. "Miles," I mumble against his mouth.

"Yeah, Queenie?"

"I need more."

His hands stop their roaming as he swallows deeply, staring into my eyes. "I can do that. Take off your pants. Leave your underwear on."

I oblige, standing quickly to peel them off my legs, my eyes never leaving his as he removes his shorts and takes himself out of his boxers, running his hand down his shaft once with a hiss. He reaches behind him, getting his wallet from his shorts and finding a condom, covering himself, all the while I stand in front of the boy I love, about to have sex in the middle of the yoga studio. Who on earth am I?

"Queenie, baby, come here," he says, snapping my attention back to him and his gloriously naked body. The use of *baby* with my nickname has my knees almost buckling as I sink back onto his lap, my center grazing against his covered dick. "God, you're amazing," he murmurs as his gaze dances all over me, pulling me against his warm body. The words send a thrill rippling through me, and I grip his shoulders, needing to feel him closer.

His fingers slip underneath the fabric of my sports bra that I'd forgotten to remove. "I need this off too," he says, then pulls it over my head.

As soon as our eyes lock again, I lift up and blindly reach beneath me until I find him right there. He lifts me higher, one hand strong under my thigh, as the other digs into the skin of my opposite hip. I pin my legs closer to him, anchoring myself as I feel him there, as he shifts my lace thong to one side, then

I sink down in a move that makes the air evaporate around us. There's a wildness in his eyes, a barely contained storm that's mirrored in the pounding of my own heart.

"Fuuuuck," he whispers, his fingers digging into my hips.

I lift up again to sink down, and the burn from him being at a different angle sends my nerve endings into a spin. I'm trembling, my pulse racing, every thought I had before now completely drowned out by the sheer intensity of being with him again.

His hand moves to my clit, pushing against my aching core, giving me the pressure I crave. I can't escape the moans that he draws from my lips as he pushes up into me while touching me, making me come undone. "You're incredible." His voice is hoarse, as if he's on the edge of control. His words send a shiver along my limbs, and I reach down, pulling him back to me, needing to feel him close, to erase the space between us.

We move together, the rhythm building, growing at a speed I can barely keep up with. There's nothing left but the way he makes me feel like I'm falling apart and being put back together all at once. "Miles, I-I..." I pant, desperate to catch my breath, but unable to stop. I trail off as everything snaps in a burst of pleasure, exploding over my entire body like a tidal wave.

I collapse into him as he thrusts twice more, then deftly lifts me up to my knees, pulling out of me. His hands encase my face as he holds my gaze. "Do you trust me?"

"Yes," I say without hesitation, feeling hazy from my orgasm.

Shuffling behind me, his movements deliberate, as his hand trails down the length of my spine, leaving a tingling warmth in its wake. My breath hitches as he gently pushes me forward, guiding me into position.

"Hands flat on the mat, Queenie," he instructs, his voice low and firm, with a commanding edge that renews my desire tenfold.

I lower myself, pressing my palms against the cool surface of the mat, feeling the tremors still echoing in my body. His hands ghost over my hips, as I hear a muttered curse, then feel his fingers slip into the sides of my panties. The lace flutters down my skin, as he drags them over my ass and lets them pool at my bent knees with a satisfied growl.

He shifts his weight, and I can feel his presence behind me. Desire pulses like a flashing beacon inside my belly, desperate for him to touch me and take me over the edge again. Then I feel it, the tip of his cock nudging against me, just before he hesitates right there. "You know I'm not made of glass, Miles. You can do what you want with me."

"And what is that?"

"You tell me. Or better yet, show me."

This time, he doesn't hold back. He plunges in deeply, making me gasp as the air rushes from my lungs. His hand glides over the curve of my ass, giving it a gentle squeeze.

Everything feels so much more like this, exposed, vulnerable, but I also feel safe with him. When he pulls out and pushes back in slowly, the sound of him losing his control has my body responding instinctively, adjusting to his movements as if guided by an invisible thread.

I sink into him, letting all the sensations rush through my body. Not a care in the world that someone, anyone, could walk past because I'm wrapped up in him, losing every single ounce of restraint for this boy.

Then I feel his hand snake between my legs, pressing against my clit again, working me up higher and higher. "Miles, I can't—" I moan, unsure if I can get there again. This is new to me, all of this pleasure so intensely woven together, and I'm overwhelmed.

"You can, baby," he growls behind me, grounding me with one hand between my legs, and one hand firmly kneading my ass. He thrusts over and over, his fingers working in time, and the flutter begins low in my belly. "That's it, give me another one. Squeeze this pussy around me. Let me feel it."

"I-I..." I whimper, unable to cope with everything. The feel of him inside me, our skin slapping in the empty room, his scent all over me. It's too much, and I fall over the edge once again, crying out my release. "Oh my god..." He loosens his grip on my ass, smoothing the skin rhythmically now.

"Still trust me, Queenie?" he pants, his voice hoarse.

"Always," I whisper.

I feel his hips stutter behind me as my body tries to clench around him. Then, in an instant, he pulls out. I hear the snap of rubber and the bristle of his hand against skin, pumping just before he groans, guttural and deep as a warmth explodes onto my back, marking me with his release.

I shift slightly, trying to get a better glimpse of him. His chest heaves as he focuses on my back, eyes glinting with a wild expression that makes me silently whimper.

"Fuck, you look pretty like this, ass up and covered in me." He makes a noise so deep and masculine, I think I melt a little. "I need this image as my screensaver."

"Miles!" I chastise weakly, still reeling.

"I'm joking." He chuckles. "There's no way I'd let anyone else see you like this. This is all for me."

All for me. The words are stuck on a loop in my head. Does that make me his? He's told me he's mine twice now. Is this his way of showing me too? The thought feels like a branding burn on my heart.

As I feel the liquid starting to shift, my back arches slightly. "Don't move, I've got you." He places a hand on my hip, grounding me.

I feel him wipe my back with a soft cotton material, and it's not until I look over my shoulder that I see he's used his underwear to clean me. "I promise we can shower when we get back to my dorm," he whispers into my ear as he pulls me back against his body.

His breath on my neck and the softness of his touch makes me hope like all heck he's claiming me as his own, just as I've claimed him.

Chapter Thirty-Eight

Miles

I don't make it a habit to drive my truck much when we're in school. It's mainly used for trips that need to be fast when we can't walk, burger runs when we're all starving after practice or, lately, when me and Quinn go to one of our various activities that are making a rainbow of my phone calendar.

Hence why, this morning, I'm outside her dorm, engine idling, waiting for my girl.

Miles

I'm here xo

Queenie

Two seconds xo

An email comes through as I'm swiping off her message, and my body immediately tenses, the buzz from the notification making my bones rattle more than I'd like.

> From: Mark Cooper
> Subject: Call me.

Call me. Two words I plan on ignoring for as long as possible. You know what, Dad? Since our last phone call went so swimmingly, I think I'll pass. I don't even have to open it to know what's inside because I already know. Like muscle memory, my body remembers the effect he has on me, my knuckles turn white from the grip around my phone. The panic attack I had last week still so fresh and raw in my mind.

The door to my truck creaks open, breaking the silence that had settled over me like a heavy blanket. I turn, and there she is—the one person who pulled me out of that darkness when I thought there was no escape, who helps me without question or hesitation. Her red hair is pulled back with a white bow, revealing her face free of makeup, allowing every freckle to stand out in perfect clarity. The sight of her makes my heart flip-flop, a jolt that shakes loose the fear and anxiety trying to grip me. As she looks directly into my eyes, all the panic I felt moments ago melts away, replaced by the steady, calming presence she always brings.

"Hey, Queenie."

"Hey, Miles."

She climbs in, and I notice how she hesitates for just a moment before settling into the seat. She's so full of sunshine that when it dims like it is right now, it's like her entire self stops glowing.

Pulling the door shut with a soft sigh, she rests a hand on her stomach.

"You okay?" I ask, my brow furrowing. "You're tense."

"I'm not, I'm okay." She waves me off, but I can tell there's something up.

"Is it your ankle again?"

"No," she breathes out, as I pull out of the school parking lot, trying not to be too distracted by her.

"Queenie, I've known you our whole lives. I can tell when something's off. Talk to me."

"I'm really fine." But her voice wavers just enough to give her away.

I twist my mouth as I think of the best plan here. "Well, I'm going to keep driving until you spill. And according to my calendar, I've got an afternoon that's supposed to be spent volunteering at the shelter again, so you can talk, or we can be late."

"It really is nothing," she mutters. "Let's just get there."

"Humor me," I coax gently.

She groans, and I feel the weight leave her. "I just have...cramps, okay? I'm tired, and this morning, I cried at a car commercial I saw on social media. All I want is the worst, greasiest food I can find—preferably a burger and fries with a milkshake to dip the fries into, and I don't want anyone telling me it's weird because I'll just cry again. I want to sit and watch the new Taylor Swift tour movie for the seventh time because it makes me happy, and maybe I'll cry at that too because it reminds me I didn't get tickets to that tour—who knows at this point." She pauses, taking a deep breath, as if to steady herself before continuing. "But we have other things to do, so I'm dealing. We're going. I'm being an adult, even though I really don't want to."

Realization dawns on me that this version of Queenie usually only happens once a month. Ahead, I spot a right turn after the stop sign and make a decision. I swing the truck into the road, and from the corner of my eye, I see Quinn grab the 'oh shit' handle above her head. Her eyes are wide as she turns to me. "Miles! What are you doing? We're going to be late!"

"No."

"No?" she repeats, incredulous. "No to what?"

"I'm calling you in sick," I say with a determined grin, making a mental note to steal the number from her phone in a minute. I don't think Quinn has ever let anyone down with a sick day in her life, but that ends today. "We're going to Lakeside to get your burger, fries, and milkshake. Then, we're heading back to my dorm, where you can watch Taylor on my big-ass TV. We can cry together, and you can dip those fries into the milkshake as many times as you damn well please."

Jeez, now I was the one monologuing. What is she doing to me?

"You're going to make me cry again." She sniffs as she fights back tears. "I'm supposed to be the one helping you."

"And sometimes, Queenie," I say, reaching over to squeeze her hand, "I want to be the one helping you."

My tires squeak to a halt at another stop sign, and I turn to see Quinn looking at me, her eyes shimmering with unshed tears. For a moment, I wonder if she'll argue. But then, she just nods, and my heart does a little victory dance.

A few minutes later, we pull into Lakeside Diner parking lot, the familiar neon sign glowing against the fading afternoon light. When we head inside, the mouthwatering smell of fried food hits me. I'm about to break my in-season diet plan and I couldn't care less. Especially not if it makes the girl next to me feel better.

"Hey, man," Brad, the owner, says as he sees me. "You want a table?"

"Nah, just takeout today."

He nods. "Good luck in the semis next week. We're rooting for y'all." He smiles, and I know he means well, but a light prickle of awareness has my skin itching as we make our way down to the takeout counter. I force a smile and take Quinn's hand in mine without a second thought of who sees us because I need her to ground me. Even after we've ordered, his words linger in the forefront of my mind, stirring up a restlessness I can't quite shake. Making that pressure return to sit on my chest like an invisible barbel I can't shift. "Hey, you know you didn't have to do this for me. We can still go to the shelter."

I blink, bringing my attention to her. "No, I want to do this for you. Everyone needs a break sometimes. Even you."

She rolls her eyes but doesn't argue. I know she gets it, but she's trying to put me first again. I'm not okay with that when she needs someone to take care of her. Today, I'm that person. The food arrives, and we take it back to my truck, driving to my dorm.

"I have a heating pad in my room if that'll help you?" I say, as we open the door to my room. She flicks on the light and walks over to my desk, placing our food there. "I can put it in the microwave, and it smells like lavender."

"Does it also happen to be in the shape of a sausage dog?" She chuckles quietly.

"It does. How...?"

"Mom got them for everyone last Christmas. I'm guessing you got one too. But yes, I'd love to use it, if you don't mind."

I lean down under my desk and pick up the long bean-filled dog. "Wanna set up food and the TV while I warm this up?"

"On it," she says, and I disappear into the hallway.

I quickly warm the dog in the microwave, and with a couple of minutes on the clock, I'm back in my room with my girl. As soon as she sees me, her face lights up, and I feel like I'm running down the sideline with seconds left on the clock, the end zone just within reach, ball snug in my hands and I cross that line. She makes me feel like I can do pretty much anything when she looks at me like that.

"I hope you weren't joking about letting me cry while watching Taylor and dipping French fries into my milkshake, because all of that is on the horizon, buddy."

"Buddy, huh?" I muse, closing my door with a soft snick. "Is that what I am? Your buddy?" I can't help the grin tugging at my lips as I move closer to the bed where she's curled up. There's a spark in her green eyes that makes my heart race, and before I can second-guess it, I toss the heating pad aside and dive onto the bed. She squeals as I tackle her, laughter bubbling up between us when I tickle her sides, her hands weakly swatting at me in protest.

"You're not my—oh my god!—you're not my buddy!" she squeals, her voice breaking with laughter as my fingertips dig into her sides, her most ticklish place.

"Oh no?" I taunt while keeping her pinned beneath me. "Then what am I?"

As soon as the words leave my mouth, it feels like someone hit the pause button in the room. Her laughter dies down, and I'm hovering above her, our faces just inches apart, the rise and fall of her chest echoing the rhythm of my own breathing. Her eyes, still shining with the traces of her laughter, meet mine, and the world seems to still for a moment.

I should say it. The words are right there, on the tip of my tongue. I can feel them, taste them even, but something stops me. Fear, maybe. The fear that once those words are out, there's no taking them back. That everything could change. That things between us could change. Hearing Quinn tell me she loved me would make me realize I'm wholly unworthy of her. When was the last time someone told me that? Jesus, I don't remember.

But the thing is, she gives me the strength to make me want to fight to be worthy of her because the thought of not having her now? I hate it.

Her eyes search mine, as if she's trying to read my mind, and for a second, I'm sure she knows what I want to say. But then she smiles—a soft, almost shy smile that tugs at something deep inside me, and lifts up to rub her nose against mine. "You're not just my buddy, Miles." Her breath hitches slightly, and I see the faint blush that colors her cheeks. She opens her mouth, as if to say something else, but then closes it, her expression a mix of uncertainty and something that makes my heart skip a beat.

"Tell me," I whisper, imploring for her to say something that I think she feels too. Silently begging for her to take the lead here.

"You're..." she starts, her voice barely above a whisper as her throat works on a swallow. "You're...everything."

The words hit me like a ton of bricks. I'm speechless. Everything? The way she's looking at me, like I'm the only thing that matters in the world, makes me feel like I could actually be that for her.

I feel the overwhelming urge to close the tiny gap between us, to show her just how much those words mean to me. But before I can act on it, she presses her lips to mine, cutting off any thoughts I might have had. This kiss is different—deeper, more certain. It's as if she's pouring all the things she can't say into this one moment, and I can feel it in every fiber of my being.

My hand moves instinctually from her waist to cradle the side of her face, pulling her even closer. The kiss is soft and urgent, tender and fierce all at once.

When we finally break apart, her forehead rests against mine, both of us breathing heavily. My heart pounds harder, trying to sync with the chaotic rhythm of hers I feel underneath me.

"Everything, huh?" I say softly as a small smile tugs at the corners of my mouth. I brush a thumb over her cheek, feeling the warmth of her skin under my touch.

She nods, her smile mirroring mine, and I want to make sure that I can be her everything, always because she's my First Down: All the way girl.

CHAPTER THIRTY-NINE

Miles

THERE'S A FAINT BUZZING sound, like a bee hovering dangerously close to my ear. I need it to stop because I'm in the middle of something with Quinn. She's pinned against the locker room door, moaning my name as my hands explore her body—*buzz, buzz, buzz*. Seriously, what the hell is that noise?

"Do you hear that?" I ask, my voice rough with frustration. But Quinn doesn't seem to notice. She's too busy leaving a trail of hot kisses down my neck, her breath sending shivers along my spine. *Buzz, buzz, buzz.* The sound is relentless, clawing at the edges of my mind.

I try to ignore it, try to stay in this moment with her, but it's getting louder. Reluctantly, I pull away from Quinn, the loss of her warm body jarring, and turn to face the source of the noise. Suddenly, I'm not in the locker room anymore. I'm on the field, and Seb is there, hurling something toward me.

"Cooper!" he yells, and I see it—a giant, furious bee zooming right at me. It's all buzzing wings and stingers, and I really don't want to catch it. But Seb's my QB, and I never back down from a pass. I spin, my instincts taking over, but instead of the ball, I crash face-first into the cold, hard floor of my dorm room.

"Urghhhh," I groan. Peeling my face from the carpet, I struggle to lift my sleepy body from the hard floor. "What the hell," I say gripping the side of my bed for support. "Jesus." I wince as I rub my chest.

Buzz, buzz, buzz.

"Fuck! What is that?" I curse, the sound louder now. Just as I pull myself up, I see my phone lit up on my bed, telling me my alarm has been going off for the last thirty minutes. Great, I'm running late for our pre-game team breakfast at the dining hall. Of all the days to sleep in, it had to be today.

Throwing on a pair of shorts and a shirt from my drawers, I grab my phone, swallow some mouthwash, and run like my ass is on fire.

"There he is, sleeping beauty himself," Hudson teases as soon as I step foot inside. The smell of buttered toast, eggs and bacon assaults me and my stomach groans in response.

"Morning," I mumble, wandering over to the breakfast bar, piling my plate with everything on offer.

"Dude, your shirt is on backwards," Seb calls out, just as I pick up an orange juice.

Glancing down at myself, I notice he's right. "Fuck it, never mind." I shrug.

"Is there a reason your late, and a reason you're wearing your shirt the wrong way?" Seb asks, mischief lacing his words. And boy, oh boy, do I wish he didn't ask me that. I can almost feel my cheeks heating, and I am not about to blurt out "oh yeah, your sister was moments away from fucking me in my dream" the morning of the semi-final championship game. I'm smarter than that, at least.

Instead, I brush it off. "Pfft, like you can talk. I could hear you and Indie allllllll night across the hall," I lie to deflect any attention away from me.

The guys' laughter erupts around us. "*Oh, Seb, you're not as big as Hudson's monster cock, but I can ride him later,*" Hudson jokes, putting on a high-pitched voice which earns him a slap from Seb.

"What the fuck, man?" Seb grumbles.

"I can imagine you getting all growly, really showing her that *captain* side to you," Hudson replies with zero filter.

"Firstly, how did this become a me thing?" He points to me. "He's the one hooking up and not getting shit for it. Secondly, why the fuck are you so invested in my sex life, Huds?"

"Sex is amazing. I want to know that my friends are having great sex."

"Weird, man," I mutter through a mouthful of eggs.

"Really fucking weird," Seb agrees.

After eating our body weight in breakfast, we head over to the stadium for warmups and a team meeting.

At the stadium, the field is dewy, glistening in the winter sun. The stands around us are empty now, but you can almost feel the energy that'll fill them later. We hit the field, getting into our warmup routine. The sound of cleats on the turf, footballs smacking into hands, and coaches shouting instructions fill the air. Everyone's shaking off the stiffness, getting focused, and building up the intensity for the game ahead.

One thorough warmup complete, we all head inside to clean up and get ready to review strategy. As soon as I'm dressed, I hear my phone ringing. My heart does a little leap in my chest because I hope it's Quinn. Stepping outside of the locker room, making sure I'm not followed down the hall, I answer the phone. "You know, I missed you this morning. I think we need to make a rule that you always sleep in my bed the night before games."

The line is silent. Not a cricket makes a sound until I pull the phone away from my ear to check who is calling and the name makes my fingers go cold.

"Dad," I croak.

He clears his throat. "Well, it's good to know where your priorities lie on game day, letting cleat chasers occupy your time."

Fuuuuck.

Realization hits me like a slap to the face. In my haste to leave this morning, I forgot to block his number.

My mind races as I desperately search for something, anything, to say that'll get me out of this. "We're about to have a team meeting, Dad. I really have to go."

"Don't you fucking dare hang up on me," he snaps, his voice so sharp and venomous that it's like a punch to the gut. My throat tightens as I try to swallow, and I can practically hear that familiar vein on the side of his head throbbing through the phone. He sighs, long and irritated, a sound that makes my stomach churn. "I'd like to say I know why my son is ignoring me, blocking my calls and emails, but the truth is, he evidently has no fucking respect.

"No respect for what I've done. No respect for how much time and effort I've put into making sure your career doesn't end in college. Instead, you'd rather fuck around, wasting your time on girls who'll drop you the second they realize you're not going pro. Ask me why, Miles. Ask me why that won't happen." His voice drips with anger, and I can feel myself shrinking inside, every part of me pulling back, trying to escape. But I know there's no getting away from him.

"Why?" I whisper, barely able to keep my voice steady.

"Because you missed a fucking meeting I set up with an agent this morning," he roars, and my shoulders slump under the weight of his words. "Not only are you playing like shit, but now you're dragging my name, my reputation, through the fucking dirt. Do you have any idea how humiliating it was to explain to Taylor fucking Lawrence—one of the top agents in the business—that I had no clue where my own son was, or why he didn't bother to show up at the coffee shop?"

Taylor Lawrence. Shit. I know that name. Coach mentioned him a few times. He's a big deal. A really big deal.

"Dad, I'm—"

"Don't fucking apologize." He's cutting me off before I can even get the words out. "It means nothing. Why the fuck didn't you show up to the meeting? I emailed you the details. All you had to do was be there."

My mouth goes dry, and for a moment, I'm completely paralyzed, my brain scrambling to find an excuse, a reason—anything that'll make this right. But there's nothing. Nothing except the truth I'm too scared to say out loud.

"You think this is a joke, Miles? You think you can just coast by, and everything will fall into place? You think you've got time to waste, pissing away opportunities like they'll come around again? Newsflash: they won't. And you're sure as hell not getting any younger. Every mistake you make, every chance you blow, is another nail in the coffin of your so-called career. You're fucking lucky you've got a dad who actually gives a damn, who's been busting his ass to keep you on track. But maybe I've been wasting my time. Maybe you're not cut out for this, after all."

My mind snags on one word. *Lucky*. He thinks I should feel lucky.

Something hot and angry bubbles inside me. My heart starts to pound a dangerous beat, but not in the way it does before a game. This is something else, something darker, twisting inside me, feeding on every bit of doubt and fear I've ever had.

"I... I didn't—" My voice is barely a whisper, trembling as I try to get the words out, even though I'm not sure what I was going to say.

"Didn't what? Didn't mean to fuck up? Well, congratulations, because you did. And you're not just screwing up your own life, but you're dragging me down with you. Do you think people don't know who your father is? Do you think my name isn't attached to every move you make? When you fail, I fail. And I'm not going to let that happen. So, get your head out of your ass and start acting like someone who gives a shit. Or else you're going to lose everything before you even realize what you've thrown away."

My thoughts start to spiral, sinking deeper into that dark place where every insecurity, every fear I've tried to bury for the last few weeks, comes rushing back up to the surface. I'm drowning in it, suffocating, being blinded by it. The ground feels like it's slipping out from under me, and I'm desperately trying to hold on, but there's nothing to grab onto. Just his voice, and the overwhelming certainty that no matter what I do, it'll never be enough.

"Nothing to say?" he barks with a sadistic laugh. "Typical. Well, you should know, Taylor is in the crowd tonight, but I doubt he'll have any interest in you after the stunt you pulled this morning."

He hangs up before I can respond, not that I had any plans to. I stare at the phone in my hand, feeling numb. The reality of everything starts to sink in, and I feel like I'm being crushed under the pressure.

Taking a shaky breath, I look around, realizing that I'm still lurking in the hallway. The rest of the team is probably already inside, getting ready for the meeting, while I'm here, completely falling apart. My chest tightens again, but this time it's not just anxiety. It's fear. Fear of what happens next, fear of what I'm becoming, fear that maybe my dad is right—that I'm not cut out for this, that I'm throwing everything away.

I force myself to move, my legs like lead as I head toward the locker room. Each step feels heavier than the last, and by the time I reach the doors, I'm barely holding it together. I push through, trying to keep my face neutral, trying not to let anyone see the mess inside me.

But as soon as I step into the locker room, the noise, the laughter, the energy—it all feels like too much. I can barely hear the conversations around me, the pounding in my head drowning everything else out. My teammates are joking around, hyped up for the game, but it feels like they're in a different world, one I'm not a part of.

I slip into my spot, attempting to stay invisible, but I can't shake the feeling of eyes on me. I try to focus, try to pull my-self together, but my mind keeps spinning, replaying my dad's words over and over. Every mistake, every missed opportunity, every time I've fallen short—it all comes rushing back. The panic rises, making my blood rush around my body, but I push it down, forcing myself to breathe, to calm down.

I try to picture her. Try to hear her voice. Feel her touch. Smell her cinnamon scent. The desperate need I have to make sure I'm worthy of her.

The more I try to push it away, the stronger it gets, until I feel like I'm going to explode. My hands start to tremble, and I quickly shove them under my thighs, hoping no one notices.

"Miles, you good?" A voice cuts through the chaos in my head, and I look up to see Seb staring at me, concern etched on his face.

I nod quickly, giving him a tight smile. "Yeah, just... I just need a minute," I mumble, my voice barely steady. "Big game tonight."

He doesn't look convinced, but as soon as his mouth opens, Coach walks in, and the meeting starts. I go through the motions, nodding when I'm supposed to, but it's all just a blur. All I can think about is what happens if I fail—if I let everyone down, if I prove my dad right.

I should be listening to the plays we're doing, I should be paying attention, but I can't keep track of my thoughts. When coach says we can break and be back here in an hour for suiting up, I practically sprint out of the locker room.

I'm so wrapped up in my thoughts that I barely notice when someone bumps into me outside, hard enough to knock me off balance. I stumble, catching myself just before I hit the ground, and when I look up, my heart skips a beat.

"Whoa, easy there, big guy," he says, then recognition flickers in his eyes. "Miles, man, I haven't seen you around."

Levi stands in front of me, his usual cool demeanor on like armor. "Levi." I nod, trying to sound indifferent.

"You look like you've seen a ghost." He chuckles as he takes a step closer to me. "I'm glad I ran into you, today."

That makes one of us. The last thing I need right now is him in my face. Especially not when I'm already hanging on by a thread. When I don't engage, he pushes more.

"Because you know, I figured you might need something from me, like old times…"

I stiffen, my mind flashing back to last year. The semi-championship game, the first time I'd taken anything. I'd been a mess then, too—pressure, nerves, everything piling up until I felt like I was going to implode. Levi had been there, offering something to take the edge off. And it had worked, hadn't it? I played one of the best games of my life. We won and my dad was briefly happy. I think.

"I'm good," I say, side-stepping him.

"Really?" he guffaws. "You don't look good. You look like you could fall apart." He stares at me, those dark eyes making me shudder. "Come on. You remember how it helped last time, don't you? Got you through that game, made you a hero for a night. I've got the same stuff, maybe even better. Just a little something to calm those nerves, help you focus. You need it, man—I can see it in your eyes."

My stomach twists as the temptation is stronger than I want to admit. He's right—I do remember how it helped. How everything had seemed to slow down, how the panic had melted away, leaving me sharp, focused, unstoppable. But there's a vision of red hair, green eyes, and perfect freckles that's stopping me. Everything good in my life right now is because of her, and I can't do that to her.

"I'm not doing that anymore, Levi." I'm trying to sound firm, but even I can hear the doubt in my voice.

He gives me a knowing look, his smile widening. "Yeah? You sure about that? Because from where I'm standing, it looks like you could use all the help you can get. You're not gonna let one rough day ruin everything you've worked for, are you? Think about it—your dad, the team, your future. All of it, just a little bump in the road if you take care of business. And I'm offering you the way to do that."

Glancing up, I meet his eyes, and for a split second, I see a way out. A way to push the fear away, to silence the doubts, to be the player I'm supposed to be. To stop all this shit with my dad.

"Tell you what..." He reaches into his back pocket and pulls something out. "I'm giving you these for free, because we're friends, and if you ever need anything else, you come see me."

He leaves, and my hand tingles with a familiar plastic bag that feels like it holds my entire future inside it. A decision I know should be easy, easier than breathing, because what I want to do isn't the right thing. But I feel like a caged animal, desperately seeking relief from being locked up. I know I shouldn't take it... I know that. I stare at the bag, my mind racing. I know I shouldn't. I should turn around, go find Quinn, or just get the hell out of here. But Dad's words are still echoing in my head, gnawing at me, tearing me down. *No one would know, no one needs to know, this is a one-time thing.*

And my last thought is that I hope she can forgive me.

CHAPTER FORTY

Quinn

GLANCING AT MY PHONE, I see Miles's name with five missed calls next to it. Immediately, I check the text thread with my brother to see if anything is wrong. But there's nothing. A wave of worry washes over me as I hastily leave the shelter, annoyed that I'd left my phone in the office the entire time I was there. And then on top of that, some of the usual women wanted to talk peach cobbler recipes with me, and now I'm hauling ass across town to get back for cheer warmups.

Pressing his name on my phone, I wait for the ring to start, but then I hear his voicemail. *Hi, you've reached Miles, you know what to do.* Followed by the echoing beep, my feet quicken the pace even more. I manage to make it to Indie's truck she lets me borrow sometimes, and hope that I don't get caught speeding, because the more I try Miles's number and it goes to voicemail every time, the bigger the knot in my stomach gets, and the harder my foot hits the gas.

I try my brother too, which also goes to voicemail. And then I look at the clock and remember they're probably suiting up now, which means no distractions.

I'm sure he's fine; he probably just wanted to check in before the game. It's all fine.

Everything will be fine.

So, why do I have this feeling in the pit of my stomach?

It doesn't go away when I get to my dorm and pick up my cheer bag.

It doesn't go away when I warm up on the field with my team, knowing he's mere feet away from me and I can't go to check on him.

It doesn't go away even as the crowd begins to liven up, and both teams come out onto the field, and I see his face for the first time today.

The face that looks like something isn't quite right. Something is on his mind. Something that I wish I could help him with. I watch him with rapt attention, analyzing his every move during final warmups. My palms felt clammy, gripping onto my burgundy and white pom-poms like my life depends on it.

Look over at me, just once, Miles. Let me see your eyes.

But he doesn't, and a weight settles on my chest, pressing and pushing down every time he almost glances my way.

Miles still runs routes and makes plays, but his movements aren't as sharp as they usually are. He fumbles the ball, and a gasp ripples through the stands behind me. I watch him scramble to recover, and my stomach twists more painfully. This isn't like him. Not at all.

He lines up for the next play, but his posture is off, like he's fighting against an invisible force. I squint, trying to read his expression from here, but it's no use.

I see Miles in the middle of the play, his usual confident stride faltering slightly. There's something off about him—a tense set to his shoulders, a hitch in his step.

Then, in an instant, it all goes wrong.

The opposing player, bigger and more aggressive, slams into Miles with a force that makes my breath catch.

Miles goes down hard, crumpling to the ground. His body lands awkwardly, helmet off his head, limbs splayed out in a way that makes my heart stutter. He doesn't move.

And he doesn't get up.

The noise of the crowd fades into a distant murmur as I watch, frozen in place, locked in this moment of horror. My nails bite into my palms as I clench my fists, my heart now pounding so hard I can feel it in my ears. The shriek of a whistle echoes around us, and the game pauses, but my focus is solely on Miles. Coaches rush onto the field, Seb and Hudson right by his side, but nothing about my brother's urgency getting to his best friend tells me this is okay.

I feel a lump in my throat that threatens to choke me as I hold back the sting of tears.

I need to get to him.

My feet move before I can process where I'm going, and I'm halfway across the field with my squad yelling my name behind me.

The closer I get, all I see is his body sprawled out on the grass, unmoving as medics rush to him too. There's a screeching sound, and I don't even realize it's being ripped from my throat like a wild, untamed animal.

I barely register arms wrapping around my middle, hauling me backward, moving me farther away.

"Hudson, get her out of here!" Seb shouts somewhere, but I can't see him. I can only see the love of my life lying lifeless on the grass.

"I know, I know," Hudson soothes in my ear. "It's okay. He's going to be okay."

My breaths come in ragged gasps as Hudson pulls me away from the scene, each step feeling like my heart is breaking more and more. "No, no, no," I mutter to myself as the medics bring out the stretcher.

"It's protocol, Quinn. They need to get him off the field safely."

I know this. In my head, I know this, but seeing it happen to him, everything feels like I'm upside down, torn apart from the inside out. "H-he's going to be okay, r-right?" I sniffle.

"He's going to be okay."

Even though his words are meant to calm me, they don't, they wash over my head and do little to stop the fear gripping me. Even though I know this is all protocol, I can't seem to marry up the idea that its Miles out there and he's the one who needs help.

Because if I let myself lose control, I fear I won't come back from it.

My hands cling to Hudson's like a lifeline, grasping for something, anything, as I watch the stretcher come onto the field. I watch them haul his body onto it, and my focus flicks briefly to my brother, who's helmet is off and he's wiping his face. Something inside me snaps and tears fall freely, like a river that broke its dam. The closer Miles gets to the medics exit, the more

I cry.

"Sssh, it's okay, I swear, it's just protocol. He's okay."

He's okay. I repeat the mantra in my head over and over. Hudson stays with me and just lets me sob into his shirt as players all amble around the sidelines.

"Shit, I've gotta go to Coach. Will you be okay?"

"I'm here. I'm here." Indie rushes over, pulling me into her arms. "It took me some serious convincing to get down here, and I'm pretty sure I owe someone money, but I'm here."

The tears come back with a vengeance, fresh rivulets soaking into her sweater, but I can't let her go. Because somehow my best friend knew I would need her, and here she is, showing up for me. "I've got you." she whispers, wrapping her arms just as fiercely around me.

"I need to see him," I mumble into her, the words being absorbed by the noise around us, but she hears me. Her hand strokes my back.

"I know, and we will. Hudson, go find out where he's gone, please."

"But—"

"Now," she growls, and I hear his feet scurry away.

Indie lets me go and offers me a tissue from her backpack. "Thank you."

"You don't need to thank me. As soon as I saw him go down, I knew I had to get to you."

"I just need to know he's okay," I say shakily.

"We will."

Two seconds later, Hudson comes bounding over to us, breathing heavily. "He's in the medic's room, but they're following concussion protocol, and he'll be going to Oregon General." He swallows, hesitating, and I see something flicker in his eyes.

"What is it?"

"I don't—"

"Tell me, Hudson," I snap, feeling like I'm going to be sick from the look on his face.

"He's out cold. There's an ambulance on its way."

And in this moment, I realize that nothing will ever be the same again.

CHAPTER FORTY-ONE

Quinn

INDIE DROVE LIKE SOMEONE possessed to the hospital. Seriously, I've never seen her so road ragey before, but I'm grateful.

Or at least I was until two seconds ago.

"I'm sorry, I can't give out information unless you're family," the receptionist, who's only doing her job, tells us. I'm sure she gets this all the time, but I can't help but snap.

"I've lived next door to him my entire life. He's spent ninety percent of our childhood in my house, he *is* my family." Tears sting my eyes as I try desperately to hold them back. I'm his family, dammit. In every way that matters, I'm his family. But the receptionist doesn't know that, and it's not her fault that she has to follow the rules.

She gives me an apologetic look. "I'm sorry, honey. There isn't anything I can do right now."

Frustration wells up inside me, a tight knot forming in my

chest. I glance over at Indie, who's pacing back and forth, her anxiety almost palpable. The sterile smell of the hospital, the harsh fluorescent lights, and the murmur of distant conversations only add to my sense of helplessness.

I take a deep breath, trying to keep steady, going for gold this time. "Please," I say, my tone softer now, almost pleading. "I just need to know if he's okay." My voice cracks on the last word, and I hate myself for it, because I need to be strong, but I can't help it.

The receptionist's expression softens, and for a moment, I think she might bend the rules, might just give me something—anything—to hold on to. But then she shakes her head, her professional mask slipping back into place. "I really wish I could help, but I can't."

Indie stops pacing and comes to stand beside me, her hand resting on my arm in silent support. "Let's wait," she says quietly.

I slump into one of the uncomfortable plastic chairs, my head in my hands. The minutes stretch into what feels like hours with no updates. He could be in surgery, he could be *alone,* and that thought is what has me sobbing into my best friend's shoulder again.

"Quinn?" My brother's familiar voice breaks through the haze of anxiety, making my head snap up. I blink through my tears and see him standing there, still in his jersey, mud covering ninety percent of him, sweaty and exhausted. His face is a mix of concern and something else—relief, maybe, or disbelief.

"Seb," I say on an exhale, wiping at my face with the back of my hand, trying to pull myself together. He doesn't hesitate; he's by my side in an instant, dropping down to kneel in front of me. "They won't tell us anything. We aren't family."

"He's going to be okay, Quinn," he says, though I'm not sure if he's saying it to convince me or himself. "I know he will."

"I can't lose—"

"Don't," Seb cuts me off, taking my hand in his. "Don't even think it. Miles is tough, he's got this. He'll be okay. We're not losing anyone."

I want to believe him, I really do. But the fear is still there, gnawing at me, refusing to let go. "Did you see more than me? I just saw him get hit."

"I saw him go down too. He landed"—Seb swallows with a wince—"awkwardly. I think his arm might be broken, but I don't know. He was out cold. They wouldn't let me go with him." His voice shakes, hanging on by a thread like I am.

My chest tightens. "Do you know who went with him?" I don't know how much longer I can feel like everything is falling apart, it hurts so much. I lean into Indie's side again and silent tears begin their descent once more.

"Team medic, I think."

That does nothing to soothe the anxiety I feel. I haven't seen the medic in here. Would he be waiting here? Would he be somewhere for family and friends? I have no idea.

"I need to move," I say, standing and shaking out my hands.

Hours crawl by. My feet pound the floor as I pace back and forth, the repetitive motion sending dull aches through my legs. I clench and unclench my hands, shaking them out until a tingling numbness sets in. My cheer uniform clings to my skin, uncomfortable and sticky, adding to my frustration. Seb taps away at his phone, trying to reach the coach, but eventually, he lets out a sigh and shoves it back in his pocket. No doctors approach, no one offers any updates. The weight of exhaustion presses down on me, sinking me further into a restless, anxious state.

"Seb?" A guy in CLU training gear appears as he rounds the corner, his expression tense. The word "medic" is emblazoned across his hoodie, and I feel a small wave of relief wash over me.

"Jake, fuck, thank god you're here. Have you been here the whole time with Miles?" Seb asks, standing to greet him.

He nods. "In the family waiting area, over there." He points behind him. "I asked Coach to call Miles's family because he's had to have surgery on his arm. It was a displaced fracture so they went in to mend the bone. It went well, though."

"Is he going to be okay?" I ask, my heart thudding in anticipation.

Jake hesitates, a shadow crossing his face. "He's got concussion too, but...I need to talk to his parents first before I tell you anything else."

"Just his dad," I correct, my voice dropping. "His mom passed when he was younger."

Jake's expression softens. "I'm sorry. I know you are all close. You should definitely talk to his dad after he's seen him."

"Wait, what do you mean 'before I tell you anything else.' There's more?" my brother asks, eyebrows drawn.

"I can't say right now. But talk to his dad."

Anxiety swirls in my gut. What if he took something? He wouldn't, right? He's been doing so good. But then, when I think about how he was on the field, he wasn't himself.

"Can we see him?" I ask, desperation seeping into my tone.

Jake shakes his head. "Not yet. They're keeping him under observation for a bit longer. He's stable but sleeping. They want to be sure before they let anyone in."

"I'm calling Coach again," Seb says, phone in hand.

He walks away, and I just stare at his back as he talks into his phone, head down.

"Coach says he's called Mark, and as far as we know, he left hours ago so he could be here any time."

He releases a ragged breath, and Indie takes his hand. "Let's go get Miles some clothes to change into, maybe something good to eat that isn't hospital food too," she suggests, giving me a look that says she's taking him away for my benefit.

Seb nods, pulling her into his chest, holding on to her for dear life.

And then less than an hour after they leave, the one person who has the ability to make Miles's world implode walks through the elevator doors.

CHAPTER FORTY-TWO

Miles

MY EYES BURN AS I try to open them. Harsh, sterile light of the room greets me as I manage to blink once, a stinging pain shooting through my arm when I try to move. My head feels heavy, like it's been stuffed with cotton, and there's a dull ache pulsing behind my eyes. I blink to focus, but everything is blurry around the edges.

Where am I? The last thing I remember is the football field, feeling a bit dizzy, then...nothing.

I move to lift my arm, but a sharp pain stops me. Glancing down, I see a heavy plaster cast encasing it. Well, that's new.

I shift slightly, wincing as the movement sends another wave of pain ricocheting through my head. The pain is relentless, a burning, searing ache that radiates from my arm and spreads like wildfire throughout my entire body. Every breath feels like it's being dragged out of me, each one more painful than the last. I can't escape it; no matter if I move or stay still, it's there, gnawing at me, refusing to let go. My head pounds with every beat of my heart, a dull, rhythmic thud that makes it hard to think about anything but the agony. My throat is dry when I swallow, my mouth a desert, and I'm terrified that if I move even an inch, the pain will swallow me whole.

"Jesus," I croak, giving up and lying back down, looking up at the bleak white squared ceiling.

The door to the room bangs open, making me jump, and my dad storms in, his face twisted in anger. Behind him, I can hear the frantic shouts of nurses and doctors telling him to calm down, to stop, but he ignores them, his eyes locked on me.

"What the fuck did you do?" he sneers, his eyes bloodshot and full of fire.

I want to defend myself, but I'm guessing with the toxin screening, the docs found something in my blood. Something that definitely wasn't amphetamines. Not even I know what it was, but I know it wasn't my usual.

"Dad," I begin, my voice weak and husky. I close my eyes, trying to block out his rage, but it's impossible. It's always impossible.

"Look at me!" he shouts, and I flinch, my eyes snapping open. "Look at me and tell me you weren't on something."

I know, he knows, we all know, I can't do that. But hell, I can barely think straight, my head throbbing with every beat of my heart, but he doesn't care. He never cares. I take responsibility for what I did tonight, but I can't pacify him. Whatever I say won't matter. He wants to hear me say it, that I'm finally the fuckup he thinks I've been all along.

"Mr. Cooper." The doctor's commanding voice cuts

through the noise. "You need to leave now, or I will have security escort you out."

For a moment, my dad just stands there, glaring at me, his chest heaving like he's about to explode again.

"Mr. Cooper," the doctor repeats, and my dad relents, spinning around and stalking out of my room.

The doctor sighs, rubbing a hand over his face before turning to me.

"Are you okay, Miles?" he asks, his voice gentle now. He grabs my chart and stares at the machines next to me while making notes.

I nod, but the truth is, I don't know. I don't know if I'm okay, if I'll ever be okay again. All I know is that my head hurts, my arm is broken, and the last thing I remember is playing in one of the biggest games of my life. And now...everything feels shattered.

"I don't want to pressure you, especially after that. But I need to know how long you've been mixing amphetamines with cocaine."

My mind races to process the question. And then my stomach churns. "I—" I look up, meeting the concerned eyes of the doc. "I didn't know it was cocaine. I thought it was just amphetamines. I've only been using it for a couple of months, and I didn't realize what else was mixed in. But this is the first time I've passed out."

He nods thoughtfully. "I need you to be honest with me, because all I'm here to do is help."

"I swear that's the truth." I swallow, my throat feeling like glass. "I took amphetamines at the beginning of fall, but I've never had a reaction like that before. I haven't used for weeks now. But..."

"Your dealer may have given you a mix without telling you. That mix is fatal and we're seeing a rise of people overdosing across the country. It's serious, Miles. You're lucky to be alive."

A cold shiver snakes down my spine, making me flinch. My shoulders tense up, and I feel the hairs on my arms prickle. "I'm sorry."

"It's not me who you need to apologize to, it's you." Folding the chart back at the foot of my bed, he levels me with a look. "Do you want to get better?"

"I do."

"Good. We'll start by keeping a close eye on your vitals and making sure there are no immediate health concerns, and book physio for your arm," he explains. "Once we're confident that you're stable, we'll discharge you and connect you with a counselor who specializes in substance abuse. They'll help you navigate through this and find ways to cope with the pressures you're facing." His gaze softens, a hint of empathy in his eyes. "It would also be beneficial if your father was included at some point too."

My throat tightens at the mention of him. "Do you think he needs to be involved right away?"

"Not immediately, but at some point, I think you'll need to address whatever is going on between you both."

I look away to collect my thoughts, picking at a thread on the sheet draping over me. "I just don't know if he'd understand or even want to be involved."

The doctor nods once more. "That's something you can address when you're ready. For now, focus on your health and getting through this. We'll help you with the resources and get you support you need."

"Thank you," I say quietly, feeling uncertain and so exhausted. How did I let myself get this far? How can I come back from this?

And then a flicker of something echoes in my mind, like remembering you found treasure on the beach as a kid. Except my treasure has red hair usually tied back with a bow, and incredible green eyes and the most beautiful smile. "This might sound odd, but is there a girl outside?"

"A girl?"

"Probably in a cheerleading uniform. Probably looking real fucking scared right now."

The doc smiles knowingly. "If I can find her, you want me to send her in?"

I nod, which hurts like hell. "More than anything."

He leaves, and I let myself relax for a second, only to tense right back up with anxiety. What if she's not here? What if she doesn't want to see me? What will she think when I tell her I messed everything up?

Then the door opens and my whole world centers around those piercing green eyes of hers.

I'm lost, so fucking gone for her, that I never want to find my way out.

"Miles," she cries, her voice breaking on a sob, and then she's moving toward me.

The moment she gets to me, everything else fades away. The pain, the fear, the guilt. All I know is the feel of her body against mine is like coming home. And I never want her to leave.

"Oh god, I'm so sorry. Am I hurting you?" she rushes out, backing away from me.

It takes all the strength I have to hold on to her. "Don't even think about moving away from me," I plead, pulling her close and burying my face in her hair.

Quinn's breath hitches, and for a moment, there's silence between us. She shifts slightly, her voice soft but firm. "I'm not going anywhere, Miles. Not now, not ever."

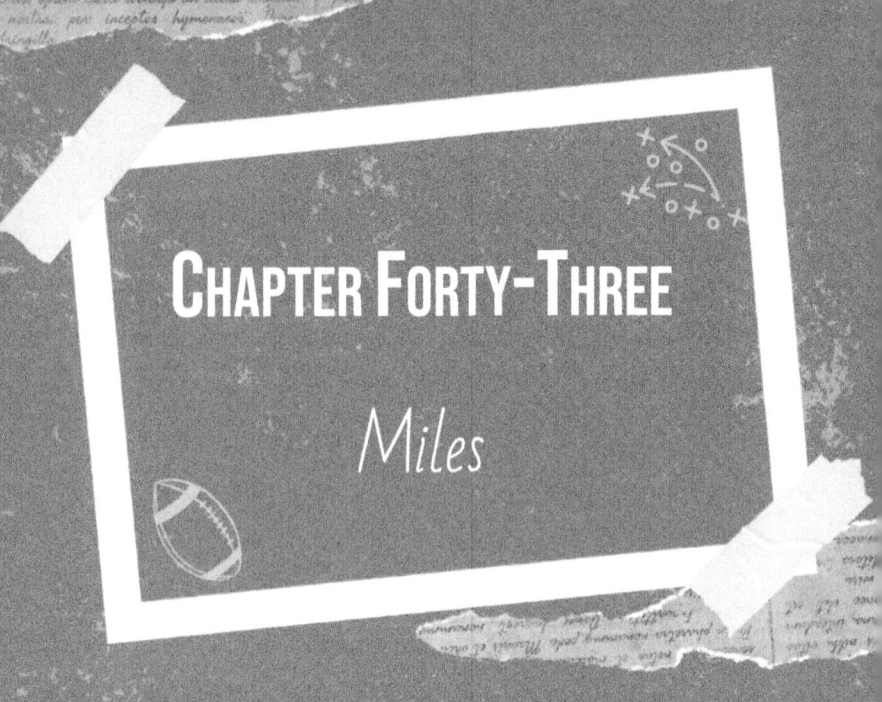

CHAPTER FORTY-THREE

Miles

SOMETIMES WHEN LIFE PRESENTS you with a decision, we can choose to fight or fall. The idea that I have to stare Seb straight in his eyes and admit everything that has happened over the last few months is terrifying, but losing him is worse. I need people who love me, who believe in me, who aren't afraid to show me that it's going to be okay. But most of all, I need to be honest with everyone and let them see how much I need their support.

I don't want to be the person who runs from the hurt, who hides behind the temporary comfort of a substance that only drags me down further. I want to feel alive, to face the world with open eyes, even if it means feeling every single emotion—no matter how overwhelming. I want to be free from this grip, to live a life where I can breathe again, where I don't have to rely on something outside of myself to get through the day.

Vulnerability doesn't come easy to me, but I'm willing to try if it means keeping people I love in my life.

Approaching Seb's door, I feel the weight of all my decisions standing next to me like shadows looming, attempting to swallow me whole. I have no clue how I'm going to start this, because it wasn't just my captain I've let down, it's my best friend, and to admit that I messed up and I've been sneaking around with his little sister too...

Jesus, I really took the crown of fucking up.

Exhaling a shaky breath, I lift my non broken arm and a rap my knuckles on his door.

Every second I wait, my heart beats louder, my blood pumps harder around my body. Maybe I'll pass out and make all this real interesting. As soon as the door swings inward and I see his face, I know I have to face this head on.

"Miles, what the hell are you doing out of bed?" he chastises, always worrying about others, just like his sister.

He ushers me inside, careful not to touch my cast. My pulse hammers in my neck like a wild beast and there is nothing I can do to stop what I was about to say.

"I need to talk to you."

"Okay?" He eyes me, skeptical. "Sit down. I don't want you passing out on me."

I take one more deep breath as I perch on the end of his bed. "I've fucked up." I sigh, running my free hand through my hair. "I have a meeting with Coach tomorrow. He knows already, but I need to tell you face to face..." I pause to compose myself. "I've been using amphetamines for most of this season."

His eyes narrow as he shakes his head in disbelief. "Wait, what? Did I hear that right?"

I nod solemnly. "Yeah, I made some pretty bad decisions after my dad gave me a fuck ton of his pep-but-not-peppy-talks. It messed with my head in a big way. I didn't want to let you down, didn't want to let him down." The weight of my demons presses down on me relentlessly, making it hard to breathe. "I thought I could manage it, that it would give me an edge and help me keep up with everything. But it just made things worse, and I knew I needed to stop, I knew it, but I didn't want to fail, and I stupidly saw this as something no one would find out about."

I shake my head, guilt racking my brain.

Seb rubs the back of his neck, his gaze intense as he tries to make sense of what I've just said. "Drugs, Miles?"

"I know," I groan.

"You... *Fuck*!" His voice rises. "You should have told me sooner. We could've figured something out."

"I know that," I say on a sigh. "But I wasn't about to drag you down with my shit."

"Are you kidding?" He pins me with a look full of hurt as he stands. "You're my best friend, you've been my best friend my entire fucking life. If you're going through something you lean on me, that's how it's always been." He paces the room, blowing out uneven breaths. "I'm not going to pretend I know everything about how your dad treats you, but I know enough, I've seen enough, and I'm—" He pauses to swipe down his face. "Fuck—I'm sorry for being wrapped in my own shit to not be there for you."

"Seb," I say quietly. I don't want him blaming himself.

"No, I really missed the mark here. You needed me and I wasn't the first person you went to."

"I had help," I admit without a thought.

"From who?" He stops pacing, staring at me. "Who helped

you?"

The loaded question, the one that is going to punch him in the gut yet again. I steel myself as I wait for my courage to kick in again. "Quinn."

Surprise flashes across his face. "She did?"

I nod.

"Of course she did. She loves to take care of people; it's her love language."

"Seb?"

"Yeah?"

"There's something else." I swallow deeply as I get ready for the finale. "I love her, okay? I'm in love with her. This isn't me messing around. I've managed to fuck things up epically, but I'm not going to lose her. She's... She's everything to me."

Seb just stares at me for what feels like the longest time. His eyes don't leave mine, searching for any hint of deceit, but he won't find it. I might not have told Quinn in those exact words, but I know how I feel about her is permanent.

I notice his jaw flex once. "You're in love with Quinn?" he asks, confusion marring his words.

Without backing down. "Down bad, man."

His mouth presses into a thin line. "How long?"

"Since that night she went on a date with Alex."

"Months?" His face twists with disbelief. "You've been fucking around with her for *months*, and I didn't know?"

"I know," I groan, dragging a hand through my hair in frustration. "I should've told you."

"Damn right, you should've," Seb snaps, eyes blazing. "Why didn't you? I'm your best friend, Miles."

I shake my head as I feel the weight of his words. "Exactly that.

I crossed a line we agreed I wouldn't. Because...you've always said no one's good enough for her and that included me. So, we decided not to say anything for a while, figure things out until we were ready to tell you."

Seb's glare doesn't waver. "And you thought screwing around, taking drugs, and going behind my back somehow makes you good enough?"

I flinch, the accusation hitting hard. "I deserved that," I admit, my voice low. "I messed up. I know I did."

For a moment, Seb's anger is unrelenting, his eyes like steel. "Fuck!" he shouts, spinning around and pacing the room aimlessly.

"You probably want to punch me right now, and normally, I'd let you, but"—I point to my head—"concussion and all, I'll have to write you an IOU." I'm hoping I can ease some of the tension between us.

Seb huffs a laugh, crossing his arms over his chest, giving me a stare that I've seen from his dad plenty of times. It makes my skin itch. He still doesn't say anything, and I feel as though I'm being suffocated more and more by the second. His eyes bore holes into me, and I think I might explode.

"Or maybe you want me to leave and that's the end of our friendship because I fucked everything. But I need you to know, I can't lose her too. Ideally, neither of you."

Seb's scowl deepens, and I definitely think he could give his dad a run for his money. I'm downright shuddering.

But then something shifts, softening the hard lines of his face. He exhales deeply and shakes his head. "I'm pissed," he mutters, voice quieter but still tense. "But this is a clusterfuck. Quinn, your dad...it's messed you up, and I should've..." he trails off, looking away.

I swallow hard as guilt swirls in my gut. "No, don't do that. I made those choices, and I messed up. I can own that. Yeah, it was rough, but I'm here now, and I'm going to be better."

Seb pauses, finally meeting my eyes again. "I get it. But Miles, with Quinn. You don't get to screw up when it comes to her."

"I'm not going to," I say, conviction filling every word. "I'm done screwing up. She means everything to me." Emotion prickles my throat.

Seb looks at me for a long moment, and the fight in him seems to fade just a little more. "If you really mean that, you better show her. Don't mess this up, or I swear…" He lets the threat hang, but it's less harsh this time, almost like he's hoping I won't.

I swallow hard, trying to keep my voice steady, but the lump in my throat makes it almost impossible.

"Listen," he says, widening his stance slightly. "Did you fuck up? Yeah, you did. Do I wish you'd told me about things? Yeah, I do. But if you think for one second that I'm going to leave you, let you deal with all this alone? You've got it all wrong." He sighs loudly. "I'm pissed, sure, but you don't get to decide when this friendship ends—because it doesn't end. Not now, not ever. Captain or not, teammate or not, dating my sister"—he shudders—"which, by the way, I do not want details of. We're in this together, and that's how it's always going to be. You hear me? It doesn't end."

"Yeah, man," I manage to say, the words barely escaping through the tightness in my chest. "I hear you."

But even as I say it, a part of me resists, doubts creeping in like they always do. How the hell do I deserve this? His loyalty, his forgiveness, his faith in me... I can't shake the feeling that, sooner or later, he'll get tired of my bullshit.

"Especially not because now you know you're going to marry Quinn, right? Like, that's the only option here," he says with a pointed look, and I can't decide if he's serious or joking. "Then we'll be family for real and forever."

Seb's words hit me like a punch, but not in the way he probably expects. Marry his sister? The old me would've freaked out at the idea—too much commitment, too much pressure. But now? I feel a weird calm settle over me, like it's the most natural thing in the world. The thought of spending forever with Quinn doesn't scare me. It actually feels...right.

I let out a breath, a small smile tugging at the corner of my mouth as I meet Seb's pointed look. "Yeah," I say, voice steady. "I'd do it. I'm all in."

Seb's expression cracks—just slightly. He raises an eyebrow like he's trying to gauge how serious I am, but he doesn't say anything. I think he expected me to stutter, panic, backtrack. But I don't.

Because deep down, I know, if anyone's my forever, it's her.

Maybe it's because I've been a part of their family my whole life and they're always there for me. Or maybe it's because I've got the girl I never knew I wanted. The girl that has always been mine, without me even knowing.

"Just don't go all 'dad' on me again," I tease cautiously, wondering if he's okay with joking with me again.

"Shit." He chuckles and rubs his jaw. "I did, didn't I?"

"Yeah, but get the practice in now for when you and Indie make little mini humans, because they're going to be wild little things."

"Jesus, that's more terrifying than you marrying my sister." He laughs, but there's a pause, and he looks at me with something more serious in his eyes. "You know, I'm trusting you with her. That's not easy for me, even though I know you. You've got to prove you're good for her."

"I know, and I won't let you down."

Without a word, Seb steps forward and pulls me into a hug, his arms firm around me. I hug him back without hesitation, gripping his shoulder with my good hand.

He pulls back, giving me a final once-over, like he's making sure I mean everything I've said. And I do.

CHAPTER FORTY-FOUR

Quinn

I'M AT MY DESK, textbooks spread out in front of me, I even got my scrapbook out too as a distraction, but my thoughts are miles away. My pencil taps absently against the page as I worry about Miles. Is he resting? Probably not. Is he okay? Does he need anything? Ugh, I should go to him. Or text him, at least.

I get up and grab my phone, sending him a quick text. Just as I'm about to turn back to my notes, the door to my room creaks open, and I look up in surprise.

"Oh my god, what are you doing here?" I blurt out, my heart racing.

Miles leans against the doorframe, causally, like he wasn't in a hospital bed yesterday, just like he doesn't have anywhere else he'd rather be. His hoodie is half-draped over his injured arm, the white cast peeking out, but it doesn't diminish him in the slightest. If anything, it adds to his rugged appeal. There's a hint of stubble shadowing his jawline, and for a split second, I catch myself thinking that I wouldn't mind if he kept it. But it's his smirk that really gets me, tugging at the corner of his lips like he knows exactly the effect he has on me. Man, oh man, he's breathtaking.

"Jeez, you sound like your brother. I'm fine." He rolls his eyes playfully, pushing off the doorway and stepping toward me.

"But you need rest. You got knocked out and broke your arm, or did you forget?"

Miles looks at me with such intensity, I almost lose my footing. His gaze shifts to my lips before he leans in and brushes his briefly against mine. "Hmm, you smell good."

My brain catches on his earlier words before I lose myself in his kisses. "Wait," I say as I pull back to look at him. "You saw my brother today?"

He reaches back, digging something out from his hoodie pocket. "I did," he replies with a nod. "I hope you aren't thinking about him as I kiss you, though."

"And?" I'm too anxious for his playfulness right now.

"And I told him everything." He sits on my bed, pushing off his shoes, holding up the bag of gummy worms he's got for me. My eyes dart to the bag of candy in his hands, but my mind is stuck on what he said. Oh god. My chest tightens at the thought.

"E-everything?" I stumble, unable to keep the nerves from my voice.

"Come sit down with me." He pats the side of my bed, but I don't miss the way he ignores my question. In an ideal world, it'd all work out and everyone would be happy with the situation, but I have no idea how Seb would feel about everything and that scares me a little.

Still, I go to Miles, because I can't not. He's my person.

"For you." He places the bag of candy in my lap, and I just stare, dumfounded, at the gesture. He went out of his way to get these after being in hospital. My mind can't comprehend why he would do that.

Before I can say anything, he gently tilts my face toward his, his finger under my chin, and leans in to press a firm kiss to my lips. "And that was for me," he murmurs against my mouth.

I'm speechless, overwhelmed by the urge to blurt out how much I love him, how much he means to me. The words are on the tip of my tongue, burning to escape, but all I can do is stare at him, my heart overflowing with emotions too big to put into words. Story of my life with this boy.

"You know, your brother has a mean 'dad' face. It's scarier than your actual dad's."

Clearing my throat, I manage to find my voice. "He does? Huh. Wait, does that mean he got all philosophical on you too?"

"No." He chuckles, shaking his head. "But we talked, and it's good."

"Good?" I question. If he's not going to give me answers, I might burst.

He nods, taking my hand and pulling it into his lap. His eyes fix on our intertwined fingers, as if he's drawing strength from the connection, grounding himself. "Queenie, there are some things we didn't talk about at the hospital. And I don't know how to say this, so I'm just going to say it." My heart skips a beat when he calls me "Queenie." Normally, it's playful—him trying to get under my skin—but this time, there's something different in his voice, something that puts me on edge. He exhales a shaky breath, his brown eyes locking onto mine. "Before the game, I had a rough phone call with my dad. He was...well, his usual charming self, and it got to me. I spiraled hard." His voice cracks, and he swallows thickly. "Then I bumped into Levi. I tried to shut it all out, tried to focus on you, on how far you've helped me come...but I messed up."

My heart sinks, the weight of knowing choking me because I already know what he's going to say.

"I took two pills that Levi gave me." He sighs, deep and tortured. "I thought they were the same ones as normal, but it turns out, they'd been laced with cocaine and that's what caused me to feel so bad on the field. I started to feel off after the first touchdown, but didn't stop, and then when that player knocked me, I was out cold."

The ache in my chest grows as I try to stay calm, but I struggle because what if I lose him to this again. What if I can't be enough for him? He pauses, his eyes filled with a mix of shame and regret.

"I take full responsibility for what I did, because no one forced me to do it. I could've, no I should've said no. But I didn't." He looks down at his arm, the white cast stark against his black hoodie. "I'm 99% sure I've lost my spot on the team. I'm waiting to hear from the dean to see if I'm going to be expelled too. I'll find out everything in the meeting."

I don't realize how tightly I'm gripping the bag of candy in my hands until I start to breathe again, and the plastic crinkles under my skin. I'm relieved he's told me, but it doesn't make the words any easier to hear. This is everything I didn't want for him. But at the same time, I can see the guilt that's eating away at him. When he hurts, it feels like the pain slices through me too.

"I can't keep screwing up like this," he whispers, his voice trembling with a raw vulnerability that shatters something inside me. It takes every ounce of strength I have not to crumble, not to fall into his arms and let the tears I've been holding back spill down my cheeks.

But I never want to be another person who's disappointed in him.

Steeling my emotions, I purse my lips with a swallow.

"Miles, I see the struggle in your eyes every day, the way the weight of the world presses down on you, and I wish I could carry it for you. But I want you to know that you're not alone in this." I cup his face in my hands, holding his gaze, telling him the only thing I know to be true. "I'm here, every step of the way, not just to pull you back when you're about to fall, but to walk beside you as you find your footing again. Even when you can't see it, I see how strong you are. I see the good in you, and I'm not giving up on that, on you, because I know you can do better for yourself."

His eyes start to well up, but he's still trying to hold it together. I lean in closer, so close I can feel the unsteady rise and fall of his chest.

"You're stronger than you think," I whisper. "And I'm here to remind you of that, every single day."

Pressing my lips to his, I make sure I'm gentle, but he has other ideas, as he one-handedly scoops me up into his lap, claiming my mouth with passion that has me breathless.

When we break apart, there's a look on his face that fills me with hurt for him. "You know, my dad always says, 'you don't get diamonds without pressure.'" He laughs, but it's empty.

"Even that made me feel like I wasn't good enough."

My heart aches at hearing the emptiness in his voice. I reach out, placing my hand over his, squeezing. "But you're not a rock, Miles, you're human," I say, trying to catch his gaze. "And if taking care of your mental health means letting one person down, let them down. You are more important."

He finally looks up at me, his eyes filled with shadows. "I don't deserve you, and I know that. I broke your trust, but I'm too selfish to give you up. Just like I know you're too stubborn to give up on me." His voice trembles. "You saw the worst of me, and you still loved me."

"Love," I correct, needing him to hear me.

"Huh?"

"You said loved, as in past tense." I take a breath as I prepare to bare my soul to him. "There's nothing past tense about how I feel about you, Miles. I've loved you since I was five years old."

Miles's breath catches in his throat, and for a moment, he's speechless. His dark eyes search mine, desperate and vulnerable, like he's trying to grasp something just out of reach.

"I—" he begins, but his voice falters. He swallows hard, his eyes never leaving mine. "I don't know what I did to deserve this kind of love from you. I don't think I ever will. But... God, Quinn, I want to be the man you believe I can be."

His hands wrap around my waist, holding me as though he's afraid I'll pull away. But I don't. I can't. "You deserve someone who will love every version of you, on your good days and your bad days."

"I've made so many mistakes," he whispers into my chest. "But if you can still love me after everything...maybe I can learn to love myself, too. I can be better, for you, for us."

There's a rawness in his eyes, a desperate need for reassurance. All the walls he's built up over the years are crumbling, and he's laying himself bare before me.

"I don't need you to be perfect, Miles." I take his hand from around my waist and clasp it in mine. "I just need you to be honest. With me, and with yourself."

I stand and walk over to my desk, my heart pounding as I pick up the open scrapbook. It's turned to a page where I've sketched some of his tattoos, with a polaroid of us tucked into the corner from a few weeks ago. Without saying anything, I carry it over to him and hold it out. "Look," I murmur softly. "See how I see you."

He hesitates for a second before taking it, his fingers brushing mine. Slowly, he begins flipping through the pages. Each sketch, every note, and memory is a piece of him, of us. And with each page he turns, I can hear his breath catch in his throat, the weight of what he's seeing settling over him.

I watch his expression change—softening, becoming more vulnerable—as he takes in the little moments I've captured, the way I've seen him all along. "I know it's a lot to take in..."

He exhales a shaky breath, dark eyes locking onto mine, and I can see the relief wash over him, mingling with hope. Then, his voice drops even lower. "Quinn...baby, I love you. I might not be good with fancy words, but I sure as hell can show you exactly how much I love and adore you, if you'll let me?"

Tears prick at the corners of my eyes, my throat tight as the moment I've been waiting for—the one I've dreamed of for so long—is right in front of me, telling me he loves me too. Those three sweet words play like a melody in my head, one that I want to listen to every second.

Leaning forward, I brush my lips lightly against his. "Show me how you love me, Miles."

It's like an invisible thread pulls us together, and when our lips finally meet again, it's filled with all the emotions we've been holding in. The kiss starts delicate, almost cautious, but in a heartbeat, it becomes something untamed—teeth, tongues, and a longing that's finally fulfilled and I'm back on his lap, back in his arms again.

The world outside fades away, leaving just the two of us. And as we fall onto the bed, lips never parting, the only thing I can think is that this is where I'm meant to be. With him.

The rest of the night blurs into a haze of tender whispers, shared breaths, and the kind of love that's been years in the making. Finally, after so long, we're not just falling—we're in freefall together, and when we land, it feels like home

CHAPTER FORTY-FIVE

Miles

"FUCK," I SHOUT, CURSING the tape that's currently sticking my fucking fingers together for the hundredth time. I've somehow in the last few days become the guy who scrapbooks non-stop, and I can't say I like it much, mostly because it's fiddly and messy and Quinn was right—I don't have an artistic bone in my body, apparently. But I can't mess this up. Not after everything she showed me from her scrapbook. Pages and pages of how intertwined we've been our whole lives and how long she'd felt more for me. I didn't have words, I still don't, hence my situation.

My phone buzzes on my nightstand, and I see my girls name pop up.

Queenie

> Good luck today. Remember if you need rescuing, crow like a bird.

I smile at her message.

Miles

> Thanks Queenie, I feel like I might puke.

Queenie

> 10/10 don't recommend that unless it's all over your dad's suit.

Miles

> I love you, y'know.

Queenie

> You can tell me that as often as you like.

Taking a deep inhale, I lock my phone and stand, stretching out my good arm, and remove my sling slowly. I can't actually straighten the arm because the break is just behind my elbow, and all I want to do is stretch it out and lie on my bed like a starfish. But sometimes having the support off helps to rotate my shoulder, if nothing else.

I need to change out of my old t-shirt and make myself look a little more put together, because today I face the dean of the school. Today, I have to explain why I did what I did and how I plan to repent for my actions. That, and I also have to hand over the name of the dealer because word got around, and he knows it's on campus. I don't agree with what Levi is doing, but I also don't know how it's going to affect me if I tattle on him.

My phone buzzes again, but this time, it's not Quinn.

Hudson has added you to "Textual Healing" group chat.

Opening the notification with a laugh, I see Seb, Hudson, and Jay are all in the chat too.

Jay

> Do we need another group chat, Huds?

Hudson

> Yes we do, because it's criminal we don't have one with just the guys.

Jay

> I have three different group chats with you now, it feels like overkill.

Hudson

> Nothing is overkill with me.

Seb

> Everything is overkill with you, dude.

Hudson

> Whatever. The reason I'm doing it is because I love you guys and I want to tell you nice things when I wake up in the morning because you're all awesome.

Seb

Wait.

Is this just so you have more people to save you from hookups gone wrong?

Jay

Nail on the head.

Hudson

No! I'm upset that you think so little of me.

Miles

It totally is.

Hudson

Oh there he is, my favorite person.

Jay

Why you gotta break my heart like that.

Seb

Such a suck up.

Miles

Don't hate me 'cause you ain't me.

Hudson

How's the arm feeling?

Miles

Sore, but I'm hoping it'll heal fast and I can get this cast off, it's itchy as fuck.

Seb

Today's the meet with the dean, right?

I hover my fingers over the buttons, not wanting to burden them but realizing that these people care about me.

Miles

Yeah, I'm about to get dressed and head over.

Hudson

We're here for you, man.

Jay

Every step.

Seb

What they said. I'll swing by later.

Hudson

What if he's getting it on with your sister later?

Seb

You just had to go there.

Hudson

> Spoiler: that won't be the last time I go there either.

Smiling, I exit the chat, feeling my nerves settle. Doesn't matter what happens today, these guys will still have my back.

Reaching into my drawers across the room, I choose a clean black shirt and slip it over my head, pulling my cast free, mentally preparing myself for the walk across campus to the dean's office.

As soon as I'm outside the foggy glass door, I drop into a seat across from it. My leg starts bouncing uncontrollably, the jittery motion betraying the nerves I can't quite shake. My fingers tap restlessly against my knee, and I rub my palms together, trying to calm the anxious energy. A shadow suddenly falls over me, and I freeze, quickly straightening up as I look up to see who it is.

Only when I do, I'm met with eyes that are the exact shade of brown like mine. Shoulders set with the same broadness and a jawline that I recognize because I see it in the mirror.

"Dad," I say with a nod, keeping my voice even.

"Miles," he repeats, echoing my cool demeanor.

I haven't heard from him since the day he was asked to leave the hospital. No call, no text, no emails. Nothing. The bitterness I feel toward him is warranted, but the hurt and pain that's also making my chest feel like it might cave in isn't something that I expected. Mostly because I've been conditioned to disappoint him and now all I feel is hurt.

It doesn't matter that I have feelings or show emotions. They were for the weak and, according to my dad, Cooper men weren't made to be weak. We were meant to be bulletproof. Except I felt like glass, fragile and breakable. In fact, everything in my life felt fragile. My relationship with my dad, my football career, my childhood. But there's one thing that always felt steady and constant and that was Quinn. She was there. As sure as the sun rose every day, my girl showed up for me.

Damn, I wish she were here right now.

"Miles. Mr. Cooper?" The dean stands in his doorway, observing us, probably wondering which one of us will snap first. Well, it won't be me, not today. I hope.

Dad swaggers over to him, fingers touching his suit buttons until one perfectly manicured hand extends to him. "Jared, it's good to see you again. I'm sorry it's not under better circumstances."

Well, fuck. There it is. Venom that stings.

"Miles." He extends his hand to me too, and I take it with a firm shake, because Seb's Dad always told me a good handshake is the foundation of impressions, first or last.

"Mr. Nesbit, sir."

"Come in, both of you. Have a seat," he says, gesturing toward his expansive mahogany desk.

We follow him into the room, the rich scent of polished wood filling the air. As we take our places in the sleek, leather chairs positioned before the imposing desk, silence falls over us.

"So, we all know why we're here today."

My dad hums, and I have to resist rolling my eyes. Of course that hum is the most judgmental sound he could make.

"Miles, I understand you've had a lot to deal with since the weekend game, what with your injury and concussion." He steeples his fingers on his chest. "How are you feeling now?"

I try my hardest to ignore the fact that he is more concerned about me than my own father has been. "Sore, but okay. Thank you, sir."

"Good. I'm glad to hear you're doing better." He takes a breath. "Now, there is something your coach and medic disclosed to me, and that is that you were under the influence of illegal substances while on the field."

I swallow hard, feeling the heat radiating from my father beside me.

"You understand that we have a zero-tolerance policy for drugs on campus, but especially as you are an athlete under government of the association, they have given us notification that you are to be removed from the team indefinitely."

I nod solemnly, because I expected that. The confirmation doesn't lessen the blow. It hurts like fucking hell to know that I did this, but I accept it, because I know I messed up.

My dad makes a noise that sounds as though he might be choking. Wishful thinking, perhaps.

"I need to apologize on behalf of my son. I'm sure there's a reasonable explanation as to why—"

"He had class A drugs in his system? I think even if he had a valid reason, I'm not prepared to bend the rules for any student, Mr. Cooper."

Jeez, that told him. I could high-five him for putting my dad in his place, if I wasn't the subject here.

"Right, of course," my father says, backing down, and I glance to him in my peripheral. I've never known him to back down before.

"Now, there are things to discuss here, Miles." The dean sits forward, moving his pen to align with the paper pad on his desk. "One is the matter of your place here at Cedar Lakes. There are no school rules that state you will lose your place here, and given that it's your last year next year, I would prefer if we could come to an agreement instead."

"I'm listening, sir."

He nods. "I understand you are majoring in Sports Science and Physiology. Correct?"

"Yes, sir."

"Your professors have very complimentary things to say about you, and your grades reflect hard work too. It would be a shame for you to leave here with an uncompleted degree, in my humble opinion. Don't you think, Mr. Cooper?"

My dad clears his throat, pushing his palms into his knees. "I wasn't aware that Miles had declared a major."

I can't help the scoff that leaves my mouth, but I regret it as soon as both sets of eyes swing my way. "Sorry." Gritting my teeth, I turn to my dad. "I decided to declare at the beginning of last year after speaking to Mr. Dawson."

"Sebastian's father?"

"Yes. He gave me some sound advice, and I wanted to make sure I had a contingency plan in case I ever got injured in a game." I make a point to emphasize the last words, and I know they hit as intended because I see my dad's eye twitch. Yeah, that's right, Dad, I'm not going to end up bitter like you. His eyes bore into mine, full of disdain and darkness that I'll never fully understand.

"Right, well, it was a smart move. It meant that people want to vouch for you in this school; they want to see you succeed," the dean says, allowing my attention to snap back to him.

"I'm grateful."

"Yes, I wouldn't be so grateful just yet, because if you are to stay in this school, there are some requirements you'll need to adhere to, without fail."

My chest eases for the first time since walking in here. "I'll do anything."

He smiles and places his glasses on his face, looking down at his notepad. "The first is that, as well as your doctor ordered counseling, the school also has a weekly meeting for students who require additional support with any mental health subjects. You will need to join this group and attend every week without fail."

"Done," I say without hesitation.

"You will also have to name the person who sold you the drugs so we can deal with them accordingly."

Now I hesitate. I knew this would happen, but I feel guilty for possibly signing someone's future away here, or maybe he did it himself anyway.

"Don't be stupid, Miles. Tell him," my dad snaps.

"It's not that—"

"It's that you had planned on using him again and you don't want to give up your connection at school. It's convenient having a dealer just down the road, and now you don't have football, you may as well give up."

His nostrils flare with every harsh breath he takes, spitting his words like daggers at me. I try to control my anger, clench my fists until my nails dig into my palms, but it's no use.

"You know all of this started because of you, don't you?" I hiss quietly but lethally. "Yeah, because you have constantly made me feel like shit, like I'm nothing but statistics to you, and even when that delivers to your standards, it's still not enough."

He holds my gaze, unwilling to back down, to take what I'm saying as truth. "And you know what else? It fucked with my head enough that I thought the only way I could impress the great Mark Cooper, the only way I'd get my own flesh and blood to accept me was to take some fucking pills that might make me focus better, stay more alert. And look where it got me! Fucked up in the hospital because the last pill I took after you called me on Saturday was laced with cocaine and I had no fucking idea."

"Miles," the dean begins, but I'm on a roll.

"No, please, sir, I will do everything you've asked, but I need to get this out." I take a breath and wait for him to nod before continuing. "You know the only person who was willing to help me was Quinn. Her family has always been there for me, for my entire life. They picked me up when you let me fall. They stood by me at every event that wasn't football, the ones you missed because you checked out after mom died." I pause, taking a shaky breath. "And I get it, I do, but I fucking miss her too," I admit, my voice cracking slightly. The ache of her absence feels like a void that's impossible to fill. "Since she's been gone, all I've gotten is a version of my dad I don't know but have no choice in loving anyway because you're my dad and you're all I have."

My dad stands, threading a hand through his hair. The soft thud of his suit shoes against the hardwood floor is the only sound as he paces around his chair.

"Mr. Cooper, if you'd rather I leave—" The dean stops immediately when my dad holds his hand up, gaze locked on me, and I can feel the pain he's going to inflict before he even says it.

"I have done nothing but support you. You wanted to go to

this school because Sebastian did, you got it. You wanted to stay in the house where I lost your mother, you got it. You wanted to play football just like me, you fucking got it, Miles."

"But you never fucking loved me, Dad!" I explode, my hands trembling. He can tell me all the ways he's helped me in the past, but none of them compare to the ways he's torn me down over and over.

He staggers backward as though I've physically struck him.

"I think we should reconvene," the dean interrupts wearily. "Miles, if you're free tomorrow, I'll have my receptionist set up an appointment with just you and I."

Heavy breathing fills the air with so much tension, I feel as though I'm balancing on a tightrope above a flaming volcano.

"Thank you for your time today, Jared," my dad says, slipping his mask back in place, straightening his suit jacket with a shrug. "If you could let me know the outcome, I'd appreciate it."

And then he's gone. And I'm left with the broken pieces once again.

CHAPTER FORTY-SIX

Quinn

I DON'T THINK IT's healthy the amount of times I've tapped my phone to check if Miles has messaged me. I'm going to give myself carpal tunnel with the repetitive action. I'm up to at least two hundred now. Maybe more. *Tap.* Yeah, two-hundred and one.

I let out a deep sigh as my professor talks to us about the varied therapy approaches that we can study over the remainder of the year. It was part of the assignment this semester to pick a therapy style and explore it.

"Miss Dawson, you had some interesting insight in your last assignment. Would you like to come and share with the class?"

Would I ever. "Uh, Mr. Lambert, I think—"

"I insist."

Okay, looks like I'm going up there. I don't have many qualms about talking in front of groups of people—in fact,

I like it—I just hadn't planned to do it today when I'm so distracted. Clearing my throat, I stand and head toward the podium, just as the professor steps aside.

I take a deep breath, willing myself not to run back to my desk and tap my phone again. *Focus, Quinn.*

"So, in my assignment, I posed the question: Is art therapy really therapeutic?" A few people nod in the front row as I continue. "We all know that there are prescribed techniques we'll be teaching when we work within a practice. There'll be things we recommend and rules we follow to help patients heal and recognize their strengths in order for them to move forward. We have an arsenal of techniques to use." I look around the room at my fellow students. "But what about the patients who don't want to communicate? Imagine, you can give them said tools, and none of them work for that patient. What if we used a medium that allowed them to connect with another part of their brain, to give them new perspective and help them use another medium to communicate?

"Art therapy isn't only beneficial for creative minds, but it can allow logic, fear, and pressure to be removed from any situation. Art is subjective. What you see will be different to what I see, and that's the beauty of it. The uniqueness that anyone creates also resides within the artist."

"Exactly," Mr. Lambert adds, stepping beside me. "Do any of you have questions?"

Dylan, in the front row, raises his hand. "What if part of your reason for therapy is that you're a perfectionist. Do you think that doing something they aren't well versed in might lead to feelings of inadequacy or failure?"

"Miss Dawson?"

"Or we can look at it in a different way. The idea of art, in whatever form you create it, is to create something unique, that doesn't have conceptual perfection attached to it. To channel any emotions that you can't articulate into whatever artistic medium you decide. Studies have shown that it can improve self-esteem, empowerment, and self-discovery. Not to mention, it can significantly reduce stress levels and increase relaxation."

Another student raises their hand. "How can that compare to something like Cognitive Behavioral Therapy? Studies behind art therapy are miniscule by comparison of the scientific evidence for CBT."

"Arguably, it can enhance the effects of such a process. Instead of thinking about it replacing a therapy, think of it as enhancing what clients can put into practice, another tool to use in their program." I step to the side of the podium. "The perfect example is a marine who is suffering with post-traumatic stress and they're unable to communicate because voicing their emotions feels too raw and overwhelming. Then let's begin by giving them another medium—"

"But how do you implement evidence-based practices? Surely, that client might think they're able to avoid talking and not complete the therapy side of CBT or anything similar? Instead, they can just bake a cake, or paint a picture."

"The opposite, actually. By giving the client another medium to express themselves, you can discuss their work and see what they've created with their mind when it wasn't focused on their trauma, and tap into the emotions and their subconscious that way, bringing them to a sense of realization that they *can* communicate, it just might take some longer to express themselves verbally. I agree that we should still rely on all forms of therapy in order to assist clients with their journeys, but we also need to keep an open mind on how our brains work, especially when dealing with trauma. There's no one-size-fits-all, but there is enough out there to help everyone."

"Very nicely debated. Thank you, Miss Dawson."

I take my seat, striding back to my desk with a sense of confidence I thrive off of. It was a good distraction, until I'm sitting down again, and my phone has no new notifications.

As the professor carries on, bringing up another student to the podium, more debates echo around me, but I'm lost in thoughts about the time I've spent with Miles over the last few months and how I've seen him relax when baking with me at the shelter. How I've seen him embrace yoga classes and even scrapbooking. All of these things are allowing him to express himself in a way that he wouldn't normally.

Deep down, I think watching Miles grow up without his mom and with a father who was barely there left a lasting mark on me. Even as a kid, I could sense the emotional void in him, something that needed healing, even if I couldn't fully understand it at the time. I didn't know the weight of what he was going through—I hadn't lost a parent—but I knew, instinctively, that Miles needed someone to be there for him. Looking back, it might seem naïve to think that movie nights or silly distractions could help someone who was grieving, but maybe that's exactly what he needed. He needed to look at things from a different perspective and I offered that to him. Maybe all he needed was to escape from his own mind for a little while and to feel that someone cared.

As we've grown up, I've come to realize that, in some way, shape, or form, we've always needed each other. There's an understanding between us that runs deeper than words, a friendship that's made us stronger. It's almost as if our relationship was inevitable, like we were two halves destined to find each other and become a whole. And maybe that is partially wishful thinking because I've loved him for so long and so deeply; I never wanted to see a life without him in some way shape or form. If we never progressed into more than friends, I would've still loved him and cared for him and wished him a life of happiness. I feel incredibly lucky that everything worked out the way it has.

As if the realization has struck me by lightning, I need to see him. I have to.

"Mr. Lambert?" I ask, raising my hand. "May I be excused? I'm suddenly not feeling well." I shouldn't lie, but I have to leave.

His eyebrows draw together as he regards me. "Of course, feel better."

Before he can finish his sentence, I'm already out of my seat, my hands gripping my textbook so tightly that my knuckles turn white, and my backpack haphazardly slung over one shoulder. My heart races as I push through the crowded hallway, weaving between oblivious students. The campus blurs around me, the only thing on my mind is getting to Miles as fast as I can.

I barely notice the stairs as I take them two at a time, my breath coming in quick, shallow gasps. By the time I reach his dorm, I'm practically shaking. My hands fumble for the spare key he gave me months ago, as I tap it on the magnetic strip.

As the door swings open, I speed walk toward his door, holding my breath before doing a final swipe of the key to open his dorm room. The moment I see him, lying in his bed, eyes closed, earbuds in, I breathe a sigh of relief. His chest rises and falls in a steady rhythm, his muscular arms resting at his sides, the tension of the day clearly melted away. The usual intensity he carries, both on the football field and around campus, is replaced by a calm stillness. His dark hair is slightly disheveled, as if he'd just run a hand through it absentmindedly, and his strong jawline relaxes in sleep. My grip on the textbook loosens as I take him in, letting my breathing regulate again.

My backpack falls from my shoulder, landing to the ground with a thud, alerting him of my presence. His eyes spring open, and the moment they lock onto mine, it feels like the air is sucked out of the room. When he realizes it's me, the look he gives me is so intense, it could set my entire world on fire. Removing his earbud, he sits up, propping himself on his good arm. "Hi, baby," he breathes, his voice low and raspy from sleep, sending a spark tingling down my spine.

"Hi," I manage to reply, but I'm barely holding myself together under the weight of his gaze.

For a moment, we stay still, taking in every inch of each other. His eyes lock onto mine, and the space between us feels too far, too empty.

"Come here," he murmurs, his voice still a rough whisper.

I hesitate, my heart pounding, but the pull is undeniable. Slowly, I step closer, feeling the warmth of his presence drawing me in. His hand reaches out, fingers brushing against mine, as he shifts his strong body closer.

The weight of his gaze is almost unbearable, yet I don't want to look away. "You're okay?" I ask, concern flickering in my mind.

"Yeah." He smiles, and I feel my body melt into him. "I am now." He's so close that I can feel the warmth radiating off him, the scent of his cologne and just him, wrapping around me like a hug. "I was going to text you, but I didn't want to distract you in class."

"I'm always going to be distracted when it comes to you." My voice is surprisingly steady, considering my inside are trembling. "Besides, I couldn't just sit there in class wondering if you were okay. I had to see you."

His eyes glisten as he looks at me. "I missed you."

"I missed you more," I reply without hesitation. Gone are the days when I play it cool around him, because everything I feel is right there on my sleeve.

Something shifts in his expression as he reaches up to tuck a stray strand of hair behind my ear. The touch gives me instant butterflies, and I can't help but lean into him more, exhaling a quiet moan. "I doubt that," he murmurs, his hand lingering against my cheek, his thumb brushing lightly across my skin.

I close my eyes for a second, enjoying the feel of his touch, the closeness of him. When I open them again, he's watching me with that same intensity, as if he's memorizing every detail of my face. "Do you know that I have a favorite freckle of yours?"

My throat suddenly feels thick as I swallow hard. "I did not know that."

He hums, letting his fingertip move from my cheek until it's dusting the skin underneath my left eye. "Right here," he says, almost reverently. "This little cluster looks like a heart."

I barely breathe as he continues.

"I remember looking at it when we were kids," he says, a soft chuckle escaping him. "Your mom always said, 'some people wear their hearts on their sleeves,' but I always thought no...Quinn has hers on her cheek."

My heart swells three sizes in my chest, my pulse quickens under the heat of his touch. There's that invisible thread again, tugging at us, tightening and pulling us closer, binding us together in a way that feels undeniable. I try to say something, anything, but the words catch in my throat. All I can do is look at him, really look at him, as though seeing him for the first time, yet remembering him from a thousand moments before. Every shared memory, every laugh, every unspoken feeling I've had for him feels magnified, like we've been circling this moment forever.

His hand comes up to cup the back of my neck, fingers threading gently through my hair, making my skin prickle and igniting something deep inside.

I can almost taste the faint hint of mint on his breath, feel the way his heart pounds just as wildly as mine. It's like we're both standing on the edge of something, and in a way, maybe we are. I suppose I've been here my whole life waiting for him. And now he's finally here too.

As his forehead rests against mine, for a moment, we're caught in the stillness of it—our bodies, our breaths, our hearts in sync. His lips hover so close, and just when I think he might close the gap, his voice breaks the silence, a whisper against my lips.

"Why do you keep saving me?" he breathes, his voice strained with emotion. "I know I don't deserve you."

He doesn't see what I see when I look at him. All he sees are the cracks, the flaws, the mistakes he thinks define him. But to me, those cracks are where his light shines through, the imperfections that make him real, that make him human. He's been through so much, carrying burdens that would crush most people, and yet he's still here, still fighting. How could he not see how incredible that is?

I want to tell him that he's worth saving, that every part of him matters to me. But instead, all I can do is promise, "I will always save you. No matter how deep you go, I'll be right there to pull you out."

As I say the words, I mean them with every fiber of my being. I would dive into the darkest depths for him, face any challenge, because he's worth it.

"Just don't let me go, okay?" I say, my voice softer, almost pleading. I need him to hold on, to trust that I'll be there for him, no matter what. Because as much as I'm trying to save him, he's saving me too.

"I love you," he whispers tenderly against my ear. "I need you, more than anything or anyone else."

As much as I want to ask him how it went with his dad and the dean, as much as I want to know every detail, I need this—I need him too. I need to feel him, to reassure myself that he's really here, that this is real. His good hand finds my waist, pulling me closer until there's no space left between us.

"I love you," I say against his mouth as he presses another kiss to my lips. And nothing else matters but him.

CHAPTER FORTY-SEVEN

Miles

BEING HERE IN THE stadium, not feeling the buzz of my team around me, not having to go through the routine of pre-game practice and nutrition, has been one of the hardest things to accept today.

My team, my teammates, are all in the locker room, gearing up for the championship final against Idaho. I should be there with them. I should be on that field. But I'm also lucky to be here at all. After the meeting with the dean and my dad went sour, the follow-up was much calmer. Essentially, I'm allowed to stay in the school if I attend their version of group therapy every week, check in with my counselor, and have bi-monthly meetings with the dean himself. I also had to hand over Levi's name and I heard he's been expelled.

This morning, I attended my first counseling session. It's not easy letting go of addiction, but it's sure as hell easier than letting go of fear, inadequacy, and resentment. Those feel rooted in my mind, and I know even without therapy, the only way I'll overcome them is when I talk to my dad again, which I haven't done since the day he stormed out of the office. It needs to happen, but I'm not ready to let him in yet.

"Hey." Indie walks up to the empty seat to my left and passes me a large Sprite.

"Thanks," I say, taking it from her.

She nods. "You feeling okay?"

"I'm not gonna lie, this sucks."

"Yeah, I get that."

"But I know they'll win today. The team is strong, and my guys won't back down."

"They'll miss you out there, without a doubt, but you're going to be fine. Especially with my girl looking out for you." She nudges my shoulder.

"I don't know how I got so lucky with her."

"I feel the same a lot of the time. Those Dawsons are a different breed, I swear. But if you tell her I said that, I will personally make sure you regret it." There's a warmth in her voice, though, a genuine affection that softens the playful threat. It's clear she cares about Quinn just as much as I do, and that thought settles something inside me.

I chuckle, holding my hands up in mock surrender. "Your secret's safe with me. I wouldn't dare."

"I'll hold you to that."

Game chants start as teams are announced and players begin to charge from each locker entrance. The deafening rumble of the crowd barely lets up as the championship game unfolds on the field below. The pang of longing makes my ribs damn near rattle in my chest, but as I look down, searching for something—anything—to steady me, and that's when I find her. Quinn. Her eyes lock onto mine, as if she's been waiting for this moment, knowing exactly what I need. She gives me a little wink, her lips curving into the softest smile, and then she mouths, *I love you*.

My heart stumbles, then starts pounding so hard I can feel it in my throat, like it's trying to escape and race straight to her. I swallow the emotion threatening to rise, but I can't hold back the smile. With a subtle nod, I mouth back, *I love you too*, my gaze never leaving hers. In that second, it feels like the crowd, the noise, the game—everything—fades. All that's left is her.

She owns every single piece of me.

From the stands, I watch the game unfold, my breath hitching with every play. My eyes stay glued to my team—*my guys*—fighting with everything they've got. And even though I'm not on that field, every tackle, every pass, every sprint feels like a part of me is still there, right alongside them.

The clock ticks down, the score tight and the tension even tighter. But as the final minutes approach, our team pulls ahead with a brilliant play—a last-minute touchdown from my replacement that seals the game. The crowd erupts in cheers, the booming noise of victory echoing around the stadium. I can't help the swell of pride that rises in my chest as I watch my team, our team, celebrate the win we've all worked so hard for.

The guys are hugging, shouting, some even dropping to their knees in disbelief. I can see the sheer joy on their faces, the culmination of months—no, years—of effort, dedication, and relentless determination. Indie's screaming and jumping next to me. I chuckle because this is the girl who refused to come to

Seb's game at first, and now look at her.

Just as I'm soaking it all in, Coach suddenly turns, scanning the stands until his eyes land on me. For a moment, I'm not sure what he's thinking, but then he motions for me to come down. At first, I hesitate, unsure if I should, but the look in his eyes is insistent, and I know better than to piss off our coach.

"Get your ass down here, Cooper," he shouts, and my feet move as though I'm running drills for him, muscle memory taking over as I weave my way down to the field.

"Coach, congratulations on the win," I say as I approach him.

"You might not have been out there today, Miles, but this win is yours too," he says, his hand landing on my shoulder with a firm, reassuring grip. His eyes meet mine, filled with sincerity, and I can feel the weight of his words sinking in. "You helped build this team. You belong down here with us, son."

His honesty hits me like a punch, knocking the air out of my lungs. I can't speak for a moment, my throat tight, the familiar ache of always striving to meet my dad's expectations suddenly feeling so distant, so small in comparison. This—what I'm feeling right now—is different. It's like something has shifted inside me, a relief taking over that has nothing to do with the victory on the field and everything to do with the people around me.

I glance around at the guys, at the way they're grinning and celebrating, but still keeping me in their orbit, not as an outsider but as one of them. Even though I haven't been on the field, haven't worn the jersey today, they're including me like I was right there beside them, every step of the way.

It's more than just friendship; it's something deeper, something I never knew I needed so badly until this moment, yet

I've had it all along. This is belonging, pure and simple. It's not about the goals I've been pushing myself toward, the ones that were always tied to my dad's approval. No, this is about being seen, being valued for who I am, not for what I can achieve on the field. These guys, my team—no, my family—they're here for me, whether I'm on the field or not. And that realization is like a breath of fresh air after being underwater for too long.

Coupled with the fact that I know I've got my girl by my side, and I didn't know I could feel so lucky.

I swallow hard, trying to find the right words, but all I can manage is a nod, my voice lost somewhere in the flood of emotions swirling inside me. But that's okay. The look in their eyes says enough, and for the first time in a long time, I feel like I'm exactly where I'm supposed to be.

Then the guys are pulling me in, slapping my back, ruffling my hair, and suddenly I'm surrounded by my teammates, by my brothers.

"Miles!" Hudson shouts, grabbing me in a tight hug. "You're here."

Seb is practically bouncing with excitement, jumping into the group hug. "Man, this is unreal. Two years in a fucking row, baby!"

"Guys, I need to breathe." I laugh as they finally let go. "I'm so fucking proud of you guys," I say, grinning from ear to ear.

"We're so fucking proud of you, too," Seb says as he pulls me in for an even bigger bear hug than Hudson.

"Jeez, you all look like you love me or something," I tease, patting Seb's back.

He releases me, his eyes green eyes shining. "We do. We're serious about us all being there for you."

"Yeah," Hudson adds. "Just because you carry it well, doesn't mean it's not heavy, Miles. We've got you."

"Dude, that's profound coming from you." I chuckle, but the sound is watery, full of emotion.

Hudson smiles. "I know, I have my moments." He slaps my shoulder, then says, "Now, I don't know about you two, but I need to get my perfectly peachy ass to a party."

"Perfectly peachy ass?" I laugh, because that's more like it.

"You know it's true."

"I don't make a habit of looking at your ass, Huds."

"You should, it's delightful."

"Peachy, I've heard."

Benny, my replacement, jogs over to us. "Hey, man, great game. That last touchdown was something else." I offer my hand to him.

"Thanks, Cooper. That means a lot. If I can be half the player you are, I'll be happy."

Hearing that makes something tighten in my chest. *Half the player I am?* I'm not sure how to take it. Part of me feels a rush of pride—yeah, I spent years on this team, worked hard to get here, to be someone they look up to—but another part feels...uneasy. Like they're seeing me as something more than I am, or more than I ever was. How my career ended was less than ideal, but I take full responsibility for it, and if I can pass on any wisdom to anyone...

I slap his shoulder, keeping my hand there. "Stick to the path, even when it feels like everything's falling apart. Trust your team—they'll get you through the rough patches."

He grins at me, that familiar sparkle still in his eyes, and I know this kid will go far.

"Oh, and get us to the playoffs again next year, yeah?"

As we walk off the field, I feel like I achieved so much more than the win tonight.

CHAPTER FORTY-EIGHT

Quinn

SEB'S VOICE CUTS THROUGH the noise, louder than anyone else's. He's got Hudson in a headlock, both of them grinning like idiots as the rest of the team surrounds them, cheering and whooping. It's pure chaos, but the best kind.

"Look at those idiots," Indie says beside me, shaking her head but grinning. She's leaning against the wall, a drink in her hand, looking as relaxed as I've ever seen her. "You'd think they'd never won anything before."

"I think this win meant more to them," I reply, catching Seb's eye as he spins Hudson around like they're in the middle of some strange, football-themed waltz. He shoots me a wide grin, and I can't help but laugh.

Indie nudges me with her elbow. "So, where's your boyfriend?"

I glance around the room, searching for Miles in the sea of

faces. It doesn't take long to find him—he's on the other side of the room, talking to one of his teammates. But even from across the room, he feels close. No matter how far apart we are.

"There he is," I say as I nod in his direction. As if sensing my gaze, Miles looks up and catches my eye. The smile that spreads across his face sends a flutter through my stomach, the kind that I've felt for so long, but to see him reciprocating the same look makes it feel so much more intense.

Indie follows my gaze and smirks. "You two are disgustingly cute, you know that?"

I roll my eyes, but I can't hide my smile. "Says the girl who's literally glowing every time my brother looks at her."

She laughs and takes a sip of her drink. "Touché."

Minutes turn into hours as the guys enjoy their win.

The energy in the room is infectious, and I find myself bouncing from one conversation to the next, soaking in the joy that seems to radiate from everyone around me.

At some point, I feel a hand on my shoulder and turn to find Miles standing there, a soft smile on his face.

"Hey, baby," he says, his voice just loud enough to be heard over the noise.

"Hey," I reply, my heart doing that little flip it always does when he's near.

"You wanna get out of here for a bit? I have something I want to show you."

I raise an eyebrow. "Sure. What is it?"

His smile widens, but there's a nervous edge to it. "You'll see."

I glance over at Indie, who waves me off with a knowing smile. "Go. I'll be fine. I'm just waiting for your brother or Hudson to break something, preferably not a body part, and then I can go home."

With a laugh, I let Miles lead me out of the crowded dorm and into the quieter hallway. The noise of the party fades as we walk down the corridor. We reach his room, and he pauses for a moment before unlocking the door and taking a deep breath, which only makes me more curious. When he pushes the door open, I step inside, the familiar scent of his room wrapping around me like a warm blanket.

Miles follows me in, closing the door behind us. He walks over to his desk and picks up a wrapped package. Turning to me, he holds it out with that same nervous smile.

"I made something for you," he says, his voice a little softer than usual.

I stare at the package in my hands, my heart skipping a beat as I feel its weight. He's never been the type to make grand gestures, so this catches me off guard. His hands are shaky, and that only makes my chest tighten even more.

"You didn't have to do that," I say, my voice softer than I intended, trying to keep the surprise out of it.

"I wanted to," he says, his reply immediate, almost like he's been holding it in for a while.

My fingers linger on the edges of the wrapping, and for a moment, I can't even focus on what's inside. All I can think about is how much this means—how much *he* means.

I carefully unwrap it, the brown paper crinkling under my touch, and as the last layer falls away, my breath hitches in my throat. It's a scrapbook, bound in a way that I've never seen before, definitely more professional than the ones we make at our club. This one has my name engraved on the cover in elegant script. My fingers move almost involuntarily, tracing the letters of my name as if to confirm that they're real, that this book is really meant for me.

"Miles...this is..." I swallow, trying to find the words.

He smiles, a hint of relief in his eyes. "Open it."

Flipping open the book, the first thing I see is a Polaroid of us from when we were kids. We're standing in front of the old treehouse in my backyard, both of us grinning like we've just conquered the world. I'm looking up at him, my hair tied into braids, face covered in mud. His arm is slung around my shoulders and he's just as filthy as me. I remember that day so clearly—how we'd spent hours completely lost in our own little world.

And then at some point, I scrapped my knee, and he carried me inside, and looked after me like I was the most precious thing he'd ever known. I knew I felt something so strong for him then that I'd never be the same again.

That day changed everything.

As I flip through the pages, more memories unfold before me—pictures of us at school when I'd finally caught them up being a year later, notes we'd written to each other over the years, ticket stubs from movies we'd seen together. Every page is a reminder of how much we've shared, how deeply intertwined our lives have always been.

"Ever since Mom passed, I had this keepsake box, and last year, I brought it to my dorm." He inhales sharply. "Well, I found so much of you inside it, of us, of our childhood. And after you showed me your scrapbook the other day, I knew I needed to show you mine."

Tears prick at the corners of my eyes as I reach the last page, which holds a photo of us from just a few weeks ago, on his bed, and I'm looking at him in the exact same way I did in the first picture.

"Miles, this is... I don't even know what to say."

Stepping closer, he takes the scrapbook from my hands and sets it on his desk. His fingers brush against mine, sending a shiver down my spine. "You don't have to say anything. I just wanted to remind you how much you mean to me."

I look up at him, my heart swelling with so much emotion I can hardly breathe. "You mean everything to me too, Miles. You always have."

He smiles, that crooked, boyish smile that never fails to make my heart race. "I'm not letting you go, ever, Queenie."

And then he's kissing me, his good hand gently cupping my face as he holds me closer.

I melt into him, my hands sliding up to wrap around his neck as I press myself against him. His lips are soft and warm, and the way he's kissing me—slowly, deeply—makes me feel like I'm the only thing that matters to him in this moment. It's overwhelming in the best way possible.

When we finally pull back, we're both breathing hard, our foreheads resting against each other's. Miles looks into my eyes, his gaze so adoring it's like he's trying to memorize every detail of this moment. "I might have one more surprise for you."

My eyes widen in surprise. "Another one?"

He nods, tugging at my hand gently, guiding it under his shirt. My fingers skim over the hard ridges of his abs, each muscle firm beneath my touch. My breath catches as I explore, the heat of his skin seeping into my palm. But then, I reach a spot that feels different—smooth and unfamiliar, like plastic. I pause, frowning, trying to understand what I'm touching.

"What is that?" I ask, my voice barely a whisper.

He doesn't answer right away, just looks down at me, a small, almost shy smile playing on his lips. Slowly, he lifts his shirt, revealing a tattoo covered over with plastic wrap that I've never seen before. My eyes land on the design—a queen's crown inked over his left pec, bold and intricate.

My heart skips a beat as I take it in, my fingertips grazing over the ink. "You...got this for me?" I ask, my voice shaky, half disbelieving.

He lets out a light laugh, his eyes never leaving mine. "Who else would it be for, Queenie?"

My heart swells as I trace the crown again, barely able to breathe. "You're insane," I whisper, looking up at him, but there's no denying the warmth spreading through my chest.

"I love you, baby," he whispers, his voice shaky but certain.

My heart swells to the point where I think it might burst. I'll truly never get tired of hearing those words from his lips. "I love you too. So much."

He kisses me again, and I know that whatever happens next, whatever the future holds, we'll face it together. Because this—what we have—is real. It's solid, and it's ours.

And I wouldn't trade it for anything in the world.

CHAPTER FORTY-NINE

Miles

THE SUN CASTS A warm golden glow over everything it's touching. The air is thick with the smell of pine trees, fresh water, and the unmistakable smoky scent of a fire burning in our little make-shift pit. It's perfect, the kind of evening you only get in Oregon right at the cusp of summer down here by the lakes, where the days are long and the nights are just cool enough to remind you that spring hasn't completely let go yet.

Quinn sits in front of me, legs tucked up as she plays with the label on her beer bottle, the condensation making her fingers glisten in the fading light.

"This view never gets old," she says, her voice almost lost in the gentle rustle of the trees. She leans against me, her arm brushing mine, and I can feel the tension from the past year slowly melting away like it has been for the last few months. Slowly, but surely, I'm beginning to feel like myself again. I'm allowed to be the twenty-year-old—or I guess twenty-one to-morrow—who can live life the way I want to. And with her by my side is exactly where I want to be.

"Yeah," I reply, taking in the way the sunlight catches in her hair, turning it into a halo of copper and gold. "It's like everything else disappears out here."

Across the fire, Seb crouches down, coaxing the flames high-er with a few more sticks. Indie sat beside him, marshmallow skewered on a stick, her curly hair spilling over her shoulders as she grins at something Seb whispers in her ear. The two of them have always been a force together—quiet, steady, but with a spark that makes you think they could set the whole world on fire if they wanted to.

Hudson, meanwhile, is busy cracking open another beer—his fourth, maybe? He's laughing at Jay, who's halfway through telling us a story about his most recent gym trip.

"And then," he says, shaking his head as if he still can't believe his own stupidity, "I hit the 'increase speed' button instead of the stop button, and next thing I know, I'm face-first on the floor, the treadmill just spitting me out like some kind of—"

"Some kind of human slingshot?" Quinn suggests, her voice laced with amusement as she takes a sip from her bottle.

"Exactly!" Jay exclaims as he points at her with the hand holding his beer. "But, you know, less cool and more 'please someone kill me now.'"

"Why you suddenly working out so much, man? Huh?" Hudson teases, nudging his arm.

Jay turns a shade of pink I haven't seen on him before. "No reason, just you know...because."

"It hasn't got anything to do with G—"

391

"Hudson, shut it," Jay interrupts and places his hand over his mouth.

Quinn chuckles beside me, and I feel the sound vibrate through her body and into mine. "I think maybe Jay's got a secret crush..."

"Tell me all the gossip later," I say, pressing a kiss to the top of her head.

"I'm still not used to this." Hudson waves his hand in our direction. "But you're cute and I'm jealous. Just a little bit."

"Aww, Huds, you want to sit in between Miles's legs?" Quinn laughs.

"No, no, this spot is reserved for you only, Queenie. Birthday boy rules." I hug her closer to my body, kissing the side of her neck.

"Maybe I want a little something like that." Hudson pouts as he shrugs.

"My boy is growing up so fast." Jay sniffs, wiping a fake tear from his eye, and everyone erupts into laughter. "Soon there'll be no hookups at all, and then I can finally sleep soundly."

"Shut up, you all suck. I need new friends."

"Don't be salty, princess." Seb stands up, brushing his hands off with a satisfied smile as the fire crackles to life. He glances over at Indie, who is toasting her marshmallow to a perfect golden brown, and grins. "You're up, marshmallow queen."

Indie lifts the stick, the marshmallow glowing. "Who wants s'mores?" she calls out, her voice light, carrying a hint of that carefree joy that's been missing for too long.

"Right here," Seb says, reaching out, but Indie playfully pulls the stick back just out of his reach, sticking out her tongue.

"Patience," she teases. Grabbing a graham cracker and a piece of chocolate to complete the s'more, she hands it to him. Seb takes a bite, and the chocolate and marshmallow ooze out of the sides, smudging the corner of his mouth. Without missing a beat, Indie swipes the goo with her thumb and pops it into her mouth, grinning.

"Okay, who's next?" Indie asks as she looks around the circle.

"I'll take one," I say, grabbing a cracker and chocolate from the stack next to us, taking the stick as Indie passes it over.

Quinn leans in close, her breath warm against my ear as she whispers, "Make me one too, baby?"

I freeze for a split second, the word "baby" hanging in the air between us. It's the first time she's ever called me that, and it hits me like a jolt of electricity. I can feel my heart skip, then pick up speed, my pulse thrumming in my ears. It's such a simple word, but coming from her, it feels like a small shift in the universe, like things between us just clicked into a new gear.

I turn my head to look at her, my eyes searching hers, trying to read the expression on her face. She's smiling, just the faintest curve of her lips, like she knows exactly what she's said. I can't stop the grin from spreading over my face too, as I quickly kiss her lips.

"I've only got one good arm, and it's my almost birthday, shouldn't you be making me one?"

"Listen, I know exactly what you can do with that good arm of yours. Besides, the cast is off now, and your physio says you should be exercising it," she whispers, dipping her face closer to my ear, "and I know exactly how to celebrate your birthday with you later."

"That a promise?"

She nods, and my body reacts, her smile wicked and I'm here

for it.

"Hey, what's the plan for tomorrow?" Jay asks, bursting our little bubble. "Hiking or chilling here?"

Quinn tilts her head, looking at the group again. "Definitely hiking," she says. "We've been cooped up too long studying. I need to stretch my legs."

"I'm down," I say. "But if anyone bails halfway through, you're on your own." I give Hudson a pointed look, and he immediately throws up his hands in mock surrender.

"Hey, I've learned my lesson. No more late-night benders before a hike. Scout's honor."

"Were you even a scout?" Seb asks, arching an eyebrow as he pulls Indie closer, his arm slung casually around her shoulders.

"I got kicked out for setting the scout leader on fire during our overnight camp out."

Everyone falls into more fits of laughter. Faces turn red as everyone doubles over, clutching their sides, unable to contain their amusement. "Of course you did, Hudson," Indie laughs out. "I wouldn't expect anything less."

A couple of hours later, the fire crackles, sending up a shower of sparks as Seb tosses on another log. The sky is a deep, inky blue now, with the first stars beginning to peek through. Jay is talking about some trail he read about—something with a waterfall at the end—while Indie leans into Seb, her eyes half-closed as she listens. Hudson is sprawled out in his chair, looking up at the sky with a content expression, and Quinn is still between my legs, her hand resting on my knee.

I feel lighter than I have in months. This—this is what I'd been missing. The laughter, the teasing, the feeling of being surrounded by people who know me inside and out, who'd seen me at your worst and still wanted to hang out by a lake with me on a Friday night.

Quinn leans her head on my shoulder, and I can feel her smile against my skin. "This is nice," she murmurs, just loud enough for me to hear.

"Yeah," I agree, resting my chin on her head. "It really is."

As I hold her, I realize that this moment, this feeling, is what I've always wanted. It's not about the perfect words, it's not even about being perfect. It's about being with the person who means everything to you and knowing that they feel the same way.

And in that simple truth, I find everything I need.

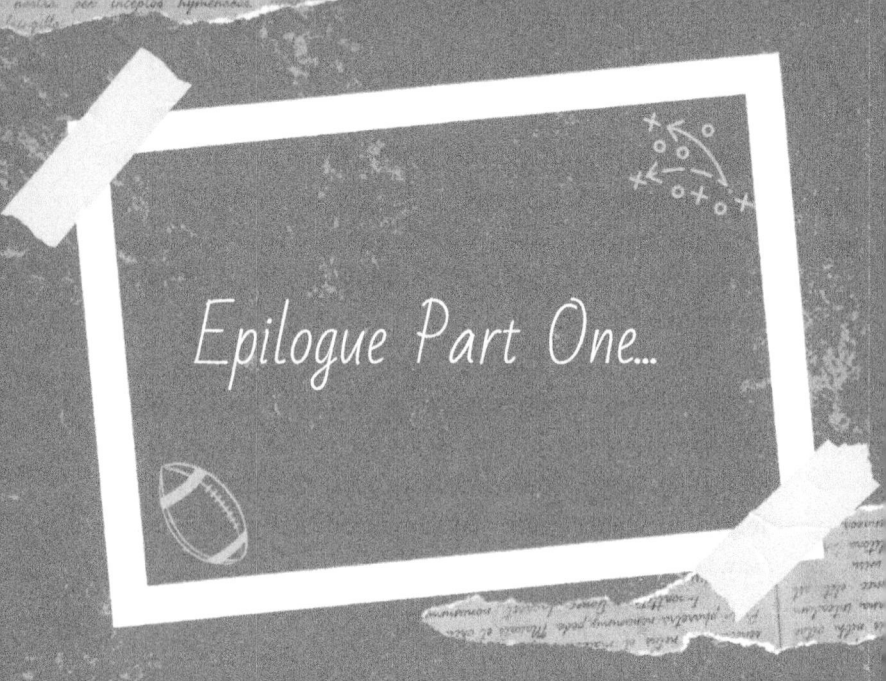

Epilogue Part One...

Miles

I STARE AT MY reflection in the mirror, running a hand through my hair for what feels like the hundredth time. My new apartment is quiet, save for the hum of the AC kicking in, but my heart's racing, like I'm about to suit up for a game, but this isn't about football anymore. This is something else entirely—something bigger.

I haven't seen Dad in over a year. It's been long enough that I've almost forgotten what his voice sounds like when he's not yelling. Almost. The memory of our last conversation still sits heavy in my chest, like a stone I've been carrying around, pretending it wasn't there. He walked out of my life the same way he'd always tried to control it—without warning and on his terms.

But that hasn't stopped me from living. It hasn't stopped me from trying to move on because my life is pretty damn good.

"Here you go." Quinn breezes around the corner from the kitchen with a fresh cup of coffee in her hands for me. Her shrewd gaze takes in my outfit of an Oregon Beavers hoodie, repping my job as Team Physio Assistant that I'm starting in a couple of weeks, and she smiles. "You're sure you don't want me to come with you?"

Extending my hand, she takes it without hesitation, and I pull her toward me, wrapping my arms around her legs, resting my chin on her stomach. "I love you for offering, but this is something I want to do by myself."

Her hands run through my hair gently. "I'll be here when you get back."

I nod, gesturing for her to lean in and kiss me, and she does, making all my nerves disappear for those few sweet seconds.

"I love you," she says, and I'll never get tired of her telling me.

"I love you too, Queenie."

With one more kiss and the deepest breath I can muster, I'm out the door and on my way to the coffee shop in town. As soon as I've parked, I stroll across the street and breathe in the smell of freshly brewed coffee coming from the building. Pushing the door open, I head straight to the counter and order a black coffee.

A few minutes pass as I watch the steam rise from my coffee cup in front of me, unable to take a sip yet. Every time the door swings open, I glance up, half-hoping, half-dreading that it's him.

The door opens again, and this time, it's him. Dad stands there for a moment, scanning the room until his eyes lock onto mine. There's a pause, like we're both trying to figure out how to do this—how to meet after everything that's happened. I can see the tension in his shoulders, the lines on his face that weren't there before. He's also not in his usual Mark Cooper suit. Instead, he's in jeans and a plain white t-shirt. I don't know the last time I saw him out of his formal wear.

When he sits down across from me, the silence between us feels thick, almost visible.

"You look good, Miles," he says finally, his voice low, cautious.

"Thanks," I reply, trying to sound casual, but my throat feels tight. "You too."

I pick up my cup, swirling the cold coffee around unsure of who should talk first.

He looks down at his hands, his expression hard to read. He seems nervous, and I don't think I've ever seen him like this. When he looks up, there's something I definitely haven't seen before in his eyes. Regret, maybe. Or guilt.

"I'm sorry, Miles," he says, and there's a raw honesty in his voice that catches me off guard. "I need to say this and be honest. I didn't realize what I was putting you through. I didn't see how much it was hurting you."

His words hang in the air between us, and I feel a knot in my chest start to unravel. I've waited years to hear him say something like this, to acknowledge that the pressure wasn't just in my head. It wasn't me being weak—it was him being too blind to see what he was doing to me.

"I pushed too hard," he admits abruptly. "I thought I was helping, but I see now that I wasn't listening. I wasn't paying attention to what you really needed."

Not trusting myself to speak just yet, I simply nod.

"I know I have a long way to go and things between us aren't going to be perfect, but I'm trying to improve. I've taken sabbatical at work, and I'm seeing a therapist. I'm trying."

He's trying, I remind myself. And I can see that. He set this up; he wants to make amends, so the least I'll do is hear him out today.

I finally swallow as I hold his gaze. "Growth is uncomfortable, Dad. I know. I've spent the last year facing situations that are hard, growing and becoming a man who mom would be proud of. I've made a life that I'm proud of with someone who loves me exactly as I am."

"Your mother would be proud of you, without a doubt." He pauses to look at me, but his eyes are filled with emotion. "You're just like her, you know, resilient and caring…" he trails off, and I know he's thinking that he misses her because I do too. "I'm not looking for forgiveness yet. I know that's earned, but my behavior has been unacceptable, and I see that now. I just want you to know that I wish I'd handled everything differently."

I think about what my therapist said to me in my last session with her, and I take a deep breath. "I do forgive you, because I need to, because I held on to so much anger and fear for too long, and I need to forgive you so I can move on." His eyes drop down to the floor in disappointment before I add, "Before *we* move on."

The look he meets my eyes with is full of hope and something I haven't seen in him for a really long time—acceptance. "I never thought I'd hear those words," he says quietly, his voice thick with emotion. "I didn't know if I deserved to. But…thank you, Miles. It means more than you know."

I nod, feeling the weight of what's happening between us. It's not just about forgiveness—it's about rebuilding, about finding a way to coexist without all the old wounds tearing us apart again. My therapist told me that forgiveness isn't about erasing the past; it's about freeing myself from the grip it has on me. And I'm finally beginning to understand that.

"I'm not saying it's going to be easy." I continue steadily, even as my heart races. "We've got a lot of stuff to work through. But I'm willing to try too."

He nods, swallowing hard, as if he's trying to keep his emotions in check. "I want that too, Miles. More than anything. I want to be there for you, the way I should have been all along. I know I can't change what happened, but I want to make things right. I want to be better."

There's a sincerity in his voice that makes me believe him. It's not just empty words or another attempt to control the situation. It feels real, like he's finally seeing me—not just as his son, but as a person who has struggled, who has fought to find his own way.

"I think we both have to be better," I say, offering a small, tentative smile. "I wasn't perfect. I should've asked for help instead of finding other ways to cope. I have a lot of regrets over that. But I don't regret my life now. I'm happy and I'm loved."

He listens, absorbing my words. "I'm glad to hear that."

I take a breath, feeling the weight of what I'm about to share. "I've got a job, too," I say, and I can't stop the excitement from creeping into my voice. "I'm training to be an assistant physiotherapist with the Beavers."

Something flickers in his eyes—pride, I realize. It's subtle, but it's there, and it makes my heart swell a little. "Here in Oregon?"

he asks, looking down at my hoodie.

"Yeah." I smile, feeling a warmth spread through me. "Quinn's doing her master's at CLU, so I wanted to stick close by. We've been through a lot together, and being near her just feels right."

"Quinn Dawson?" he asks, raising an eyebrow. "Are you two—?"

"She's my everything," I cut him off gently, but with a certainty that leaves no room for doubt.

For a moment, Dad just looks at me, his expression softening in a way I haven't seen in years. There's no judgment, no critique, just genuine emotion. "I'm glad you have someone like that, Miles. Your mother always said you two were like magnets."

"Thanks, Dad," I say, my voice a little rough. "That means a lot."

He nods, looking down at his hands for a moment before meeting my eyes again. "I'm proud of you, son. Not just for the job or finding Quinn, but for finding your way through all of this. For standing up for yourself, for learning to be happy on your own terms. I know I didn't make that easy."

The words hit me harder than I expected, and I realize how long I've waited to hear something like that from him. It's like a balm on an old wound, soothing some of the pain that's lingered for so long. For the first time in a long while, it feels like we're on the same team—not the one he tried to force me onto, but one we're building together. I feel something shift inside me. It's not just the release of the anger and fear I've been carrying—it's the start of something new, something better.

Epilogue Part Two...

Miles

Her body trembles beneath my fingertips, subtle shivers that urge me to explore every inch of her, mapping out the places that make her sigh or catch her breath. I kiss my way down her body, savoring the warmth of her skin under my lips. She arches slightly, wordlessly urging me on.

When I reach the spot just below her navel, I pause, letting the anticipation build. Her breathing quickens, shallow and expectant. I want to take my time, to savor her reactions, to feel the way her body responds to my touch, to listen to the soft sounds that escape her lips. But I also want to devour her.

I dip lower, my mouth finding her with a gentle, teasing stroke. She gasps, her hands tangling in my hair, pulling me closer. A smile tugs at my lips as I deepen my touch, exploring her slowly, deliberately. I want to give her everything, to make her forget the world beyond this room, to lose herself complete-ly.

The taste of her is intoxicating, and each sound she makes drives me deeper into my own desire. I love how responsive she is, how every flick of my tongue draws a new reaction from her. It's a conversation between us, one that doesn't need words—just the sounds of her pleasure and the way her body moves beneath me.

She's getting closer, her moans growing louder, her grip in my hair tightening. I can feel the tension building within her, the way she's on the edge, and I'm determined to take her there, to watch as she comes undone because of me.

Her hips lift, her back arches, and I hold her steady, ground-ing her as the waves of pleasure crest. I keep the rhythm steady, unrelenting, until finally, she breaks. A breathless cry fills the room, her body tensing, then releasing in a series of shudders. I stay with her through it, not stopping until I feel her coming down, her breathing slowing, her grip on me loosening.

I kiss my way back up her body, taking in the sight of her—her flushed skin, her half-lidded eyes, her parted lips. She's beautiful like this, raw and vulnerable, completely in the moment.

I brush a kiss across her lips, tasting the remnants of her pleasure on mine. She sighs into it, her arms wrapping around me, pulling me closer. "That's one way to begin the day."

"It should be the only way for my Queen."

"Seriously, I think I'm floating."

I chuckle. "Glad to be of service."

"I'm going to be glowing at the commencement today."

"I can make sure you're extra glowy, if you want?" I press

a kiss to the tip of her nose. She giggles again, this time more fully, and it lights up her entire face. I know how much this day means to her, but there's something else I've been thinking about—something that's been on my mind for weeks now.

Something I'm hoping I'll have time to discuss later with her.

Her phone buzzes on the bedside table, breaking our perfect morning bubble. When the ringtone for Saweetie & Doja Cat's "Best Friend" starts playing, I have to laugh. "Did you set that for her?"

She gets up, giving me a perfect view of her mostly naked body. "Yeah." She shrugs, and the tiny strap of her sleep camisole falls down her shoulder. I want to reach up and pull her back into bed with me, but when I hear her next words, I know my morning is thwarted. "Okay, I'll be there as soon as I can."

She hangs up and swirls around with the grace of a cheer-leader. "I've gotta shower. Indie has a hair emergency; she needs my help." She pops out of the room, only to peep her head back in. "Join me in the shower?"

She doesn't have to ask me twice.

***

Freshly showered and with a bigger glow to her cheeks, we drive in my truck to Quinn and Indie's dorm. We don't spend evenings here much together because since I got my new apart-ment a year ago and the job, it made more sense for her to stay at mine. But she doesn't spend every night at mine, and I like that we've got a balance. I'm ready to be selfish with her, though.

Pushing the thoughts aside, I let Quinn go in ahead to help

her best friend, thinking of my own best friend, who's been living in Seattle for the last year. He got his pro career like he always wanted, and damn is he still the best QB out there. Pulling my phone from my pocket, I bring up his number and press call.

"Dude, do you have a sixth sense?" he answers, his voice full of amusement.

"Were you just about to call me?" I ask, grinning.

"Yeah, but only because I'm about to get into a ride to go to campus."

"You're here?" I ask, surprised.

"Yeah, I'm surprising Indie," he says. "I thought I'd drop by since she's graduating. I told everyone I was in pre-season training, but I had to sort out the new apartment. Training starts next week, but since Indie's moving up here, I got us a bigger place."

"Damn, man, that's some graduation gift," I guffaw.

"That's the plan," he says. "Are you at your place?"

"Nope, I'm on campus. The girls had a hair emergency, so I'm just hanging out," I explain.

"Perfect timing, then," he says. "Meet me at Mug Life in about fifteen minutes?"

"I'll be there."

"Awesome. See you soon."

I tuck my phone away, a grin on my face as I head toward the coffee shop. Within fifteen minutes, he walks through the door, and I stand to hug him.

"You've filled the fuck out, look at those gains," I say, slapping his back.

"I've got a nutritionist who manages my food life these days."

"And all that training, you're looking strong man."

"Thanks." He smiles. "I've got you some tickets again for opening game."

Something twinges in my chest, reminding me that we should've been doing this together, on a field, the same team or even competing. But my life has taken a different path, one that I am truly happy with, but I still love the sport. "Thanks, man," I say genuinely. "I'm hoping I can fly out for the weekend, so long as Oregon aren't playing it should be good."

"I don't know if I've said this, but I'm pretty fucking proud of you, being a big shot physio."

I chuckle, shaking my head. "Shut up, you're the big shot, always have been."

An hour later, we're all in the outdoor auditorium where Quinn, who's graduating with honors today, is about to deliver the opening speech for the ceremony.

Quinn steps up to the podium, and even from here, I can see how comfortable she looks.

Her hair falling in red waves around her face, her graduation hat on her head. She looks perfect.

"Tomorrow…" She pauses, looking around. "That might feel like a scary word for some of us. Not everyone is a planner, but there's a beauty in knowing and not knowing, because tomorrow for all of us is the start of something completely new.

"I wish I could promise that none of you will face adversity, heartbreak, or loss. But what I can promise is that overcoming these challenges will shape you into the person you are destined to be. There's no single right way to navigate life; it's all about how we learn and grow along the way.

"What you do have control over is how you use the time

you're given and the people you choose to surround yourself with. Seek out those who allow you to breathe yet hold you close. Choose those who feel like home but also give you space to express yourself fully. Be with those who light your heart on fire but also watch you grow.

"Because one thing I know is that every single person sitting here today is worth the kind of love that we all deserve and that includes loving yourself.

"The journey ahead is yours to shape. Congratulations, Class of 2024, and may tomorrow be the start of something wonderful."

The crowd erupts into cheers and clapping, including me and Seb. We're on our feet, my gaze glued to my girl, and as soon as those beautiful green eyes find me in the crowd, she smiles the most breathtaking smile. That's all for me.

I think about how lucky I am to have her in my life—someone who challenges me, makes me feel at home, and gives me space when I need it. Hearing her say all this makes me realize just how right our journey together has been.

Just how right our future is going to be.

After the ceremony, we're all gathered around the lake. The graduates, Quinn, Indie, Hudson, and Jay, all graduated the same year and there're a few extras in our group tonight.

I manage to sneak Quinn away from the group for a second, toward the lake, where the sun is setting behind the trees.

"I can't believe we're all going separate ways now. No more scrapbook club."

"I think that'll still happen," I say, kissing the side of her neck.

"We did agree to do it virtually, and I'll still run the club while I'm here doing my master's too."

"You wouldn't be you without it, Queenie."

The water laps around us, gently meeting the lake's edge as we stand together, watching the sun disappear. I can't stop the urge to ask my girl the one thing I've wanted to ask her since we woke up this morning. The words have been on the tip of my tongue all day, and now we're alone, my skin is tingling.

I turn her around, taking her hand in mine, my voice steady despite the nerves. "You know, I spent so much time being blind to you, to what was right in front of me my entire life. I don't want to waste any more time. I want to wake up to you every morning, I want to make you coffee with that awful peppermint creamer you love, I want you and me to make a home together."

She looks up at me, her eyes reflecting the fading light. "You really mean that?"

I nod, feeling a lump form in my throat. "Will you move in with me, Queenie?"

A smile lights up her face. "I thought you'd never ask."

She pulls me into a kiss full of promises, and I know I want to spend all of my tomorrows with her, because she's the one who taught me that sometimes being fragile is what makes us strong.

***

Thank you for reading Fragile. This book means a lot to me, and I hope you enjoyed it <3

Want to know more about Jay's story? It's coming early 2025!
Pre-Order is live.
Follow me on social media for more CLU updates IG:
@meghanhollieauthor

Acknowledgements

THANK YOU TO YOU, yes you! for picking up this book and taking the chance on me. I love creating fictional worlds for people to find new characters to fall in love with. It was so so good to get back to this world, I hope you loved it.

The process of writing this book was tough. Miles had a character arc that I'd not written before and there were times when I thought I'd never be able to make it all worth it in the end. Thankfully, my amazing Alpha/Beta team pulled me out of many a dark hole when I starting doubting myself. Mhairi, Jessi, Clare, Tash, Tasha and Isabella I mean it when I say I'm truly grateful for you all.

My editing team, Kenzie and Lisa, you're both an absolute dream to work with and I can't wait to continue this series with you!

My street team – I adore every single one of you and I'm so happy to be on this author journey with you all!

My husband and children who not only support me in my

writing but always give me time to get jobs done. I'm more grateful for you all than you'll ever know <3

About the Author

Meghan lives in rural England with her family – a husband, two children and a yappy dog!

She works in Education by day but writes romance novels by night.

To keep up to date with new releases and exclusive snippets sign up to Meghan's newsletter today.

https://www.meghanhollie.com/

And follow her on social media for even more exclusive content!

https://linktr.ee/meghanhollie

If you enjoyed this book, please consider leaving a review on Amazon and you'll be thanked in virtual hugs forever!

Also by Meghan Hollie

Book three of Cedar Lakes coming early 2025 and the couple will be.... Jay and Georgia!

Pre-Order here https://mybook.to/CLUCollide

Other books in this series

Trouble

Fragile

Collide – Releasing 2025

Pieces – Releasing 2025

Riptide – Releasing 2026

***

Meghan also writes new adult, contemporary romance...

The Ladies Of London Series (Interconnected stand-alones)

All Of My Lasts (Second chance, Childhood friends to lovers)

All Of My Firsts (Reformed playboy, Frenemies to lovers)

All Of My Heart (Brother's best friend, Age gap, Marriage of convenience)